PENGUIN BOOKS

BULIBASHA
King of the Gypsies

Witi Ihimaera is of Aitanga-a-Mahaki, Rongowhakaata and
Ngati Porou descent, with close affiliations to Tuhoe, Te
Whanau-a-Apanui, Kahungunu and Ngai Tamanuhiri. He
is the author of *Pounamu, Pounamu* (awarded third prize
in the Wattie Book of the Year Awards); *Tangi* (first prize in
the Wattie Award); *Whanau*; *The New Net Goes Fishing*;
Maori; *The Matriarch* (winner of the Wattie Award); *The
Whale Rider* and *Dear Miss Mansfield*. He is also co-editor
of *Into the World of Light* and general editor of the five-
volume *Te Ao Marama* series, the first volume of which won
second prize in the Wattie Awards in 1993.

After serving with the Ministry of Foreign Affairs in
Canberra, New York and Washington, Witi Ihimaera now
lives in Auckland and lectures in the English Department at
Auckland University. He was awarded a Scholarship in
Letters in 1991 and spent most of 1993 in the south of France
as the Katherine Mansfield Fellow.

BULIBASHA
King of the Gypsies

Witi Ihimaera

PENGUIN BOOKS

PENGUIN BOOKS

Penguin Books (NZ) Ltd, Cnr Rosedale and Airborne Roads, Albany, Auckland, New Zealand
Penguin Books Ltd, 27 Wrights Lane, London W8 5TZ, England
Penguin USA, 375 Hudson Street, New York, NY 10014, United States
Penguin Books Australia Ltd, 487 Maroondah Highway, Ringwood, Australia 3134
Penguin Books Canada Ltd, 10 Alcorn Avenue, Toronto, Ontario, Canada M4V 3B2

Penguin Books Ltd, Registered Offices: Harmondsworth, Middlesex, England

First published by Penguin Books (NZ) Ltd, 1994
This edition first published 1998
5   7   9   10   8   6

Copyright © Witi Ihimaera, 1994

Typeset by Egan-Reid Ltd, Auckland
Printed in Australia

The author thanks Allans Music, for permission to quote from 'Ramona'
(Gilbert/Wayne); Southern Music for 'Rock Around the Clock'
(Freedman/De Knight); and J. Albert and Sons for 'River of No Return'
(Darby/Newman)
Other works quoted in the text are Sir Walter Scott's 'Lochinvar' from
Marmion, 5th Canto, XII; and Denis Glover's 'The Magpie Sings'.

Prologue

It was Tobio who gave the name Bulibasha to Grandfather. I was twelve then and still obedient. My father Joshua had been shearing at a station near Matawai. He was on his way home when he saw Tobio weaving this way and that on the roadside, and he stopped the car to help this drunk Maori before he got run over. As he approached, however, Dad realised that Tobio wasn't drunk at all. Tobio was dancing, a queer dance with slaps to the chest, stamping of feet, flicking of wrists and snapping of fingers. And Tobio wasn't a Maori.

– *Komm Zigany, Komm Zigany, spiel mir was vor* –

'Are you all right?' Dad asked.

Tobio stopped in mid-click and mid-stamp. He grinned at Dad, revealing white teeth in a rich red mouth. He tossed his black curls. He had green eyes and wore a golden ring in his right ear. He was in his early twenties.

'I dance to be happy,' he said. He put his arms around Dad and burst into tears.

Dad brought Tobio home to Waituhi. Grandfather was doubtful about having him around, especially with three spinster daughters. He was even more concerned when he found out where Tobio was from – Romany.

'A gypsy,' Grandfather said.

'Yes!' Tobio replied. He had a fierce and proud look in his eyes. 'Romany yes, gypsy yes.'

And he proceeded to tell us, amid copious tears, the sorry story of how he had come to be in New Zealand.

'I was born in Romania,' he began, 'in Salonta, not far from the Hungarian border. All our family we live the gypsy way, you know? We travel all year round from Salonta to Oradea to Marghita to Carei and back again. Winter, summer, spring, autumn always the same. My father break horses, my mother sell fine clothings to rich ladies. We *never* steal and *never* take pretty babies –' He gave a sly look at my youngest sister Glory. 'Except now and *then*!'

5

He shouted, grabbed Glory and started to kiss her all over. Then he burst into tears again.

'So sorry,' he said. 'She look so like my little sister, you know? Well, life not too good in Romany just now with communisti takeovering of Hungary, and my father say, "You go to Oakland in California. We have uncle there. You go, stay there, work for uncle, then send for us." So that what I promise to do. I cry –' He showed us. 'I do not want to leave Salonta, my beloved Apuseni mountains. I travel many days alone to Timisoara then Craiova to Bucuresti. Cry *all* the time–' He showed us again. 'I have many bad adventures. Then at Bucuresti I meet a man who tell me go to Constanta, the port. So I go. And *there*, I hardly believing my eyes what I see, is ship leaving for Oakland! So I work my passage many months and arrive –' Tobio looked at each of us sorrowfully. 'I arrive in this country, not the America Oakland but the New Zealand Oakland. You know? *Au*-ckland.'

'E hika,' Mum said.

Tobio stayed with us all that year, working for Grandfather who, despite his earlier misgivings, discovered that Tobio had the same gift for breaking horses as his gypsy father. During that summer Tobio became part of the Mahana Four gang, bossed by Uncle Hone, travelling from one shearing shed to the next.

The Pakeha owners of the stations were intrigued by Tobio's presence among us. They often invited him to stay with them rather than with the clan in the shearers' whares. At first Tobio was flattered, then puzzled and then understanding. He began to refuse the offers.

'They think I same as them,' he said. 'Is better here with you. Maori and Romany are same people. Same blood.'

Tobio was a bit crazy. He was a strange, wilful, passionate presence among us. He sometimes caused fights between his lovers and was often found in the middle of them, laughing for joy. He had a great need to be loved, and would often encourage jealousies among those who wished to woo him.

He loved Maori life and the family, and greatly admired Grandfather Tamihana.

'This is like my own family, you know?' he said to Grandfather. 'You are like my father. You live just like us, wandering all over. I am at home here but I am not at home. And I am not yet at Oakland.'

By the end of that year we had come to love Tobio. We thought he was happy with us. However, when winter came he began to dance more frequently, a lone dancing shadow on our landscape.

– *Komm Zigany, Zeig heut was du kannst –*

He was lonely for his own kind. We knew that if he did not find them soon, his heart would break.

Tobio had earned sufficient to get by ship to Hawaii, and had organised a visa for America. When Grandfather gave him the extra to get him to California, he burst into tears.

We all went to the bus station to see Tobio leave for Auckland. He was excited, childish, unbelievably innocent, rushing from one of us to the next and showering us with kisses. When the time came for him to board the bus he grew grave and dignified. He bowed before Grandfather.

'In my country,' he said, 'all the gypsy peoples they go to the monastery in Bistrita. Thousands of the Romany go. Some from Hungary too, from the Ukraine, from the Bulgaria, all go. My father –' Tobio paused, gulping, 'he take me there once.' He stood up straight. 'There, all the gypsies agree who will be their leader. We crown him King of the Gypsies. Bulibasha.'

He took Grandfather's hand and kissed it. Then he was gone. Soon after he left my conflict with Grandfather began.

Part One

Part One

1

In those days, if you wanted to get to Waituhi from Gisborne, you had to cross the red suspension bridge over the Waipaoa River just past the Bridge Hotel. The hotel is still there but the bridge was long ago replaced.

Dumped on land now owned by the region's premier vintner, Matawhero Wines, the bridge is a worrying reminder that things shrink as you get older. I remember it as an imposing superstructure which cast shadows over our Pontiac as we drove across. When the river raged in winter the swollen silt-laden waters slammed tree trunks against its pontoons. In reality, the bridge was very small and short, redolent of the times before constant flooding of the Gisborne lowland compelled engineers to slash shortcuts across each S-bend and to open out the river's width like a gutted stomach. Back then the river had a narrow course – a slender eel threshing toward the delta at the sea.

Something else happened when human engineers simplified that complex landscape of river bends. With every sculpting movement of bulldozer and grader, they stripped the river of its mythology. Engineers control it with scientific and analytical precision, monitoring its rise and fall by computer, taming its wilfulness by the flick of a button. This simplification has led to an acceleration of time. The epic dimension that existed when you travelled at thirty miles an hour maximum on a twisting, turning road has gone. Once it took almost two hours to get to Waituhi. Now the journey takes half an hour.

Once you crossed the bridge, you turned either left to Hukareka or right to Waituhi. Most people turned left because that was the main highway across the Whareratas to Napier, Hastings, Waipukurau and, eventually, Wellington. Hukareka just happened to be on the way. But if you turned right, Waituhi was your only destination. There was something superior about that, as if our small village was as important as Wellington. Certainly it was more important than Hukareka which was like a horse's fart, a strong smell of processed hay in the air which you passed in a hurry.

The road to Waituhi alternated between tar seal and shingle. My sisters and I used to watch out for the shiny black surfaces and, as we approached, would yell, 'Kei konei! Te rori Pakeha!' Look! The Pakeha road!

For a glorious few seconds the air would clear of dust and we would be able to gulp its freshness.

The first piece of tar seal came at the showgrounds, that privileged place where the Pakeha farmers brought their horses to jump. Our father Joshua would sometimes slow down as we passed to allow my sisters and I to peer at the red and white figures on their prancing horses. We called the Pakeha the silver people because they always had silver knives and forks while we used tin. They paraded shining silver horses too, with names like Queen's Guardsman or Lady Jane or Vanity Fair, not Pancho Villa, Blacky or Piebald like ours. Their horses had saddles and bridles, and their riders got dressed in hunting coats and cute little caps; everybody clapped when a Pakeha horse jumped a fence. We hoped nobody clapped when we rode ours, otherwise the owners would know we were borrowing again. You wouldn't see three or four Pakeha jumping on one horse as you would on a Maori horse, either.

The second section of tar seal came at Patutahi where there was the local hotel, the general store selling everything from sweets to saddles, the blacksmith, the petrol station owned by Mr Jenkins and, most hated of all, Patutahi School. There was also a movie theatre which was bigger than the one at Hukareka by a mile, and sportsgrounds for rugby and hockey. Once part of Maori country, Patutahi was owned by the descendants of those soldiers who had fought against Te Kooti Arikirangi in the 1880s. Pakeha were in power here. The publican, Mr Walker, was a Pakeha and so were the skinny spinsters Miss Zelda and Miss Daisy who owned the general store with their brother, Scott, but that was the preordained order of things. The whole township of Patutahi proclaimed Pakeha status in that no-dust zone. Pakeha were served first at the hotel. Pakeha imposed their language on all the signs. Pakeha were always boss.

We were taught by Pakeha. Mr Johnston – we called him Three Legs on account of his randiness – was our headmaster and Miss Dalrymple taught us English, history and something called music appreciation. Miss Dalrymple also caned us out of our culture and gave us lines if we spoke in Maori. She was not unkind; some belief

12

in Christianity and British Empire made her assume she knew what we wanted. The irony was that although our teachers were our superiors, they were in a minority among us. Perhaps this explains the zeal with which they imposed their beliefs. Convert the Maori before they rebel.

The Pakeha also happened to be our creditors, giving us our groceries and petrol and beer on the tick in those long lean winter months when there was no work. I doubt if any of us managed to get out of debt during the summer. There always seemed to be money owing on the tally which Miss Zelda had displayed above the counter at the general store.

Once past Patutahi there was no more seal. From here to Waituhi was dust and more dust, the constant characteristic of Maori country. As a consequence everybody, including our father, drove in the middle of the road, kept in front of other cars and wouldn't let anybody pass. Better to be in front where the sweet air was than behind in a dust cloud kicked up by another car.

Some sense of spitefulness used to overcome my sisters and I whenever we were on the road in our Pontiac and a car came up from behind. Immune to the honking and the swearing – 'Get over, you bastard! Let us pass!' – we fluttered our eyelashes, shocked at the swearing, as if we were the Royalty of the Road. Oh how we hated it if a car managed to squeeze past. We would wind down our windows and pelt the back with stones we carried specifically for that purpose. As for our father, he would drive on oblivious to all until we had arrived at Waituhi. Then, if the cars behind happened to belong to some of our relations, he would wind down his window and feign surprise –

'Aue, kia ora, cuz. I didn't know it was you behind me.'

Sometimes there'd be reckless races along those roads by young men like my handsome cousin Mohi. 'Yahooo!' The boys would hang out of the cars or ride astride the mudguards, eyebrows and hair caked in dust, their arms slapping at the doors as if riding wild mustangs.

You could always tell when you had reached Waituhi. On the left of the road was the terraced hillside where the Dodds' house stood, a two-storeyed white colonial house which thought it owned the hill. On the right were the tall maize cribs like a wall curving around the road. Then, there it was, the village of Waituhi – a road with houses on either side and, in their back yards, the best maize, kumara,

13

pumpkin and watermelon crops this side of Heaven. And, to one side was the Waipaoa River, ruling all our lives. It had the sweetest-tasting water in the world.

First came the Pakowhai part of Waituhi, with the small church and muddy road along which were grouped the houses of Pakowhai marae. The houses here were four-walled boxes painted red or green or, on a bad day, both red and green with some yellow and purple added in just for fun. Sometimes you'd see an old kuia smoking in the sun.

Along the straight was the Rongopai part of Waituhi. Here the houses were strung amid flax and huge Scotch thistles, the symbol of our warrior prophet Te Kooti Arikirangi for whom Rongopai marae was built. That was in the 1880s, after the government pardoned him and we expected him to be allowed to return to us. Although he was stopped by police, his presence still lived among us – as did that of the artists who created Rongopai. The houses here were more brightly coloured than at Pakowhai, as if the owners wanted you to know that they were the ancestors of the people who had painted the interior of the meeting house. A riot of red, green, yellow, purple *and* blue, the houses proved that artistry isn't always inherited from generation to generation. You might see a farmer urging his horse to pull a flat dray from one field to the next.

Around the corner from Rongopai was the Takitimu part, with Takitimu marae just beneath the village graveyard. Here the houses were built away from the road, appearing like solitary ships on a heaving sea of yellow grain. Except for the indomitable Nani Mini Tupara, who looked like an old Incan princess, Takitimu people were more constrained than the rest of Waituhi, and that showed in their colour schemes – they left all other colours out except purple and green.

Further along was the Wi Pere part of Waituhi. Here my granduncle Ihaka lived in the old Pere homestead with my grandaunt Riripeti, whom some called Artemis. It was Riripeti who took on Te Kooti's mantle after he died, and who held Waituhi together through the First World War, the great flu epidemic, the Depression, the Second World War and the post-war era. That was why Granduncle Ihaka lived with *her* rather than she with him. She headed the Ringatu part of Waituhi, and when she said *jump* we all jumped – including Grandfather Tamihana. Although a woman, Riripeti was the only one Grandfather acknowledged to be above him. Her line of ancestry was higher.

14

Our home, where my sisters and I lived with our father Joshua and our mother Huria, was in the Rongopai part of Waituhi. There we lived with Grandmother Ramona and Grandfather Tamihana.

2

There was surely no better place to live in the whole world than Waituhi. That is, unless it was Sunday. On that day the roosters worried about crying 'Cock a doodle doo!', fearing that too loud an utterance might bring down the wrath of God and get them thrown prematurely into the cooking pot. The dogs, too, were silent. Sometimes I would look out the window and even see people pushing their cars past the homestead to start them up further down the road.

As if He lived here.

What made Sundays even worse was that Glory and I had to get up earlier than usual to milk the cows because church meetings started at eight. I wished I was Maui the demigod who tamed the sun, and that I could either stop Sunday from coming or else hurry us all to Monday. No such luck.

'Simeon? Are you awake?'

'No.'

'The cows are waiting,' Glory said. 'I've already got them in the bail. Hurry up, otherwise we'll be late for prayers again.'

'I've decided to take the day off.'

'Si-*meon*.' Glory came in, eight years of sunshine and innocence. 'Come on. If we're late today of all days, Grandfather will get really angry.'

'Anybody would think the sun shone out of his bum,' I said.

Glory gasped. 'Wash your mouth out with soap and water!' She began to pull at the blankets.

'Ouch,' I said. 'You go on.'

When she left I lifted the blankets and looked down at myself. I punched the air. Yay, I wasn't going to be a eunuch.

Thank you, God, thank you, thank you.

Ever since she was born, Glory and I have had a special relationship. I never realised it at first, regarding her as all brothers do their younger siblings – as a brat. When she was a baby my two elder sisters Faith and Hope thought she was *ador*-able, until she shat in her nappies. After that they wanted nothing to do with her. As for me, I was already used to shit in the cow bail and shit in the sheep pens and shit whenever my father Joshua and I had to fill in one dunny hole and move the outhouse over another. It was second nature to change Glory, and at least her shit smelt passable. By the time she was walking it seemed only natural that I would assume responsibility for her toilet training, her feeding and her bedding down. My cousin Mohi, the Stud Who Walks, once commented drily, 'You should have had tits, man, then you could've weaned her too.'

That put me off Glory for a while, but by that time she had latched on to me. Wherever I went, she went. Whatever I did, she wanted to do it too – including helping me with the milking.

One morning I had just finished bringing in the cows from the far paddock with our sheepdogs, called Stupid, Hopeless and Dumb because they never obeyed instructions. Despite his limited intelligence, however, Stupid had learned to perform tricks.

'Roll over, Stupid,' I said, and he did.

'Shake my hand,' I said, and he put out his paw.

'Sing a song, Stupid.' He started to howl.

That's when I heard Glory behind me. She was five at the time and she was howling along with the dog. I smiled, thinking nothing of it, and threw Stupid a watercracker.

'Woof.'

I looked at Glory. She was eyeing me dangerously.

'*Woof*,' she growled again.

Woof?

She tilted her head at my pocket and I started to laugh. 'You want a biscuit too, darling?' I asked. 'Of course you can have one.' But I didn't catch on until I said to Stupid, 'Okay, play dead now.'

Stupid gave a whine and rolled on to his back, his four paws pointing at the sky.

So did Glory.

I shucked on my work clothes and crept out of the bedroom past the Frog Queens, the nickname I had for my two elder sisters. They were, as usual, fast asleep with their mouths in their customary position – open.

16

Mum was just waking. She looked up and over Dad's stranglehold around her neck, pushing her hair away from her face.

'Kei te haere koe ki te miraka kau?' She smiled and illuminated my life.

'Ka pai. Good.'

Then I was out the door, over the stile and across the back paddock to the cow bail where Glory was waiting with Red, Brindle, Blacky, Ginger, Albino and Tan, pausing a moment to breathe the fresh air and to see the mist drifting off the hills. Magic was still about at that time of the morning, wraiths and kehua reluctant to give up their domain to the sun; lingering with their memories of battles between iwi and iwi or with Pakeha; still singing the old blood songs of revenge, heart songs of love and lonely songs of death; still reaching out to us, disturbing our dreams, lingering, saying, Never forget, never forget –

I raced up the rise and took another deep breath before going into the cow bail. Glory had already washed and greased Red's udders, and she stood aside as I placed the stool beneath Red, butted my head into her right flank and put the bucket between my legs.

'Okay, Red,' I sighed.

There is nothing worse for a young boy with the whole world before him than to be faced with cows' udders every morning.

'Phew,' Glory said as we humped the last milk bucket into the kitchen of the homestead. The milk frothed and foamed, warm and pungent. The smell of newly drawn milk is like no other in its sweetness and freshness. I grinned at Glory and jokingly threw her a watercracker. Although she had grown out of pretending to be a dog, we still kidded around with the fantasy, sometimes using the 'Drop dead' routine to get us out of trouble.

Glory looked at the biscuit and sighed. 'We're not allowed,' she said.

'Good girl,' Mum said.

We always fasted on Sundays, and that was another reason for hating them. On Sundays, so Grandfather said, God's food sustains even the most famished soul. That might be true, but it wasn't my soul that was hungry. And today was going to be worse – no kai until *dinner* time.

The side door slammed. 'Get out of the way, Useless.'

My nemesis, Mohi, was dressed already – of course, *he* had no chores in the morning – and snaking his way out to the De Soto, grabbing a piece of bread and munching on it in front of Mum and my aunts, knowing they wouldn't tell. Eighteen and already a prick.

'Glory, you better go and have a wash,' my mother said. 'Your sisters are already in the bathroom. Tell them to hurry up. As for you Simeon, you can use the outside pump. Kia tere!'

She had her eye on the clock. Five-thirty. We would be expected in the drawing room of the homestead at six, and she and my aunts were running five minutes behind schedule.

From the window she saw me shambling over to the pump, taking off my shirt and loosening my braces. I thought she wasn't looking so just dabbed my eyes, enough to get the pikare out.

'No you don't, Simeon,' she yelled. 'And don't forget behind your ears and under your arms.'

In the distance that sonofabitch Mohi was doubling over with laughter because I looked like the skinny guy whom Charles Atlas was always exhorting to try his muscle-building course.

Can't a person have any privacy?

3

'Kia tere,' my mother said. 'Kia *tere*.'

She was stooped over, trying to get the seams of her stockings straight, her hat in danger of falling off. My father was slicking down his hair and putting his black jacket on.

'Simeon? Oh, pae *kare* –'

I was struggling, as usual, to put a windsor knot in my tie.

'Here,' Mum said. She loosened the tie, began to knot it for me and hesitated. 'Why do you want to wear *this* one?' It was the tie my cousin Haromi had bought me for my birthday and had Hawaiian hula girls all over it. 'You know your grandfather hates this tie. And look at your hair! I told you to get it cut last week.'

Yes, I know you did, Mum, but tough.

'You know how important this day is,' Dad chimed in.

'Mu-*um*,' Faith interrupted. She pointed airily at the clock.

Two minutes to six.

'Oh Hi-*miona*,' Mum said, as if it was all my fault.

It was always the same performance on Sundays, but it was even worse today, for this was the first October Sunday before shearing. Today, together with Uncle Ihaka's and Zebediah Whatu's families, we had thanksgiving. We had to get over to the main house at six for prayers and the family service, and then go on to church. The only consolation was that we wouldn't be the only ones running around like hens with our heads chopped off. My uncles Matiu, Maaka, Ruka and Hone, named after the first four saints of the New Testament, would be well on the road to the homestead by now. As would be my aunts Ruth and Sarah, named for goodly women from the Old Testament; no doubt Aunt Ruth would be haranguing Uncle Albie, and Aunt Sarah would be giving both Uncle Jack and her daughter Haromi hell. Following close behind them on the road would be my uncles Aperahama and Ihaka, after Abraham and Isaac in Exodus, and their families. All of them had been given land to live on by Grandfather.

Under the circumstances we, being my father Joshua's family and his three youngest sisters, could count ourselves lucky we lived on the premises. That's if you *do* count living with Grandfather Tamihana and being tied to him by pecking order and obedience a blessing. Oh yes, *our* names had been inspired by the Bible too. I had been named after a saint, not that it seemed to do me much good.

'Himiona!' Dad was calling. 'Stop your daydreaming, son, and get over here.'

He was standing at the front door of the big house with Mum and my sisters. My mother had managed to pull on her white gloves and secure her hat. We were all in our Sunday best, and only half an hour ago I had been in cow shit.

'And do try to get on with your grandfather,' Mum said. 'No answering back.'

Me?

Just then, cars and trucks arrived from all directions to deposit frazzled uncles, aunts and cousins on the front lawn. My father knocked on the door.

One minute past six.

The door opened. A glittering eye looked down on us. It was slightly skewed and tilted over on a bad left leg. Behind the eye, my aunts Sephora, Miriam and Esther.

'You're late,' the eye said. 'Zebediah Whatu and his family are here and so is Ihaka and his family, but my own family never gets here on time.'

19

'Sorry, Bulibasha,' my uncles and their wives, aunts and their husbands and my cousins whispered as they filed past Grandfather and into the sitting room. One after another, bobbing their heads.

SorrySorrySorry sorrysorry Bulibasha.

Under and around the eye and bad left leg. Subservient. Meek and mild. Everybody stooped, developing sore backs all of a sudden. Deferential. Not looking the Lord of Heaven in the eye. Then my turn. Hastening past him.

Kiss my arse, Bulibasha.

'What did you say, Simeon?' He clipped me over the ear.

'Sorry, Bulibasha.'

In the corner, my cousin Mohi was pissing himself with mirth.

Left ear ringing, I filed in with the rest of the family and, like them, began to take off my shoes. As I bent down I pointed my bum accidentally on purpose in Mohi's face and farted.

'You little bas –' he began.

I looked at him innocently – who me? – and took my place with my mother and sisters just beside Dad, ninth child and seventh son, and next to Aunt Sephora, tenth child and third daughter.

There was always a hierarchy in the family. Whatever the occasion, Uncles Matiu, Maaka, Ruka and Hone and their families were nearest to Grandfather, but in that sequence. The rest of us followed suit according to order of birth, and if anybody got out of sequence, *watch out*. Aunt Ruth told me once that that was the way our great-grandfather had organised his even *bigger* family; it was the only way in which he could tell if anybody was missing. Grandfather had merely perfected the notion, so that it implied degrees of worth. The older you were the more important you were, and therefore you were placed closer to him; the younger you were, the more worthless you became. What other explanation could there be for Dad and Aunts Sephora, Miriam and Esther being so far away from the throne?

I thought, What's the use of our being here? Especially as there seemed to be some time delay in Grandfather's words reaching us way down at our end of the room. It was like the echo effect you sometimes get on an overseas telephone –

'*Hello*? Elloellello? *This is God* odododo *speak* speak *ing* inging ing.'

My mother jabbed me in the side. Grandfather had been walking from one end of the room to the other. He had stopped, giving me a penetrating look.

'Is something bothering you, Himiona?' he asked.

I pretended that his clip over my ear had made me momentarily deaf. Then I beamed him a smile. 'My ear seems to be okay now, Grandfather.'

Grandfather turned swiftly to Mohi. 'Tell your cousin what I was saying.'

Mohi was faking a look of penitence. 'Bulibasha was asking us a question. If the Lord our God had said all His faithful could come through the gates of Heaven at six –'

'And if *you* arrived at one minute past six,' Grandfather continued, 'would He let you in?' He looked at his sons in turn.

'No Bulibasha.'

NoBulibasha Bulibasha bashabasha asha.

'Well?' Grandfather was asking me now.

I opened my mouth to answer. I was merely going to point out that the question was entirely supposition and that –

My mother went, Shush.

'No, Bulibasha.'

Grandfather paused, unsure about the quality of my answer. I had the ability to make my negatives sound quite the opposite.

'Good,' Grandfather said. 'Everybody will be here on time next Sunday –'

The Lord our God hath spoken.

'Turituri!' Mum hissed in my ear.

'But let's get through today first, be one as a family, go to church as a family and ask God's guidance.' Then, for good measure, 'Joshua, see that your boy gets a haircut. He's starting to look like a girl.'

The blood rushed to my cheeks. I watched as Grandfather sat down on his throne. His seating himself was our signal that we should kneel. Bulibasha looked in the direction of the bedroom. There was a white linen curtain across the doorway which stirred like a veil as Grandmother Ramona came in. Without looking left or right, she took her place in the vacant chair beside Grandfather.

'Kua tae mai te wa,' Bulibasha began, 'kua timata ta tatou karakia.'

We began to pray.

'E to matou Matua i te rangi,' Grandfather leading.

'Kia tapu tou Ingoa,' we intoned.

'Kia tae mai tou Rangatiratanga,' he continued.

'Kia meatia tou e pai ae,' we followed like submissive sheep jumping through Heaven's gates before it is closed. All the while the minutes ticked away, tick tock, ho hum, yawn, fidget, scratch, *ouch*.

'Behave yourself,' Mum glared. I had begun to indulge in my favourite pastime during prayers – picking my nose. After all, what else is there for a boy to do when he's bored? That was the trouble with our prayers. They went on for so long, as if Grandfather wanted to make sure that God actually heard us.

Then prayers were over and our family thanksgiving began.

4

All family sagas need a sense of history. For us, the descendants of Tamihana Mahana, this was imparted at the October thanksgiving and usually told by Uncles Matiu, Maaka, Ruka and Hone, Grandfather's eldest sons. In deference to Grandfather's mana, the rest of us remained kneeling throughout the proceedings. It was the only way to ensure that our heads were never higher than his. If we had anything to ask, we shuffled forward on our knees to request permission to speak.

'Yes,' my uncle Matiu said, 'it was in 1919, straight after the Great War, that our family established itself as a shearing gang, and it was our father Tamihana who had the dream.

'In 1919 our father Tamihana travelled to Tikitiki to see Ta Apirana Ngata, the Maori member of parliament, to ask him for a loan to get started in shearing. Ta Apirana had a scheme going at the time to help Maori farmers. He had heard of our father's sporting exploits and respected him. Our father was twenty-three, married to our mother Ramona, and already had four children, all boys – myself, Maaka, Ruka and Hone –'

'And I was on the way,' Aunt Ruth grinned.

'Ta Apirana respected our father. Both were deeply worried at the situation for Maori people in those days, especially on the land. Ta Apirana agreed to advance the loan. Soon after Father returned to Waituhi, he had a message to go to the branch of the Native Affairs Department in Gisborne where a cheque was waiting for him from Apirana Ngata. That cheque was for £200, a prince's ransom in those days, and it was to be paid back at the rate of £25 per year, plus interest. The man who gave your grandfather the cheque was Floyd Chapman.'

Uncle Matiu was meticulous in setting out the history. In so doing he was saying, We must never forget even the smallest detail, for it has its role in maintaining our memory. This is what those monthly meetings were about – ensuring that we did not lose our memory, for otherwise we would also lose the understanding that in the beginning there had been only a dream.

'Father Tamihana took that cheque to the Bank of New South Wales. The bank manager was Mr Stephen Watson who asked our father what he wanted to do with the money. Mr Watson said he would help by providing an additional £100 if this was required. He gave our father an interest-free loan for three months and he also gave him some valuable advice. This is why our family has continued to bank with the Bank of New South Wales. A business relationship must always be between two people who respect each other. We never forget our friends.'

Uncle Maaka coughed. It was his turn to take over the saga.

'With that money our father contracted his brother Ihaka and his friend Zebediah Whatu to shear for the 1920 season. This is how the Whatu family became our partners in our shearing gangs. Our uncle and Zebediah both accepted the deal, and our father guaranteed a payment of £50 in advance and £5 for every hundred sheep shorn. Remember, these were the days when sheep were shorn with hand clippers.'

'Our father,' continued Uncle Ruka, 'then asked our mother if she was well enough, having just had her fourth child, to be the fleeco. Our mother said, 'Yes.' She was the first fleeco and wool classer for the family. Wherever she went, we went.'

'By then I was the baby,' Aunt Ruth said.

'And I was on the way to join my sister,' Aunt Sarah interjected.

By this time I was being swept up with the story, laughing along with everyone else, especially since Aunt Sarah was so competitive and it was just like her to be chasing after her eldest sister.

'My big brother Matiu was the first sheepo and he was helped by Maaka and Ruka who were then three and two years old,' Uncle Hone said.

'And me and Hone did the dags,' Aunt Ruth continued, holding her nose.

'So was the first family shearing gang formed. But that was just the beginning –'

23

'Times were hard in the 1920s.' Uncle Matiu took up the story again. 'Farmers could not afford to squander their money on shearers like father Mahana whose work they didn't know. He might be good at sport, but a shearer? So our father walked from farm to farm that winter, offering the services of our gang. Time after time he was turned away. Then he came across the station of Mr William Horsfield, who said that although money was tight, he would try our gang –'

'Our father shook Mr Horsfield's hand,' Uncle Maaka continued, 'but he made a bargain with him. He said, "Because times are difficult I will shear your sheep free for the first year on condition that you give me the contract to shear your sheep for the next three years and the option of renewal." This was the advice that Mr Stephen Watson of the Bank of New South Wales had given him. Not to work year by year but always by contract and three years in advance. Nobody else was doing this in the district. Our father was the first.'

'Mr Horsfield agreed,' Uncle Ruka added. 'He said, "You are either an honest man or a fool." But he was so impressed that he told another farmer, Mr David Collinson, and he became the second farmer contracted on the same basis – one free year on condition of a three-year contract.'

'So in 1920,' Uncle Hone said, 'our father began our family operation. He had managed to get seven contracts for the season. He, our mother, Uncle Ihaka and Zebediah Whatu walked to every shed. At each shed they worked free and they did quality shearing and quality classing. The work with hand clippers was long and hard. There was no room for error. At the end of that season our father went to pay Uncle Ihaka and Zebediah Whatu what had been agreed. But they shook their heads, saying, "Ka tika. We know that the money is running low. If you pay us what you promised, your own family will starve all the winter months. Let us share the money between our families so that we will be in a working position for next year."'

'So we *all* starved that winter,' Zebediah Whatu laughed.

'This is the second lesson,' Uncle Matiu continued. 'The Horsfield and the Collinson contracts are still ours and, over the years, we have had to take the good times with the bad. Some years we have accepted that they cannot pay us but we have still shorn their sheep.'

'And,' Uncle Maaka interrupted, waving to Zebediah Whatu,

'the third lesson is that when you find a family like the Whatus, who are prepared to go hungry with you, treasure them. We will never forget what you did for us in 1920, Zebediah Whatu.'

There was a pause. Smiles were shared at the warmth of a common history. Zebediah Whatu tried to shrug it off but was deeply affected. He took out a huge handkerchief and blew his nose. Next to him his grandson, and my best friend, Andrew Whatu, grinned proudly.

'Indeed,' Uncle Matiu began again, 'that winter was very bad and the £300 that our father had been given was used up entirely. So, with heavy heart, our father went to see Mr Stephen Watson to ask if his first repayment could be delayed. He said he would put up our family land as collateral. But Mr Watson simply answered, "Your integrity is the only collateral I need, Mr Mahana. You already have seven contracts for the next season and that will be collateral enough. You may have your extension."'

'Thus it was in 1921,' Uncle Maaka said, 'that our father was able to obtain the first income from his shearing operation. In that year he added another five farms to the contract because they had heard of his fair dealings and his quality of work. By 1923 he was able to pay the Bank of New South Wales and the Department of Native Affairs its first loan repayment. He remortgaged and bought a truck for the gang to get around in, Grandmother Ramona being pregnant again –'

'This time with me,' Uncle Ihaka said from the back. 'And my brother here –' he jabbed Aperahama, 'wasn't far behind either.'

'By 1925,' Uncle Ruka continued, 'we had another three contracts and work assured for the three years to come. We were finally on our feet. Father paid off both loans, increased his gang to three shearers and added another fleeco. Eight of us children had been born and we helped at the sheds. Father's brother, Ihaka, and Zebediah Whatu had also had children and they too joined the family gang.'

'Then in the 1930s,' Uncle Matiu concluded, 'the four remaining children were born – Joshua, Sephora, Miriam and Esther – and Father Tamihana established a second shearing gang. By 1940 he had another two gangs operating. The gangs were known simply as Mahana One, Mahana Two, Mahana Three and Mahana Four. In the 1950s, Father vested their leadership in the four eldest sons, Matiu, Maaka, Ruka and Hone. We were the largest shearing gang in Poverty Bay.'

The meeting ended in a rosy glow. But I couldn't help muttering, 'The only other gang as big as ours was Rupeni Poata's of Hukareka.'

Dad clipped me over the ear. 'You're asking for trouble, boy,' he said as we filed out of the homestead to our cars.

As if I cared. There was church to get through yet.

5

As with all things, the order in which the cars drove to church was prescribed by family ranking. Grandfather and Grandmother were in the first car, the De Soto, driven by Mohi; by virtue of being the eldest spinster daughter, Aunt Sephora accompanied them. Next were Uncle Matiu and his family in the latest model Jaguar; Maaka and his family in the latest model Chevrolet; Ruka and his family in the latest model Rover, and Hone and his family in the latest model Austin. Then came Aperahama and Ihaka, in second-hand Ford and Chevrolet respectively and who, because they had wives but no children, took my aunts Miriam and Esther. Last in the cavalcade was my father Joshua's Pontiac, the oldest model of the lot, which had been Grandfather's own car until traded in for the De Soto.

To make matters worse, this was the order that had to be maintained all the way to church in Gisborne. Thus the De Soto was in the fresh air, and the dust increased further down the cavalcade. By the time it hit us it was a duststorm of Sahara proportions. In the early days Dad had tried to make light of this by making us imagine that bringing up the rear was the most important place to be. He would refer to wartime movies like *The Dam Busters* where the tail-end gunner had to keep those dratted Messerchmitts away from the rest of the bomber squadron, or to westerns like *Charge at Red River* in which scalp-hunting Indians attacked the last wagon first. My sisters and I sat keenly watching our rear, waiting for Indians – we always sided with the cavalry in those days – or for the dastardly Hun to come at us from out of the dust. As we grew older we realised it was all a con job. We were not at the rear to save the wagon train but because our father was the youngest. Nor would any amount of success in saving the wagon train ever increase our chances of moving up a car or two. We were last and always would be last. No wonder we looked forward to the two stretches of te rori Pakeha as we made our stately procession from Waituhi and Patutahi, over the red suspension bridge into Gisborne.

No sooner had we stopped outside the church than the pastor came rushing down to our cars, his black robes flapping like Batman's.

'Happy Sunday,' he beamed as we all stepped out. 'My, we have a large congregation this October day! Happy Sunday, sister Sarah, how's that be-*eau*-tiful voice today? And sister Sephora, my, you look good in green. Brother Ihaka, I've got you down as one of the ushers today, is that correct? Oh g-*ood*. And father and mother Mahana, it is so wonderful to see you both. Father Mahana, sir, you will read the lesson? Praise the Lord, what would our humble church do without the fine Mahana family to get us through the day?'

What indeed. Not only were we a devout family but every Sunday we all had some duty to perform. It was no good just praising good works; we also had to do them. This meant that my aunts Ruth and Sarah had been raised to be in the choir from the moment they were born; such a long career in singing had absolutely ruined their voices. My uncles Matiu, Maaka, Ruka and Hone were raised to be deacons and then part-time pastors in the church. Aperahama, Ihaka and my father Joshua were always on ushering duty, and Miriam and Esther came in every week to do the flowers. Whenever there were bring-and-buys, our table was the largest. If donations were required, the Mahana collection outdid everybody else's. And because this was in the days of the tithe, before church collections became automated so that you could have tax rebates, our one-tenth of income was so magnanimous as to ensure our entry into the Kingdom of God.

I'm leaving the worst until last. Aunt Sephora was the organist unless, like today, I was 'giving her a rest'. Today we were *all* on deck.

The bell was ringing as the family hurried up the path and into the church. To the left I saw that Granduncle Ihaka and his family were there in force, all with the exception of Riripeti who, of course, would never come *here*. No doubt Granduncle Ihaka had asked her dispensation for this special Sunday. Ihaka had sired even more children than Grandfather Tamihana had; like me, they seemed to be still waking up, trying to blink the pikare out of their eyes. To the right were Zebediah Whatu and his descendants, dressed as usual up to the nines. As the pastor came in with Grandfather Tamihana and Grandmother Ramona everybody stood. The preacher knew they weren't standing for *him*. Grandfather bowed gravely to everyone as he walked to the front. My uncles, aunts and their spouses and families followed him. At the last moment Andrew Whatu and Haromi, my favourite cousins, peeled off from the main entourage and snuck back to the last pew, as far away from Jesus as possible.

'Did you see the pastor's new false teeth?' Andrew asked. I had wondered why he was looking like Francis the Talking Mule. 'They're so Kolynos white,' Andrew continued.

To which Haromi gave a droll look and lowered her sunglasses. 'You don't think I'm wearing these for nothing,' she said in her low, hoarse voice, the product of too many smokes at too early an age.

'I'll see you two afterwards,' I said.

'Oh no you won't,' Aunt Sarah said. She had come to get Haromi to sit with her up the front. 'I've got my eye on you three. You should be ashamed of yourself, Simeon, leading Haromi up the wrong track –'

What had I done now! Me leading *her* up the wrong track?

'Where there's smoke there's fire,' Aunt Sarah continued, resorting to her usual platitudes. 'Haromi is coming straight home after church with me.'

I shrugged my shoulders and went up to the organ, pumping it so that it wheezed and coughed into life. The choir was taking its place and the pastor was standing in front of it. Grandfather himself had instructed that I learn to play the organ. He had said, 'What else is Simeon good for? Anyway, playing the organ will put his hands somewhere we can see them –' whatever that meant. No doubt, given his crack about my hair, playing the organ was also an appropriate pastime for a –

The bell stopped. The congregation began to settle down. The pastor turned and flashed a smile which sunburnt everybody in a trice.

'And now, brothers and sisters, to begin our service today on such a be-*eau*-tiful day –'

'Amen to that,' somebody said.

'We will have a rendition of "Love at Home" by our very own choir.'

Everybody went 'Aaaah'. The choir stood up. Yes, mostly Mahana. The family that sings together stays together.

'There is beauty all round –' the choir crooned. 'When there's love at home –'

Aunt Sarah, as usual, was the soloist. Her tonsils were in fabulous form. Her vibrato was so wide she was singing every note between D and G at once.

'There is love in every sound –' I crescendoed, just to make Aunt Sarah work a little harder, 'When there's –'

Aunt Sarah cast me dagger looks. She gasped for deeper and deeper breaths, her lungs expanding.

'Loo-*oo-ve* –'

I slowed the tempo down too. Aunt Sarah was making frantic hand signals to speed it up. No Auntie, attagirl, you can do it. And anyway this will teach you for your crack about Haromi –

'*Love at home*!'

Way to go! Everybody was holding on to their hats. Auntie's tonsils were working like mad, her voice like a train roaring out of a tunnel. *Guinness Book of Records*, here we come.

And after all that, there was a hush as Grandfather Tamihana came forward and up the steps to the podium.

'Brothers and sisters,' he began, 'this is a special day for all of us and particularly for the Mahana and Whatu families. The shearing season is upon us. Today, the first Sunday of October, we have all come to thank the Lord, in His own house, for all that He has given us. We also ask His blessings on us as we face the new season.'

It was always the same words and the same text. I wanted to roll my eyes with resignation. Then, as Grandfather Tamihana started to say the words, I found myself looking up at him, for the text itself was simple, dealing with simple and true emotions. It was a text written for country folk, containing within it all the values and trust that we placed in our God to look after us. It held the shared understanding of all rural communities that sometimes our trials and tribulations can only be faced by trusting to Him, having faith that the Lord will provide.

'Brothers and sisters, the Lord was a shepherd and we are the sheep of His flock. Over all these years He has kept us in sickness and in health, in good times and bad times. Please say with me –

> The Lord is my shepherd
> I shall not want
> He maketh me to lie down in green pastures
> He leadeth me beside the still waters
> He restoreth my soul . . .
> Yea though I walk through the Valley of Death

I will fear not
For He is with me
His sword and His staff comfort me
And I will dwell in His house
For ever –'

6

Finally, Sunday service came to an end. Grandfather and Grandmother were making their farewells to the pastor and his wife. The
rest of the family were milling around waiting for the movement
order back to Waituhi. Aunt Sarah, who had lost her voice, was
guarding Haromi from my clutches. Then Uncle Matiu coughed and,
pointing to his watch, drew Grandfather's attention to the time.
Swiftly Grandfather looked up at us and nodded.

'Okay,' Dad said. 'Me haere tatou.'

We dispersed to our cars.

The tar sealing lasted until we came to Makaraka and then, as
usual, we were back in Maori country. My father could have fallen
back from the cavalcade but kept his speed up.

'Can you see them?' Dad asked. He wasn't referring to the cars
in front; he was pointing to the road on the left that intersected ours.

'No,' I said.

The pace had quickened in front and, alerted by it, Mum nudged
Dad.

'Keep up, dear,' she said. 'We're lagging behind.'

Dad nodded and accelerated. 'Bulibasha's putting his foot down,'
he muttered. The needle on the dial was steadily increasing from 27
miles per hour through 32 to 38 to – golly whizzikers, we were flying!

'Just keep up, dear,' Mum repeated. We wished she was driving;
she had a certain touch that drove cars crazy.

'I'm up as far as I can go,' my father said. Indeed he seemed to
be playing a dangerous game of touch and go with Uncle Ihaka's
back numberplate. 'Father must have seen something –'

Sure enough, through the drifting dust to our left we caught a
glimpse of another cavalcade approaching the T junction ahead. Not
far beyond it was the red suspension bridge.

The Poata family from Hukareka. They were coming back from

their church in Gisborne, returning home to Hukareka as we were to Waituhi. Kicking up a dust like clouds and flying through it like enemy aircraft.

Our mother said, 'Hang on, darlings.'

The race to the bridge was on.

My heart was pounding fast. I tried to be Dad's extra pair of eyes, looking through the dust for him and willing him to stay on the road and keep up. I imagined that I was pilot Gregory Peck's sidekick in *Twelve O'Clock High*; Greg had suddenly become blinded and Japanese kamikazes were diving out of the sun and I had to see for him. It was all up to me. We *had* to get to the T junction before they did, otherwise the Poatas would have the advantage on the approach to the bridge. It was going to be close –

Bang. The Pontiac hit the back of Uncle Ihaka's Austin and ricocheted off.

'Keep on the road, dear,' Mum said. Stones and gravel were clanging and spraying the Pontiac.

'I'm trying my best, Huria,' Dad answered. 'But the car needs new wheels and –'

'We're gonna get there first!' Glory squealed.

Sure enough, we were almost at the T junction. We were in front by some ten precious yards and, ahead, Mohi was broadsiding into the stretch, then Uncles Matiu, Maaka, Ruka, Hone, Aperahama, Ihaka and –

Bang. The Pontiac broadsided into the straight as well, ricocheting off one of the Poata cars. I caught a glimpse of startled faces, a fist being shaken and grim expressions.

'Well, after all, it's an old car,' Dad said of our Pontiac, 'and the wheels need changing and –'

'Just keep up, dear,' Mum said.

A gap was developing between us and Uncle Ihaka. That was dangerous, because the Poatas could get in between and try to cut us out. If that happened, who knows *what* they would do to us and our mother?

And now the Poatas were coming up on the outside, trying to get ahead of us and, agony, they were gaining. With growing despair my sisters and I watched as one after another the grim faces of our enemy edged past us and in front of us. The first car, a Buick, had Rupeni Poata in it, as ugly as sin. The second was being driven by his eldest son, Caesar Poata, whose kids were flattening their faces against the windows at us. Then came the third car with Poppaea –

31

or 'The Brute' as we called her – and her daughter the divine Poppy making cross-eyes at me. Ahead was the bridge.

'Run them off the road, dear,' Mum said. Run them off the road?

'I don't think I should do that, Mum,' Dad said.

'Yes you can,' she answered.

The bridge was looming up fast. My heart was in my stomach. Did I forget to tell you it was one way?

I closed my eyes. One of us had to give in, either us or the Poatas. I heard a squeal of brakes. I opened my eyes.

All the Poata cars were slewing into a skid. A little old lady in a Ford Prefect was coming their way and they were on the wrong side of the road.

Oh, *thank* you, Lord, thank you.

Even if ours was the last car, the Mahanas had got to the bridge first. I looked back. The Poatas were gesturing ineffectually at us. Poppy was raising her fist.

Eat our *dust*.

By the time we stopped at Patutahi my daydreams about Poppy had just about subsided. It didn't matter that she was three inches taller than I was, skinnier than a rake and had freckles – or as we called it, bird shit on the face – Poppy was the girl of my dreams. Perhaps it was because she was unattainable, being from Hukareka, just as Rhonda Fleming – my favourite actress – was also unattainable, being older and living in Hollywood. Whatever the case, to me Poppy was as lovely as Rhonda Fleming who played Cleopatra in *Serpent of the Nile* and just as tempting. I would have laid all of Waituhi at Poppy's feet had she not been from Hukareka.

Dad pulled the Pontiac into the petrol station and went off in search of Mr Jenkins. One of Dad's responsibilities was to get the oil for all the lamps in the homestead.

Mum watched him go. Then, 'Let's get it over with,' she said.

She gathered herself together, dusted herself off, checked her hat in the mirror and went into the general store. Having on her best Sunday clothes made her feel better when dealing with Miss Zelda and Miss Daisy.

Although my sisters and I liked nothing better than to dawdle in the general store, my mother's exchanges with Miss Zelda, who took care of the business side of things, were always too brief.

'I – I – I,' Mum began to stutter.

'Why, good afternoon, Mrs Mahana,' Miss Zelda answered, 'what a pleasant surprise! Daisy? Scott? Mrs Mahana has come to visit.'

Visit, huh?

'I think I know why Mrs Mahana is here,' Miss Daisy said to her sister. 'To pay her account.' She pointed to the huge tally board on which the names of families with overdue accounts were marked in red. 'Well, Mrs Mahana, you can thank your lucky stars you're not in the red.'

Being in the red was awful. It meant having to go in to discuss a further extension on your loan, often while other people were around. It was like grovelling.

My mother took her purse from her handbag. She looked at me.

'This is all we can afford this week, Miss Zelda,' I said.

Miss Zelda peered down at the coins, poking them around on the possibility that there might be a £1 note beneath. Sighing, she reached under the counter and pulled out a huge ledger book. My mother's lips trembled.

'Now,' Miss Zelda said, leafing through the pages, 'Mahana E, Mahana H, ah here we have it, Mahana J, for Joshua.' She shifted the book so my mother could look at the ledger. 'You can read for yourself, Mrs Mahana, that you owe us £45 already and you are getting very close to being in the red. Can you see? Last week you bought a sugarbag of flour and –' Perspiration beaded Mum's face. Obediently she followed Miss Zelda's pencil, nodding as it went down the figures. I wondered whether she saw the look of contempt on Miss Zelda's face. 'But this will help pay off some of the interest,' Miss Zelda said. 'You couldn't perhaps pay off more? No? Well, anything is better than nothing. Perhaps Mr Mahana might be able to work a little harder. Or you might be able to find some work for yourself, Mrs Mahana. Good day.'

Miss Zelda offered us four aniseed balls. Free.

I said, 'No thank you, Miss Zelda, my sisters and I don't eat sweets.'

Nothing would induce us to be beholden in any way, to be in emotional as well as financial debt.

Back at the car my father was waiting.

'Next time, darlings,' my mother said to us. She knew we would have loved some lollies.

'They're mouldy old sweets anyway,' Hope said.

'All done?' Dad asked.

My mother nodded. Both of them seemed afraid. Dad took Mum's hand and squeezed it. She squeezed back.

My mother couldn't read. My father couldn't read either. They knew it only too well. So did Miss Zelda.

7

That night at dinner we broke our fast with a simple ceremony of bread and water, knowing that in the households of Granduncle Ihaka and Zebediah Whatu the same ceremony was happening.

Then Grandfather nodded his head and Aunts Sephora, Miriam and Esther, assisted by my mother, began to bring the food out from the kitchen. The table, which Grandfather had made himself, was three huge slabs of kauri which could be fitted together or taken apart depending on how many people needed to be served. Tonight the three parts had been pushed together, end on end; we were seating thirty of the family and some of our shearers. The food was simple country fare: lamb chops, potatoes, kumara and pumpkin, peas and beans, all smothered in rich brown gravy. Jellies and ice cream had already been placed on the table. Jugs of red and orange cordial were there also, with small jugs of cream. Plates of paraoa rewana and other Maori breads, plastered with slabs of butter, were spaced at regular intervals.

My aunts sat down. Together we held hands around that large table. I noticed one of the shearers, a handsome nineteen-year-old named Pani, was sitting next to Aunt Miriam. He crimsoned when she went to hold his hand. I wondered why – Aunt Miriam was a plain woman who at twenty-five was much too old for him. Yet she was blushing too.

Grandfather signed for Matiu to bless the food.

'Lord, we thank you for Father Tamihana and Mother Ramona and ask you to protect them with your love. At the same time, we ask you to bless this food and the hands which prepared it, in Jesus' name –'

'Amine,' we said.

Then Grandfather Tamihana said, 'We are all family. The family comes first. The family always comes first –'

YesBulibasha YesBulibasha Yesyesyes.

Even I found the words readily on my lips.

'And are we all ready to begin our new season?'

'Yes, father,' Uncle Matiu said. 'Mahana One will start at the Horsfield station next Wednesday.'

'Mahana Two will be at the Wi Pere estate,' Uncle Maaka said. 'I rang the station manager up. Bob said they're bringing the first sheep in tomorrow.'

'We go up to Otara station,' said Uncle Ruka about Mahana Three. 'I've asked Maaka if he can spare one of his boys as Lloyd is in hospital.'

'When did he go in?' Grandfather asked. Lloyd had been shearing with us for four seasons. He was a muscular man with the sun in his smile and all the world before him. Always eager to please, he adored Grandfather as most of the young men seemed to do. He would have walked on water for Grandfather, or placed his life in Grandfather's hands.

'Last week. He might have appendicitis. Something has been bothering him.'

'You should have told me,' Grandfather reproved. 'He's not working, but he stays on the payroll. He has a family just like the rest of us.'

'Yes, Father,' Uncle Ruka said.

'And Mahana Four,' Uncle Hone coughed, 'we start at the Collinsons'. No sweat.'

'Good,' Grandfather Tamihana said. 'We must all work hard. There must be no slackening. Any problems should be brought to me immediately. Don't leave it to the last minute. That's when problems happen. Kua pae?'

'Kua pae,' we agreed.

'The family –'

'Comes first,' we said.

There was a pause. Grandfather picked up his fork. The sign to eat.

As I was climbing into bed that night I heard the dogs beginning to practise for Monday with little squeals and yelps, clearing their throats for tomorrow's dawn. Our rooster was also in rehearsal, preening his feathers and doing his scales – do, re, mi, fa, so, la, ti, *cock a doodledo*! The whole universe seemed to breathe a sigh of relief as if to say, Roll on Monday.

I heard Glory calling out, ' 'Night Mummy, 'night Daddy, 'night Faith, 'night Hope, 'night Simeon –'

She did this every night, a childish mantra to set her world right before she could sleep, a special piece of magic to get us through the night. I heard the others call back, including Dad, with, 'Go to sleep, Glory.'

I decided to pretend I was asleep. Sure enough, I heard the pitter-patter of little steps and a small shape jumped on me.

'I won't play dead any more,' she threatened.

'Night Glory,' I squeaked.

'That's better.'

A kiss and she was gone.

8

Monday, and sometimes if I was lucky I managed to get into the bathroom before going to school. On those days I was able to see something of myself, for this was the only place, apart from Grandfather's own bedroom, where there was a mirror. Grandfather regarded mirrors as devices of the devil, leading to vanity and selfishness.

The mirror in the bathroom at the homestead was hung so high on the wall that usually all I ever saw was my forehead. This was because Grandfather Tamihana was over six feet tall and so were most of my uncles. As a consequence my forehead became the most well-known part of my body and I have watched it grow higher as I have grown older. In those days, though, my forehead was pretty close to my eyebrows but not so close that anybody could accuse me of having werewolf ancestry.

A couple of blocks of wood to stand on did the trick. There I was. All five feet six inches of me. At fourteen I wasn't handsome, but I wasn't plain either. My hair had a tendency to stick out all over the place but at least it hid my big ears. I couldn't do anything about that big Mahana nose, but all in all, not a bad looker – and all *man*. All *sex machine*. Eyes that could look soulful and wicked at the same time. A nose that flared at the nostrils like a stallion. Lips perhaps a little on the generous side but you wouldn't be able to miss those beauties in the dark.

Mohi, The Magnificent Turd, came in. 'Once a short arse,' he said, 'always a short arse.'

He proceeded to elbow me out of the way and to bend – like my uncles he too was at least six feet – to comb his thick wavy hair. A few self-regarding winks and smiles later, and a poking out of his tongue to see if it was yellow and –

'If you've got it, you've got it,' he said.

'Why all the fuss?' I asked. 'You're only going to the shed.'

Mohi had left school three years previously. He was free, out of jail and on the payroll with his father's shearing gang, Mahana One. My cousins Andrew and Haromi and my sisters and I still had to go to school for another month before helping out in Mahana Three.

Mohi gave me a smirk. 'It's the early worm,' he said, indicating his crotch, 'that catches the birds.'

Oh, *gross.*

'Hey, Mohi!' I shouted when he was safely out of hearing. 'You forgot to shave your palms!'

Roll over and die, Mohi.

Across the sunlight, I caught a glimpse of Grandfather Tamihana. He was standing with his walking stick today; his leg must be playing up. Beside him were his brother Ihaka and Zebediah Whatu, and they were talking with Uncles Matiu, Maaka, Ruka and Hone. The shearers were loading up the truck and cars, each of which bore the simple logo: MAHANA. What more needed to be said?

Mohi walked over to Grandfather to say goodbye. Grandfather feinted at him with his left fist and Mohi weaved and feinted back with his right. I envied Mohi his easy familiarity with Grandfather. Then Grandfather rolled up his sleeve and offered Mohi his right arm. They started to Indian wrestle, Mohi straining to beat Grandfather. But slowly Grandfather forced his arm down in defeat.

'I'm going to get you one day, Grandfather!' Mohi yelled.

Grandfather laughed. Then he saw me and waved my father over to him. Dad nodded and came over to where I was standing.

'Simeon,' Dad said, 'you're going to have to look after the homestead while I'm away. Be obedient to your grandfather and grandmother, especially your grandfather. He is remaining behind because he still has a big job to do sorting all the paperwork and making sure everything goes smoothly. He has his job and you have yours.'

'Yes, Dad.'

'Look after your mother, aunts, sisters and the rest of the family.

37

It won't be for long, son. Once school is over we'll close up the homestead and you can all come out and join us.' He went to put his arms around my shoulder but I shrugged him off. I looked at Grandfather still talking to Mohi.

'Why couldn't Grandfather have told me himself?'

'He asked me to tell you.'

'If he had told me, everybody would realise my job was as important as theirs.'

'When my brothers and I were your age we all had to take our turn looking after the women and children.'

I shook my head. 'No, Dad. *You* did, but not the others. Now I have to do it.'

'I don't want any arguments. Goodbye, son.' My father walked back to the truck.

I ran after him. 'Hey, Dad,' I said, 'you're the greatest shearer of the lot. The best!'

He smiled at me. 'How come then,' he asked, 'I'm still on the Number 2 stand?'

It was on the tip of my tongue to say, Because Uncle Hone is older than you and the boss. But just then Pani called out, 'Aren't you coming, Simeon?'

Grandfather Tamihana turned to him. 'Better for all of us that Simeon stays here,' he said. 'He'll only want to read his schoolbooks at the shed and forget about being sheepo.'

I guess he meant it as a joke, but I felt embarrassed, especially as Mohi was cackling with scorn. I knew full well Grandfather's contempt for education; after all, he hadn't been educated, and look at him now.

Grandmother Ramona came to my rescue. 'Leave the boy alone,' she said to Grandfather. Mum and Aunts Sephora, Miriam and Esther joined her to say goodbye to the men; Miriam blushed when Pani looked across at her. There were no kisses, no sentimental goodbyes. This was simply something that had to be done.

Grandfather raised a hand.

'Ma te Atua koutou e manaaki,' he prayed.

'Amine,' the shearers replied.

9

There are some souls, like Grandfather Tamihana, whom God signs contracts with before they are born. You can tell who they are when something shows up in the manner of their birth or in their accomplishments as young men or women.

How else can you explain why some people are blessed in terms of physical attributes and others not? Why some are tall and others are short? Why some have fabulous hair which they will keep all their lives and why others, like me, will always worry about losing theirs before they are thirty? God also marks such souls with a special blessing. In some cases it is astounding beauty, like Helen of Troy or red-headed Rhonda Fleming. In my grandfather's case, it was physical strength and sporting prowess.

This is why, although sometimes stirred by the sentimentality of our family meetings, I always hated the homestead drawing room. It was a shrine to blessed people, a testament to physical prowess and virility, neither of which I possess.

Look at all the photos on the walls – Grandfather as teenage sports champion in boxing, wrestling, track and field, javelin, discus; as representative team member of rugby, hockey, swimming, sprints and even playing polo with the Pakeha at the showgrounds. He is a stunning sight, his physique scarcely fitting into his clothes. He has the wide open smile of a careless youth with the entire world at his feet.

Now look at the photo of Grandfather with his parents. They are short and stunted, unlike their god of a son. See? He was born that way.

And look at all the silver trophies and shields. Not all of them have been won by Grandfather, yet he so inculcated his sons and daughters with the drive for physical and sporting excellence that, as they grew, *they* began winning prizes for *him*. That too is part of his physical triumph. His physical achievement lives on in us.

Did I say us? In this holy of holies, it is strength rather than intelligence which is worshipped. You will find no trophies of mine here, though there may be a couple of certificates for being third in class stuck away in a drawer. This room makes it clear: I am no use whatsoever to Grandfather.

I was in a foul mood when I walked in to breakfast. With all the men gone, the only ones left in Waituhi were old women, girls or the useless.

'How come,' I asked Aunt Ruth, who was packing up the cutlery for Mahana Two, 'we pray all the time?'

'The family that prays together stays together,' she said in a singsong way. 'You know that.'

Yeah yeah.

'But we weren't always like this,' Aunt Ruth said. 'Not as pious, and church-going. If your grandfather hadn't met the angel –'

Glory dropped her spoon. 'Met the angel?' she repeated, her eyes widening.

Aunt Ruth sighed, looked at her watch and glared at me as if it was all my fault.

'In those days,' Aunt Ruth said, 'the sky wasn't cluttered with planes and satellites. God's angels were still able to get through to earth with messages for the faithful.'

Aunt Ruth had an unswerving belief that the First World War was when human beings began to lose their godliness. It had something to do with the use of mustard gas on the Western Front; God's voice had come through pretty regularly until then. The gas infiltrated into His Kingdom and affected His throat, then just when He recovered He found all the frequencies jammed by radio.

'Your grandfather was twenty-three in 1918,' Aunt Ruth said. 'He wasn't exactly an ungodly man, but he wasn't a godly man either. He was an ideal choice for a visitation by an angel. He bowed to no man and he bowed to no god. He believed in what he saw and he believed in a man's strength. He thought man was an animal like any other beast of the field or fowl of the air' – like all the Mahanas, Aunt Ruth had a penchant for the well-turned biblical phrase – 'and that at the end of your life you went away, found a place to die, and got on with dying. Furthermore, there was no Hereafter. How could there be? You couldn't see God, could you? Therefore God could not exist. You couldn't see an afterlife, could you? Therefore that did not exist either! Yes, a man's own strength, that's what your grandfather believed in.'

Aunt Ruth pointed through the door of the kitchen into the drawing room. She motioned to one of the photographs of Grandfather, the one hanging next to the oval photo of Grandmother Ramona in 1914. In it was the evidence above any other that Grandfather was exactly how his reputation has captured him. 'Tamihana Mahana, Wrestling Champion, Gisborne District, 1914–1920, undefeated.'

Standing with feet apart, Grandfather balances on the balls of his toes, head tucked into shoulders, arms outstretched. He had the art, even then, of appearing twice as large as he was. He did not merely enter a space; he claimed it. Territorial, he expanded his arms and decreed, This is mine. If he saw something he wanted, he took it. He was a Samson of a man.

'The irony was,' Aunt Ruth said, 'that although your grandfather was ungodly, your great-grandfather was the *very* godly minister in the Ringatu church, second only to Riripeti Mahana, its priestess. When they saw that a Samson had been born into their midst, ka tika, they agreed he would help to lead the people out of bondage to the Pakeha and into the land of milk and honey known as Canaan. But if only he could believe in God. Oh, he was a trial to them!

'All through the war, your great-grandfather and Riripeti waited for him to take up the jaw of an ass and smite the Philistine Pakeha. But he just didn't seem interested in anything else except sport, women and –'

'Why women?' Glory asked.

'Never you mind,' Aunt Ruth answered. 'By the time the war ended they had almost lost hope that your grandfather would bring the Temple of Dagon down upon the Pakeha. So when that angel came, they took it as a good sign. At last God would let Tamihana *see* Him through one of his angels. Then your grandfather would turn to the paths of righteousness and help to fulfil the Ringatu destiny.

'So it was that on a summer day in 1918 –'

Tamihana Mahana was behind the plough in the maize fields when the angel visited him. It was a Sunday, and coming on to midday. Tamihana didn't care much about the Sabbath. There was work to finish, a crop to be sown. Very soon there would be another mouth to feed. Ramona was with child again, her fourth, whom they would name Hone if he was a boy or Ruth if she was a girl.

'Hup!' he called to the two draught horses. 'Hup!'

The day was peaceful and quiet. Most of the people in the village had gone to karakia, to church, at Mangatu. There was nobody around except old man Kuki who was sick and Maggie who had taken the chance to tell everybody, 'I'll look after Kuki.' What she really meant was that she wanted to stay by the window, watching Tamihana. Tamihana grinned to himself. He had taken his shirt off so that Maggie could really see what he was made of. He was proud of the V shape of his shoulders and the washboard tautness of his glistening stomach.

The horses came to the end of the field. 'Ka mutu,' he shouted. He took off his hat and sweatband, unhitched the team and let them head for the long grass on the side of the field. Perspiration poured from his brow and into his eyes. The ploughing should have tired him, but it didn't. His body had never let him down, and in this he knew he was unlike other men. When they dropped by the wayside or fell out of a race, he kept on going. He relied on his physical strength to get him through life, to till his land and, more important, to secure cash work from the Pakeha farmers in the district. Now that he was a married man and a father, he relied on the crops from his land to feed his family. But obtaining cash work was harder. What he needed to do, he realised, was to create a business, something that would bring the work to him.

Perhaps I should pray, Tamihana thought. If I ask God, He might tell me what I should do to prosper. He started to mumble some words to God. Then he shook his head – only fools and old women prayed. He looked up at the sun and was momentarily blinded by sweat and sunlight.

Huh? He aha tera?

Printed on his retina was an after-image. The clouds had rolled back, revealing a blue kingdom. Something golden was fluttering down from the sky.

'So the angel had wings?' Glory asked.

'Of course,' Aunt Ruth responded. 'How do you think angels get down from Heaven?'

'Was it a man angel or a lady angel?' Glory continued. 'Or was it a baby cherubim?'

'Shush,' Aunt Ruth said, 'don't you see? Even though our father only managed to get a tiny bit of his prayer out, it was answered. Now keep still, because you're spoiling my story –'

Tamihana shook his head again. He took a cloth from his trouser pocket and wiped the sweat away.

'E hika,' Tamihana exclaimed.

The angel was standing on the roadside. He was blond and had blue eyes and looked like Jesus in a cotton suit.

'But I thought you said the angel had wings,' Glory said accusingly.

'The angel folded his wings away,' Aunt Ruth answered. 'After all, what would you do if you saw an angel with wings on the road. Would you believe it was an angel?'

'No,' Glory said after pondering this for a while. 'I'd probably think the man was on his way to a fancy-dress party. Or had forgotten it wasn't Christmas yet.'

'That's *right*,' Aunt Ruth said.

'Kia-a- orai-a, ee hor-a,' the angel said in an American accent. He had a hideous midwestern crewcut and looked like he'd just flown in over the rainbow from Kansas City or Salt Lake.

'Kia ora,' Tamihana replied.

The angel came closer, leaned on the fence and blew away a feather that had fallen on his shoulder. He plucked a straw and began to chew on it. Still blinded, Tamihana saw golden rays emanating from the angel.

'Ko ko-ay a Tamihana Mahana?' the angel asked. His Maori accent was atrocious.

'Ae,' my grandfather nodded.

The angel smiled, a sweet smile which showed perfect white and even teeth. 'Ah,' the angel said. 'Ten-ay ko-ay.' The golden rays began to shimmer, spilling their radiance across Tamihana's face. They spun across the sun, whirling like spokes in the sky. 'I couldn't be sure,' the angel said. 'That was a pretty quick prayer you said there!'

Tamihana laughed. He must have said something out loud and this Pakeha walking along the road had overheard him.

The angel shook his head. He gave a lazy sigh and then stood proudly, pointing a finger at Tamihana. 'The Lord has great work for you to do, Tamihana Mahana. He has blessed you with great strength and sporting prowess. Such men or women are valuable to the Lord and because of this suffer temptations beyond those of ordinary mortals. That is why He, the Lord thy God, has sent me.'

43

'He aha?' Tamihana asked.

'He wants you to use your strength to be a living witness and testament unto all your people that God lives.'

'However,' Aunt Ruth said, 'your grandfather wasn't going to believe any angel that came along the road, least of all a Pakeha angel! So he said –'

'How do I know you're an angel?'

'I have wings,' the angel said.

'So do birds,' Tamihana answered, 'and devils.'

He paused, suspicious. The angel was smiling with those clear cornflower-blue eyes, amused. Tamihana knew that he had to test the angel.

'And what do I get if I help God?' he asked.

'Why, what you prayed for! The Lord will help you to prosper and, as He did with Israel, bless the fruit of your loins all their days.'

The slick-sounding promises left Tamihana unconvinced. 'My people tell me I am their Samson. They say God gave me this strength. I will wrestle you, for nobody has ever beaten me. If you are truly an angel, God will take my strength away so that you can defeat me.'

The angel roared with laughter. 'I accept your challenge,' he said.

'The best of three falls?' Tamihana asked.

'Yup,' the angel answered, spitting on his hands.

'So it was,' Aunt Ruth said, 'that in the middle of the day your grandfather Tamihana wrestled with the golden angel –'

'Wingless like a crispy chicken,' I interpolated.

'But an angel all the same,' Aunt Ruth continued, swatting at me with her hand. 'They wrestled all that afternoon and soon Grandfather realised he had met his match and that this indeed was an angel. He hoped that Maggie wasn't looking out her window to see him getting beaten.'

Then the angel executed some pretty unorthodox moves. With

horror, Tamihana felt his strength suddenly leave him. He fell to the ground. Once. Twice.

'Oh my God,' Tamihana said, stunned. He went down on a bended knee.

The angel was panting. 'No, I am not God,' the angel said, 'but I have been sent by Him. Will you now agree to undertake your part of our bargain?'

Tamihana hesitated. He was humiliated by his defeat.

'I ask again,' the angel said, 'will you agree to our bargain?'

'Yes,' Tamihana said.

The angel put his hands on Tamihana's head and Tamihana felt the strength pouring back into him. It was a new kind of strength, godliness was in it, and he felt like crying for joy.

'You will be blessed, as Abraham was blessed,' the angel said, 'and so will your children and your children's children for ever. And you yourself will prosper from this day forth just as your family prospers. So, Tamihana, thou servant of God, do as the Lord has commanded.'

The angel let Tamihana see his brilliant golden wings, so glorious that they filled the sky with their radiance.

'So the angel *did* have wings,' Glory said.

'Did I say it didn't?' Aunt Ruth sighed.

Tamihana became a Samson all right. The trouble was, the angel wasn't a Ringatu angel. He was a Mormon angel.

Within the space of two decades Tamihana converted all the Ringatu members of the Mahana family, with the exception of his father, Riripeti herself and his brother Ihaka – though Ihaka began to weaken in the 1950s.

However, the conversion of part of the Waituhi Valley began a great Ringatu–Mormon conflict. Huge splits appeared between the four sections of Waituhi itself, and the Pakowhai, Rongopai, Takitimu and Pere families involved; Nani Mini Tupara was so angry about it. I even used to think that this same conversion was the cause of the trouble between our family of Waituhi and the Poata family of Hukareka. There, the Ringatu religion remained powerful. Was I ever wrong?

My Grandfather Tamihana was at his physical peak in 1918 when he met the angel. There was no task that he could not accomplish. However, God had now set Grandfather a task – to raise his family so that it was an exemplar to others. God had also promised him that he would prosper. But how?

These were the great questions which Grandfather set about to answer. It was his twelve days in the wilderness.

The prospects for young Maori men living in rural areas were not promising. Much of the Patutahi block had been confiscated by the Pakeha, and by 1918 many communities had had their lands alienated because of their inability to pay the rates. Riripeti had been one of the lucky ones in that her ancestor Wi Pere had maintained an estate for her family. The Mahana clan, however, were only one of a number of dirt farmers eking out a subsistence living on small patches of land alongside the Waipaoa River. All around him Tamihana could see the results of Maori poverty. The Great War had claimed some lives, the 1918 flu epidemic had just ravaged the district and people were saying that a world depression was on the way. Although his sporting reputation had kept him regularly at work as stockman, scrubcutter, forestry worker, fencer, orchardist – as labourer for the Pakeha – even those sources of income were diminishing. Land development had virtually come to a standstill. Drink, debauchery and dissolution were all around the newly converted Tamihana. How was he to prosper so that he would become a model of God's word? What did God want him to do?

For the second time in his life, Grandfather Tamihana decided to pray. He went down on his bended knees before God.

'Where's my miracle?' he asked.

The Lord sent Apirana Ngata.

At that time Ngata, the Maori member of parliament for the East Coast, was in Tikitiki, at the dedication of an Anglican church commemorating the Maori soldiers of the First World War. Ngata had encouraged his Ngati Porou people into dairying. Land development had remained his main preoccupation.

'I must go to Tikitiki,' Tamihana said to Ramona. 'If I can talk to Ta Api, perhaps his administration will agree to lend us the money so that we also can go into dairying.'

Tamihana walked and hitched his way to Tikitiki. The trip took him three days. Apirana Ngata saw Tamihana striding into the township and was taken by Grandfather's strength and purpose. Tamihana asked Ngata for a loan to get him going.

'I will see to it,' Apirana Ngata said, 'but only if you will agree to one matter.'

'He aha?' Tamihana asked.

'I will give you the money but I want you to go into the sheep industry. Wool prices will go up soon and you will be well placed to take advantage of that.'

'Ta Api,' Tamihana said, 'I do not have the wisdom to be a sheep farmer. Let me make you a counter offer.'

Apirana Ngata laughed. 'He aha?'

'If you give me the money, I will build up a shearing gang. Let the Pakeha be the farmer and let me shear his sheep.'

'So that you can fleece him?' Apirana Ngata asked, his eyes twinkling.

'Ae, Ta Api.'

So it was agreed. The story of the Mahana shearing saga began.

'So you see,' Aunt Ruth said, finally, 'our family shearing business has been blessed by God from the very beginning.'

Glory clapped her hands. 'And we've lived happily ever after!' She was always a sucker for happy endings.

'Well –' Aunt Ruth looked doubtful.

Glory's eyebrows furrowed.

'Yes,' Aunt Ruth said hastily.

10

Andrew and Haromi were waiting at the corner for the school bus, standing as far away from the small kids as possible. Andrew saw me and waved. 'Did you bring any matches?' he asked.

I nodded. We had about five minutes before the bus arrived. Quickly we went into the flax where Andrew pulled out some tobacco and Haromi some De Reszke cigarette paper. Haromi was the expert in making roll-your-owns and, in a trice, one cigarette was lit and being passed around for a puff.

'The place is fucking deserted,' Haromi said.

Haromi always looked so angry at the world, so angry at being stuck with awful parents and being a goddam Mahana. When she was younger she actually went through a phase when she would whisper darkly, 'I'm not really a Mahana, you know. Somebody made a mistake up in Heaven and mixed me up with the babies destined for Los Angeles.' Today she looked even angrier. She had eyeliner around her eyes and had hitched her skirt up around her knees. Rebellion, rebellion.

She stood up and yelled, 'I wish I could tell you all to go to Hell but we're already here!'

The kids further up the road stopped, bewildered. Then, Oh it's just Haromi again.

'Guess who's in charge of the women?' I asked, puffing coolly on the cigarette she handed me.

'Not you too?' Andrew answered in mock surprise. 'Pity they're either older or our sisters. But there's always –' He winked at Haromi and she punched him.

'I'm grounded as well,' Haromi said, 'though for different reasons, obviously. Mum thinks I'm too dangerous to be around the shearers. As if I'm interested in *them*. The only boy I want,' she sighed, 'is James.' She had seen *Rebel Without a Cause* four times and knew some of the lines off by heart.

'I could have done with the pocket money,' I said.

'It's all a plot,' Andrew said. 'They think that if we don't get any pocket money we can't get up to any mischief. So they make us milk cows instead.'

Haromi tossed her hair, working herself up into a dramatic storm. When her voice came out it could have been Natalie Wood's. 'Oh I despise everything about being a Mahana and what they're doing to me,' she emoted, batting her eyelids furiously. 'I'm just too good for this family. One of these days I'm getting on the first bus out of here. I'm going to all those places where my kind of people are. New York, Chicago, Los Angeles, anywhere except here. And you know why? Because I'm worth it. I've got talent. And I'll just *die* here, I know I will, I'll really die –' She subsided into cinematic sobs.

Yeah yeah, Haromi, yeah yeah.

'At least we have each other,' Andrew said.

Haromi stared at him as if he hadn't understood one thing she had said. Finally she nodded, 'Yes, and we'll show them.'

'Oh shit, there's the bus,' Andrew said. He stood up and stamped the cigarette out. There was just enough time for me to start our secret catechism, the words that bonded us together as the Three Musketeers of Waituhi.

'In the beginning was our patriarch Tamihana Mahana!' I yelled. Andrew grinned and Haromi took my arm. 'He was like unto Samson and known far and wide for his strength and as a man among men. All the people clamoured for him, pleading that he be their champion in rugby, hockey, boxing, wrestling and other sports. Yea, and because he was handsome to look upon, even the concubines and harlots of the city of the plains desired him. But in the land of Nod he took to wife Ramona, who was a virtuous daughter of that land.'

Andrew took over. 'Then an angel came unto Tamihana and said unto him, "Alas, Tamihana, you have strayed onto the path of the ungodly. The Lord thy God has therefore sent me to save you." '

Haromi gave a giggle. 'But Tamihana closed his heart to the angel and it was only until they had bargained and had wrestled that Tamihana verily realised that the angel was indeed a messenger of God. Yeah, he got *trounced*.'

By this time we were laughing out loud.

'Then Tamihana said unto the angel, "What is the Lord my God's will?" And the angel said unto him, "You and your wife Ramona will be blessed with many children. Raise them and all that are yours so that they may be counted among the faithful. Let others see your works so that they come to God and inherit the sweet Beulah land." '

We completed the catechism in unison. 'Thus did Tamihana know that his mission was to be the father of many children, yea, as Abraham was. His loins poured out seed and he was blessed with sixteen children, alas, four dying at childbirth. Nevertheless, Tamihana was content, saying, "Although my children number only twelve they will be as the twelve thousand. Verily I shall raise them as a family in God, for that is how He has willed it and thus it will be done." And Tamihana's children had children including –'

'Simeon Mahana!' I shouted.

'Andrew Whatu!' Andrew shouted.

'And Haromi Whatu!' Haromi shouted.

'And because we were different,' we said together, 'we were treated like shit.'

'Me,' I said.

'And me,' Andrew said.

'And most definitely me,' Haromi said.

We had reached the bus. We shared a secret glance at each other before we hopped on. 'All for one and one for all!' we cried. Then –

'Grandfather *sucks*!' we shouted.

We didn't give a damn who heard – not even the Poatas.

11

Ever since I was an infant and began to understand what people were saying the first tenet of my life had been 'The family always comes first'; the second was 'Never trust a Poata'. Had I not assumed – wrongly as it turned out – that this enmity was based on religious differences, I would have thought it the product of some ancient quarrel of biblical or Sicilian proportions.

The adult members of the two families treated the relationship with magnificent disdain. If Uncle Hone met Caesar Poata in the street he would cross over to walk on the other side; if Aunt Sarah saw Poppaea Poata in a shop she would pretend there was a strange odour in the place and walk right out. The younger members, however, were more reckless. My cousin Mohi, for instance, once goaded Fraser Poata into a drag-strip race along the sandy stretch of Wainui Beach. Late one night, with the Poata youths at one end and the Mahanas at the other, they drove headlong at one another. It was Fraser Poata who quailed and pulled over, allowing Mohi to win. He just didn't have the killer instinct. Just as well, as Mohi was driving Grandfather's De Soto.

In our younger generation, the Poata counterparts for Haromi, Andrew and I were Poppy, Titus Junior – we called him Tight Arse – and Saul. We went in for eyeballing and swaggering – you know the sort of thing:

'You're a black bastard,' we might say to our duelling threesome at high noon just before a movie matinee.

'Not as black as you,' they might reply.

'Oh yeah?'

'Yeah?'

'Oh yeah?'

At their most serious, our conflicts ended as screaming matches and fisticuffs in the main street of Gisborne, but our arenas of conflict were mainly ritualised. The race to the bridge was one; shearing was another. However, the main arena was the sportsground. Here, we could engage in gladiatorial combat which assuaged our blood lust and allowed us to put the boot in. Had it not been for sports, I am sure our conflict would have escalated.

In all this, what was at stake was the mana of our leaders – in our case, Grandfather Tamihana; in their case, Rupeni Poata.

Again, had I not assumed religious differences as the cause, I would have looked to some sporting incident at the heart of the conflict. For Rupeni Poata, like Grandfather, had been a sporting champion in his youth. Haromi, Andrew and I found this incredible, because Rupeni Poata was what my cousin Mohi would have described as a *real* short arse. At five foot two, he was more than a foot shorter than Grandfather; he was even shorter than Grandmother Ramona. How he ever managed to beat Grandfather Tamihana in wrestling and track events – which he was reputed to have done – was beyond us. Rupeni Poata was also dumpy and ugly. When Haromi and I went to see *The Ten Commandments* we clutched each other with shock at the sight of Edward G. Robinson playing the lascivious Jewish turncoat who threatened Debra Paget with a fate worse than death.

'Rupeni Poata!' we hissed.

It was all the more incomprehensible to us therefore that Rupeni Poata was reputed to be so successful with women. When he spoke there was a slight whistling sound on his sibilants. His lips were big and fleshy, and he had a gap between his teeth. He was a snappy dresser, though, I have to say that for him. He had a habit of wearing dark suits and a fedora with its brim rakishly pulled to one side. He also drove a Lagonda.

'But he has another car,' Andrew told me.

'What kind?'

'An old Model T Ford,' Andrew said. 'It's locked in one of the sheds on his farm.'

'What would Rupeni Poata be doing with a Model T?'

'He must collect vintage cars,' Andrew shrugged.

In 1918, Rupeni Poata married a woman of high rank from Waikato; he knew how to get ahead. His wife's name was Maata and together they raised fourteen children. Although Rupeni began having children later than Grandfather Tamihana, his household overtook Grandfather's by having two sets of twin boys to begin with. Whether this should be taken as an indication of rampant sexuality I don't know, but if so, Rupeni was obviously on par with

Grandfather Tamihana. The twins were Uncle Ruka's age now, big, fierce men who had taken their physical size from their Waikato mother; and their names were all from Roman history: Caesar, Augustine, known as Augie; Titus, or Tight Arse Senior, and Alexander. They were an answer to their father's prayers, forming as they did a rugby front row of equal size to ours. To witness them against our front row of Uncles Matiu, Maaka, Ruka and Hone was to witness a battle between Leviathans.

The twins were followed by eight sisters: Julia, Agnes, Helen, Virginia, Gloria, Anna, Carla and Poppaea – she was the one we called 'The Brute' because of her strong hockey tactics. The Poata women, too, were big and fierce, and endowed with qualities which were suitable for men but which tended to tilt the women towards masculinity – moustaches on their upper lips and lots of hair under the armpits. They all seemed to marry tiny men, similar to their father, but they bred big children. Two brothers followed them, Bill and John, named as if Rupeni couldn't be bothered with the Roman any longer.

Had I not known better, I would have suspected that Rupeni bred his big family on purpose, to challenge ours.

The Poata homestead was right in the middle of Hukareka, next to the War Memorial Hall. It wasn't as big as ours, but because of Rupeni Poata's considerable reputation among the Ringatu community, it was the centre of attraction. Maata also brought her own mana and glory to Hukareka, and that amplified her husband's fame.

When Maata died in 1947, Rupeni Poata remained alone at the house, unmarried despite the interest of a number of widows. Unlike our family, none of his children lived with him. Rather, they took houses nearby in Hukareka. They were apparently devoted to their father, despite his evil and manipulative nature. Of course they believed everything he said, and thought everything we said was a lie.

Rupeni's constant companion was his granddaughter, the beauteous Poppy. How she was ever born from The Brute is God's own secret. I think that Andrew was as much in love with her as I was, and I venture to suggest that it was because she was so like our own Mahana women. She danced in Maori culture competitions with fire and spirit. She played hockey like Boadicea, her stick an instrument to mow people's legs off. She carried herself most of the time as a Maori princess.

As for Tight Arse Junior and Saul, weight for weight and height for height we were similar. This made them well-matched opponents, but I sometimes wished that God hadn't given them one asset we didn't have – longer arms. When Andrew and I got into fist fights with them, we sometimes came off worst. If God was truly on our side, how come *we* didn't have the longer reach?

In sum, the Poatas were worthy challengers for the House of Mahana. The stage was always ready for some good punch-ups.

12

Apart from Sundays, the only other time when Waituhi wasn't the best place in the world was when the shearing began. As the only working male left in the homestead, I was like Audie Murphy in *The Siege of Fort Petticoat*, defending the women as well as the crippled, the lame, the elderly, the ill and decrepit against Injuns.

'This is the way it's always been,' Aunt Miriam consoled me. It was six in the morning. I had already finished the milking and lit the copper in the washhouse. 'Every morning all his life your father has had to do this. Milk the cows, chop the wood, fill the copper for the washing –'

Aunt Miriam was carrying out the baskets of sheets, towels and clothes, including Grandfather's longjohns. Today they'd all be soaked, boiled in the copper and taken down to the creek to be rinsed, slapped against the rocks and pegged out to dry.

'And it's going to get worse,' Aunt Sephora joined in. 'The shearers will be sending in all their clothes soon.'

'Why *you*, though?' I asked my aunts. 'Why has it always been like this for you and Dad?'

'It's our job,' Aunt Miriam answered. 'We're the youngest. Anyway, what else have we got to do!' They laughed together.

I could never really think of my three aunts as separate women. Where there was one, the other two were nearby.

'But you could get married,' I said.

Aunt Miriam blushed. Aunt Sephora gave her one of her glances.

'We're too busy to do that,' she said. 'Bulibasha wouldn't let us anyway.'

'You get used to it,' Aunt Miriam said. 'Being us, I mean.' There was a pause.

'Enough talking,' Aunt Sephora instructed. 'We're running late. Esther, you better help Simeon fill the copper.'

It was on the tip of my tongue to say No. Instead, I nodded, and together Aunt Esther and I began ferrying the buckets from the outside pump to the copper.

At breakfast, Grandfather Tamihana said to Aunt Esther, 'I saw you helping Simeon.'

'It was nothing,' she answered. I wasn't being reprimanded. Esther was.

'You do your job, Esther. Let Simeon do his.'

'Everybody has their job,' my mother Huria said a few days later. The washhouse was on the go morning, afternoon and evening. The wood pile was diminishing fast and I was constantly chopping more wood. Now, just as I finished, Grandfather yelled, 'We're running low on meat, Simeon.' The criticism was implied: you are supposed to be the provider but you are slacking on your job.

I sharpened the butcher knife on the whetting block. Dad had chalked a mark on one of the sheep. I separated it from the flock and, in the yard near the homestead, slit its throat.

'It's the way it's meant to be,' my mother continued. She was watching me in the yard. The dead sheep was hanging from the hooks and I was skinning it, punching the skin from the carcass.

'Why is it meant to be!'

Mum shifted uneasily. 'You are always questioning things, Simeon. Can't you just go along with the way things are?'

The carcass was swinging crazily from the hooks and blood was spraying everywhere.

'If I had been Uncle Matiu's son,' I challenged, 'would this be the way it is meant to be?'

'No. But Matiu's not your father. He's –'

Slice, slice, slice with the butcher knife. 'Mohi's dad, I know, and Mohi is therefore the eldest grandchild. When Grandfather dies, Uncle Matiu will be the chief. When he dies, Mohi will be the chief. In my generation he will be *my* chief.'

'Your grandfather loves all his grandchildren –'

'Not equally, Mum.'

The skin fell away. I made a cut down the underbelly. The guts of the sheep, still steaming, fell on the concrete.

Mum hesitated, not wanting to agree or disagree.

I pressed on. 'Nor would this be the way things are meant to be if I was the son of Maaka, Ruka, Hone, Ruth, Sarah, Aperahama and Ihaka.'

'But you're not their son, either,' Mum tried to laugh, and stood to help steady the carcass. I was almost finished.

'No,' I answered, my voice firm. 'I'm yours and Dad's son. I'm the first born of the ninth child and seventh son. Now –'

I let the carcass down and carried it to the chopping block. One blow of the axe and the carcass split in two.

'Please don't play this game with me, son,' Mum said.

But I couldn't let it go. 'Another example,' I continued. 'Look at Dad's elder brothers and sisters. Why don't they live here at the homestead?'

One half of the carcass was on the chopping block. I took up the butcher knife again.

'They've got their own land,' she answered.

Slicing through the ribs. One rib after another.

'And who gave them their land?'

Heaving the other half on to the chopping block.

'Grandfather Tamihana.'

Cleanly, swiftly slicing.

'And why, Mum,' I asked, 'do we and Aunts Sephora, Miriam and Esther still live with Grandfather Tamihana and Grandmother Ramona at the homestead?'

My mother would not answer.

'I'll tell you why,' I said.

I was heaving with the exertion. I put the meat into the safe. Now there was meat enough for the next few days. My mother had taken up the bucket of water to sluice the blood off the concrete.

'There's no more land for Grandfather to give us. Even if there was, he wouldn't give us any –'

Tears were brimming in Mum's eyes. I took the bucket from her.

'And you know why, Mum? Do you really want to know why? It's all a matter of mana. Of our place in the order of the family.'

Flies were already feeding off the thick congealed blood. They rose angrily, buzzing around my head.

'Turituri to waho,' Mum whispered. 'It is an honour to stay with the old people and to look after them.'

I shook my head. I took up the yard broom, intending to sweep the concrete clean of the blood.

'We're here not because of the honour. We're here because the others in the family are older and have been given land and there's none left for us. There's something else too. Grandfather likes to have us here. We're trapped. He won't ever let us out.' My mother tried to take the broom from me. 'No, Mum. After all, this is my job, isn't it? It's the way it's meant to be, isn't it? We're here because in this life there are chiefs and there are Indians. We're the Indians.'

She gave me a long, fierce look. Her hand came up and slashed me across the face.

'I never want to hear you say that again, Himiona.'

Just to make sure, she hit me again.

'Never.'

That night at dinner, my mother and I were not speaking. Glory kept on kicking me under the table but I refused to take any notice. Glory hated it when we weren't playing Happy Family. Later, I was doing homework in my bedroom when Grandfather came in. He looked at my books.

'Why do you want to learn about mathematics?' he asked. 'And why do you read all these books? This one about China, for instance? What will that do to get you a job?'

'Why?' I answered. 'It's called getting an education. What I read in books helps me understand the world.'

'The best education is right here,' he said. 'This is where your world is. This is where your job is. The only time you need to use mathematics is when you want to tally the sheep. I already have people to do that. Reading books isn't going to help you put meat on the table. Books will only make you whakahihi, a know-all.'

Anything you say, Grandfather. Three bags full, Grandfather. As if, like my father and aunts, I was going to stay here all my life.

Grandfather told me that one of the cooks in Mahana Two had injured his hand, so the meat would have to be sent up to the gang every morning. I would be butchering every night.

'Do you want me to get someone to help you?' Grandfather asked. 'So you've got time to read your books? I could tell Mohi to come back.'

Yes, that's right, Grandfather, throw Mohi in my face. You know I'll say no.

'I'll be okay,' I answered.

After all, it was my job.

13

The punishing work schedule put me in a rebellious mood. I was also at a stand-off with my mother, who had not forgiven me. She did her job, helping my spinster aunts; I did my job.

Up every morning at five to milk the cows, *sir*. Separate the milk, deliver all the cans to the kitchen, take one can over to Zebediah Whatu's house, *sir*. Get the copper going for the washing, *sir*. At six, butcher one beast, skin, prepare for the kitchen and Mahana Two, *sir*. Wash and have breakfast, *sir*. Make sure that all the lamps have kerosene and do any other jobs as required, *sir*. Catch the bus at eight and go to school and have a nice long rest, *sir*.

After school, make sure nobody misses the bus, *sir*. Chop wood for an hour, *sir*. Feed the dogs and the pigs, *sir*. Move the sheep in rotation from one field to another, *sir*. As required, do some work in the maize garden or bag potatoes or kumara, *sir*. Have dinner and, if I'm lucky, May I now go to the toilet to have a shit, *sir*!

And always, Grandfather Tamihana was keeping an eye on me, making sidelong comments like:

'Having a rest, Simeon?' (I'd only sat down for a minute), or:

'Not bad for you, Simeon' (in other words, as good as can be expected), or:

'I've told you before, Simeon, get your hair cut' (that is, you're weak like a girl).

Just to keep me on my toes.

'He's like that with everybody,' my Aunt Sephora said. 'He's just testing you, to see if you've got spunk.'

Testing? Aunt Sephora wasn't kidding. I was supposed to be a good samaritan, too.

'Simeon,' Grandfather said, 'I want you to take some meat and maize over to Maggie's place. After that call at Pera's. The old fella phoned me. He needs help.'

To get through this one, I'd asked Andrew to help me.

Maggie's old shack was on the other side of the maize fields.

'This is my lucky day,' she slobbered. '*Two* young boys, and juicy too.'

'Cut it out, Auntie,' I said. She roared with laughter, showing her black teeth. She was eighty if she was a day.

'Huh? I must be losing my reputation!' She looked at the meat and maize and sniffed approvingly. Then, 'You got to hand it to Bulibasha,' she said. 'He looks after his women.'

This was Andrew's chance. 'You mean women really went for him?'

'Did they what?' Maggie answered. 'My boy, when the word spread about the size of it –' She made a guess with her hands, shook her head, expanded the gap between her hands, and shrugged. 'Oh how can I possibly be expected to remember.' She yawned. 'I've had so many.'

Andrew broke up laughing. The last thing I wanted to hear, however, was yet another exaggerated claim about Grandfather.

'I'll leave you two sweethearts,' I said.

The company wasn't any better at eighty-three-year-old Uncle Pera's.

'Thank you, boy,' he said when I went into his bedroom. His chamberpot was full to the brim. I had just enough time to take it to the outhouse, pour it down the stinking hole and take it back to him. As soon as I returned he was wanting to slide off the bed and on to the pot. His old body burst into a series of farts, hiccups and splashes of piss and shit into the bowl.

That's right, Granduncle, go ahead and make my day.

'Sorry, mokopuna,' he said.

'That's all right, koro,' I answered.

'My daughter, she usually come to fix me up but, hullo, her car lie down and die today.'

'No problem, Uncle Pera,' I mumbled. I wished he wouldn't talk to me. I was trying hard to hold my breath. My words came out more like NopoblemuncaPera.

Afterwards, eyes and nose averted, I wiped his bum and got him to lie down while I washed him all over with a sponge. I'd done this with him before so knew where he hurt and where he didn't. What always surprised me was that his skin was so smooth and dark, polished by age and the sun to a shining ebony. It was a privilege, really, to touch him, and know he was my kin, my own flesh and blood.

I changed Uncle Pera's sheets, put him into a new nightgown and back into bed. In the lean-to kitchen I found some Maori bread and boiled up some broth of watercress and kumara. Uncle Pera didn't know where his false teeth were so I had to break his bread for him, soak it in the broth and feed him that way.

'That grandfather of yours –'

Slurp.

'He's a great man.'

Not again.

'I remember when we all go down the river to be baptise. All us peoples –'

Munch.

'Down the river. Singing our heads off. Long time ago. All dress in white like the peoples of Israel. We were so happy. The elders all there. We wade right in up to here –'

Spill, slurp, munch.

'They raise their hands and ask us, "You want to receive the Holy Ghost?" I nod and down I go. All the way under.'

He started to cry. He pushed his plate away and clutched me. His body rattled like a hollow gourd.

'If it wasn't for your grandfather, boy, I wouldn't get close to the gates of Heaven. You thank him for me, boy. I be Heavenbound soon and he the one saved my soul.'

By the time I got back to the homestead, the family were already sitting down to dinner – Grandfather, Grandmother Ramona, Aunts Sephora, Miriam and Esther, Mum and my three sisters. I washed quickly but as I came into the dining room Aunt Sephora shot me a warning glance. She got up to get my plate from the kitchen.

'He can get it,' Grandfather said.

Aunt Sephora sat down again.

I'd had enough. It was Aunt Sephora's job, not mine, to get me my plate. But *he* was saying now it was *my* job. As if the kitchen was my place, too. As if I was a woman. As if I was useless.

'I'm not hungry,' I said. I stalked out and slammed the door.

All of a sudden there was an eruption behind me and women's screams. The back door flew open. I *knew* the fucker was running behind me, hip *hop* hip *hop*, and I hoped he would trip on his bad leg. My heart was pounding, but I kept on walking steadily onward. Fuck him, *fuck* him.

Then he was on me. He lifted me up by the scruff of the neck. He pulled me back, half strangled, into the kitchen.

'The food that is put on this table was given to us by the grace of God –' his voice hissed out. 'Your father, uncles and aunts are all out there shearing so that *this* food can be put into your belly –' The pots were steaming on the stove. 'I will *not* have anybody in *this* house refuse food that good hands have prepared –'

He opened one of the pots. He pushed my face into it.

When my head came up it was covered in puha and mashed potatoes. I was too stunned to care about what came next. It was the humiliation more than anything else. The humiliation of being too weak and too young to fight back. The humiliation of having my mother, sisters, grandmother and aunts as witness. I know it was idiotic but I looked at Aunt Sephora and said, 'Mmn, nice.'

Grandfather threw me against the wall. 'You're getting too big for your boots, Himiona.'

Grandmother Ramona tried to reach Grandfather, to stop him. 'Hoihoi,' she reproved him, 'he tangata porangi ke.'

She was too late. He raised a hand to hit me.

I saw Glory and semaphored to her. Play dead, Glory, *quick*!

She screamed and crumpled to the floor.

I wrenched away from Grandfather and ran out into the darkness.

Above the moon and stars. Below the earth.

Glory found me in the cowbail, crying my eyes out. She cradled me. 'There, there, Simeon.'

We went back down the hill towards the quarters. My mother Huria was waiting for me. When she tried to hug me I pushed her away.

'Kua mutu,' she said, 'Kua mutu. Stop this, Himiona. I won't have this anger between us.' Her eyes were haunted. 'I know how you're feeling,' she said. 'I feel that way sometimes about your grandfather. But he is Bulibasha.'

Faith and Hope joined us. My mother grabbed us all in a fierce embrace.

'We have to remain a family,' she continued, piercing me with her eyes. 'You, your sisters, your father and me. Perhaps one day. Perhaps –'

It was all a zigzag of lightning in a summer sky. The next day there was no mention of the incident. Grandfather got on with his life and his job; we got on with ours. I guess Grandfather could have piled more work on to me, but he didn't. Nor did he go out of his way to avoid me, as I did him. Life went back to normal, whatever that was. However, Grandfather *did* think that Glory should see a doctor about her fainting spells.

At the end of the third week the Mahana shearing gangs returned to the homestead. It was the beginning of a new month and another family meeting, the opportunity for a huge feast. My mother was overjoyed to see my father Joshua. She didn't tell him what had happened between me and Grandfather.

'You've done well, son,' Dad said. 'I'm proud of you. Your grandmother has told me how good a job you did.'

Grandmother, yes. But not Grandfather.

There was a full gathering at the family meeting. Ihaka Mahana and Zebediah Whatu were there as well as the shearers and shedhands. Grandfather opened with a karakia. Then, 'The first month of the shearing is ended. My sons, let me have your reports.' He indicated we could get off our knees and that Uncle Matiu should begin.

'Well, Father,' Uncle Matiu said, 'it took us a while to oil our rusty joints –' Everybody laughed. 'But the boys did well and our shearers were soon up to their three hundred-a-day tally.'

'Yes,' Grandfather nodded. 'Jack Horsfield rang me to say he's very pleased with your work. He told me he's increased his shearers' positions on the board by one extra.'

'That's right,' Uncle Matiu said. 'Lucky we had the man for the job. Mohi's got the makings. His first season, Father.'

'Good on you, boy,' Zebediah called out. Mohi grinned proudly.

'We've another three or four weeks up at Horsfield station. Then we go on to Brian Smedley's.'

Grandfather nodded. 'Mahana Two?'

'We had a bit of a surprise at the Wi Pere station,' Uncle Maaka began. 'The wool was full of bidibid and the fleeces are pretty greasy this year. Our handpieces worked really hard and we were sharpening the blades a lot. It's going to take us a while to finish there. I've asked Mahana Three if they can give us a hand after they've finished Williamson station. Then we had to find a replacement for Lloyd.'

'Mother Ramona and I are going up to the hospital to see him soon. There have been complications –' Complications? I had an image of Lloyd jumping off the top diving board at the Peel Street baths in Gisborne, holding his nose and sailing down to make a huge splash. 'And the problem of our cook – thank you, Simeon, for doing our meat.'

'Himiona was just doing his job,' Grandfather cut in. 'Mahana Three?'

I surveyed all the people in the drawing room and wondered what was it about Grandfather that made them so respectful and obedient? There in the front were Uncle Matiu and Aunt Sophie, for ever stuck in the role of exemplars for family. Pious churchgoers, they lived only to please Grandfather Tamihana; their seven children were going the same way. Next to them were Uncle Maaka and his wife Barbara, pregnant with a fourth child; Maaka had suppressed his own eagerness for a career in the army when Grandfather ordered him to return home to Waituhi. Further along was Uncle Ruka, reputed to beat up on poor Aunt Dottie and their five children; Aunt Dottie had never quite recovered from coming from a small sane family to such a huge and insane one as ours.

Squeezed in with them was Uncle Hone, my favourite, with Aunt Kate. In the second row Aunt Ruth was sitting with Uncle Albie. Of all the family, theirs was the saddest story. Something was wrong with Aunt Ruth and she couldn't have children. My Aunt Sarah at least managed to have one child – my fabulous cousin Haromi – before kicking Uncle Jack out of her bed. No wonder he was rooting around with other women. Uncle Jack also went to the pub and drank hard liquor. In the third row – of course – was my father Joshua with Mum and my sisters, and my three spinster aunts. They were the ones who stayed at home and to whom no land would be given because there was none left to give. Their inheritance was the crumbs from Grandfather's table.

The place of the spouses in all this was interesting. They held a ranking second even to my own. If they had any opinions, they voiced them through Grandfather's children. For instance, my mother Huria never spoke to Bulibasha direct, and certainly never before Dad had spoken. Normally, if she had anything to ask, she got Dad to ask for her. If he wasn't there to deliver her request, she buttoned her lip.

All these people would follow Grandfather to the end of the earth? Why? And why did they stay?

The next morning the shearers went back to the sheds. But before leaving, Dad came to sit with us in the quarters. The others in Mahana Four were whistling for him.

'Hey Joshua! Shake a leg!'

'Didn't she give it to you last night!'

It was good-natured ribaldry, but my mother's sensitive nature made her blush.

'Don't listen to them, dear,' Dad said.

He coughed. Then he took his first pay packet of the season from the shirt pocket closest to his heart. 'He koha o taku aroha ki a koe,' he said to Mum. 'Please accept this gift of love.' He put the packet halfway between them.

Trembling, our mother picked it up. 'Tena koe mo to awhina aroha ki ahau,' she answered. 'I accept this gift of love.'

My mother opened the packet and divided the notes into two piles, one of which she returned to Dad. The other was the housekeeping money for the next month, and would also be used to pay off the huge debt that had accrued at the general store. By custom, Dad divided his pile in half and returned half to our mother. 'After all,' he said, 'what have I got to spend it on except beer and wild women!'

With a kiss he was gone. The euphoria of having the shearers at home went with him.

Later that day I heard Grandmother Ramona talking to Grandfather about going to see Lloyd in Cook Hospital.

'What's the matter with you!' she scolded. 'Lloyd's been in intensive care for two weeks now, and we still haven't seen him.'

'Every time I think of hospital I think of death. You only go to a hospital to be born or die.'

'But we'll only be visiting!'

'Even so, Death's presence is there.'

'Oh, for goodness *sake*!'

Grandfather Tamihana could easily have not gone to see Lloyd. In the end, however, Grandmother Ramona taunted him about being a coward and said that *she* was going – and she was just a woman. So Grandfather plucked up the courage and told Mum to bring the De Soto around to the front of the homestead.

'Simeon can come with us,' Grandfather said. 'He can keep an eye on the car while we are visiting. I don't want anyone to scratch the car, Himiona.'

On the way into Gisborne, Grandfather became increasingly nervous and agitated. Grandmother tried to calm him.

'You're Bulibasha after all,' she said. 'There's not many people who have an angel looking after them.'

'Ae,' Grandfather agreed. 'But does Death know that?'

Outside the hospital, I stood guard by Grandfather's precious De Soto. I watched as he went with Grandmother Ramona and Mum up the stairs into the lobby. My mother was very pretty in dark suit, gloves, high heels and cloche; she was wearing a buttonhole of flowers that Glory had picked. All of a sudden she reappeared on the steps and waved to me. For a moment I thought that Grandfather had died already.

'Himiona, haramai,' she said. 'They've moved Lloyd to a ward upstairs. You know your grandfather – he's got that bad leg but he won't take the lift. You'll have to help him up the stairs.'

Grandfather still wasn't too happy about being there, or about needing my support. As soon as we were up the stairs he pushed me away. He was sweating profusely.

'Shall I go back to the car?' I asked.

'You think I'm stupid?' he snapped. 'You want me to fall down the stairs when I leave?'

Be my guest, I shrugged.

He motioned to me to accompany him along the shining corridor. It was almost as if he needed me to protect him. We came to a large white door.

'Ah, you're here to see Mr Lloyd Donovan,' the charge nurse said. 'Please come in. He's expecting you.'

The door opened. Grandfather gave a loud, terrified moan. The room was silent, except for breathing. A silver barrel like a huge cream urn was in the middle of the room – but something was wrong about the urn.

A man was in it.

All I could see was his head. Then I saw a mirror slanted above the man's head so that he could look at us. I will never forget his eyes. They widened, their irises opening out to enfold us all in his helplessness.

'Buli-bash-aaa –' As if only Grandfather could deliver him from the polio that had begun to cripple him. Or, failing that, give him death.

We didn't stay long with Lloyd, but it was long enough for Grandfather to realise that Death was not after *him*. He calmed down and was strong and supportive to Lloyd, who was being transferred, at his parents' request, to Waipukurau where they lived.

'The Mahana family never forgets the people who join us,' Grandfather said. 'For as long as you live you will stay on the payroll. We will make sure that you have the best medical care to help you return to full health. Kia kaha.'

'Th-ank y-ou,' Lloyd stammered, his eyes wet with tears.

We left soon after. Grandfather, Grandmother and Mum kissed Lloyd on the forehead. Outside, Grandfather washed his hands at a tap and sprinkled himself with water. We set off back to Waituhi, and the further away we got from Cook Hospital the more Grandfather's spirits revived. He'd come away from the House of Death unscathed.

Then, as we were going across the red suspension bridge, we saw a car coming from the other side. Oh no. Rupeni Poata's Buick.

Mum started to slow down but Grandfather, buoyant, said, 'Go faster, Huria. We were on the bridge first.'

Mum put her foot down. So did whoever was driving the Buick. Mum pressed the horn of the De Soto. There was an answering blare from the Buick. Mum dipped the lights: make way. The Buick's lights dipped: *you* make way.

We were more than halfway across before Mum put her foot on the brakes. The De Soto skidded to a halt. So did the Buick. Just inches separated the two cars.

'Back up!' Caesar Poata yelled. Next to him were Tight Arse and Saul, blowing on their fists and indicating where they'd like to place them on my face.

'*You* back up!' Mum yelled back.

'We were on the bridge before you!'

'Oh no you weren't. See? We're already over halfway, and that proves it.'

'You maniac woman!' Caesar yelled.

While all this was happening, Grandfather was sitting in the back seat laughing to himself. Rupeni Poata was doing the same in the back of the Buick. Grandmother was silent and still. After a moment, Grandfather got out.

'Keep the motor running,' he said to Mum. His manner was breezy and lighthearted.

He walked over to the Buick. Rupeni Poata got out of his car. They faced each other like Burt Lancaster and the Clayton gang in *Gunfight at the OK Corral*. To add to the tension, traffic was piling up on either side of the bridge. Impatient drivers were sounding their horns.

Grandfather had his walking stick. He raised it above his head and – *bang*. He slammed it down on the Buick's engine cowling.

Rupeni Poata looked at the damage and shook his head sorrowfully. He had a walking stick, too. Gauging his stroke, he lifted it and – *bang*. He slammed it down on the De Soto's cowling. Amused, Rupeni Poata then bowed to Grandfather and indicated that he could boot one of his headlights if he wished. Grandfather indicated that Rupeni could do the same to the De Soto.

Stalemate. The two men tipped their hats and retired.

Grandfather got back into the De Soto. He smiled at Grandmother and then, 'Gun them down,' he ordered Mum.

Before Caesar Poata had time to start the motor or put on the brakes, Mum had engaged the Buick's front bumper. Rupeni Poata had just enough time to leap ignominiously into his car.

'Hold on, son,' Mum said.

Tyres squealing, we pushed the Buick back across the bridge with the De Soto.

'You crazy bitch!' Caesar Poata yelled.

Did I forget to tell you that my mother could not abide bad language? At the words, murder came into Mum's eyes. She pressed the accelerator right to the floor. It was all Caesar could do to keep the Buick from boomeranging off one side of the bridge and on to the other.

At the other end of the bridge the waiting cars scattered. The Buick skewed off in a cloud of dust. I caught a glimpse of Saul and Tight Arse's frightened faces as the car came to a halt. Wouldn't you know it? Rupeni Poata was obviously enraged, but with his face in rictus he looked as if he was laughing his head off.

'Don't call *me* a bitch,' Mum whispered to herself. She was so wonderful when she had her wild up.

'That will teach Rupeni Poata to come onto the bridge when we're on it,' Grandfather muttered.

15

As if still recovering from her last car ride with Grandfather, my mother came on the school bus to Patutahi when she wanted to pay off some of our account at the general store.

'Do you want me to come with you?' I asked when the bus dropped us off.

'No.' She bit her lip. 'You go on to school. Not long now before you break up, ne?'

'Two whole weeks,' I moaned. 'Are you sure you don't –' I knew she was trying to change the subject.

'Haere atu,' she said.

I watched nervously as she hesitated, then walked up the steps and disappeared into the store.

'Why, Mrs Mahana!' I heard Miss Zelda say in her bright tinsel way. 'Daisy? Scott? Mrs Mahana has come to visit.'

'It's so wonderful,' Miss Daisy chimed in. 'Since the shearing started, Zelda, all our Maori customers have been to see us.'

'I don't think we have one customer in the red any longer,' Miss Zelda replied. 'As I always say, Mrs Mahana, pay as much of your account now, because when that nasty winter comes –'

My mother didn't say a word. I had a mental picture of her standing there, immobile, while the two sisters chattered to one another. She was a clockwork doll that had stopped working – an automaton with a silly smile on her face, mesmerised by what the sisters were saying, opening and closing her mouth but with no words coming out. I rushed inside. Sure enough, there she was, trying to talk, the perspiration beading her forehead, her cheeks crimson. I felt you only needed to give her a slight push and she would topple to the ground.

'I – I – I –'

Miss Zelda and Miss Daisy were staring at Mum. 'Isn't that right, Mrs Mahana?'

'Good morning, Miss Zelda,' I said, breaking the spell.

Miss Zelda gave a cry. 'Oh you startled us!' she said.

Mum swayed. Blinked. Then recovered. 'Yes, Miss Zelda,' she said evenly. 'That *is* right.' She reached into her purse and passed the money that Dad had given her. Miss Zelda counted it.

'My mother would like a receipt,' I said.

Miss Zelda obliged.

'Thank you.'

Mum and I walked out into the sunlight. She looked at me, pressed my shoulders and ran her fingers through my hair.

'I wish you'd get your hair cut,' she said. 'Your grandfather is always talking about it.'

My mother sighed and began to walk back to Waituhi. I watched her reach the edge of the tar seal. She looked so lonely. A slight windstorm swirled around her, like a miniature tornado. She crossed over into dust country.

16

The day finally came when school was out for the year. We were *out of jail*. Andrew and I wrestled all the way to the bus. Even before Haromi had left the playground, she'd slashed her lips with lipstick.

'When do we pack up to go to the shed?' Glory asked Mum that night.

'The shearing gangs come to collect us in the weekend,' she said. 'Once testimony-bearing is over, we'll return to the sheds with them.'

Glory was getting into her costume for the tiny tots' parade. It was the night of our school break-up ceremony and Glory was going as Little Bo Peep in a blue satin dress that had once been a blouse. On her head was a baby's bonnet, and in her hands were a crook and a small felt lamb.

'Don't forget,' I warned her as she twirled around, 'when you sit down, hold your dress like so –' I had made a hoop to go under her dress so that it would stand like a Regency ballgown. 'Otherwise, your hoop will flip up and everybody will see your pants.'

'We wouldn't want *that* to happen,' Mum said.

The tiny tots' parade was first on the programme and, in the excitement, Glory forgot her instructions. Not only that, but whenever she bumped into anybody the hoop would slip backwards or forwards. Very soon all the little boys were bumping into Glory accidentally on purpose. When she eventually punched persistent Rawiri Jones on the nose, it was time for the hoop to come off.

Next was the school choir, conducted by a stern Miss Dalrymple. All the Maori parents in the audience winced as their daughters strained and screeched through 'Cherry ripe, cherry ripe, *riii-ippe I prrayee*!', enunciating in clipped plummy voices as if they were English broadcasters. That, however, wasn't as bad as 'In Dub-leen's fairrr cit-eee, where the girrls are so prrre-tee –'

Ah, Miss Dalrymple. She had tried so hard with her elocution lessons and this was her one moment of triumph – her chance to reveal to the parents that every last Maori vowel and consonant had been knocked out of their girls. Or so she thought.

The end-of-year prizes were given out by Mr Johnston and required him to use both his hands. It was strange to see them so exposed rather than in his trousers. The certificates were read out in order, from the lower primer classes up. Every time a Pakeha got a certificate, there was a polite smattering of applause and compliments. When a Maori got one, the Maori parents copied Pakeha behaviour.

Clap, clap, clap of gloved hands. Oo, yaas, we ore ve-rry prr-ow*dd*, which translated meant, Pae kare, we thought our kid was a dumb cluck.

I was second in my class after Richard Jenkins, the red-haired son of the garage proprietor. When I went up to get my certificate, Andrew whispered, 'Brainbox!' Haromi was hiding in a corner, disassociating herself entirely from me and the whole prizegiving. Even in coming second, I was being embarrassing. Becoming more Pakeha and less Maori somehow, because being Maori meant being dumb, always coming last and not caring about it because everybody else was dumb or last too. Or, as Grandfather would say, becoming whakahihi. Too big for my boots. Not staying in my place.

I didn't care. Miss Wallace had told me what my prize would be and I wanted it desperately. Another H. Rider Haggard novel, *Allan Quartermain*.

Nor did I care that only the women of the homestead were at the break-up – Grandmother, my three aunts, Mum and my sisters. There were very few men at all in the hall, and certainly not

Grandfather Tamihana. He said that school prizegivings were like flower shows. Let the women attend; the men had better things to do. I didn't mind. It was the active support of women – the showing up, standing up and eventually petitioning for changes in Maori language and culture – which would, in future, change all our lives.

Our father Joshua and the other shearers returned on the Saturday night before the first Sunday of the month. As usual, we were late for opening prayers at the homestead.

Sorry Bulibasha sorrysorrysorry.

Then we were off to church. On that day I realised the real reason why we all met beforehand. It was so that we would make a marvellous procession on our way from Waituhi and people could admire us for our godliness. Mind you, we were looking particularly impressive today, in keeping with the spirit of testimony-bearing, the monthly highlight of church life when the faithful bore their testimony to God and the church, and unburdened their guilt in the process.

Outside the church the pastor was pumping everybody's hand, greeting his flock with his usual exuberance. 'Good *morn*-ing father Mahana! Hasn't our Lord produced a *wonder*-ful day? You will give the lesson again? Praise be to God! And don't you look just di-*vine*, mother Mahana, mm-*mmmm*! Oh, and before I forget, mother Mahana and father Mahana, may I thank you both for your *oh so* generous contribution? Praise be to those little white woolly sheep!'

Aunt Sephora was playing the organ today, which meant that Andrew, Haromi and I could hide in the back pew. Haromi was in absolute misery, wearing her largest pair of sunglasses and turning her collar up in an attempt to escape notice. Our one consolation was to find humour in the opening hymn, which had the line 'And God's love will never leave a sting behind'. When Haromi wet her pencil, crossed out the g in sting and replaced it with a k, we thought it was hilarious.

Grandfather gave the lesson. The text was taken from the parable about the good shepherd who has one sheep missing from his flock. He leaves his flock to find that sheep.

'Amen, Father, amen,' the faithful said.

'Nobody's to come looking for me,' Haromi hissed. 'Got that, guys?'

The congregation settled down into testimony-bearing. The

70

procession of the faithful up to the microphone began. There they paused –

'Brothers and sisters –'

Yes? What's it to be today?

'I have *sinned*.'

The catalogue of guilts, grievances and ills came pouring out. Swearing, shoplifting, carnal desire for the neighbour's wife – you name it, somebody enunciated it. The sins also included grievances against members of the family – a spouse's lapse from godliness, a son's descent into Hell because he'd gone into the billiard saloon, a daughter's first steps on the path to who knows where because she had drunk a cup of coffee. There were infinite variations on tear-filled eyes, trembling lips, groans, moans and shrieks and, at the end of it all, a pleading to God for forgiveness. As the woeful tales were told a collective sigh of regret wafted from the audience.

'Amen, brother,' or 'The Lord forgive you, sister.'

Around the halfway mark, people's testimonies began to be punctuated by muffled sobs from the pews.

'Here we go, guys,' Haromi said.

Two-thirds of the way and Aunt Sarah's sobs had given way to explosions of agony, loud blasts on her handkerchief and gestures of melodramatic proportions. She was magnificent. Every time a brother or sister mentioned a particular sin, she would clutch at her left breast. Or swing around to nod at her nearest neighbours. Or put on her sunglasses and, a minute later, take them off so that we could see her tear-streaked face. Sometimes she would emit a gagging sound as if she was spewing up the Devil himself.

No testimony-bearing was complete without the testimony of Aunt Sarah. She was always the last to speak, and she was always the *best*. Accordingly, there was always a respectful half a minute or so of silence, the podium empty in front, after the second to last person had left the stage.

We all waited.

The world waited.

The universe waited.

Until with a loud wail up and down three octaves, Aunt Sarah forced herself up and out of her seat. Clutching at one pew after another, buckling under the weight of the accumulated sins of her month, Aunt Sarah staggered to the microphone. There, she stood like a shattered monument.

'Hang on to your hats,' Haromi said.

71

Tapping the microphone to make sure it was on, Aunt Sarah began –

'Brothers and sisters –' Sobs and quivering lips. 'I have such woes to tell you today –'

'Oh, poor sister Sarah,' the congregation moaned.

'I don't know why I should deserve this –' Shouting. 'Lord, why have you *forsaken* me?'

Hysterics, then once everyone's attention was hers –

'Brothers and sisters, my husband Jack goes to the pub and gets pissed –' Poor Uncle Jack, scowling away in the corner. 'He looks both ways, brothers and sisters, before he goes into the pub, but you know what?'

'What, sister Sarah?'

'He forgets to look *up*!'

More hysteria.

'And he *smokes* and when he lights up his smoke he looks both ways but –' Shouting. 'He forgets to look up! You all know he smokes –'

'What do you expect?' Haromi whispered. 'You *tell* them every month.'

'But even if you didn't know –' Looking up to Heaven. 'God knows. He knows, brothers and sisters –'

'Amen to that, sister Sarah,' the congregation intoned.

'Then there's my eldest daughter, Haromi –'

'Let's get out of here,' Haromi hissed.

'Trying to sneak out while her mother is talking. Yes, *there* she is, brothers and sisters –' An accusing pointed finger. 'I should have listened to my father. He told me that naming my daughter after Salome was asking for trouble. I should have listened to you, Dad –' Clutching the podium with both hands. 'She sneaks out the window and goes to dances and parties and God knows what else. She's like her father, looks both ways and forgets to look up! That's where the Lord is, brothers and sisters, up there, and he sees everything. Even my daughter Haromi in her short skirts *without pants on*, exposing her house of children to the world –'

'Oh Ker-rist, Mumma!' Haromi exploded.

Shock. Horror. Just what Aunt Sarah needed – something to bring down the curtain, and in the best eyeball-staring, tears-streaming, mouth-agape, Joan Crawford style. Even Bette Davis would have clapped.

A loud shriek, a clutch to her heart (I've told you before, Auntie, it's on the *left* side) and Aunt Sarah collapsed on her knees. The pastor rushed up to rescue her. Everybody's eyes swivelled around to look at Haromi and, by extension, the two sinful boys beside her. As if we had just murdered Aunt Sarah.

Why, the thought never crossed our minds.

17

Wouldn't you just know it, but on the way back from testimony-bearing we saw Rupeni Poata's family at Makaraka.

'E hika,' my father said, 'they must have been waiting here for two hours.'

'They want their revenge,' Mum said, nodding at me wisely.

A SECOND WORLD WAR TWO-SEATER FIGHTER PLANE. FLIGHT COMMANDER JOSHUA IS IN FRONT WHEN HIS CO-PILOT LIEUTENANT SIMEON SPOTS SOMETHING COMING OUT OF THE SUN.

SIMEON E Pa, Hapani rere rangi waka!
(Subtitles: Japanese aircraft at two o'clock, sir!)
JOSHUA Kei whea? Kei whea? Ka, titiro ahau.
(Subtitles: Where? Yes! I see him now!)

SUDDENLY FLIGHT COMMANDER JOSHUA GIVES A CRY OF PAIN. A SHARP RAIN OF GRAVEL ON THE WINDSCREEN.

SIMEON (ALARMED) He aha te mate, e Pa?
(Subtitles: What is it, sir?)
JOSHUA Aue, ka kaapo aku kanohi.
(Subtitles: I've suddenly become – blind.)
SIMEON (GRIMLY) E Pa, maaku he kanohi mou!
(Subtitles: Then I shall be your eyes for you, sir!)
JOSHUA Te mutunga taua mahi kei roto i o ringaringa ... e hoa ...
(Subtitles: The success of our mission depends on (gasp) you ... Lieutenant ...)

As soon as they saw us, the Poatas scattered to their cars. They waited for us to draw level and we traded insults and jeers, spitting from one window to the other.

'We'll get ya this time!' Tight Arse Junior yelled.

'You can try,' I answered.

'Oh yeah?'

'Yeah.'

'Oh yeah?'

Somebody gave a loud whistle and we were off, neck and neck to the bridge.

'Keep up, dear,' Mum said.

Of course the Poatas had taken the inside lane which meant that it was difficult for us to pass them and get ahead.

'Run them off the road, dear,' Mum said.

It was no use. There was too much traffic coming down our side of the road. We had to keep on cutting back behind them. I saw the delectable Poppy give a V sign of triumph.

'Hukareka sucks!' my sisters and I screamed.

FLIGHT COMMANDER JOSHUA (REGAINING HIS SIGHT) Kei te pai tena.
(Subtitles: You did well.)
LIEUTENANT SIMEON (GRAVELY) E ta, ko te mahi a te tangata ko te mahi te tangata.
(Subtitles: A man's got to do what a man's got to do, sir.)

We watched as they pulled ahead, spraying us with dust.

'We live to fight another day,' Dad said. 'But first things first. Shearing time –'

By the time lunch was over it was well after three o'clock. The gangs were in a hurry to get back to their sheds and shortly after dessert most of the Mahana family and shearers had departed from the homestead. They were soon followed by Grandfather Tamihana and Grandmother Ramona, who were joining Mahana One, the top Mahana gang. Aunt Miriam was a fleeco and Pani a shearer with Mahana Four. Before leaving the homestead, Grandfather Tamihana said, 'Miriam? You're coming with us. Ruth? You take Miriam's place with Mahana Four.'

'Dad has seen the way Pani looks at sis,' my father Joshua whispered to Mum.

'Bulibasha's trying to split them up,' she replied, 'just like he tried with us.'

After that, everything fell strangely quiet. My father Joshua and Aunts Sephora and Esther, helped now by Aunt Ruth instead of Aunt Miriam, were always left to close up the homestead. It was their job and their place. Even so, it was a difficult duty, disturbing and fretful. Only when Aunt Sephora turned on the wireless and filled the place with noise did we feel any sense of relief.

My aunts busied themselves in the kitchen doing the dishes, closing the rooms and locking the windows, while my sisters helped Mum to pack our belongings. We were to go in two cars – the Pontiac and Pani's Chrysler. Dad and Pani tied the mattresses, blankets, pots, pans, suitcases and provisions anywhere they would fit. We needed all the room inside the two cars for *us*. While they were doing this, Glory and I herded our cows over to Zebediah Whatu's place; he was looking after our dogs and small flock of sheep.

'I wish I was coming with you, boy,' he said.

'Somebody's got to look after the fort,' I smiled.

'Yes,' he saluted. 'I guess they do, Kemo Sabe.'

By the time Glory and I returned, dusk was setting in. The cars had been transformed into strange-shaped carriers. Mattresses were tied to the sides and back; the spare tyres were transferred to the front where they were lashed to the radiator. The blankets, pots, pans and boxes of food were on the top of the car. Legs of mutton swayed over the windows. Petrol cans were roped to the runners. Mum had decided to take some laying hens, and put their cage on top of the Chrysler. Their husband, the rooster, was going crazy trying to get at them.

'We better get going,' Dad said. 'It's getting dark.'

'A long way to go, bro,' Pani answered. 'You follow me.'

Somebody turned the wireless off. Mum and my aunts came running out, shivering. Without people to give it life, the homestead was somehow frightening. Mum made one last check of the quarters, slammed the door and locked it. The report echoed across the darkening hills.

'We're all ready, dear,' she said. Her lips were trembling, as if she wasn't sure.

My aunts got into Pani's Chrysler. His tyres were fit to bursting. With a laugh, Aunt Ruth came back to join us in our car. She got in just in time – there was a *whump* as the enraged rooster, still after his hens, hit the door.

75

'You're for the pot when we get back,' Aunt Ruth threatened.

Dad beeped his horn. Pani beeped back.

'Don't get too far behind us,' Dad yelled. 'One of your headlights is crook.'

Pani waved, Okay.

The sun had turned the sky red. The cars moved out and on to the road. I closed the gate behind them. I caught a glimpse of Nani Mini Tupara waving from far away. She was picking maize and wore a big straw hat.

'Bye, Nani! Keep Waituhi safe for us!'

I ran to our Pontiac. Silhouetted in the red dusk, our cars looked like gypsy caravans.

18

In those days the whole of Poverty Bay, the East Coast and Hawke's Bay was covered by a grid of roads which wound further and further from the main towns of Gisborne, Opotiki, Whakatane, Napier and Hastings along the coast or up the steep valleys into the interior. On the way were small Pakeha-run settlements similar to Patutahi. They marked the beginning of Pakeha history when a whaler or English trader settled there and began the process of bringing civilisation to the natives. Later, after the land wars and two world wars, the towns became the focus of more settlers when parcels of land around them were granted to rehabilitate soldiers who had fought for King and Country; war memorials of a soldier bending over his rifle sprouted in every town. The settlements had names like Tolaga Bay, Tokomaru Bay, Tikitiki, Te Karaka, Mahia or Nuhaka and they comprised a hotel, petrol station, general store, small community hall where a dance or film was shown at weekends, church and graveyard, rural school and stockyards – and their roads were tar sealed te rori Pakeha. Further out, and you were in dust country. There the settlements were villages like Waituhi, Waihirere, Mangatu and Anaura Bay – brightly coloured houses around a drab meeting house, with not a Pakeha in sight.

Right at the back of beyond, along the even dustier roads which zigged up the valleys and zagged down over culverts, through cattle stops, across fords, through gates that you opened and closed on your way in and out, around hairpin bends and over rickety one-way swing bridges, at the very top of the valleys, were the big sheep and cattle stations. Regardless of their isolation, the big stations and their ability to produce meat and wool for export were the edifices upon which the entire economy of Poverty Bay, the East Coast and Hawke's Bay depended. Without them, and the constant stream of cattle and sheep trucks which brought their stock and produce down the valleys, there would have been no need for the settlements, freezing works, ports, towns and industries which had grown up to support them.

The big stations knew their self-importance. They were capped by huge two-storeyed houses with names like Windsor, The Willows, Fairleigh or Tara. Some had been constructed of stone shipped from England, France or Italy. They were characterised by wide entrance halls, their floors shining with paving stones that had been hauled in by bullock teams. They had imposing staircases and hallways panelled with English oak. The furniture, four-poster beds, linen and sculptures were all English and had been collected during regular visits by steamship to the Home Country. The master's study was filled with leatherbound books; there was always a deer's head over the fireplace. Gravelled driveways led up to the big houses. Rose trellises and arbours of English daisies bordered the driveway. In the middle, a clipped green lawn. The glass in the windows was handmade and shaped like diamonds. From the windows you could see the big red-roofed shearing shed, cattle yards and sheep yards.

To ensure an appropriate distance between station owner and station worker, the quarters for the foreman, musterers, cattlemen, shepherds and their families and all those who were on regular pay were on the *far* side of the shearing shed. Furthest away were the whares – crude, rough-timbered bunkhouses and kitchen-dining room – for the itinerant workers, the scrubcutters, fencers and, of course, the shearing gangs. They had no ovens, no running water and no electric lights.

My sisters and I loved the shearing season. To this day I don't know why. Why, for instance, would anyone love all those dusty three- or four-hour journeys to the sheds? Usually we had to travel in convoy to ensure support for one of the other cars just in case it broke down, its radiator boiled over, tyres were punctured, batteries ran flat or an axle snapped under the weight of our accumulated baggage. One year Uncle Hone's old car gave up the ghost entirely.

Dad hitched a tow line which broke as we were going up a steep gradient and Uncle Hone's car careened back in a wild ride down to the bottom of the hill. It had no brakes. In the second attempt to get the car up the gradient, Dad lashed a spare tyre to the front bumper and our car *pushed* Uncle Hone's car to the top of the hill. Uncle was supposed to wait for us at the top so we could get in front of him and prevent a dangerous no-brakes descent. Uncle must have forgotten, because no sooner had he reached the top than down the other side he went.

I can still remember that car as it rocketed out of control down to the bottom of the gradient. How Uncle managed to hold the road was a mystery – we agreed later that it must have been because the weight of all the people inside kept the car from flipping on the corners. On our own way down we had to stop every five minutes to pick up pots and pans, bedding, boxes of food and tin plates that had come loose on that pell-mell descent. What else could we do except dissolve into gales of laughter when we reached the bottom ourselves?

Then there were the fords, where one car would get stuck in the middle of the river. My aunts would yell out, 'I could do with a swim!' Out they'd get, their muscled arms heaving away until the car was free. My Aunt Sephora discovered that she had natural flotation when she slipped and went arse over kite down a waterfall and along the deep river.

'Help!' she cried. She couldn't swim. She bobbed along, kept afloat by her natural buoyancy, her red dress inflated by trapped air like a balloon.

After that, my uncles used to sing in jest, 'When the red red robin goes bob bob bobbin along –'

More dangerous were the swing bridges when some of the boards gave way and the car's wheels went through. We'd all get out, carefully unload the car to make it lighter, lift the car up from the holes in the bridge and load up again once the car had reached the other side.

Finally there were roads that had been washed out or blocked by slips or peppered with mud-filled potholes. Some places had no roads at all. When such hazards or challenges presented themselves, Uncle Hone would say, 'She's right. Let's have smoko.' Uncle Hone was the boss of Mahana Four. After smoko, while we kids were skinny dipping in the river, he would korero the problem with the adults and, by the time we got back, something had been worked out. Off we would go, backtracking or sidetracking or driving down to the river bed and motoring along it until we could get back onto the road.

We drove, pushed, pulled and sometimes carried our cars piece by piece to get to the sheds.

'It was easier when we had packhorses,' Grandfather Tamihana said.

My mother never liked travelling at night. We had a four-hour drive ahead to the Williamson station and 'Amberleigh' at the back of Tolaga Bay.

'As long as we get there by midnight,' she said.

Like many Maori, Mum believed that kehua – ghosts – were abroad at night; humans were therefore taking their lives into their hands when they traversed the kehua's domain. She was calm enough for the first part of our journey across the red suspension bridge and through Gisborne, but when we left Wainui Beach she started to get nervous. The darkness fell very quickly and the only lights were those from farms floating away like ships on a dark sea. Even the moonlight on the road was intermittent. Dark clouds boiled up from the south. To cap it off, it began to rain.

'E koe,' Mum said, nodding her head. 'I knew this would happen.'

The rain didn't last long – luckily, as we didn't have a tarpaulin for the hens on top of the car – but then there was a *bang* and Pani's car skidded to a halt. A burst back tyre.

'E koe,' Mum said again. All her fears were being confirmed. 'The kehuas want us to go outside so they can jump from the scrub and eat us.'

Dad scoffed at her. He positioned our car close behind Pani's and, in the light of the headlights, they jacked the car and began changing the tyre. No sooner had the engine stopped than we heard the noises of the bush, *alive* with bird calls, wild pigs rooting in the scrub, the sounds of the hunter and the hunted.

I got out to help. Glory wanted to come with me, but, 'You stay in the car,' Mum said to her. 'You're just the right size to be taken by a flying kehua to its nest of hungry chicks.'

We arrived at Tolaga Bay at around eleven that night. Half an hour out of Tolaga, just as Pani's car got to the top of a precipitous road, its radiator boiled over.

'E koe,' our mother said between compressed lips. 'We're never going to get to Amberleigh by midnight.'

79

That meant that we would all be eaten up by kehua. Ah well, nothing else to do except have our last feed on this earth. So out came the food basket, and we ate and drank as if it was the final supper – Maori bread buttered with margarine and golden syrup, washed down with raspberry cordial.

Out of the darkness, Aunt Ruth began to tell a story about the family. There were always stories during the shearing; they leavened our work with fun, excitement and a sense of history. The stories recounted the life of the family, our travails and triumphs, defeats and victories. But this was a story I had not heard before, telling the reason why the Mahana and Poata families were always fighting. It had nothing to do with religion at all.

Grandmother Ramona was sixteen and Grandfather was nineteen when they met, just before the Great War, in 1914.

'Your grandfather tried to enlist,' Aunt Ruth said. I already knew this; Grandfather carried a grudge against the army when he was refused. 'It wasn't his fault. His parents wouldn't have let him go anyway. Why should they let him go to fight a white man's war? We'd only just finished one *against* him!'

Grandfather was visiting Grandmother's village. They took one look at each other, and it was love at first sight.

'They were struck by the lightning rod of God,' Aunt Ruth said. 'If that lightning strikes, you're the dead duck.' Poor Aunt Ruth – the Lord hadn't pronged her and Uncle Albie with his divine sign, that's for sure. 'The trouble was, Mother Ramona was already engaged to be married to a soldier who had just joined the Pioneer Battalion in the First World War.'

You guessed it: Rupeni Poata.

'It was all jacked up between Mother Ramona's family and Rupeni's family,' Aunt Ruth said, 'but Mum never loved Rupeni. However, her people told her, "Poor Rupeni, he could get killed and have no children", or "This is a great sacrifice Rupeni is doing, so can't you make his last days in our village happy?" Despite her love for our father, she agreed to marry Rupeni. Of course Dad was heartbroken. He tried to dissuade her. She said it was too late. She had to honour her family's wishes and marry Rupeni. Our mother was supposed to be the innocent sacrifice to Rupeni's lustful desires.'

'What's lustful desires?' Glory asked.

'Ask your brother,' Aunt Ruth answered, casting me a murderous glance. Why me?

'The day of the wedding came,' Aunt Ruth continued. 'Our father rode his white horse over to Mum's village to ask her once more not to go through with the wedding. He arrived just as she was setting off to the church. She was wearing a beautiful long wedding dress, the one she has to this day locked in her memory chest. She was on the verandah with her father and family. Her father was outraged to see our father and got his old rifle. He didn't want any young buck from another village, especially Waituhi, to soil his goods. But our mother restrained him from shooting our father –'

I've mentioned before the two photographs of Grandmother Ramona and Grandfather when they were young. Although badly hand-tinted (Grandfather had been given green eyes and curly brown hair) the coloration cannot disguise my grandmother's innocent beauty or my grandfather's handsome pride. As Aunt Ruth was talking I imagined a scene straight out of a silent movie.

RAMONA IS ON THE VERANDAH OF AN OLD HOUSE. HER PARAMOUR, TAMIHANA, STANDS IN THE STIRRUPS OF HIS WHITE HORSE AND, TEARS STREAMING FROM HIS GREEN EYES, CUPS HER CHIN IN HIS HANDS AND KISSES HER.

TAMIHANA E Ramona, kaua koe e haere ki to marena.
(Subtitles: Ramona, I beg of you, do not do this.)
RAMONA Aue, e Bulibasha, tenei taku whakamutunga.
(Subtitles: Alas, my love, this is my destiny.)
TAMIHANA Engari, kahore koe e aroha ana ki a ia.
(Subtitles: But you do not love him.)
RAMONA Ae engari, ko hoatu te honore ki toku papa.
(Subtitles: That is true, but I do this for the honour of my father and because it is his wish. And Rupeni has only a week before he must journey to the war.)
TAMIHANA (CLOSEUP, IN DESPERATION) Ka pehea atu ki au?
(Subtitles: What about me?)
RAMONA (WITH PROUD RESOLUTION) Ahakoa taku aroha ki a koe, ake, ake, kaore he aroha mo maua. Haere atu.
(Subtitles: Although I will love you for ever and for all eternity our love can never be. Go.)
TAMIHANA (WITH AN AGONISING CRY) Ramon-aaaaaa –
(Subtitles: Ramon-aaaaaa –)

'Your grandmother and grandfather had one last sweet kiss,' Aunt Ruth said. Hupe was dribbling from her nose – she was such a romantic. 'Then your grandmother pulled the veil over her face. She was never more lovely. "Although another man may own my body," Ramona said to our father, "you will always possess my heart." A single tear trickled like a falling star down her left cheek.'

Meanwhile, Rupeni had arrived at the church. He was an ugly, squat young man with a big bulbous nose, huge fleshy lips and legs so short he looked like he was walking on his knees. He was at least three inches shorter than Grandmother. Whoever heard of a hero who was shorter than the heroine?

'Did you know there was a song named after your grandmother?' Aunt Ruth asked. 'Well, a small trio outside the church – a violinist, pianist and bass player – started to play that song:

"Ramona, I hear the mission bells above, Ramona –"

'The guests were mainly Rupeni's family and all those he had managed to fool. Huh! He was as heroic as my bum! Everybody knows he didn't lob that grenade at the Turks, it was somebody else. Just as he was going through the door with his groomsmen he heard the karanga. He turned and saw his bride coming –'

This is what Rupeni saw. An old kuia, one of the guests, stepped forward and began to call, 'Haere mai ki te wahine na, haere mai, haere mai, haere mai.' Her voice was high-pitched, formal. Far in the distance, along the road which ran through the maize fields, the bridal party was coming. Ramona was escorted by her weeping mother, father, sisters, brothers and relatives. She was in the middle, her face veiled. A beautiful feather cloak was over her shoulders and white wedding dress.

From that distant bridal party came the reply, 'Karanga mai, karanga mai, karanga mai.' The reply was pitched even higher, and throbbed with emotion. Everybody knew that Grandmother was making a sacrifice. Rupeni was oblivious to all except his own lust and passion.

Ramona walked with her head held high; the rest of the bridal party were watching the road so they could avoid the horse shit and potholes. Ramona was silent, unlike her sisters who were yelling out to the mangy old dogs that dashed out to snap at them. Her pride had made her inviolate to such barking creatures. She was otherworldly, seeming to float above everything crass and mundane.

Rupeni heard the voice of the priest beside him. 'You should come inside now and wait for your bride at the altar.'

Rupeni shook his head. He was entranced by Ramona's beauty and sadness. He waited. Finally she was there. He looked upward into her eyes. The boldness of her stare made him look away.

By this time, Ramona was having a change of heart.

I watched Aunt Ruth's lips. I felt like switching her voice off, as if it was a radio, and mouthing along with her lips.

Rupeni heard Ramona say, 'Mother take the cloak from my shoulders. It is a royal cloak and should not be sullied by such an event as this.'

Rupeni laughed. His lips curled into a sneer. He saw Ramona's tears of anger.

'Although you weep for another man,' Rupeni said, 'you will always be mine. I own you as surely as I do my horse, my cattle, my sheep, my farm.'

Defiant, Ramona answered, 'I marry you only to give you the comfort of my body for a week before you leave for Europe. Yes, I might have a child by you and, if so, I will love that child. I do this for my family and yours. You could have spoken against the arrangement. Instead you take advantage of me because I am the most beautiful girl you have ever seen and a virgin. You are a rogue, a cur and a bounder, sir, and I hate you. Will you not let me go?'

'Never, *never*,' Rupeni hissed. 'I will take you to my bed and make you mine.'

'So be it,' Ramona said, 'but never assume my throes will be passion. I spit on your bed and I spit on you. Though you may take my body repeatedly in the night, my innermost soul and my heart will never be yours. Never, never, never, *never*.'

'The preacher coughed for attention,' Aunt Ruth said. 'He began to beckon everyone inside the church.'

That is when it happened.

A thrumming of hooves came echoing along the road between the fields of maize. A handsome young lover was seen, spurred on by passion for his woman.

'It was our father,' Aunt Ruth continued, eyes afire. 'The thought of losing our mother was too much to bear. Impetuous, he rode his white horse right to the church steps –'

The tinted oval photograph comes to life again.

'Ramona-aaaa –'

Ramona gives a cry. She sees the sunlight flashing in Tamihana's curly brown hair and the desperation in his sparkling green eyes. She turns to her father.

'Forgive me, e pa –'

Tamihana is galloping in slow motion, scattering the crowd, his horse's hooves scything the air like silver swords.

Rupeni's groomsmen try to stop Tamihana. They grab at the reins of his white horse. He eludes them and in a trice is reaching for Ramona. Only Rupeni is between him and his prize.

A gasp comes from the crowd. Rupeni has a knife and he slashes at Grandfather's face. Blood beads Tamihana's left cheek, spilling dark red rubies on Grandmother's white dress.

'Oh my love –' Ramona cries.

Laughing like Douglas Fairbanks in a swashbuckling movie, Grandfather leans down, knocks Rupeni to the ground with one heroic blow, scoops Grandmother up into his arms and turns his white horse away.

Glory clasped her hands with delight at Aunt Ruth's story. As for me, was I surprised? Was I what!

'True love gave your grandparents the wings of eagles,' Aunt Ruth said to Glory. 'They rode and rode –'

'Into the sunset,' I murmured.

'And Rupeni couldn't find them,' my aunt continued, trying to poke me with her foot. 'He left for Europe and by the time he returned from the war your grandparents were already married and raising the family in Waituhi.' She paused. 'And of course,' she added hastily, 'they lived happily ever after.'

Aunt Ruth's voice drifted into the darkness. The radiator of Pani's car popped and hissed as it cooled.

An hour later we were able to pour some water into it and get on our way again. It was getting on for half-past twelve. Then, *crack*. Pani's second headlamp went out.

'E koe,' we said before our mother could open her mouth.

'Aue,' she agonised, 'Kei te haramai a Dracula ki konei!' Dracula will get us now for sure. She had been to see Bela Lugosi in *Dracula* a month before. Dracula was even worse than kehua because he sucked your neck.

We stopped again. Dad went over to talk to Pani.

'We should shoot your car,' Dad said, 'and put it out of its misery. Never mind. You follow us. And look –' He pointed to the moon, rising full across the sky, lending silver light to the road ahead. 'Who needs lights when we have the moon to show us the way?'

My mother wasn't so sure. A full moon meant that Dracula would find us easy.

By that time our mother's anxiety was affecting us as well. We kept on saying, 'Hurry up, Dad, make the car go faster.' Dracula was already following us. He was coming over the hills. His mouth was opened and his fangs were starting to grow and –

Saved! Ahead was the sign for the Williamson station and, beyond, the track leading along the side of the hill past the two-storeyed house where the boss lived, to the shearing shed and shearers' quarters beyond. But what was that? Luminous green eyes staring at us from out of the darkness! Vampires! We screamed.

Only sheep. Phew.

A lamp was shining in one of the quarters.

'Is that you, Joshua?' Uncle Hone called.

'Ae,' Dad said.

'Good,' Uncle Hone continued. 'Early start tomorrow. You and your family are in with Sam Whatu's family. Pani, you're in bunking with the single men. Sephora, you and Esther are in with Auntie Molly. Ruth? Albie's over in the quarters next door. He's been waiting eagerly for you all night.'

'I'll bet,' Aunt Ruth said.

By torchlight and moonlight we unpacked the two cars – the bedding first, so that my aunts and Mum could make up the beds for us; then our belongings, stores and provisions for the kitchen, twenty-five yards away next to a small stream. Finally, Dad and Pani took out the handpieces, blades and assorted equipment they would need for tomorrow's shearing. I could hear them talking as they worked; Pani sounded unusually anxious. Apparently Mahana One, on their way to Horsfield station, had come across Poata Three.

'Are you sure?' Dad asked.

'That's what Maaka told Hone,' Pani said.

'Could he have made a mistake?'

'No. They came around a bend in the road and, hello, there were the Poatas as plain as day. They looked like they'd just come from the Horsfields. Anyway no sooner had they seen Mahana One than they scooted off in the other direction.'

'They're way out of their territory,' Dad said.

'Ae,' Pani nodded.

'Has Dad been told?'

'Aua,' Pani shrugged. 'That's up to Matiu.'

Dad paused. 'Something must be going on. I don't like the sound of it.' He was pensive. The moonlight glinted on his blades.

'Come to bed,' Mum called, interrupting him.

We had arrived.

19

'Okay, sweethearts, rise and shine,' Aunt Ruth yelled the next morning. I opened one eye and then another. No, this wasn't a nightmare, this was *real*.

'Come on,' Aunt Ruth repeated. 'This is second call, you fellas! The cook is cooking and the shearers are already over at the shed. *Get to it.*'

Aunt Ruth roused the single men who were still in bed in the bunkhouse. I looked around. Dad and Mum had already gone, and so had Glory. We had arrived in the middle of the night and four hours later were straight into work.

'Faith! Hope!' I said. 'Kia tere. We're late.'

Aunt Ruth poked her head in through the door. She was scrubbed and energetic. She had tied a red scarf around her hair. She wore green overalls.

'Good, you're up, boy. No hurry. The sheep are in the shearers' pens but they haven't started the engines yet.' Aunt Ruth's eyes twinkled. She had caught me unawares and I had dreamt one of *those* dreams. 'Is that your stick to whack the sheep with?' she laughed. She could be so embarrassing.

Her eyes returned to Faith and Hope. 'Come on, girls! You two are on kitchen duty.'

I dashed down to the creek to wipe the pikare out of my eyes. When I was ready I walked past the kitchen, cocky this year because Willie Whatu was the poor shit taking my place there – and he was already quailing under Auntie Molly's orders. Affectionately known as Good Golly Miss Molly, she had been Mahana Four's cook for *ages*. Behind her was Aunt Esther as second cook and, entering, the Frog Queens as the female kitchen hands.

'Oh my giddy aunt, Willie,' Molly was growling. 'Get a move on, boy. Bring that pot over here. Not over there. Over here.' She turned to Faith and Hope. 'Where have you two been! Don't be late tomorrow morning or you'll have your pay docked. Esther? You show the girls how to peel the spuds the way we want them, ne? Thank goodness you're here. I don't know how I could manage without you – just look at this kitchen! Oh for crying out *loud*, Willie –'

Aunt Molly sat in the doorway, trying to escape the worst of the smoke as it billowed *down* the ineffectual chimney. All shearers' kitchens were variations on *bad* and, boy oh boy, by midday they turned into a smoky fiery furnace.

'Good morning, Aunt Molly!' I called cheekily. 'Isn't it a lovely day to start a new shed? The birds are singing and the bees are humming –'

Aunt Molly tried to be stern. She was physically enormous. She never did any cooking herself but, rather, directed from afar. She sat all day in one place, ordering you around, and if you didn't do your job properly she had a switch that stung your legs.

'Don't think you can laugh at me, Simeon Mahana! You think you're on easy street now, ne! I can still get you back in here for one more year!'

I grinned and blew her a kiss. 'I love you too, Auntie!'

I ran along the track to the shearing shed. The Pakeha shepherds were saddling up to bring in the sheep from the far paddocks. Sheepdogs scampered and barked and squealed around the horses' hooves, daring the horses to kick them. The shepherds had whistles shaped by sovereigns in their mouths. The air was filled with the excitement of their whistling and the barking of the dogs.

I took a quick look at the sheep yards at the back of the shed. Good – they were filled with sheep and there were two shepherds there.

'Kia ora,' I said to them. 'My name's Simeon and I'm the sheepo.' *Me*. Wow.

The shepherds nodded. They were in their late teens.

'Gidday,' the red-headed one said. 'My name's Mick. This here's Phil.' We shook hands. 'We'll keep the sheep coming. If they're coming in too slow, give us a whistle. Okay?'

'Sounds good to me.'

I saw Uncle Hone and he winked at me. Then, into the shed.

There was nothing like the first day at a shed before the engines started up. Outside was the yelp of dogs, swearing of shepherds and constant bleat of sheep. Inside was purposeful preparation. Aunt Sephora was Mahana Four's wool classer, but now that Aunt Ruth had been assigned to us she was deferring this position to her elder sister. Apart from the mana of the position, it also brought in more pay.

Aunt Ruth smiled. 'No, sister,' she said, 'everybody's used to you.'

My mother and Aunt Kate, Uncle Hone's muscular wife, would be working with Aunt Ruth and Aunt Sephora on the table. Two on each side. Mum waved me over.

'Did you say your morning prayers?' she asked.

'Yes,' I answered. Under my breath, Wethankyouforthisday-inJesusnameAmen.

'Ka pai,' she continued. 'You ready to do your job?'

'Ae.'

I waved to Mahana Four's pressmen. David and Benjamin were the eighteen-year-old twin grandsons of Zebediah Whatu. I would become a pressman when I got to be their age; they would have moved on to being shearers. I saw Glory sitting close by Uncle Hone, two clapper boards in her hands. Peewee and Mackie, her male cousins, were glaring at her. There had been a fight to wrest the boards from her.

Glory gave me her look. Do something.

I walked over to Uncle Hone, who was on the top gun or ringer's stand. He was dressed in the usual black woollen singlet, woollen pants tied at the waist with string and jute moccasins. Although he was big and fat, Uncle Hone was one of the best shearers in the family. His bulk gave him reserves that kept him going way after everybody else had called it quits. Uncle Hone had just finished sharpening the blades of his handpiece, the sparks arcing like fireworks from the grinding wheel. He was talking to Dad on the Number 2 stand. Dad, of course, was the *champ*, except that he pretended not to show it; out of respect for his elder brother, he always lagged one or two sheep behind. Sam Whatu, David and Benjamin's father, was on the Number 3 stand, Pani on Number 4 stand, and on Number 5 was Uncle Albie, who was cutting out new moccasins and sewing them up.

'Eh Albie!' Aunt Kate called. 'Sew up your fly while you're at it and give Ruth some peace!'

'I should be so lucky,' Aunt Ruth muttered.

The two sweepers on the boards were my cousins Haromi and Frances. I was surprised to see Haromi because she was usually with Mahana One.

'Morning, boy!' Uncle Hone said. 'I saw you talking to the shepherds. That's what I like – a sheepo who knows how to do his job. I want the sheep to come in nice and steady. Not too slow. But don't push us, all right? The sheep look like they're pretty clean, so they'll be sweet to shear, but that doesn't mean we should increase the pace. Slow and steady does the job.'

'Yes, Uncle.'

'I don't want my pen less than half empty, okay?' he continued.

'Nor mine,' Dad said.

'Nor mine,' Uncle Albie said.

Uncle Hone laughed. 'But *mine* gets filled before anyone else's!'

Behind me, Glory coughed. Uncle took me to one side. 'That sister of yours has been giving me the glad eye ever since I got here,' he whispered.

'She wants to be in charge of the dags.'

Peewee and Mackie jostled forward. 'Glory's only a girl,' they complained. 'She can't work as fast as we can.' The boys were punching each other out in an attempt to get in the front position.

'What do you think?' Uncle asked me.

I nodded at Glory. She was ready to murder. 'Possession is nine-tenths of the law,' I answered, referring to the clapper boards in her hands.

'*And* I got up,' Glory said, 'at three o'clock in the morning to get here before they did.'

Uncle laughed. He looked at the other boys. 'Looks like you boys will have to help Simeon in the pens.'

I smiled at Glory. Satisfied? No, she kicked me in the legs. She mouthed a word – Pee-ay-why-ar-oh-ell-ell-

'Does that mean that Glory's on the payroll?' I asked.

'Hmmn, you tell her she's on trial.'

Glory wasn't having *that* on. She shook her head.

'No trial,' I continued.

Uncle hesitated.

'In that case, everybody else's dags will get swept away –' I paused – 'except yours.'

Uncle was trying not to laugh. 'I call that blackmail,' he said. 'But –' he turned to Glory, 'it's a deal, babe.'

Mr Williamson, the owner of the station and Amberleigh, arrived. With him was a young Pakeha boy of my age. One of the shepherds later told me his name was Geordie. He was the Williamsons' youngest son, home on holiday from boarding school in Nelson. It was five minutes to six.

'Good morning Bob,' Uncle Hone greeted him. It was all right for Uncle Hone to use Mr Williamson's first name, but the rest of us were not accorded the same privilege.

Mr Williamson nodded. He was a tall, austere man with a badly sunburnt appearance, as if he didn't really belong in this climate. His skin was scaly, flaking off in huge yellow patches. He raised his hat to our women and then shook Aunt Sephora's hand. As wool classer, she had responsibility for maintaining his reputation as a producer of wool of the very finest grade. She introduced to him the women under her charge – she had been doing this every year, and Mr Williamson still hadn't remembered their names.

'Well, gentlemen,' Mr Williamson said, 'and ladies, welcome to Williamson station again. We have always counted on Mahana Four for quality shearing and quality classing. When buyers look at my wool bales they know they will be of premier excellence. Your work has always secured us top price. I know that, as in the past, we will continue to have your sterling service.'

Murmurs. 'Thank you, Mr Williamson.'

Uncle Hone nodded to Benjamin.

'Excuse me, boss,' Benjamin said as he went past Mr Williamson into the engine room.

Phut . . . phut . . . phut – with an explosion of blue smoke the machine started. The belt whined, accelerated, revolving the driveshaft to greater and greater speed.

'Timata!' Uncle Hone yelled.

The shearers walked swiftly into the pens and grabbed their first sheep of the day. They dragged them out and settled them within the curve of their legs. With one hand the shearers reached for their handpieces. With the other they pulled on the cord which would send them power.

Bzzzzz – the first cut. Right on six o'clock.

20

One of the reasons I liked the shearing was that it took me away from Grandfather. The work was just as hard and relentless as at the homestead but, for a small space of time, I escaped Grandfather's daily subjection. I think this is how my parents, sisters and spinster aunts felt as well. We all commiserated with poor Aunt Miriam for being with him in Mahana One.

There was a second reason for liking the shearing, and that was that Mahana Four was a second family. For six months of the year the family was mine and I was theirs. I had always been theirs – even as a baby, watching from the wool and having my nappies changed by whoever was nearest.

'E hara, Huria,' aunts or uncles would say, 'he tutae ano.'

As a toddler I became a runner for whoever needed me – the shearers, pressmen, wool classers and cook.

'Get me an orange cordial, boy', or:

'Wipe my face for me, son, the sweat is in my eyes', or:

'Tell the sheepo to bring some more sheep into the pen.'

No doubt I made a thorough nuisance of myself running here and there through the legs of the shearers, among the brooms of the sweepers, and around the dresses of the wool classers. Nothing prepared you better for the shearing shed than being able to negotiate the minefield of activity without tripping anyone up.

Then I graduated to helping the sheepo keep the pens tightly full for the pressmen or fleecos –

'Come and jump in the sacks, boy, and push the wool down.'

Finally I worked my way up to my first *real* job and seeing my name on the payroll – picking up the dags with the clapper boards. I was so keen to get at any sheep with a dirty bum! I waited until the sweepers separated the bum wool and dags, scooped them up and took them to my special place where I sorted through and salvaged as much wool from the dags as was possible. There was always a place and a price for any sort of wool.

From the dags I had descended into Hell by becoming the skivvy for Aunt Molly. That had been the *worst* job. Keeping the kitchen clean. Chopping wood – lots of wood – for once the fire was started it stayed on until the shearing was finished. Cutting the meat, carrying water, peeling potatoes, carrots and cabbage – phew. I had been first up in the morning and last to bed at nights. But now I was sheepo. And my sister Glory was on the payroll too. I felt proud that she had attained that status this season. She had earned her position in charge of the dags. From now until the time she decided to give up shearing, she was a paid member of Mahana Four. Her pay might be only ten shillings a week, but it was hers. There was no greater accolade.

Two hours after we had begun, Uncle Hone gave a nod to Benjamin and the engine was switched off – phut . . . phut . . . *fart*.

'Kua pai?' he asked. It was time for breakfast.

'Kua pai,' everybody agreed.

The shearers downed their handpieces, taking a breather, having a smoke. The sweepers swept the board tidy. The last fleece was thrown on the table for my aunts to skirt, class, fold and place into holding bins. David and Benjamin cranked the top onto the wool press. Aided by Peewee and Mackie, I took the opportunity to fill the pens tight with sheep. Peewee and Mackie were doing pretty good. I had said I'd give them ten shillings each a week from my pay. Glory, eyes clinched in concentration, was being absolutely impeccable with the dags.

My father picked her up. 'Come on, babe.'

However, as we approached the cookhouse – 'Uh oh,' Uncle Hone sighed.

A huge commotion was coming from the kitchen.

'Come on, girls, kia tere! The engine over at the shed has gone off. Oh my giddy aunt, *Willie*! Where's the hot water for the cocoa? You boiled the potatoes in it? What you want to do that for!'

Aunt Molly was on the warpath. Bangs, crashes, shrieks and foul imprecations issued from the kitchen. She looked out the door and saw Uncle Hone and the rest of us standing there. Arms akimbo she roared, 'Hone? Hone Mahana, you just get your big black arse over here, you bastard!'

Although church-going like the rest of us, Aunt Molly had never been able to stop swearing. She did her repentance every First Sunday.

Poor Uncle Hone. He trotted over to Auntie Molly as meekly as a lamb and went into the kitchen.

'What seems to be the trouble, Aunt Molly?'

Aunt Molly's voice issued from the depths of the kitchen. 'Don't think you can sweet talk me, you bastard! You told me I would have a good kitchen this time and –'

Clang as something was thrown against the wall.

'I find the same fucken place as last year. Didn't you talk to Mister High and Mighty Williamson about it? Not only that –'

Crash of something on the ceiling.

'How am I going to feed all you buggers when there's only four hooks to hang the pots from! Then there's the little matter of the stream –'

Splat as something, probably Uncle Hone, was spilled onto the floor.

'The water is too fucken far away, the safe is broken and there's not enough air in here for even one person, let alone my girls and my boy Willie. What the *hell* do you expect me to do! I can't work miracles, you know, only *God* can do that and even *He* would have a hard time in *this* –'

Smash as something was booted by her foot.

'Place. What do you think I am Hone? Eh, you tell me that! You tell me –'

We waited outside while Uncle Hone tried to pacify Auntie Molly as best he could. She was worth her weight in gold. Many a time Mahana One, Two and Three had tried to capture her, but her loyalty to Mahana Four was legendary. Not even Grandfather had been able to persuade her to come over to the top gang.

'I'm sorry, auntie,' Uncle Hone began. 'I don't know how you put up with us, year in and year out. Goodness knows we can't manage without you.' Grease, grease, Uncle. 'All we ask is that you do your best, Auntie Molly, that's all. And if the food is not up to scratch, even the crumbs off your table are better than a big kai at Mahana One, Two or Three.'

Auntie Molly began to sniff. Uncle Hone edged around the doorway and beckoned us to hurry up and come in. As we did so, we patted her on the shoulder –

'Never mind, Auntie.'

'We love you, Auntie Molly.'

To one side, Aunt Esther was waiting, and Faith and Hope were grinning with pride. So was Willie. The cookhouse may have just been a one-roomed tin shack with a long table down the middle but, despite her fulminations, Aunt Molly had organised the most splendid breakfast ever – porridge, sausages, bacon and eggs, Maori bread straight out of the oven, cocoa and cordial.

That was always the way with Aunt Molly. She loved us so much that nothing she did was ever good enough.

We sat down to breakfast – and could we eat? Could we what! And as we ate, the bantering and stories began again, arising easily out of the camaraderie, as if any silence had to be filled in. Uncle Hone started to reminisce about how beautiful Grandmother Ramona had been as a young girl. As he was talking I began to revise my image of her – young boys don't go around thinking about their grandmothers as sex symbols. She must have been some looker to have two men fight over her.

'She's where I get my looks from,' Aunt Ruth said, striking a pose.

'Gee, sis,' Uncle Hone answered from the head of the table, 'our mum and dad made you on a *bad* day.'

'Huh,' Aunt Ruth retorted. 'At least they made me during the day,' referring to her fair complexion, 'rather than at midnight!'

Everybody laughed. Then Uncle Hone began to tell how the great conflict between Rupeni Poata's family and the House of Mahana began.

'Never underestimate Rupeni Poata,' he said, picking up a fork and waving it at us in warning. 'He is a formidable opponent and his family have the advantage of his excellent training, just as ours has from our father.'

'Ka tika,' Aunt Ruth nodded. 'You may think that as a young man Bulibasha had the greater mana, but Rupeni Poata was his equal. They had known each other before Dad took Grandmother Ramona from Rupeni and had been good friends.'

Friends?

'It's true,' Uncle Hone confirmed. 'Not only that, but in those days Rupeni Poata's achievements as a sportsman were as good as our father's.'

The older ones nodded sagely. 'They were twins on the sportsfield. If Grandfather won –'

'Rupeni was second,' Uncle Hone said. 'If Rupeni won –'

'Grandfather was second,' Aunt Ruth continued. Whenever they were racing, boxing or wrestling, people took bets on who would win. Some sports our father excelled in –'

'Like swimming and sprints,' Uncle Hone continued, 'but there were other sports that Rupeni excelled in. Although he was smaller and shorter than our father, he had great reserves of power. His upper arms, for instance, were much more developed. This gave him the advantage in wrestling or in shot put or javelin.'

'In field games too,' Aunt Ruth said, 'they were eager competitors. In rugby, our father played in the forwards –'

'Rupeni was a halfback,' Uncle Hone continued.

'Our father played centre in hockey,' Aunt Ruth said.

'Rupeni was a winger,' Uncle Hone added.

'They were always against each other in the games between Hukareka and Waituhi,' Aunt Ruth continued. 'Luckily, the representative games weren't competitive, so sometimes they found themselves on the same side, and they *were* friends –'

Uncle Hone nodded. 'It is important to remember this,' he said, 'because our father bore Rupeni no ill.'

'Rupeni Poata gained as much fame for his sporting prowess,' Aunt Ruth underlined, 'as our father did. Our father had no other peer than Rupeni. His house in Hukareka is likely filled with as many trophies as our homestead at Waituhi.'

There were murmurs of doubt that this could possibly be so.

'However, everything changed between them when Dad took Grandmother Ramona from Rupeni,' Uncle Hone said. 'Although both of them wrote to Rupeni in Europe seeking to mend any ill feeling, there was no reply. They waited for Rupeni Poata and the boys who had gone to the war to return.' There was a pause. Uncle Hone looked up at the clock. Starting time was in a quarter of an hour. 'What do you think, sis?' he asked Aunt Ruth.

She nodded. 'Tenei korero he korero tika,' she said. 'Everybody must understand.'

Four years had passed since Rupeni Poata had left for the war. Now he was returning with the other soldiers to a heroes' welcome at the railway station. His home crowd from Hukareka was there in force. They proposed to swing into a haka of acclamation as soon as he stepped from the train. When Tamihana and Ramona arrived with their three children, Matiu, Maaka and Ruka, and others of the Mahana clan, some of the Hukareka people were hostile.

'Must you rub Rupeni's nose in your offence to him?'

'We have come to welcome our hero also,' Tamihana said. 'Bygones should be bygones.'

Some of the Hukareka people agreed. 'Ka tika,' they said. 'The world has turned four times and cannot be returned to the way it was. A reconciliation would be a good way to begin in the new world. There is so much to challenge us all. Let us go forward having resolved the unhappinesses of the past.'

Then Grandfather discovered that another taumau marriage had been arranged for Rupeni with a woman from Waikato named Maata. A letter had been sent to Rupeni to ask if he would accept the arrangement and he agreed.

Maata stepped forward to greet Ramona. She was a proud and handsome woman with stars in her eyes. 'I wish only to serve Rupeni,' she said. 'He has already written to me about the death and the destruction he has seen. Men have been blown to bits on the battlefield. They have been suffocated by the deadly gas used in the trenches. He wishes only to return and to find peace. My arms are ample. They will bring him the peace he seeks. My hips are big and will bear many sons.' Maata told Grandfather and Grandmother they should remain.

The train came into view. Smoke was pouring from the engine. Fathers, mothers, wives and children waved patriotic flags. The town band played 'God Defend New Zealand'. There wasn't a dry eye in sight. Finally the train was there, and steam hissed from beneath the couplings. The soldiers began to disembark. Still under command, they formed a line along the station platform, waiting for the colonel to dismiss them. The suspense was awful.

Then it was done. The Hukareka people launched into their great haka for Rupeni Poata. His mother and sisters ran weeping towards him and flung themselves into his arms. Maata was brought forward. She knelt before him. He smiled down at her.

Then out of the corner of his eye he saw Ramona. His face crumpled with grief. Then he saw Tamihana. He saw their children.

Maata tried to act as the go-between in healing the rift between Rupeni and my grandparents. Rupeni pushed her to the ground. He still had his bayonet and he drew it. People screamed. But Rupeni's anger was unchanged. Raising his bayonet, he slid it between his lips so that his mouth filled with the blood.

'With these, my blood words,' he said, 'I vow undying vengeance on you and all who spring from your loins. Let there always be enmity between you and yours', he pointed to Tamihana and the children, 'and me and mine.'

21

Sometimes when I think of Grandmother Ramona I remember a moment in summer when I watched her unobserved. The day was hot. I had come into the kitchen for a glass of water and to escape the heat. I thought I was alone in the homestead and pondered sneaking into the drawing room to turn on the wireless and listen to 'Dossier on Demetrius'.

I heard a sound. I went through into the drawing room. The door to Grandfather and Grandmother's bedroom was open. Grandmother Ramona had just come back from her hives. She was removing her beekeeping veils.

Although Grandfather Tamihana had no land left in Waituhi – or so he said – Grandmother Ramona had five acres of the richest meadow down beside the Waipaoa River. Annual flooding had not leached that land where the river looped, and instead had layered the meadow with dark earth from further inland. Grandmother Ramona grew her fruit trees – quince, fig, apple, orange, feijoa and nectarine – and cultivated her strawberries and raspberries on that land. The primary glory, however, was the meadow itself, wave upon wave of green grass speckled with wildflowers. There, Grandmother Ramona kept her hives.

Grandfather Tamihana hated bees, and although he would have loved to have taken Grandmother Ramona's land, stayed well clear of it. He said in jest that he would not risk being pursued by every bee in Christendom.

'I think your grandmother goes down there,' Nani Mini Tupara once told me, 'because she knows Grandfather won't set his foot in the place! She can be by herself there and do what she wants.'

With the exception of Mum and Dad, everybody else in the Mahana clan hated 'Mum's bees' too. In the beginning, I had an aversion to them as well. I marvelled at Grandmother Ramona's courage as she went down to take honey from the hives. I sometimes went with her as far as the edge of the field, but watched from afar as, dressed in her long beekeeping veils, she went about her work. The bees were like the Furies, buzzing and circling angrily over her.

'They're all noise,' she told me. 'They really love me, see? Titiro!' To prove it, she took off a glove and allowed the bees to swarm on her hand. 'Do you know why they love me? They know that as long as I am alive this meadow is theirs.' When she eventually peeled the bees off, like a gold and black crust, she had not been stung at all.

As I grew older I began to lose my fear of being stung and went into the meadow with Grandmother Ramona. There I would join Mum and Dad picking fruit or helping Grandmother with the bees. My mother always had stars in her eyes when she was down on Grandmother's land. The meadow was a place to dream.

'One day,' Dad told her, 'we'll have a place like this. One day –'

Grandmother Ramona harvested the honey for family eating, but its golden colour and rich taste were renowned throughout the district. To some she was known as 'Te Hanene', the Honey Gatherer, and people would often come to the homestead to ask for her honey.

'E kui,' they would say, 'homai enei hani mo taku mokopuna me taku koroua.' Grandmother's honey was regarded as having healing properties, especially for young babies or old men and women.

The windows in the bedroom were wide open. The wind was billowing the curtains like dreams. A thunderstorm was approaching. Dark clouds were boiling across the hills, pushing the hot air in front of them. Grandmother Ramona was rubbing the sweat from her neck with a small towel. A tender look came over her face. She approached her memory box at the foot of the brass bedstead and knelt beside it. She opened the lid and unfolded a dress from layers of tissue, carefully, slowly, the paper falling like doves' wings.

I glanced up at the oval photograph of Grandmother. The dress looked similar – long, white, high-collared with puffed sleeves. But I wasn't sure. When I looked back, it was too late to check. Grandmother was standing with her back to me, the dress enfolded tightly in her arms. She was staring out the windows, watching the dark clouds coming. All of a sudden there was a rush of wind through the windows. The curtains flapped like white veils. Tissue paper swirled like white birds.

Summer lightning jagged the sky.

22

'Hey, sheepo!' Mick the shepherd yelled. 'Tell them to slow down inside, eh?'

He and Phil were grinning in a harassed way. Outside, the yards were bedlam. We were on to the last of the rams, and now ewes were being brought into the shed. Mick and Phil were pushing them through the race, but the ewes were baulking at the entrance to the shed. On the way through the race they'd been divided from their lambs and wanted to get back.

'Can't keep up, eh?' I yelled.

The pace was fast enough inside. I was lucky to have Peewee and Mackie's help. Getting sheep to go through gates was worse than making a donkey trot; unlike donkeys, you can't entice sheep with carrots.

'You bloody bitches!' Peewee was scolding. Peewee and Mackie's swearing had escalated as the shearing progressed.

Now another of the ewes had baulked, afraid of crossing from sunlight into darkness. The ewe had turned the rest away from the entrance. Alerted, Mick whistled his cross-Collie – 'Hup, Skip!' Skip came hurtling over the backs of the sheep to the ones in front. She let off a roulade of barks, startling the sheep to return our way again – and *in*.

'Thanks, Mick,' Peewee called.

The large holding pen at the inside back of the shed was almost full. Just one more sheep – and Peewee was pushing the gate across, flicking the toggle shut. Mick waved good-humouredly. He took his hat off and wiped the sweat from his brow. Already more ewes were being brought down from the back paddocks. Shepherds on horseback whistled their dogs to weave back and forth across the hillsides, driving the sheep relentlessly down the slope toward the shed. No time to talk. Mick put his hat back on. He strode through the dust and the melee to bring in the sheep.

'Get in behind, Skip!'

By midday the shed was an oven at its highest heat. Outside, you could fry an egg on the inverted V of the corrugated red roof. Inside, the heat radiated mercilessly, amplifying the stench of grease, wool and sheep droppings.

'Sheepo!'

Mackie and Peewee went scrabbling along the network of railings to Uncle Hone's pen. Sure of foot, they literally ran along the tops, jumping from one rail to the next.

'You got it, Uncle!' Mackie answered.

In a trice, Mackie opened Uncle Hone's pen. Peewee began to push sheep through from the larger feeder pen behind.

'Sheepo!'

Another call, this time from Uncle Albie. His black singlet was drenched. Again my two charges went to work. The shearers were cracking on the pace.

A good sheepo had the pens filled before the shearer called. However, we were on the last of the rams. We had to push sheep to the shearers on an equal basis – say, two or three at a time – so that one shearer didn't end up with an empty pen while the others were still shearing.

'Sheepo!' Dad this time.

'I'll get him,' Mackie yelled.

The feeder pen was emptying fast. Behind, the ewes were waiting. Uncle Hone came into his pen to grab a sheep. The sweat was riveting down his neck.

'Do you want to start the ewes after lunch?' I asked. It was a question, but –

'You're the boss,' he answered.

Mackie and Peewee overheard. They sighed with relief. Great, we would have the lunch break to bring the ewes up into the shearers' pens.

I went to let Mick and Phil know that we could all take a breather. Peewee went down the board telling everybody that ewes were coming in after lunch. You had to think ahead in shearing – a new wool type meant a complete changeover in handling. The shearers changed their blades. The sweepers, fleecos, pressmen and wool classer cleared their work area. Aunt Sephora was already calculating whether the pressmen would be able to make up complete bales from the rams' wool. Wool types were never mixed.

'Sheepo!'

The cry was coming more frequently and my small mates were scurrying back and forth, pushing the rams in each shearer's pen one at a time and figuring, 'There's five in Uncle Hone's pen, three in Uncle Josh's, six in Uncle Sam's, better put one more in Uncle Albie's –' I would not have managed without them.

The shearers were down to three sheep each, then two and –

'Last sheep up!'

Time for Peewee, Mackie and me to start bringing the ewes up for the afternoon's shearing.

Meantime, one by one, the shearers yanked on the cords to stop their handpieces. They were stretching, bending, massaging tired muscles, taking throatfuls of cordial and waiting for the boss to tally their run.

David stopped the engine. The whining noise as the belt slowed would alert Aunt Molly to start dishing up the kai. Hungry workers liked their food on the plate and not in the pots. Haromi passed by Pani, sweeping the board clear of the rams' wool. Patches of dark moisture stained her armpits.

'Hot work!' Pani said. 'Plenty to sweat about.'

'Men sweat,' Haromi said haughtily, 'women perspire.'

She picked up the last ram's fleece and took it back to the table. Did I forget to tell you that Haromi usually never threw the fleece on the table properly? It would land skewered, half off the table, or – when she was in a bad mood – the wrong way up, or – when she was angry with Aunt Ruth for catching her having a smoke – missing the table altogether. This time, no doubt because we were stopping for lunch, she did a perfect throw. Swinging from the hip, she gave a mighty *heave*, as if throwing a net. The fleece began to unfold in the air and, at the last second, Haromi let it go.

Uncle Hone laughed as the fleece landed right in the middle of the table. He led a smattering of applause. 'We might make a fleeco out of you yet!' he called.

'Hardly,' Haromi muttered.

One by one the shearers began drifting back to the cookhouse. Then, once Aunt Sephora was satisfied that the fleecos' work areas were ready for the afternoon, they left the shed too, grabbing Glory up on their way over the paddocks.

'Come on, Glory!' Aunt Ruth said.

Peewee, Mackie and I finished our job.

'You guys are great,' I commended them. They gulped, grinned and were off.

The only noise left was the press. David and Benjamin were trying to catch up before we started the ewes. It would be good to clear the holding area and get the bales out onto the loading bay.

'Do you two need a hand?' I asked.

'You go on,' they said.

Except for the sheep baa-ing away, all was blessed silence.

23

Geordie and I met a week after Mahana Four had arrived at his father's station. He must have seen me climbing up to the top of the bales where I had stashed my book, *Allan Quartermain*. I always went there for a spell by myself after lunch. Now he had my book in his hand, and was supercilious. He was a fey, thin boy with a mass of blond curls. His voice was languid.

'I suppose,' he said, 'you're going to tell me this is yours.' As if Maoris didn't, or shouldn't, read books.

'That's right,' I answered, bristling.

'And how would you prove it?'

'Apart from telling you what it's about, my name is in the front.' I felt like saying, That proves it wasn't stolen, either.

'Oh.' He handed the book back to me. Then, snobbily, 'Of course *The Ivory Child* is a far better book –'

'I know –'

Yawn.

His eyes sparkled. 'You've read it? You've actually read it?'

'Yes.' Now get off my hay bale.

'But I thought I was the only one in the whole western world,' he yelled, 'let alone the southern hemisphere, to have read *The Ivory Child*!'

I looked at him warily, and started to edge away. 'So what's that got to do with the price of fish?' I asked.

He recovered quickly. He could tell that I wasn't impressed by him.

'Perhaps we should be formally introduced,' he said. 'My name is Gordon George Williamson. Most people call me Geordie.'

'I'm Simeon,' I answered, 'sometimes known as Himiona.'

We shook hands. I was still doubtful about him.

After that, Geordie started to hang out in the shed, though not while we were working. I wasn't sure whether I was happy to see him or not. At Patutahi the prosperous Pakeha farmers always sent their children off to boarding school, as if the local school wasn't good enough for them – too many Maoris keeping their children from acquiring a decent education. I wasn't all that willing to entrust a friendship to someone whose father or mother was of that kind.

Haromi was the first to notice Geordie's visits. I think she was jealous because Geordie took me away from her. Not that we had been able to get together much ourselves, even after she was assigned to Mahana Four: the protocol during shearing was that the women and the girls kept together and the men and boys did the same.

'There's your kehua friend,' she said.

'He's a kehua,' I agreed, 'but he's okay. He likes books too.'

Haromi could be mean and vicious sometimes.

'Oh, another brainbox,' she answered, 'and a sissy too.'

I suppressed my anger. In those days you could be a sissy just by liking a picture by a famous artist or classical music or ballet dancing. A sissy was somebody like Freddie Murphy, the boy at school who was in Miss Mallard's tap dancing class along with Rona Clare and Jane Taylor. He was like William Haskins who was excused playing sport to protect his fingers for the pianoforte and, as he used to explain, after being ragged 'playing the workth of Franth Litht'. Instead of being admired for the courage of daring to be different, a sissy was ridiculed.

There was another criticism too, just as implicit and just as ambiguous.

'I see you've made friends with Geordie,' my father said to me later.

'Maybe,' I said.

Dad nodded. Then, 'He's the boss's son.'

'Yes, I know that.'

'Good. As long as you remember it.'

I crimsoned. Then I got really angry. Something unfair was going on. My friendship with Geordie – if that's what it was – hadn't even got off the ground and it was being ambushed by innuendo and assumption. The usual notions of the forbidding rural God, all of the 'Thou shalt nots' which dictated relationships, were being applied. Did I even *care* if Geordie was a sissy? That by associating with him, that I was one too? And so *what* if he was the boss's son! That was the criticism that hurt most. My own father was telling me, just as Grandfather had told me, that I had my place and I should stay in it. Mine the dusty road, Geordie's the tar seal.

To Hell with the lot of them.

24

A shearing gang working at the height of summer, nine hours a day, six days a week, is like nothing else on earth. I suppose if my sisters and I had known any better, we would have grown to dislike the sheer slog, sweat and boredom of repetitive work. However, because we were born to it, shearing was simply something we did in summer. At a time when other Maori families were fragmenting, the shearing kept the Mahana clan together. It replicated the dynamics of an iwi. As long as it survived, we needed no other support system.

A day of shearing started at five in the morning and finished at five in the evening. We had an hour off for breakfast at seven, half an hour for smoko at nine forty-five, an hour for lunch at noon and another half hour for smoko at two forty-five. The three main meals were eaten at the cookhouse; smoko was delivered to us by Aunt Esther, Faith, Hope and Willie – hot cocoa, tea for the non-Mormons, sausages, eggs, fried bread, and scones with lashings of butter and golden syrup. Sometimes, after afternoon smoko, Aunt Esther would stay at the shed to help the fleecos.

Our lives were driven by the phut – phut – *fart* of the engine, the whine of the driveshaft and the loud buzzing of the handpieces. Aunt Ruth, listening one day, said, 'No wonder I hate Mum's bees!' Doors slammed as the shearers went into the pens, and the press clanked as David and Benjamin pressed the wool. People shouted all the time. In the background was the constant bleating of sheep and barking of dogs, and whistles as the shepherds moved sheep in the yards.

The shearer was king. It was up to Uncle Hone on the Number 1 stand to maintain a good steady pace so that by the end of day all the shearers had made near enough to the magic tally of three hundred on full wool ewes. Dad, on the Number 2 stand, had a role too – gently pushing Uncle Hone along by being just behind him. Shearing gangs valued a good pacemaker like Uncle Hone. From him came the rhythm which would enable the entire gang to get through the season. Better that than somebody who pushed the pace and burnt out his gang. Uncle Matiu was like that – no wonder, as Mahana One was regarded as top gang and Uncle Matiu had to be king of kings. Having Grandfather driving him couldn't have made it any easier. Shearers, of course, didn't always make their daily three hundred. Sometimes a board placing was purposely kept open for a new shearer. He too was important in setting the pace – the bottom marker by whom the median could be found. Mahana Four didn't have a new boy this season, but David and Benjamin were raring to have a go.

Older shearers liked having a new boy on the board. They helped with advice on how to hold the sheep in the right way. Or how to apply a better technique to your shearing. Or when to take broad sweeping cuts. Or how to conserve your energy. Shearing was not normally a race, and the 'guns' among the shearers were those respected for their fluid style and ability to shear without cutting or marking a sheep. Such shearers also happened to be *fast*.

It was always good to watch a gun shearer. That was how every Mahana boy learned his craft. I learned by watching my Dad. He came dragging a sheep out of its pen and propped it between his legs in such a way that it couldn't move. He'd pull on the cord to start the handpiece and he was away.

First, two strokes on the top of the head, then the shoulders and into the long blow up the back of the sheep. Haromi came to sweep the wool away into its own separate pile on the board. Short strokes on the throat and insides of the legs, and longer strokes down and around the tits or ure (be careful!) to the rump. Next, Dad bent and shore down the right of the sheep. Again, Haromi with deft movements swept this grade wool away into a separate pile; the dags were swept Glory's way, and she salvaged any wool by picking through the dags. Best not to have long fingernails for *that* job.

Then came the part I liked best – the shearing of the fleece itself. It came off the sheep in one piece like a golden coat. Dad changed the sheep's position so that it was lying with its left side facing up. He began the long curving boomerang blows along the right flank, stroke after stroke, driving the handpiece through the wool, the fleece peeling magically away. Sometimes, though, the slightest movement of the sheep would cause the dumb thing to be cut by accident.

'Tar!' The cut needed to be sealed.

Dad then moved into the sheep to prop it on its bum again and began the short horizontal strokes on the right side. At every stroke the fleece fell away. Both shearer and sheep were encircled by the fabulous golden sheep. Aunt Ruth was there by then, to pick up the fleece and –

'Baaa!' With an outraged kick the sheep was pushed out from under Dad to slide ignominiously down the shute into its outside pen.

Easy, eh! Now *you* try it!

I have to admit that although Dad was probably faster, Uncle Hone was the best shearer in Mahana Four. I loved watching his style. People didn't normally equate shearing with style: I guess that commodity was more acceptable on the modelling catwalk where the wool was displayed in its finished designer packaging. There was, however, an art to shearing just as there was to most work, and Uncle Hone was a Botticelli of the board. Once I asked him what his secret was.

'You really want to know?' he asked. His eyes were twinkling. 'Well, it's not the actual shearing of the sheep which is the secret but, rather, the relationship you make with the sheep.'

Huh?

'A sheep,' he continued, 'isn't going to like it if you charge right into your pen and wrestle it and throw it to the ground, is it?'

'Well, no –'

'So what do I do? I go to the door and I say to the sheep inside, "You called?" And I think of Auntie Molly.'

Good grief.

'When I get into the pen and the sheep starts to fight me, I say, "Now don't do that, Auntie Molly, you know I love you." Then I drag her out nice and comfortable and put her between my legs. If she starts to kick I ask, "Isn't that comfortable enough, Auntie Molly?" And I find a position that's better for her. Then, if she starts to go Baaaaaa, I say, "You don't have to swear Auntie Molly –" '

My mouth was hanging open. I had a vision of Aunt Molly being shorn by Uncle Hone. She was bleating away between his legs – 'You watch it, Hone, you bastard! Are your blades sharp? I don't want to have any tar, thank you!'

'The secret is making the sheep feel confident that you know your job,' Uncle said. I think he was having me on. Sometimes his stories were pretty tall.

At afternoon smoko Uncle Hone resumed the story of Rupeni Poata and the conflict between the families. We were lounging among the bales, letting our kai digest. Mum and Dad were lying on a pile of wool sacks, with Glory half asleep between them. Auntie Molly was sitting on the edge of the docking bay with the shearers. Aunt Ruth was keeping an eagle eye on Haromi who was hoping to flirt with or cadge a smoke from one of the shepherds.

'Well,' Uncle Hone coughed, 'may as well let some more family skeletons out of the bag.'

'Do we have to?' Aunt Ruth asked.

'Only small skeletons,' he answered. 'We'll tell about those kids Dad had *before* he married Mum some other time.'

'Turituri!' Aunt Ruth growled.

Uncle Hone laughed good-naturedly. 'I want to tell you,' he said, 'about how Rupeni Poata became our strongest competitor in the shearing.

'A month after their return from the war, the soldiers were still being feted. Gisborne pulled out all the stops to welcome our boys home, Pakeha and Maori. The mayor put on a huge reception. Every small town and village began to put up war memorials and halls for those who did not return and for those who did. Whenever one was opened, the soldiers were feted there too.'

'One soldier among them all,' Aunt Ruth continued, 'was singled out for special attention – Rupeni Poata. He was a hero because at Gallipoli he had pulled three men out from under Turkish fire. At great risk to his own life he saved them from certain death. From famous sportsman he became war hero. He was constantly asked to speak at this or that function. He was very popular.'

'When the press found out he was engaged to marry Maata,' Uncle Hone said, 'they had a field day. The mayor said he wanted to put on the wedding breakfast. Apirana Ngata himself agreed to come from Wellington for the occasion.' Uncle Hone shifted to a more comfortable position. 'Rupeni's return also happened to coincide with plans for a visit to New Zealand by a British rugby team. When was that, sis?'

'In 1920,' Aunt Ruth answered. 'Naturally the British itinerary included Gisborne, so a series of trials was planned to pick the home side. Rupeni was up for selection. The mayor asked Rupeni, "When do you want to be married?" and Rupeni said, "Why not straight after the trials?" Apirana Ngata liked the idea because it meant that he could take in the trials as well as the wedding.'

'So as you can expect,' Uncle Hone laughed, 'there was a lot of excitement around!'

Tamihana was also a trialist. Although he had given up individual sports, he still played representative rugby and hockey. Every Saturday during the trials Ramona and the Mahana clan came to watch the games. If Tamihana was on one side, Rupeni was on the other. It soon became apparent that they were going to fight their way through the whole season on the field – and off.

'Hey, Mahana,' Rupeni Poata was reputed to have said once, 'marriage is ripping your balls off. You should retire before they shoot you.'

Although Grandfather had turned to religion, he found it hard to turn the other cheek. Hot tempered, he squared off with Rupeni. Fists started flying.

'Get off my back,' Tamihana answered. 'Play the game, not the man.'

Those gladiatorial fights – like Gordon Scott against Steve Reeves in *Hercules Unchained* – became the signal for fisticuffs among the other players. The fights were legendary.

Concerned, Ramona asked Tamihana, 'Can't you two mend the rift between you?'

'Nothing would be closer to my own wish,' Tamihana told her, 'but it is Rupeni who wishes to carry on this vendetta between us.'

Came the day of the last trial – the Probables versus the Possibles. Rupeni was the captain for one side and Tamihana the captain for the other. Ramona and the Mahana family were all in the stand at the oval. Ramona was like the Princess Alisande in *A Yankee in King Arthur's Court*. Apirana Ngata was sitting with Maata and the people of Hukareka. Out on the field it was a blood bath.

There were four minutes to go and it was likely the match would end in a draw, 15-all. The game had gone back and forward, up and down the length of the field. There had been five punch-ups. The people on the stand were baying for vengeance. The referee blew his whistle and called for the team captains.

'Listen, you guys,' the referee said, 'we're almost there and I want you to tell your teams to back off. You hear me? The selectors have seen what you're made of, so there's no need to kill each other. Aren't you getting married today, Poata? Leave some strength for later! Let's finish with a good clean game. Quit the rough stuff. Okay boys?'

Rupeni trotted back to his team. From the corner of his eye Tamihana saw Rupeni talking to his players and gesturing at him. The referee blew the whistle. The game recommenced.

Tamihana gathered the first row of the scrum around him. He saw the other side doing the same.

'Scrum down,' the referee said.

The two scrums bent, approached and *locked*.

'Play ball!' the referee ordered.

Rupeni, at halfback, fed the ball. Like a raging bull, Tamihana tried to keep on his feet. He braced his legs, locking his kneecaps to maintain the scrum. The further the scrum bore down, the tighter Tamihana's legs locked to take the pressure, bracing it back up.

Then he heard a voice – 'Sorry, Tamihana, you won't be making the team.'

The scrum was being collapsed on purpose.

After that, it all happened so quickly. Somebody placed a sprigged boot just above Tamihana's right kneecap. Tamihana could see it happening.

Not my knee, *please*.

Too late. The sprigged boot slammed down. A crack. The scrum wavered. The boot raised itself again and – a second crack.

The scrum collapsed.

'On that day,' Uncle Hone said, 'our father's entire sporting career ended.'

'He couldn't shear either,' Aunt Ruth continued.

'Whenever I see our father now,' Uncle Hone said, 'I cannot but feel anger at what happened to him.'

Aunt Ruth patted Uncle's hand. 'Whenever we play against Hukareka, all I want to do is to take my own vengeance. The pastor talks about turning the other cheek. Even so –'

'Nothing was proven,' Uncle Hone said, 'but we all know that Rupeni ordered Dad to be taken out.'

'Then,' Aunt Ruth continued, 'in the afternoon, after the football match, Rupeni Poata married Maata in the largest wedding of the year. The marriage was a double celebration – Rupeni was made captain of the side that would play the British team.'

'And it was at the reception at Poho O Rawiri meeting house,'

Uncle Hone said, 'that Apirana Ngata announced his wedding gift to the happy couple. It was something that Rupeni Poata himself had requested – a substantial gift of money to begin a shearing business.'

25

Sometimes after dinner was over, if the sun was still hot, we went down to the river – the young ones first, followed by the adults who drifted down in ones and twos when they were ready.

'Look after the kids,' Mum cried, referring to Glory, Peewee and Mackie, 'and don't let them drown.' As if I would.

Going down the track the little kids slipped ahead, yelling out to Haromi, Frances and me, 'Hurry up, puh-*lease!*'

Haromi and I weren't in a hurry.

In the shed, Haromi had her job and I had mine, and she kept company with the women. We relished the times when we could enjoy our private companionship and talk about all the things that were hassling us – school, church, Bulibasha, the family, being stuck in Waituhi and, of course, Aunt Sarah.

'I'm so glad to be away from her,' Haromi said. 'I can't even look at an *old* man without Mum dumping on me. Here in Mahana Four I'm free. No jailer to keep me under lock and key.'

'Except for Aunt Ruth,' I answered.

'I can handle Aunt Ruth,' Haromi sniffed.

We talked on until we reached the river. There –

'See you later,' she said as she, Frances, Faith, Hope and Glory peeled away upstream.

'Why do they swim upstream and we swim downstream?' Mackie asked.

Peewee was scornful. 'Because they're girls and we're boys, dopey.'

A code of modesty prevailed during shearing which prevented the girls from bathing with the boys. When the adults came down the same process occurred – even if they were married.

'Women to the right,' Uncle Hone laughed, 'and men to the left.'

Every now and then we heard giggles and splashes from the

women upstream. Sometimes the water brought down swirls of soap. Once there were squeals of horror, followed by silence. A bra came floating down. Uncle Hone caught it in his fingers and lifted it up for all to see. It had hollows big enough to be used for teapots.

'Hmmn,' he said, tongue in cheek. 'Must be Molly's.'

When Uncle Hone went to return the bra, conspiratorial and offended silence greeted him. When he actually suggested it might be Good Golly Miss Molly's, she slapped him. He had overstepped the mark.

The same code of modesty also meant that, although children could bathe nude, the adults had to cover themselves appropriately – shorts for men, and slips and bras for women. I was ten when my father said, 'Put some shorts on, son.' I had started growing hair in my groin.

The code had more to do with Mormon practice than with any Maori cultural attitude to the body. I have often wondered if this was why Mormons were so sexy. Even so, I found it astonishing to watch as my uncles and Dad waded in for a swim in their long underwear.

'Gee, boy,' they shivered, 'this water is *wet*.' They never seemed to like swimming as much as we did. 'Too many eels in this river,' they said. But they didn't mind throwing white stones for us to dive after. Plop went the stone and *splash*, in we dived, following to see where it had dropped.

'Throw us *silver* stones,' we yelled, meaning shillings or half crowns. 'We can't see your stones any longer. Too dark down there.'

David and Benjamin were the best divers. Benjamin stayed under so long we thought he'd drown. Then, using the power of his legs, he kicked off from the bottom. As he leapt half out of the water he spurted from his mouth and flicked his head from side to side, spraying jets of liquid jewels. He was a Maori Poseidon, water streaming from his deltoids and runnelling down his chest.

Sometimes the shepherds came down and joined us. They were different from us, being without shame. It was astonishing to see their milk-white skin and the blond or red hair in their armpits and thighs – not to mention their you-know-whats. They lay down and started talking about women.

'Well,' Uncle Hone said whenever the talk started, 'see you boys tomorrow.'

With a piercing whistle we alerted the women that it was time to go back up the track.

The tilly lamp was hissing, casting a white light throughout the room. Aunt Molly was playing Seven Hundred with Aunt Ruth, Aunt Sarah and Uncle Albie. Auntie Molly was calling ten no trumps. She loved putting her podgy hands on that bee-oo-tiful kitty in the middle. Uncle Albie was cross because he liked having the kitty too. He was calling ten no trumps as well. This was exactly what Aunt Molly wanted him to do. There was nothing better, if you didn't have the kitty, than to take down the person who did.

Elsewhere in the room Glory, Peewee and Mackie were playing Chinese checkers. Haromi was being guarded from going out the door by Aunt Ruth. Much to Haromi's disgust, David and Benjamin were both mooning over Frances, who had her nose buried in a *True Confessions*. Somebody should have told her that two birds in the hand were worth three in a bush. Uncle Hone and Uncle Sam were just finishing a game of chess. Uncle Sam had brought a wind-up gramophone to the shed, but only two records. One was 'Hold That Tiger' sung by Les Paul and Mary Ford. The other was a maudlin monologue, much in the rage, known as 'The Deck of Cards'. The fire crackled and spat in the open grate. Then –

'This black king,' Uncle Hone said, 'reminds me of Rupeni Poata, and this white king of our father. And these queens – ' He held one up and then the other, 'they're like our mother and Maata. And this –' he held up a bishop, 'is Ngata.'

Throughout the 1930s Rupeni and Tamihana continued their battles for eminence. It soon became apparent to Apirana Ngata that in gifting Rupeni money to set up in shearing he had unwittingly expanded the arena of competition between two young men he greatly admired. Rupeni's sporting reputation had won him many shearing contracts and he had quickly established as many gangs as Tamihana.

Ramona and Maata both tried to intervene, particularly when their children began to be embroiled in the competition. What concerned the women most was that whenever a Mahana and Poata gang met on the road they would fight.

Matters came to a head when one of our Mahana contracts, which Tamihana had been slow to renew, was stolen by Rupeni Poata.

'If you can't stand the heat,' Rupeni laughed, 'stay out of the kitchen.'

That remark started a battle royal in which the Mahanas and Whatus fought Rupeni and his sons boots and all. This was the first time that the eldest Poata sons, Caesar, Augie, Titus and Alexander, had fought Matiu, Maaka, Ruka and Hone. Nobody won. The boys fought each other to a standstill.

Apirana Ngata heard about that fight. Enough was enough. On his way from Ruatoria to parliament in Wellington, he sent Tamihana and Rupeni each a message: 'Meet me at the half-way point between both your villages. At the red suspension bridge.'

'I was a teenager at the time,' Uncle Hone said. 'I remember that day like it was yesterday. Apirana Ngata and his private secretary were already at the bridge. When Dad approached him, Apirana refused to shake his hand. Then, from far off, was the cloud of dust made by Rupeni's crowd. When Rupeni arrived, Ngata refused to shake his hand too.'

It was a hot day and Apirana Ngata was perspiring. He was furious at having to delay his trip to sort out two grown men who should have known better. He faced both Rupeni and Tamihana and shook his head when he saw the extent of the bruises and wounds among their sons.

'I was the midwife for your venture,' he said, and pointed to Tamihana. 'And for yours,' he said to Rupeni. 'I made your lives for you, but I can break your lives also. The trouble is you're both intent on doing it yourselves, so no need for me to waste my time, ne? But I don't want any blood on my hands, and this is my solution.'

The scene was straight out of the Spencer Tracy movie, *Bad Day at Black Rock*. Apirana Ngata took a large stick and scored a line parallel with the red bridge. The stick grated harshly, the groove like a wound, the stick a knife opening up the earth.

'All the shearing sheds to the south of the line,' Ngata said to Rupeni, 'are yours.' He threw the stick down in a temper. 'And all the sheds to the north,' he said to Tamihana, 'are yours.'

Both Rupeni and Tamihana bristled. They were not used to taking orders from anybody, including Apirana Ngata.

'Kua pai?' Apirana Ngata asked.

Neither man wavered.

'*Kua pai!*' Apirana Ngata shouted. He jumped up and down in anger and threw his hat on the ground.

Then, 'Kua pae,' they said.

'This was how the agreement was made,' said Uncle Hone, 'about which sheds belong to the Mahanas and which to the Poatas.

Although Apirana Ngata is dead, we have continued to honour the agreement.'

The fire crackled. The embers glowed. The tilly lamp gave out its slow, steady hiss. Nightflying insects made tiny taps at the window, as if trying to get in.

26

The afternoon before Christmas Eve, Uncle Hone lifted his sweat-soaked face and shouted, 'Kua mutu.'

We gave an almighty cheer. At last we could get on the road back home and into our glad-rags to go shopping and celebrating in Gisborne. Even the shearing season has to defer to the birth anniversary of the Christ child.

Mr Williamson had arranged for an advance payout. I flushed with pride at the sight of my pay envelope. Nothing, however, prepared me for Glory's face, so assured and nonchalant.

'Why be so excited? This has been *earned*.'

Even so, I felt that Glory had better look to her mettle. Peewee and Mackie were gun workers and could take her dag box from under her if she didn't watch out.

'We'll be back the day after Christmas dinner,' Uncle Hone told Mr Williamson. 'We should cut out the shed before New Year.'

'There'll be a bonus if you do,' Mr Williamson replied.

He shook hands formally with Uncle Hone and Aunt Sephora and inclined his head to us all. Geordie was with him and gave me a grin.

'Ladies and gentlemen, my son Geordie and I wish you the best of the festive season,' Mr Williamson said.

We didn't bother to wash or pack up. Everybody wanted to exit running. We piled into the cars as we were, smelling of dags and sweat and decorated with little curls of stray wool. The men drove like maniacs, tearing around the corners, over the culverts, through the cattle stops and around the bends, down to Tolaga Bay, the first sign of civilisation.

Tolaga was booming with locals. We stopped for food – pies with peas and spud on top, or fish and chips – and to fuel up the cars. Uncle Albie, David and Benjamin snuck off somewhere. Watching them go, Aunt Ruth muttered, 'Well, as long as their tanks aren't so full that Grandfather Tamihana smells the fumes.'

We hit the road again, alternating between dust and tar seal until Gisborne. Sometimes we hit forty miles an hour top speed, golly Moses.

Haromi was in the car with us. Batting her eyes furiously, she pleaded with Dad, 'Please, Uncle Josh, puh-leez, I'll do *anything* if you'll just stop in Gisborne for five minutes. Only five minutes, oh please.'

'No,' Aunt Ruth said. 'Bulibasha will be waiting at Waituhi and if we don't get there the same time as everybody else we'll be for the high jump.'

'Oh, puh-leez!' Haromi moaned, as if her entire life depended on it. 'I haven't got anything to wear for Christmas Eve!'

'No dice,' Aunt Ruth said.

However, something Haromi said made Glory frown. She jabbed me, Do something.

'We should have a vote,' I said.

Before Aunt Ruth could open her mouth to protest, everyone including Mum and Dad and Aunts Sephora and Esther had agreed with Haromi.

'Aye!'

We didn't have any good clothes either.

The change in Haromi was instant. Her eyelashes stopped batting – she had what she wanted and a girl should save her eyelashes for the real thing. Now she began to bewail the fact that she smelled of the shed and was still in her shed clothes. There were five of us in the back seat, but she squashed us to one side as she pulled a comb from her pants and began to backcomb her hair higher and higher into a beehive. She took out eyeliner and lipstick and leaned out the back window to look at herself in the rear driving mirror. As a final touch, she undid the top two buttons of her blouse.

'Oh no you don't,' Aunt Ruth said.

A tussle ensued as Aunt Ruth tried to button Haromi's blouse back up. With a sigh, and without Aunt Ruth seeing, Haromi flicked the buttons clean off.

'Oh Auntie,' Haromi said, her eyes wide with innocence and surprise, 'look what you *did*!' She was a tricky one, was Haromi.

When the car stopped in Gisborne, Dad yelled, 'Only five minutes!'

Haromi was already out the door.

There was an art to doing five hours of shopping in five minutes. Haromi was the expert. Watching her was like looking at a movie going at double speed. The trick was knowing what you wanted. The other was to be pushy, a trait Haromi shared with her mother, Aunt Sarah. When either was in a hurry there were no 'Excuse mes.' There was no time for 'Sorrys' either.

Into Woolworths Haromi went, and out she came with cosmetics, new bra and panties. No time to shoplift; just *throw* the money on the counter as you leave. Next stop was McGruer's, and out Haromi came with an H-line skirt and a voluminous petticoat to puff it up. Third was Adams shoe store, and out she came with a pair of slingbacks. Then into Melbourne Cash for some red stockings and –

There, in the window, was an imitation leopardskin bolero jacket. Beside it was a photo of NEW TEEN STAR SANDRA DEE WHO APPEARS WITH LANA TURNER IN 'IMITATION OF LIFE', UNIVERSAL INTERNATIONAL'S NEW HIT MOVIE. Sandra Dee was wearing exactly the same bolero.

Haromi came to an absolute standstill and lost thirty seconds. I could see she was fantasising about being Sandra Dee except, of course, doing a much better job of it. She swayed, dazed, and then looked at me.

'I *must* have it,' she whispered between clenched teeth.

In we marched. The poor saleswoman was on the point of selling the bolero to a girl who would have fitted it perfectly, but Haromi yelled, 'You can't sell my bolero!' The saleswoman rocked back, surprised. 'I rang just half an hour ago,' Haromi said, 'to tell your floor manager I was on my way to get it. Didn't you get the message?'

'Well no, miss,' the saleswoman began.

Haromi chattered away gaily, peeled the money out of her paypacket – and mine – and placed it on the counter. The trick was to keep on the attack and retreat quickly before the enemy knew they'd been had.

'Don't bother to wrap it,' she said, 'I'll take it as it is.'

Out the door we went, past the saleswoman, the girl who had been on the point of buying the bolero and the other customers. Just like that, leaving them like stunned mullet. And what the heck if the bolero was three sizes too small. What were scissors for?

We all managed to get back to the car within, well, six minutes at the most. I saw Nani Mini Tupara and she gave me ten shillings and told me to spend it on something that wasn't religious. Dad had bought a new shirt, Mum and my aunts had summer frocks, my sisters had comics and lollies, and Glory had bought a water pistol. The last person to arrive was the one who hadn't wanted us to stop – Aunt Ruth, wobbling along in very unsuitable high heels and burdened down with boxes.

'If we're going to be hanged,' she said, 'we may as well make it worth it.'

Grandfather Tamihana was waiting for us. He looked as if he'd just crawled out of the bottom drawer of Hell. My cousin Mohi The Greaser was pretending he had been doing all our work. There he was, cutting the meat for dinner, as if it was a feat equivalent to climbing Mount Everest.

'So you finally decided to come home?' He Who Must Be Obeyed said. His eagle eyes saw the packages and boxes of clothes bought in Gisborne. 'Father Christmas has already been, has he?'

'It's my fault,' Aunt Ruth mumbled as she went past.

'No, mine,' Aunt Sephora said.

'Mine,' Aunt Esther said.

'No, it was mine,' Haromi said.

They were just like the handmaidens of the beautiful princess Laloumi in *Sirens of Baghdad*. To save her from a fate worse than death, all the handmaidens said *they* were the princess.

'No,' Grandfather interrupted. 'The one responsible is Joshua, and *he* must explain.'

'I'm sorry, Bulibasha.'

The door slammed. Grandmother Ramona was back from her beehives. She removed her veils and released a bee which had been trapped in the netting. The bee buzzed over Grandfather's head and he ducked, swatting at it. We all started to edge out.

'What's going on?' Grandmother Ramona asked. She turned to Grandfather. She was in an irritable mood. 'Are you still making everybody's lives a misery? Why don't we all enjoy Christmas for a change.'

'You and your bees!' Grandfather Tamihana answered.

Grandmother saw Mohi putting aside his knife. He must have thought Dad would take over now he was back.

'Mohi?' Grandmother yelled. 'You keep cutting the meat!'

If looks could kill –

117

'But –' Grandfather Tamihana began.

'No buts, Tamihana. All of you are in my way, sitting in the kitchen. Sephora? Esther? Hurry up with the tea.' She turned to Grandfather again. 'Are you *still* here? This is not your place, this is the women's. You look after your job and we'll look after ours.'

We made our escape.

Curious, I turned to Dad. 'Why do you let Grandfather trample all over you?' I asked.

'He doesn't trample over me!'

'Why do you let him do it?'

Dad looked at me, puzzled. 'I love my father,' he answered. 'As the Bible says, "Honour thy father and mother and be obedient to them in all things." '

My frustration leaked out. God had poked me with a pin.

Oh. Yes. Of course.

27

As if to pay us back for playing truant, Grandfather kept Dad, Mum and our family at the homestead until late afternoon on Christmas Eve. He knew full well that we still had our real Christmas shopping to do. Mum was almost beside herself with anxiety by the time we left – Haromi's five-minute spree was not her style. She reckoned she'd need *hours*.

'Go round the back way, dear,' Mum said when we approached Patutahi. Like everybody else in Waituhi she didn't want to see Miss Zelda's accusing stare as we slipped by the general store without paying off some of our account.

Gisborne was really hopping. The police had closed off Gladstone Road from Peel Street to the clock tower. There were people everywhere. As usual, my mother Huria prefaced each trip back and forth to the car with, 'And now I'm just going to Melbourne Cash.' She wanted to make sure we weren't there to see what she was buying for us. It was a logistical nightmare, but by six o'clock we had done it.

'Well, dear,' Dad said, 'I think we should have something to eat. How about getting some fish and chips at the Lyric Cafe and going down to the riverbank for a feed?'

This was a great extravagance but, 'Oh, why not,' our mother said. Glory was in seventh heaven.

On the way I saw Haromi in her new bolero jacket. She was parading back and forth outside Melbourne Cash's window where they still displayed the poster of Miss Sandra Dee.

'I'll meet you later,' she hissed. 'There's a late movie at the Majestic. They're showing *Rock Around the Clock* again.'

I might as well have been a dummy. Her eyes were looking over my shoulder to where young boys in black jackets were lounging around a car dazzling with silver chrome. Emblazoned across the back was the dubious message FROM HERE TO MATERNITY. Righteous matrons cast glances of outrage as they hustled their daughters past.

'Dad,' I asked, 'can I stay in town? I'll come back with Andrew. All the Whatus are staying and –'

'Don't get into trouble,' Dad said.

'And do *not* go to that rock and roll movie at the Majestic,' Mum said. 'There's a perfectly good movie playing at the King's.'

'Yes, Mum,' I said, putting wax in my ears.

April Love with Pat Boone? Vomit.

Haromi, Andrew and I loved going to the movies, especially since the latest in cinema technology – the wonders of Cinemascope, Vistavision and wall-to-wall Cinerama – had finally come to Gisborne. Grandfather Tamihana didn't exactly approve, although he didn't seem to mind if we saw films on religious subjects, like *The Robe*, *Demetrius and the Gladiators* and *Shoes of the Fisherman*. What he didn't realise was that these films were really just an excuse for actresses to show lotsa flesh. *The Prodigal*, for instance, was a ploy for glamour girl Lana Turner to get dressed up in strategically situated beads. *The Silver Chalice* had Virginia Mayo floating around in almost see-through lingerie. The greatest of them all, Rhonda Fleming, showed off one of the best figures of all time in *Revolt of the Slaves* as she ran around the catacombs of Rome wearing a dress she herself had ripped so as to bind the wounds of the hero.

There were other movies, too – westerns, crime movies, romances and comedies – and some were screened in 3-D so that you sat with cardboard glasses on and ducked as people threw spears or rocks. Best of all, though, were the new crop of films made just for *us*. The moody films of James Dean, of teen stars Fabian, Frankie

Avalon or Bobby Darin, or the rock and roll films of Elvis Presley, aimed at rebellious youth. And *Rock Around the Clock* was tops, man. Best of all, it made our parents *worried*.

By the time we got to the Majestic, Haromi didn't want to know me and Andrew at all. She was in the foyer, smoking with one hand and propping up a young drunk with another. When she saw us she made a great play of trying to hide her neck. A vampire had had a good suck at it. Andrew and I decided to make Haromi's day. We did a double take as we went past her, then –

'Isn't that the –' I said to Andrew in a loud voice.

'Yes, it is.'

'It can't be –'

'I think it is.'

By this time the whole foyer was wondering what the mystery was.

Andrew snapped his finger, suddenly remembering. 'That girl,' he whispered in a *loud* voice, 'is wearing Sandra Dee's jacket.'

There was a gasp. A little voice piped up, 'Yes she *is*. There's a picture of it in Melbourne Cash.'

Ooh. Ahh. Errr.

I winked at Haromi. You owe us one, babe.

She let her bloke fall flat on the floor – his name, I found out from Haromi later, was Mihaere – and began posing like mad.

Andrew and I managed to get some seats at the back of the theatre. Just as the lights went down I saw the delicious Poppy come in with Tight Arse Junior and Saul.

The movie was a riot. The management called in extra staff to handle the rowdiness. Fat chance *they* had. As soon as the credits started to roll, Bill Haley sang, 'One two three o'clock, four o'clock, *rock*!' The whole upstairs and downstairs began to tap their feet on the floor.

'Be *quiet*!' the management boomed.

Flashlights stabbed the darkness, which was great because then we had targets to squirt at or pelt with jelly beans – the management *and* Saul, Tight Arse and Poppy.

'Five six seven o'clock, eight o'clock *rock*!'

'Any further rowdiness will not be tolerated!' The flashlights flashed on again.

Squirt squirt and *kapow* with the jelly beans.

By this time Saul was looking around to see who had thrown the chocolate ice cream at him. Bill Haley sang on.

This time, when the flashlights went on, a very brave girl threw her panties. Everybody whistled and stamped. The management gave up.

At the movie's end, Andrew pretended he had lost something. He asked every girl who came out of the theatre to bend over and help him find it. A sweet voice said to him, 'I think *I've* found what you're looking for.'

He looked up to see Poppy – and got a faceful of ice cream.

The next morning, Christmas Day, we were all five minutes late at the homestead.

Sorry Bulibashabasha sorrysorry orry.

At church, the congregation was subdued. People were recovering from the excesses of the night before. Haromi was as ever the film star, hiding behind dark glasses and a scarf wound around her neck.

'Don't even *breathe* on me,' she winced as I approached. Her breath smelt of beer and tobacco. Aunt Sarah was muttering and glaring at me as if it was, as usual, all my fault.

Guess who was up for organ duty again. Except that I was so busy thinking about Poppy – that trick with the ice cream had only confirmed my admiration of her – I had no idea of what I was meant to be doing, and when. Dimly, I heard coughing from the congregation. My mother was making flapping motions with her handkerchief. Bulibasha had that look of contempt on his face: daydreaming on the job again.

'Simeon,' the pastor hissed. 'Page twenty-three, Hymn –'

Not 'Whakaaria Mai' *again*. Ah well, let's have some fun and games.

I brought the organ up to full volume and let it all hang out. The choir were murdering me with their eyes as they sought to sing over the volume.

'Whakaaria mai –' (and now, an octave higher, One two three o'clock, four o'clock *rock*).

The congregation were holding their heads, and not in ecstasy either.

'To ripeka ki au –' (and now, fortissimo, five six seven o'clock, eight o'clock *rock*).

By this time Andrew and Haromi were awake to what I was doing. Haromi had forgotten her hangover and was stuffing a handkerchief in her mouth to stop her from laughing too much.

'Hei konei au –' (letting it rip with the pedals, nine ten eleven o'clock, twelve o'clock *rock*).

'Ra roto i te po!' (all together now, everybody join in, We're gonna *rock* around the *clock* tonight!)

With a triumphant flourish, the walls of Jericho came tumbling down.

Take *that*, Lord.

Naturally, come rain hail sunshine or Christmas, the Poatas were ready to race us over the red bridge. We were way ahead of them and would have won if it hadn't been for Grandfather's car getting a puncture. The De Soto slewed off the road and down a bank. We ran down to see if he and Grandmother were all right.

Through the dust the Poatas emerged like ghosts. Then Rupeni Poata's Buick, driven by Caesar, stopped; the engine purred like a sleeping tiger. The other Poata cars came to a halt also. The dust drifted across the road and cleared sufficiently for me to see Rupeni Poata's face. Encased behind the closed back window, Rupeni was looking down through the glass at Grandfather's car. Poppy was next to him and he seemed to be asking her a question. When she saw Grandfather and Grandmother climbing out of the De Soto, she drew Rupeni's attention to them. He closed his eyes, leaned back and tapped Caesar to drive on.

Rupeni never saw me watching. I thought he had stopped to gloat, and I hated him. Perhaps he had hoped they'd been killed. Maybe he was relieved that they hadn't been killed so that the vendetta could continue. Who knows? At that moment I realised I had never actually exchanged any words – other than abuse – with a member of the Poata family. I had been brought up in the knowledge that they were in the wrong and we were in the right. My picture of the Poata family as our nemesis was so complete that I didn't need to know any more about them.

Christmas dinner was an affair of state with family after family presenting their family gift to Grandfather Tamihana. The procession reminded me of the story my mother wept over whenever she heard it on radio – Loretta Young's tale of the littlest angel. In the story, all the angels in Heaven, aware of the impending birth of the Christ child, give Him fabulous and expensive presents. But the littlest angel is too busy playing and being a ruffian. When the time comes for the presents to be displayed, his present is something like a shanghai, a couple of stones, and eggs that have fallen out of a bird's nest. The finger of God moves along the presents. It stops at the littlest angel's. The littlest angel expects to go splat, but instead of getting a reprimand he is surprised to find that it is his gift which is selected for Jesus, being a boyish gift for the boy Christ.

Grandfather Tamihana obviously had never heard that story. His finger paused over *our* family contribution. He poked into its depths and asked, 'What's this?' When he picked up my gift he thought it was real. He dropped it quickly, as if stung. It was a plastic paperweight with a bumble bee in it. I thought Grandfather would get the joke. Anyway, there had only been two choices in paperweights – either the bumble bee or a tarantula.

'Get your hair cut, Simeon,' Grandfather said.

Our family presents to each other waited until we were back in our quarters. My father had bought our mother new gloves and she gave him a shirt. They had bought us all the same gift – watches, so we would get to the homestead on time for Sunday morning prayers.

The turn came for my sisters and I to give our gifts to Mum and Dad and to each other. My mother's eyes lit up at every gift. Not for her any choosing which was better but, in my opinion, the best was Glory's: a small wall plaque with bluebirds and butterflies around it which said HOME SWEET HOME. Glory was always a sucker for sentimentality.

28

We returned to Williamson station the day after Christmas. Rain prevented fast progress and, by New Year, we hadn't been able to cut out as planned. The unseasonal rain made the work heavier and heavier.

Just after New Year, Geordie asked me if I would like to come up to Amberleigh. Whenever he'd asked before, I had always answered 'No', knowing that this is what my parents would want me to say. This time I accepted. I did not tell Mum or Dad. What they didn't know wouldn't hurt them.

I knocked on the front door. Maria, Geordie's Maori maid, tapped on the window and motioned with her feather duster that I should use the side entrance.

'It's all right, Maria,' Geordie said, amused. As I followed him, Maria tried to swat me with her duster. In some way I had transgressed *her* protocol.

'Who was that at the door, darling?' a woman's voice called from the dining room.

'Simeon, mother.'

His mother was taking tea with a friend. She made a vague gesture of welcome. 'One of the Maori boys from Mahana Four,' she explained. 'You know what Geordie's like. Picks up strays and orphans.' Her laughter glittered in the air.

'Don't mind her,' Geordie said.

We went upstairs, past the master's study, to – the head of a deer with huge branching antlers hung on the wall to Geordie's bedroom. Geordie's gifts at Christmas had been expensive and sophisticated. They included a tie from Harrods and some shirts from George's of London. I stared, and paused over the 3-D hand toy and 3-D discs.

'Put your eyes here,' Geordie said. 'Now, click.'

The frames sprang to life. In each frame was depicted one of the Wonders of the World. The pyramids of Gaza. The Grand Canyon. The Leaning Tower of Pisa. I could not help thinking that this was what Pakeha life was like – 3-D pictures, larger than life, bursting out of the frames in full brilliant colour.

Then Geordie asked, casually, 'Would you like to come into Gisborne to see *Twenty Thousand Leagues Under the Sea*?'

'No,' I answered. 'We're shearing and I'm the sheepo.'

'Don't worry,' he said. 'Father will talk to Hone –' He pronounced Uncle's name Hone-ay. 'I'm sure Hone will be able to organise someone to work for you. It will only be for the afternoon. I know you want to see the film.'

I must admit that I was keen to see the movie. Even so, when I saw Mr Williamson speaking to Uncle Hone and Dad I felt like somebody had just stepped over my grave.

Geordie and I caught the bus into town for the two o'clock matinee. I couldn't help the growing sense of unease, a feeling that I had done something to disturb the nature of things. I tried to pretend, for Geordie's sake, that I was having a great time. Geordie didn't seem to mind.

Summer lightning.

I was not surprised, therefore, to find that Grandfather Tamihana had just happened to choose that day to come up to Williamson station. There was something fatalistic about his visit, something Greek in the irrevocability of destiny. Zeus had been told of the misdemeanour and had come himself to render punishment. When Geordie and I returned from the film, Grandfather was talking with Mr and Mrs Williamson up at Amberleigh.

'You've got a bright lad here,' Mr Williamson said as I walked into the sitting room.

Geordie must have known how I was feeling. He tried to make it better. He put an arm over my shoulder. 'It was a superb film, Father,' he said.

Grandfather stiffened. I'm not too sure if he was more angry because I was there among Pakeha or because I was being made a fool of by Geordie who, in his eyes, was taking liberties.

'Well, Simeon, time to go down to the others, ne?'

The shearing was finished for the day. The afternoon was silent as Grandfather and I walked down the hill. When he got to the whare, he simply said, 'I'm going to talk to your father.' To Dad. Not me. This was Dad's fault.

I could see Aunt Molly, Aunt Sephora and my father; the others were still swimming at the river. I prayed they would stay down there. Grandfather's voice raised itself in the whare. It was level, controlled and definite. I never once heard my father respond.

My father came out. Grandfather was beside him, leaning in the doorway, watching. Dad walked across the sunlight, cutting a dark shadow across the light.

'I'm going to give you a haircut, son,' he said. He was finding it hard to swallow. 'Your grandfather says your hair is too long.' He wouldn't look me in the eye. 'Go and ask Auntie Molly for a chair.'

'Please, Dad –'

'Don't make this any harder, Simeon,' he continued. 'Just *go and get a chair.*'

I was sitting in the chair, a towel around my neck. My father Joshua had the scissors in his hands. He was trembling. All of a sudden there was laughter. Mum and the others arrived back from the river.

'What's going on?' Mum asked gaily.

'Simeon's having his hair cut,' Dad answered.

125

'About time,' she laughed. 'We're always on him to –' She saw Grandfather Tamihana.

Then she knew. They all knew. They stood by – Mum, my aunts and cousins and sisters, all mute witnesses. Glory wanted to come to me, but Mum held her close to her.

'Please, Dad, don't do this,' I whispered.

'Son, you know you shouldn't have gone with Geordie to the movies.' He made the first snip.

'Why didn't you stop me, Dad?' Another snip.

'How could we say "No" to the boss, Simeon? When Mr Williamson came down here and asked your uncle and me, of course we had to say "Yes." '

'I wasn't away long, Dad. Peewee and Mackie said they'd be able to carry on.'

'It wasn't their job, son. It was yours.'

'You're just parroting what *he* said to you,' I answered, gesturing at Grandfather.

'The family always comes first, son. You put Geordie before the family.'

My hair was coming off lock by lock. Then Dad took up some hand shears and began to shear close to the sides of my head. I looked down into my shadow. I was sitting on a chair, at Grandfather's instructions, in the hot sunlight. I heard Glory trying to attract my attention. I knew she wanted to play dead for me but, It won't work this time, Glory.

'Not like this, Dad,' I pleaded. 'Please. Not in front of everybody.'

'It won't take long, son. I don't want to do this to you, but you have to be punished.'

'For making friends with Geordie?'

'You should have said "No" to him from the beginning. It's because of you that we're behind in the shearing.'

My head whirled. 'You can't blame me for that, Dad. I am not to blame for the rain. For us being behind. You can't believe that.'

'I'm not blaming you. I'm just telling you how it looks to your grandfather. He was really angry to see you up there at the Big House. That's not your place, Simeon. And that boy's arm around your shoulder? That's not right, either.'

The scissors went *snip* again.

It was the shame more than anything else. All I had done was allow a Pakeha to befriend me. In so doing I had transgressed some implacable law of Grandfather's. I was being punished.

Then Dad finished. My mother started to sob. I knew I must look really bad. All the hair was shorn from the sides, leaving a tuft on the top.

'I'm sorry, son. It will grow.'

'*He still has too much hair!*'

Grandfather came hip-*hopping* across the galaxies, out of a black hole in the universe, storming from Olympus. He wrested the shears from my father.

Glory shouted, 'No!'

Before I knew it, Grandfather had chopped off the top, too. The shears drew blood.

'Whakahihi, Simeon. *Whakahihi*. You're getting too big for your boots. Maybe this will teach you where your place is.' He started walking away.

'Tar,' I whispered.

He stopped. Looked back.

'*Tar!*' I yelled at him. The blood was trickling down my face.

'Porangi,' he said.

My eyes were stinging with tears. I was trembling with rage. '*Tar! Tar! Tar! Tar!*'

Each shout echoed like a rifle volley through the hills.

Shortly after that, Mahana Four left Williamson station. We went straight to the Wi Pere estate and, from there, to Tara. By the end of the summer my hair had grown back and the scar of that day was forgotten by everybody except me. Even today, when I least expect it, I feel the tingling jab of the shears where Grandfather Tamihana cut my scalp.

In February my sisters and I prepared to leave Mahana Four and return to school. At the family meeting that month, the Mahana shearing gangs received disturbing news.

'The Poatas have broken the agreement,' Uncle Matiu said. 'They have crossed over the line drawn by Apirana Ngata. They have been signed up by the Mathewsons on our side of the river.'

There was a long and anxious debate. The earlier sighting of the Poata gang by Mahana Two clicked in our memories, and everything fell into place. Uncle Maaka made some remark which I did not understand about our inadvertently doing the same thing to the Poatas the year before. The conversation rushed over him like a river. In the end –

'Whoever's right or wrong,' Grandfather Tamihana said, 'doesn't matter. The agreement is dead.'

We prayed that evening for God's guidance and support. I had taken to staring at Grandfather Tamihana until he was aware that I was there. He looked up at me. He saw my insolence.

Yes, Grandfather, it's me, Simeon.

The gloves were off, and not only between the Mahanas and the Poatas. If I had to, I would bring down Olympus.

Part Two

29

Many years have passed since I was raised in Bulibasha's house, in those times when he ruled all our lives. His power was almost invincible. How I held out against it, I'll never know. I have never really escaped it.

If I was to admit the truth, I would say that one of the reasons I rarely go back to Waituhi is because of Bulibasha. But life in Wellington is also very full and that is another reason why I can't spare the time. This is why Aunt Ruth, now in her eighties, has taken it upon herself to be my messenger, regularly arriving from Gisborne and bringing me news of the iwi. Aunt Ruth comes by plane. When she gets off, in her black scarf and holding her flax kete, she always touches the ground with both hands.

'If God had wanted me to fly he would have given me wings,' she says. She likes to impress me with her courage. 'I take my life into my own hands.'

Time has not mellowed the absolute nature of Aunt Ruth's beliefs. Things are black or they are white. If it's not yes it's no. A man is a man and a woman is a woman and a bird is a bird.

My son showed Aunt Ruth a photograph of the Pope doing the same obeisance at an airport. For all that he was a different religion, she was pleased.

'Ehara, he copies me! So am I a fool?' Then she banged me with her kete as if it was all my fault. 'How dare you tell the Pope what I do!'

Aunt Ruth has become a revered kuia and much-loved grand-aunt, her face lined with the beauty of age. She has, however, never lost her temper and her withering scorn. After Uncle Albie's gonads had dried up on him and he gave up his floozies, she made every remaining day of his life a misery.

'No mercy, boy,' she said. 'No mercy.'

Yet, when Uncle died, she mourned him as only one who has loved deeply can mourn. At his tangi she reached up to claw the sky down and into the emptiness of her heart.

A man is alive or a man is dead.

Mark loves Aunt Ruth's visits. I think, in many ways, she comes to see him rather than me. At the slightest opportunity she retells the story of my grandparents' elopement, investing the vendetta between the Mahana and Poata families with a halting, quavering passion.

I overheard Mark with Aunt Ruth in the sitting room. My mind flipped back to 1957. When I peered in to look, it was like seeing myself with Aunt Ruth those many years ago. At first I was lulled by the memories but something wilful began to buzz inside my head. I heard Aunt Ruth ask Mark, 'Did you know that there was a song named after your great-grandmother?'

'Don't listen, son,' I said, drily. 'That song was from a silent film of the 1920s and had nothing to do with –'

Perhaps I was jealous of the intimacy that had developed between Mark and Aunt Ruth. Whatever, Aunt Ruth caught the undertone of my voice. She gave me a look of warning and went on.

'Well, just outside the church the band was playing the song. Your great-grandmother was about to get married to our arch enemy, Rupeni Poata. I spit on his memory and on all his seed. Suddenly, your great-grandfather came down the road on his white horse and –'

I couldn't help it. I was unwilling to let Aunt Ruth tell that old story in her same sentimental way.

'Yes,' I said cynically, 'Thrum, thrum, thrum, down the road on his trusty stallion came the mighty Bulibasha –'

Aunt Ruth stiffened. She stopped her narration. She cupped Mark's chin in her hands and stared into his eyes.

'Don't you listen to your father. He's always been whakahihi – ever since he left Waituhi, went to school and got some brains and then to university for more brains. When you get older, don't go to school or to the university, because you see your father? That's what happens. He thinks he's a know-all. Well, he knows nothing.' Aunt Ruth stood up, turned to me and shook a finger in my face. 'Turituri to waho,' she growled. 'Turituri! Just because you've never been struck by the lightning rod of God doesn't mean it can't happen. The trouble with you is that your schooling made you heartless. You don't want to believe any more. Every time I come here you make fun of me and our family. Of your grandfather and of our blood. What's wrong with you! You're the one who Dad acknowledged in the end. Where's your family spirit! Where's that killer instinct! Where's your mana! Am I, the eldest of the women, the only one to carry on the battle?'

I went to embrace her but she pushed me away. Mark was angry at me too.

'You're mean, Dad,' he said.

Aunt Ruth was still seething. 'You just go out there right now,' she said to me, 'and bring me back a stick.' She pointed to the elm tree. I stifled an impulse to laugh. But this time her anger was different. It was shaking her apart. Her words were spitting out.

'Not just a small stick, either, nephew,' Aunt Ruth added, tremulous. 'A big one for your big black bum. Go on now. A big stick so I can give you a good caning with it and put some sense back into you. You don't believe any more in the fightings. You don't believe any more in the protecting of the mana of the house of Mahana. Those Poata family, they're still our enemy. We still have to go to war with them.' She was shaking apart. Tears were spilling out between the cracks. 'You may be a big man now, but you're not too big for me to give you a thrashing. Even when you were fifteen you were too big for your boots. I should have given you a thrashing then.'

Then she said what she had probably been wanting to say to me for years. 'It's all your fault. What happened is all your fault. You hear me, nephew? You're the one to blame. You –' She took a swing at me. I grabbed her thin elbows. She was so shockingly thin. Her eyes were spilling with tears. She collapsed into my arms.

30

When school started I was back to being the main hand at Fort Petticoat.

'Look after your mother and sisters,' Dad said. 'Another month of shearing and then I'll be home. Be obedient to your grandfather.'

One night not long after that, I was woken from sleep by my mother.

'Himiona,' she whispered. 'Wake up. Kia tere, kia tere.' The tone of her voice alerted me. In an instant I was awake and out of bed. 'Come *on*, Himiona.'

It was raining outside. I could hear Grandfather Tamihana

bellowing and my aunts shouting and screaming in the main house. I shucked on my pants and shirt and followed Mum from the quarters. She was already way ahead of me and hurrying into the homestead. Lamplight flickered against the windows of the main bedroom. Shapes were chasing backwards and forwards across the curtains. There was a crack, the sound of a punch being thrown, and one of the shadows fell down with a thud.

I ran past my mother, through the drawing room and into the bedroom. Inside, my aunts Sephora, Miriam and Esther were battling with Grandfather Tamihana. He had already walloped Grandmother Ramona and was trying to get at her again. She was crumpled up against the wall trying to recover from the blow. My aunts were holding him back from throwing another punch.

'Bitch,' Grandfather roared. 'That's all your mother Ramona is. You hear me, bitch?'

Grandfather Tamihana's rages came out of nowhere, out of some black hole in his past. They took over his entire body. His veins knotted at his neck, his eyeballs protruded and there was foam at his mouth. He was a demented animal, and most often he took out his rage on the person nearest to him – Grandmother Ramona. Whenever Grandfather was like this, it was always Dad's job to pacify him. Now it was mine.

'That's enough, Grandfather,' I said. 'Leave Grandmother alone now. Okay?'

The words sounded absurd but they had the effect of turning Grandfather's attention away from Grandmother and towards me. Grandfather looked at me incredulously and laughed.

'Listen to the boy,' he gestured. 'Telling *me* what to do. Didn't anybody ever tell you not to come between a man and his woman?'

'Come on, Grandfather. It's all over. Time to get back to bed.'

He started for me. I looked across his shoulder and motioned to my aunts to look after Grandmother. I backed out of the bedroom, Grandfather followed after me, jabbing at my chest.

'I own you as much as I own *her*,' Grandfather shouted. 'Whenever I want her I will have her. That's the law. She belongs to me. You all belong to me. So don't you order me around.'

He reached out to grapple with me. Frightened, I chopped at his windpipe with the edge of my hand. He fell back gasping.

'You little bastard!'

Free for a moment, I took off out through the kitchen, into the rain and across the back yard. My strategy was to get Grandfather out of the house and keep him busy until his rage had gone. But –

'Look out, Simeon!'

Aunt Sephora's warning came too late. Something hit me in the back. Grandfather must have thrown a brick or a heavy piece of wood. The blow made me double up in pain and I fell against the outside pump. Then Grandfather was on me and I thought, I'm for it now. Nothing to do except hold tight to the pump and try to protect my stomach and face.

'Get up, you son of a bitch!'

Grandfather was trying to prise my fingers loose, but I held on for dear life. He began to kick me – in the side of the head, the kidneys and the back. I was gasping from the blows. My aunts were screaming. I felt like I was being murdered. The *pain*. He was hitting my head against the iron of the pump. I didn't have a prayer.

'Come on, you little bastard,' he panted. 'Stand up. Stand up and fight like a man!'

Finally he lifted me up and propped me against the pump. I was groggy, soaking from the rain or blood. I don't know which. The piledriver was coming. There was nothing I could do about it. Ah well, better me than Grandmother Ramona.

Glory, where are you, sis? Play dead, Glory, please play –

Grandmother Ramona was there, standing in the rain. She had a rifle in her hand. She reversed it so that she was holding the barrel. She slammed Grandfather over the head with the butt. Grandfather swayed, not quite ready to topple. She hit him again. With a groan he fell poleaxed to the ground.

My aunts were hysterical. They knelt beside Grandfather, trying to revive him.

'Father? Father!'

Grandmother Ramona cupped my chin in her hands.

'I'm sorry, Grandmother,' I said.

'You're going to have a beautiful black eye,' she said. 'A real shiner.'

I felt ashamed that I hadn't been able to protect her. I spat blood and a broken piece of tooth.

'You did well, Himiona,' Grandmother said. 'Nothing to be sorry about. Anything broken? Or are you just bruised?'

'I don't know,' I said.

'Huria?' Grandmother Ramona called. 'Look after your son. As for you others, leave your father there.'

'We can't leave him out here in the rain,' Aunt Miriam said.

'Just do as I say,' Grandmother commanded.

As she was speaking, Grandfather began to revive. His rage was over and, dazed, he looked up into Grandmother's face.

'E kui –'

'Picking on a boy,' she muttered. 'Just be careful that next time I don't shoot you.'

She went to walk past him. He grabbed at her nightdress and pulled himself up to clasp her around the waist. She paused, her face wan, then pushed him away and continued on into the house.

After this incident I fired my first shot across Grandfather Tamihana's bow. I chose to do it in the only way and the only place that Grandfather would understand – at church during testimony-bearing. And I scandalised the whole congregation by taking the microphone *after* Aunt Sarah had vacated it.

'Brothers and sister,' I said, 'you know that I rarely bear my testimony, so don't expect this to be a habit. I have a black eye –' There was a gasp. 'And I have bruised ribs.'

Grandfather Tamihana was staring straight ahead. Grandmother Ramona began to pull her veil across her face, then decided against it. She nodded at me.

'I went to help a woman who was being beaten up by her husband.'

My aunts were crimsoning and Aunt Sarah was flapping her hands at me in horror.

'Do you think I should have left her to be beaten?' I asked the congregation.

'Brother, no,' came the answer. 'You should take the lesson of the good samaritan who did not pass by but stopped to help when it was needed.'

'Thank you for your support,' I said. 'The person concerned is a member of this church.' There were more gasps.

'I give him fair warning that if it happens again I will seek your help against him.'

After church Dad approached me and said, 'You shouldn't have done that, son. The family can handle it.'

I saw Grandfather Tamihana in the distance. He came over to me, paused, and nodded.

'So, Himiona,' he said.

31

At the beginning of winter 1958, the family had achieved a good season. There was every chance that we'd be able to winter over without difficulty. However, no sooner had we had a chance to congratulate ourselves than my father Joshua faced two reversals.

The first announced itself when Dad was coming back from Tara, Mahana Four's final shed of the season. He heard a *clunk* and the car lurched.

'It's not my car that should be shot,' Pani said.

Pani looped a tow rope to the Pontiac, and towed it back to Mr Jenkins' garage at Patutahi.

'I'm sorry, Josh,' Mr Jenkins said. 'The repair is going to work out pretty expensive. Parts for cars like this are hard to come by and I'm going to have to get a new back axle –'

The Pontiac was a month in Mr Jenkins' garage. When the car came out, the bill was enormous. Dad's face turned white as a sheet.

'We need the car,' Mum said.

A car was really the only status symbol we had. Paying for the repairs wiped out our savings.

Then came a request from Uncle Matiu at the March family meeting. It was nearing its end when Grandfather Tamihana asked, 'Kua pai?' and Uncle Matiu coughed. He shuffled forward on his knees, his head bowed before Grandfather. He made his plaint.

'Father,' Uncle Matiu said, 'I am putting this request on behalf of the pastor. As you know, a Mormon college has been established in Hamilton for our children. The church has been calling for more funds to support the college's work, and more volunteers also. The pastor has asked whether our family might commit a tenth of our earnings to this work.'

'On top of the tithe?' Grandfather Tamihana asked.

'Yes, father. The pastor realises we already substantially support the work of the church. He hopes, however, that the shearing season has been bountiful enough so that the Mahana family will be able to –' Uncle Matiu paused.

Given Grandfather's attitude to education, I didn't think that our teeth-flashing pastor had a hope. I had forgotten that this was one of those matters which, if agreed to, would increase Grandfather's public reputation and mana.

'You may tell the pastor,' Grandfather said, 'that the Mahana family would be pleased to support such work. Kua pai?'

'Kua pai.'

Oh that was just great. Now twenty per cent of Dad's earnings was going to the church.

'Let our light,' Grandfather began, 'so shine before men that they may see our good works and glorify the Lord our God who is in Heaven.'

Blah blah bloody blah. My thoughts weren't complimentary. I looked upward. My father and our family had just been shat on from Heaven.

'So what are we going to do?' Dad asked Mum. They were whispering in the dark on the other side of the bedroom wall.

'We'll manage,' she said. 'We always manage.'

'I think we can last out till August,' Dad said. 'Money will be tight from then though.'

'There'll be seasonal work,' Mum said. 'Perhaps we can pick up some scrubcutting. If we have to, we can always ask Miss Zelda for more credit –'

'Only if we have to.'

'We'll cross that bridge when the time comes,' Mum said.

That night I dreamed my mother was standing on a stage in front of an audience of a thousand people. She looked like Edgar Bergen's dummy, opening and closing her mouth without being able to say a word.

'Please Miss Zelda please Miss Zelda please –'

Next morning I was angry enough to confront Grandfather Tamihana.

'I disagree with your decision,' I said. 'You should not have committed more of our income to the church.'

He was amused. 'Why didn't you say so at our meeting?'

'I will next time,' I answered. 'What you have done is make things more difficult for all of the family.'

'The church comes first.'

'Charity begins at home,' I hit back.

'Don't *you* start quoting my Bible back at me, Himiona.'
The words stung the air between us.

As if that wasn't enough, my physical development was bringing me into conflict with grandfather too. I was starting to sprout in all directions and, yay, was now at eye level to the mirror in the bathroom.

'That boy of yours,' Grandfather said one day to Dad at dinner, 'is eating us out of house and home.'

'Didn't you tell me once,' I responded, 'that I should eat what was put before me?'

My father nudged me. 'Don't be disrespectful to your grandfather,' he said.

Growing up was having its positive side, though. Even Mohi The Turd Who Walks was treating me with guarded respect, and girls were starting to look at me.

'It's your tight pants,' Haromi said. 'Aunt Huria should buy you some new ones. They're managing to cover everything, but only just.'

I blushed. Haromi, Andrew and I were at our usual place, waiting at the bus stop, doing our usual thing – slinging off at the family. I knew she was right but couldn't bear the thought of having Mum spend our hard-pressed cash on new clothes.

To change the subject I asked, 'Did Aunt Ruth ever tell you guys about how our grandparents met?'

'That old story about the lightning rod of God?' Andrew asked. 'Sure.'

'Huh,' Haromi said. 'I'm not going to be struck by no lightning rod of God or anything else. Any storm cloud comes along, or even any hint of a clap of thunder, I'm out of here.'

'I sometimes wonder whether they really loved one another or not,' I said, ignoring her. There, I had admitted the possibility to myself.

'Of *course* Grandmother and Bulibasha loved each other,' Haromi said. 'Look at all the kids they had!'

Oh really? As if having fourteen children was the ultimate proof of love.

Haromi turned tragedienne. 'Please, God,' she screamed to the world, 'save me from having too many kids crying at one end and shitting at the other! I'm too beautiful to have my body ruined and to end up looking like, Jesus ber-loody ker-rist, my mother!' She threw a hail of pebbles at the little kids playing hopscotch on the road. They looked up, bewildered.

Oh, just Haromi again.

In this dangerous mood I turned fifteen. That same April the annual Maori cultural competitions were held between haka teams from all over the district. The Mahana family had the first inkling of what was to come between us and the Poata family of Hukareka.

As in past years, the venue was the Gisborne Opera House, now long demolished, a two-storeyed building with upstairs and downstairs decorated in fabulous gold and red. In its heyday, at the turn of the century, the theatre hosted overseas opera and theatre companies which performed everything from Puccini and Verdi to Shakespeare and George Bernard Shaw. During the 1920s it became more versatile, even going so far as to become a boxing venue for the great Tom Heeney, a local boy, before he went to live in America. Gisborne was on the Williamson station circuit and one of its claims to fame was that J. C. Kerridge had opened the first of the great Kerridge-Odeon theatres in the town.

By the 1950s Gisborne Opera House was more a backwater venue. Although it still hosted first-class shows and the occasional visit of the New Zealand Players – valiantly dedicated to bringing culture to the provinces – it was more likely to feature local productions. Sometimes the Gisborne amateur dramatic company put on operettas and musicals like *White Horse Inn* or *Rose Marie*; Gilbert and Sullivan's *Pirates of Penzance*, *HMS Pinafore*, and *The Mikado* were also occasionally dusted off. In August the annual amateur dramatic competitions took place, and singers, tap and ballet dancers and elocutionists trod the boards of the Opera House. Little did we know in the 1950s that a bright-eyed, ringlet-covered girl with a silver voice would follow an earlier East Coast Maori singer, Princess Te Rangi Pai, and turn from being 'Tom and Mum's daughter' into Dame Kiri Te Kanawa.

The haka competition was tough. Twenty-five teams were in the open section. Last year Mahana had managed to win, receiving the glittering Ngata Cup and the Hine Materoa Shield in the process, pipping Waihirere and Hauiti at the post. Our job this year was to hold off all challengers.

So far so good. We had succeeded in getting through the first round and were now among the twelve semifinalists. Again our performance was impeccable. When the curtains opened, we were already grouped to give our traditional item, 'Po Po'. After that, our programme was fluid, moving with professional ease through action song bracket, poi, haka and exit waiata. Most of the team comprised the Mahana and Whatu families: my aunts, mother and other female in-laws all in the front row, and the Whatu women and others from Waituhi in the second and third rows. Behind them were my uncles and father, led by Uncle Ruka, and in the fifth row were the younger men including Mohi, myself and Andrew. Pani had been dragooned into joining us.

After our performance we sat upstairs in the balcony with Grandfather Tamihana and Grandmother Ramona, other teams, supporters and spectators.

'We've got it in the bag,' Granduncle Pera said, shaking our hands.

Aunt Sarah, our tutor, and Uncle Ruka thought we had done well, and of course Mohi was receiving the usual pat from He With The Gammy Leg. The women were dressed in their headbands, bodices and piupiu; the men too were in piupiu, but wearing coats or jerseys over their chests. All of us were sweating, and our grease-applied moko were smeared.

Hukareka was the final team to perform. The lights dimmed. The plush red velvet curtains swished back.

Huh? The stage was empty. Normally haka teams were already onstage in their ranks, two or three rows of women in front and two rows of men at the back.

Then, from the side of the stage, a woman's voice called out authoritatively in the karanga.

'Tena koutou rangatira ma, tena koutou, tena koutou, tena koutou!'

Aunt Sarah nodded her head. 'That's new,' she said, approving. 'The judges will give them points for originality.'

To whistles and cheers, Hukareka swept on to the stage, the men at an angle from one side, the women at a similar angle from the other. They were moving at double speed, making an X pattern. When they met in the middle, the scissoring effect was so dazzling that the hall raised a mighty cheer.

'Pae kare, they're good this year,' Aunt Sarah repeated. She should know. She had been trained by experts.

'Look at that!' Even Uncle Ruka was filled with admiration.

'A bit showy,' Aunt Ruth sniffed.

141

Aunt Sarah had her eyes on the judges. Showy, yes, but there was no doubt the judges were impressed. As Hukareka continued with their programme – the ancient waiata first, then action song, poi, haka and exit – all the judges except one known for his preference for the traditional nodded their heads in agreement. Last year Hukareka hadn't even made it to the semifinals. But this year –

That was when Aunt Sarah realised.

'They're planning to take us on,' she said. Her voice was filled with awe and respect.

It was no surprise to Aunt Sarah when the judges took so long to reach a decision on the final six. They had a heck of a job, and it would be worse on the night of the finals.

To cheers of applause the compere announced, 'The haka teams in the finals are in alphabetical order. Hauiti, Hukareka –' Rupeni Poata and his family yelled and screamed. They were sitting in the front downstairs. 'L.D.S. Mahia –' My heart lurched. We hadn't made it. 'Mangatu, Manutuke, Waihirere, Whangara and –' The compere smiled up at us. 'Sorry, Bulibasha,' he apologised. 'My alphabet was never any good: Mahana!'

We erupted into roars of relief.

'I'll wring your neck!' Aunt Sarah yelled.

The compere waved good-naturedly at her. 'See you next month for the finals.'

The red curtains swished to a close.

Just as Hukareka were leaving, Rupeni Poata looked up at us. He inclined his head.

32

At school the next week, not even Miss Dalrymple's usual greeting could pour cold water over our excitement at making the finals. We were doing English – poetry appreciation, page 17 of *Plain Sailing*.

'This is a Scottish tale,' Miss Dalrymple began. 'It is very famous throughout the *English*-speaking world.' She got out a stick and tapped like a conductor on her table. When she thought we had the beat, she said, 'Now, class, together!'

We began to read in unison. ' "O, young Lochinvar is come out of the west, through all the wide Border his steed was the best – " '

I could hardly believe my eyes. Lochinvar, a young Scottish stud, was in love with Ellen, a girl forced to marry another man. So what did Lochinvar do? He rode his horse to the wedding and snatched her up from the altar and they escaped to live happily ever after.

It was the same story as Grandmother Ramona's abduction on her wedding day.

That night the haka team met for the first time since the semifinals. As usual, Grandfather and Grandmother joined us as we assembled at Takitimu Hall, wondering what Aunt Sarah had in store for us. The month after the finals was when Maori cultural teams practised, polished, changed their repertoire and incorporated – some would say pinched – other people's ideas.

'Our main challengers are Waihirere and Mahia,' Uncle Ruka said. 'I don't know what happened to Hauiti this year. Waihirere are solid and Mahia have got some great men in their haka.'

Aunt Sarah made a sign of assent. I began to feel irritated. Everybody was afraid to say what they really thought because Grandfather was among us.

'No, our greatest challenge is from Hukareka,' I muttered.

Everybody looked from me to the Lord Of Heaven.

'The boy's right,' Grandfather said, amused.

It was just what Aunt Sarah had been waiting for. She started to crack her whip. 'Did you all see the way they came on?' she asked. 'Ka pai, credit where credit is due, that was original. You put our entrance up against that one and who wins? Not us. We have to change our entrance.'

Uncle Ruka thought this through and nodded. The haka team groaned. No sooner did we get it right than we had to start all over again.

'Notice anything else?' Aunt Sarah asked again. 'Any of you? Come on, you've all got eyes.'

'They looked different somehow?' Frances ventured.

'That's right, babe,' Aunt Sarah answered. 'They had new piupius, bodices' the lot. What have *we* got? All you girls will be busy sewing this month.' Haromi sighed. 'That's another thing,' Aunt Sarah went on. 'You know why they looked good? They weren't resting on their laurels like we were. Compared to them, our front row was as crooked as a dog's hind leg. All the hems of the piupius were higgledy

143

piggledy, especially yours, Haromi, pulled up so high. This is not a beauty contest to see who has the nicest-looking knees.'

Everybody grinned.

'Did you notice something else?' Aunt Sarah was really getting into it. 'All their front row was young. Judges like seeing young girls in front. We may have to switch some of the oldies to the back.' She began to pace up and down. 'But we must come up with a trump card. Hukareka knows they're on a winning streak so they're not going to change their programme. That gives us the edge, because they think they know ours. We've got to come up with something that will appeal to all the judges, something traditional as well as modern. Something that will get us the Ngata Shield again –' She stopped in mid-sentence. 'That's it!' she said. Her eyes were shining. Whenever she got that look, trouble was bound to be brewing. 'Tomorrow we change our programme. We'll keep the poi and the haka. But we will learn a new entrance and a new action song. The action song will be our trump card.'

'But Auntie,' Andrew moaned. 'Hukareka never even came anywhere last year. Why all the fuss?'

Aunt Ruth stepped forward. 'Never underestimate Rupeni Poata,' she said.

Aunt Sarah nodded in agreement. 'Nobody is targeting us this year,' she said. 'They all know that Hukareka is the tops. We have to target them too, as sickening as that is for me to say.'

Then Andrew asked the million-dollar question. 'And what's our new action song?'

Aunt Sarah made my day. 'Simeon hasn't composed it yet, eh Himiona? You do the melody and I'll do the words, ka tika?'

My mind boggled. Grandfather began to shake his head doubtfully.

'Okay, Aunt,' I said. 'You say, me do.'

Of course it was just like Aunt Sarah to dragoon everybody, including Mum, into creating the all-new all-stereo sound and technicolor Mahana haka team. She had four weeks to do it.

'I've had an idea about costuming for you girls,' Aunt Sarah announced one night at practice. 'Floor-length cloaks – *floor* length, Haromi, not knee-length, not even ankle length. Huria, can you drive me to the store to get some calico?'

'Not Mum,' I said quickly. 'Get somebody else.'

Aunt Sarah looked at me quizzically. 'You're getting uppity, boy. Can *you* drive the car?'

Checkmate.

'Why, he-*llo*,' Miss Zelda said as Aunt Sarah and Mum walked into the store.

'Good morning, Zelda,' Aunt Sarah answered. 'We've come for the best calico you've got in the place.' Aunt Sarah knew how to handle Miss Zelda.

'Of course,' Miss Zelda said. 'Scott? Will you bring our best quality calico in for Sarah?'

Scott came in with a roll and unfurled it over the measuring table. Aunt Sarah pursed her lips. 'I'll take it.'

'The whole roll?'

'Why, yes.'

'Cash or charge, Sarah?'

'Cash. Your interest rate is too high for me, Zelda.' Aunt Sarah turned to Mum. 'Always pay in cash if you can,' she offered.

It was a careless, innocent enough remark, but it made Mum blush with embarrassment. As my mother started the car, she saw Miss Zelda and Miss Daisy at the window. They were like eternal watchers, watching and smiling and waiting. Winter had only just begun to bite, but they knew there would come a time, soon enough, when my mother would need to go in and get herself on the tick.

33

As if the cultural competition wasn't enough, the Mahana women's hockey team found itself scheduled to play Hukareka women in the Gisborne women's senior grade section the following Saturday afternoon. Hukareka had won the last game and both teams were neck and neck in the competition.

Aunt Ruth was the Mahana women's coach and Aunt Sarah was team chaperone. Both were veterans of the field. However, as soon as Aunt Sarah found out who our opponents were the challenge of playing Hukareka was irresistible, varicose veins notwithstanding. At the very least she wanted to go in as goalie.

'You can't,' Aunt Ruth said. 'We already have a goalie. Auntie Molly's our goalie.'

'I'll be one of the fullbacks then,' Aunt Sarah said. 'You need me, sister, after that hiding you fellas got from Hukareka last time. Put me in as left fullback.'

Aunt Ruth bristled. 'A draw is not a hiding, and Sephora's already left fullback.'

'Move her to halfback.' When Aunt Sarah made up her mind, she could never be budged.

'What happens if somebody takes a crack at you?' Aunt Ruth asked. 'Who'll look after our haka team?'

'Nobody's going to take a crack at me!' Aunt Sarah scoffed. 'If anybody is taking a crack it will be me, and Poppaea, The Brute, will be on the receiving end. Boy, do I owe *her* one.'

'Sister, dear,' Aunt Ruth said, 'if you go on, who's going to be on the sideline directing the play?'

'You are,' Aunt Sarah answered. 'You're the coach.'

'Not for this game I'm not. I'm playing right fullback.'

The two sisters paused, made up their minds and shook hands. In unison they said, 'Let's both play.'

Hukareka, *watch out*.

The day of the match was cold and wet, and the rain had made the ground mucky underneath. Four other games were on at the same time, but word soon got around: 'Hey! Mahana women are playing Hukareka!' Naturally, Nani Mini Tupara, who loved hockey, was there to barrack for Mahana, even if we were Mormons.

As Andrew and I made a beeline for the pavilion I saw Mohi parking the De Soto and heard Grandfather calling to me: 'Himiona!'

I hurried Andrew on. 'Pretend we haven't heard,' I said.

Aunt Ruth was huddled with the team. She had just finished karakia, calling on God's aid in this fight against the Infidel. Aunt Miriam was centre forward. Aunt Esther and Aunt Kate – Uncle Hone's wife – were inner right and inner left, and the wings were the youngest – Haromi on the left and Frances on the right. Playing at halfback positions were Aunt Sephora, Aunt Dottie – Uncle Ruka's wife – and my mother Huria, who seemed to be a different person all togged up in her hockey outfit. The backs were the heavyweights, Aunt Ruth and Aunt Sarah, an impenetrable wall of solid flesh, with Aunt Molly as goalie. There she was, looking for all the world as if she was sitting on an upsidedown basin outside her cookhouse, splaying herself from one side of the goal to the other.

'Okay, girls?' Aunt Ruth asked. 'Are you all ready? Just keep to your positions.'

'Hit the ball,' Aunt Sarah interjected.

'And if you can't hit the ball –'

'Hit the player,' Aunt Sarah said.

Then Aunt Ruth and Aunt Sarah said in unison, 'The Brute is *ours*!'

The referee called the teams on to the field. The linesmen took their places. Grandfather Tamihana came sauntering from one entrance of the field and Rupeni Poata from the other. Rupeni Poata raised his hat to Grandmother. Grandfather Tamihana flared.

Then, 'Didn't you hear me yelling out to you, Himiona?'

'No.'

He wasn't convinced. 'I wanted you to hold the game until I got here.'

I shrugged my shoulders.

He made a motion as if to hit me. 'You're sailing close to the wind, boy.'

As if I cared.

The referee pushed his glasses on to the bridge of his nose. 'Let's have a nice clean game, ladies,' he asked, then blew his whistle.

'Come on the maroon,' came the chant from the left sideline. Maroon was the colour for Mahana.

'Come on the black,' came the chant from the right sideline. Black was Hukareka's colour. And boy, was their team formidable. Poppy was at centre forward until her mother, The Brute, saw she was up against the heavier Aunt Miriam.

'Poppy!' The Brute called. 'Change with Auntie Anna on the right wing.'

'No!' Poppy answered. 'I can beat the old bag.'

A deep rumble came from the Mahana sideline. Fighting talk and the game hadn't even started.

'Do as I say!' The Brute yelled.

It was wonderful to see Poppy's flaring temper. She stalked over to the right where, ah Heaven, Andrew and I were standing. Her opposite number was Haromi, who accidentally pushed Poppy on purpose.

'So my auntie's an old bag, is she?' Haromi smiled sweetly.

Murder was in the air.

Weight for weight, the teams were evenly balanced. The Poata women were all on deck – Julia, Agnes and Helen at the back

147

positions; Virginia, Gloria and Carla in the positions at middle field, and Poppy, Ottavia, The Brute and two other cousins of Poppy's in the forwards. The Hukareka women were leaner and fitter. But either they had forgotten about the ruthlessness of Mahana women or else they hadn't played sport with their brothers and men for quite a while.

'Hockey one, hockey two, hockey three –'

The sticks blurred and Aunt Miriam, finessing Anna by not quite touching on the third click, scooped the ball past her to where Mum was waiting to push the ball past Gloria, chasing it into the clear.

'Ref! Where's your eyes!' The Brute roared.

My mother took a look to see where Frances was. No, Haromi was better placed. *Whang*, and she hit the ball towards the right corner of the Hukareka half.

The Mahana team strategy had always been that once anybody got the ball they hit it out to the wing. The older women knew the younger girls didn't want bruises on their beautiful legs and would therefore fly down the line, keep out of trouble and then *whack* the ball into the circle of the opposing team. The theory was, of course, that the older women would be there to receive the ball. Good theory.

Haromi positively streaked along the line after the ball. The Hukareka halfbacks chased after her, but not for nothing was she the last baton runner of our school track and field team.

'*Offside*, ref!' The Brute cried.

If the ref was blind, that wasn't *our* fault.

Haromi picked up the ball, tapped it nicely, past the Hukareka backs. Only the goalie ahead. Now hit it into the centre where the aunties were – huh? Where were the aunties? Never mind. Haromi dashed into the circle. She pretended to hit the ball to Frances, and the Hukareka goalie turned to the left.

Gotcha!

Did I forget to tell you that Haromi had a wicked eye? Whether playing basketball, billiards – even though she wasn't supposed to – or kicking a goal, Haromi had an inbuilt direction finder. She needed no computer to calculate the distance divided by the width of the goal minus the mass of the goalie multiplied by the probability factor to –

Up came her stick. *Wham*. I swear that ball caught fire, it was travelling so fast. It sizzled into the net before the goalie even knew it was there.

The Mahana side of the field roared with acclamation. The Hukareka side screamed and squabbled with the ref. 'I told you girls,' The Brute screamed, 'to watch these Mahana women.'

Haromi trotted back to the centre of the field, looking at her fingernails as if she'd broken one.

'Try that again,' Poppy hissed.

Oh, they were magnificent, those Mahana women. They had skill, strategy and, if not speed, the experience of modern-day Amazons. They were like the army led by man-hating Amanda Blake in *The Loves of Hajji Baba* who rode standing up on their horses and lassooed the evil Caliph's men. Directed from the back by Aunt Ruth and Aunt Sarah, they pulled every trick in the book to keep ahead.

Both aunties liked directing the referee too. Aunt Ruth, for instance, liked to have one fullback way up to the half-way mark when the play was in Hukareka's half. That way she could often catch a Hukareka forward offside.

'Offside, ref. Offside,' she'd yell.

'Yes, I know, Mrs Whatu.'

And if a Hukareka player was in the circle and about to aim at the goal, her favourite trick was to yell, 'Sticks!'

You never knew your luck. The ref might agree with you.

The half-time whistle blew. Poppy was looking dazed, the realisation dawning that her mother was right about Mahana women. Mahana were ahead four goals to Hukareka's (very lucky) one. Mahana's tactic of hitting fast and regularly from the very start, getting as many goals as possible, had paid off.

However, the game was only just beginning. The *real* problem was that in the second half all the aunties got slower and slower. Having too many babies and standing so long at the shearing sheds had given all of them, not only Aunt Sarah, varicose veins. The Brute knew it.

Immediately after play resumed, Hukareka broke through the Mahana lines. Despite a valiant stopping attempt by Auntie Molly, Virginia managed to get a lucky hit.

'Take *that*, you big black bitch,' Virginia snarled. She started to trot back to her side.

Aunt Sarah accidentally put her hockey stick out. 'Oh sorry, darling,' she said as Virginia tripped over and ended up with a face full of mud. Aunt Sarah went to pull Virginia up. By the hair. Virginia screamed. 'Only trying to help,' Aunt Sarah said.

To make matters worse, it began to rain. The ref looked doubtful about continuing the game. He consulted the two captains. Call the game off? You've got to be *kidding*!

As the aunties began to run out of steam, the play moved relentlessly into Mahana's half. The greater fitness of Hukareka began to show as the women made lightning strikes into Mahana territory.

The delectable Poppy scored a goal. 'Take *that*!' she screamed.

'Lucky shot,' Haromi yawned.

Mahana 4, Hukareka 3.

None of this fazed the Mahana team, for defensive play in the second half had always been part of the strategy. Although one by one my aunties were coming to a standstill, their hitting power was as damaging and as accurate as ever. The objective became to stop the ball or get it off Hukareka and keep hitting it to the younger and fitter wingers who could take the ball back up the field into the Hukareka half. It didn't matter what Haromi or Frances did with the damn ball once they were up there, so long as they kept Hukareka busy while the aunties had a bit of a breather. The primary task was to guard the circle at *all* costs.

However, the rain made the field muddy and the ball wasn't running as far as it would on a flat surface. To get the ball travelling, Mahana had to resort to greater strength –

'Sticks!' The Brute cried. Or 'Raised ball!'

Each penalty against Mahana meant that Hukareka could begin the game closer and closer into the Mahana half. As Hukareka penetrated and pushed the Mahana defence further back, slowly but surely the aunties began a strategic retreat to guard the circle.

A cornered animal is always dangerous, and there was nothing more glorious to watch in hockey than Mahana women on the defensive. They were like tigers, roaring, screaming and yelling orders to each other. 'Watch the left! Watch the right! Watch the centre! Protect the flank! Keep an eye on that young winger! Cover that gap! Keep together, girls! Only another quarter of an hour to go! Kia kaha!' Mahana were wonderful, shifting and dissolving fluidly from one defensive pattern into another. The defenders stopped the ball and hit it out to the wingers. But Hukareka had them marked. Never mind. Defend again and *hit* beyond the wingers to the far corner. Defend again and *hit*.

Then Hukareka managed to get through the Waituhi defences and slam another goal home. The score drew at Mahana 4, Hukareka 4.

That *did* it. Defensive strategy descended into the arena of dubious play as the Mahana women began pulling every trick in the book – and some that weren't in the book. If the ref didn't see what you were doing, that was his problem. If he did, never mind.

If a Hukareka player is dribbling the ball and gets past you, don't worry. Stop the player, either by tripping her up with your stick, tangling your stick with hers or, if necessary, pushing her off balance as she passes. The referee might blow his whistle – 'Obstruction!' – but at least that will stop play for a while and allow the aunties to regroup. If you are standing in the clear with the ball, don't hit it straight away. Why waste a good shot? Wait until one or two Hukareka players are coming to attack you, then hit it. If there are two attacking players, you can get them both. Easy! You pretend to miss the ball on your first stroke, because that way you can whack the first player, Oops sorry. On your second stroke, *that's* when you hit the ball at the second player. She shouldn't have been in the road anyway.

Oh yes, sticks is okay if there's a Hukareka player behind you who might cop your stick on your backswing. That way she might get carted off the field and, who knows, by the time you finish Hukareka might not have any reserves left. And if all else fails and you need to protect the ball, pretend to slip and sit on it. Nobody's going to hit a poor defenceless old lady when she's down.

You never do any of the above in the circle, though, or the referee will call – 'Penalty!' But if it's really necessary, a penalty is better than Hukareka getting a goal.

The Mahana women trotted leisurely to their backline to prepare for a penalty goal attempt by Hukareka. Only four minutes to final whistle.

'Hey, ref!' The Brute yelled, 'Tell Mahana to move their big bums. They're wasting time.'

'Wait your hurry,' Auntie Molly responded.

'Better a big bum than a black one,' Haromi called.

'Keep it clean,' Aunt Ruth said.

My aunts lined up to protect the goal. Julia Poata was Hukareka's hitter. The ball would be stopped by Agnes, and The Brute would take the attempt at the goal. Aunts Sarah and Ruth joined Auntie Molly in the goal. No *way* could a hockey ball get past them. The rest waited, taking deep breaths ready to –

The ball *cracked* out from the corner and across the circle. Agnes stopped it. The Brute steadied. Mahana women were charging out of the goal.

The Brute aimed at Aunt Esther and *swung*. The ball rose – and slammed Aunt Esther in the stomach. Aunt Esther collapsed.

There was shocked silence. Mahana could do that to the opposition, but they weren't allowed to do it to Mahana – especially to the baby sister who had never hurt a fly.

Aunt Ruth helped Aunt Esther up. We were all wondering what she would do – take The Brute on herself or order a free-for-all. Aunt Ruth did neither. She smiled at the ref and smiled at The Brute and indicated that the game should continue. Her killer instinct, however, was aroused, and from the side of her mouth came the words, 'Okay girls, *kill.*'

Oh they were angry! The ref ordered a free hit for Mahana. Aunt Sephora tapped the ball gently to Aunt Miriam. Adrenalin pumping, the Mahana women began to move like a juggernaut down the field. Even Auntie Molly left her goal, twirling her stick like a taiaha. She followed Aunt Ruth and Aunt Sarah as they moved out of the Mahana circle.

'Fall back!' The Brute screamed to her women. 'Fall back!'

Mahana made an awesome sight as they came silently sweeping through the rain. They dribbled the ball amongst themselves. They were like Zulu warriors executing a pincer movement into enemy territory.

'Watch out, girls!' The Brute cried.

Mahana crossed over into Hukareka's half. Never mind about being on the defensive. Mahana women were going to war. Where was the ball? The rain was falling so heavily you could hardly see it. Ah, there it was –

'Gloria!' The Brute commanded.

Uttering a banshee cry, Gloria Poata ran at the wall of Mahana women. Silently a gap opened, and Gloria hurled herself in. It closed behind her. When the juggernaut moved on, there was Gloria Poata, dazed, going round and round in circles without her hockey stick and wondering what had happened to it.

'Helen!' The Brute squawked.

Helen rushed at the Mahana women. A flurry of sticks followed and there was Helen Poata cartwheeling head over heels out of the pack.

Meantime, Aunt Sarah somehow staggered against the referee, knocked off his glasses and trod on them. Good, he was out of the way.

'Back to the circle!' The Brute ordered. She still couldn't see the ball – only those huge solid Mahana legs like Burnham Wood come to Dunsinane.

Then Aunt Ruth let out the order, 'In you go, sis!' She flicked the ball to Aunt Sarah.

The game literally exploded.

'Keep out of the way, girls,' Aunt Sarah roared. She took the ball through the Hukareka defences. The referee still hadn't found his glasses.

Wham here, slam there, and two Hukareka women were down. The rest of the Mahana women joined the attack. The rain was so heavy that nobody could see what was really happening. Slash here and slash there, and another two Hukareka women bit the dust. Boot here and boot there, and a fist as well, and three more went reeling away from the circle.

Suddenly the rain cleared and there was Aunt Sarah, hair plastered on her face like a gorgon. Wielding her hockey stick with one hand, she gave an earth-shattering cry and *cracked* the ball. The fact that it missed the goal by a mile was not the point. Aunt Sarah had had no intention of getting a goal. She took out The Brute, who fell, clasping her mouth with horror. She shouldn't have been in the road anyway.

The referee found his glasses. Oh, look at the time. He blew the final whistle. In protest, somebody threw an orange at him.

Mahana 4, Hukareka 4.

A draw – but, boy, it was *worth* it.

34

When I look back, I realise something was happening to me in 1958 that made me wilful and rebellious – something intangible that I couldn't recognise in myself, though others could.

I was delivering calico for the cloaks to Aunt Ruth one day when –

'Hey Aunt,' I said, 'have you ever heard a poem about a young Scottish boy who steals his girlfriend on her wedding day and –'

She pierced me with a glance. 'Just because the Scottish have the same story doesn't mean ours isn't true.'

'I wasn't going to say that!'

'But you were thinking it,' she growled. 'You're getting too whakahihi, Simeon. Too big for your boots.'

I turned away from her. 'Nor was that song about Ramona,' I muttered, 'written for Grandmother. It was written for a silent screen star, Dolores Del Rio and a film she made in 1928 when she played a Spanish girl in the Old West and –'

'What's that?' Aunt Ruth asked. She was holding her sewing needle as if she was ready to skewer me with it.

'Oh nothing,' I answered.

Even Glory was affected by the change in me.

'I hate it when you're like this,' she said one day while we were milking.

Like what?

'You're always so up yourself. Always in a bad mood. You never talk any more, and when you do it doesn't come out sounding nice. At nights you're the only one who doesn't answer when I call g'night to everybody. I don't care if you don't love anyone else, but –' She pinched me, hard. 'Don't you love *me* any more?'

I looked at her, surprised.

'There,' she said, 'you're doing it again.'

Doing what? Suddenly afraid, I hugged her close to me; we clung together as if we didn't want anything to get in between. I knew Glory was right. I was changing, and I didn't know how or why.

Nobody was safe from me. At school I went around pushing little kids out of the way. I pushed my father Joshua and mother Huria away. The fearsome ones in my life, like Miss Dalrymple, were no longer so formidable.

'Do speak up, Simeon,' Miss Dalrymple said in class.

'Quardle oodle ardle wardle doodle,' I mumbled.

Even when Mohi tried to push me around, I pushed him back. Perhaps he put his finger on it: 'You're growing up, kid.'

One night the collision between new and old bordered on madness.

The family had just finished evening prayers. Grandfather was at the holy end of the room, where his throne was. Casually, Aunt Esther asked me, 'So, Simeon, what are you studying at school these days?'

'We're doing biology,' I answered. 'The theory of evolution. Did you know that we are descended from monkeys?'

Grandfather Tamihana was in the middle of talking to Grandmother. His mouth made a big O. 'Man is a special creation,' he said. The Voice of Authority hath spoken.

'There was a court case about that,' I muttered. 'In the 1930s. God lost.'

'Simeon,' my father reproved.

There was silence for a moment. I thought that was the end of it. But –

'Get me the Bible,' Grandfather Tamihana said.

'I know what it says in the Bible,' I answered.

'So you *know*,' Grandfather continued, 'that God *created* Adam and Eve?'

'I know that is what the Bible *says* –'

'And is the Bible not the Word of God?'

'No,' I answered, 'it's the Word of Man.'

Mohi started to make strange choking sounds. My aunts were blushing with embarrassment.

'I think you should leave the room,' Mum said. She was panicking. Grandfather Tamihana was growing extremely angry.

I looked around at everyone. 'Why is it?' I asked, 'that every time I say something, everybody takes sides so quickly? Doesn't anyone here, apart from Grandfather and myself, have an opinion?' My uncles and aunts continued looking at their laps. Ah well, I had tried.

155

'I am not descended from a monkey,' Grandfather said.

His comment would have been humorous, except that he was apoplectic with rage. I crossed my arms and stared at him. 'Grandfather,' I said, 'the greatest biblical scholars in the world have agreed with you. However, some of the greatest scientists have disagreed. You are right –' he nodded – 'but you are also wrong.'

There was hardly a sound. Dad was on his feet ready to clip me over the ear. Grandmother restrained him.

'Let us agree to differ.'

As soon as I said the words, I felt a rush of elation. Grandfather wasn't too sure *what* I was saying. Was I agreeing with him? Or disagreeing? It was as if suddenly I had discovered a new language, a way of saying things beyond his limited comprehension. In knowledge was power, yes. But the secret was how to articulate that knowledge.

My grandfather, despite his mana, was piss ignorant. The understanding made me feel triumphant.

My father came looking for me after prayers. I was in my bedroom doing my homework when he burst in and motioned to a book on the bed.

'Is that your biology book?' he asked.

'Yes.'

'I want you to burn it.'

Burn it?

'You can't, Dad. It doesn't belong to me. It's from our class set.' I paused. 'Grandfather wants this done, doesn't he?'

'Give me the book, Simeon.'

'Dad, this is really dumb.'

We began to tussle over the book. Laughing, I wrenched it away from Dad. He raised his fist and hit me. I couldn't believe it. I touched my right cheek. This *couldn't* be happening.

Dad took the book. I watched from the window as he handed it to Grandfather. The entire family had been ordered to watch. Grandfather doused the book with kerosene. He threw a match at it. There was a *whump*, and the book burst into flame.

He looked across at me where I stood at the window. He was laughing, and he looked maniacal. This was the only kind of reaction he could muster – physical or symbolic. I had discovered

Grandfather Tamihana's weakness. He feared anything that would destroy his world.

Later I had it out with Dad. When did I ever get to be so wise?

'Dad,' I began, 'I don't mind that you did what you did. But there are other books just like the one Grandfather burnt. Is he going to burn every book?'

'Just that one,' he answered.

'Dad, you can't stop progress.'

'Progress is not always a good thing, Simeon.'

I was getting nowhere. I tried to be kind. 'You only say that because those are Grandfather's words. You only do what you do because Grandfather tells you to. At some point, Dad, you're going to have to make a choice without looking to him first. All the family will have to make that choice one day. Are you always going to choose for Grandfather Tamihana?'

'Honour thy father and thy mother, Simeon.'

'When are you going to choose for *me*, Dad? For my mother and my sisters? For yourself? And when are you going to choose for what is right? Are you always going to take his side just because he's your father? What if he's wrong?'

My father looked at me, frightened. 'I know he's wrong sometimes, son,' he said.

'Then you're a coward, Dad.'

He raised his hand again.

'Don't you hit my son,' my mother interrupted. She had just come into the room. I thought she would take my side. Instead, she turned on me. 'You think you're so smart, Simeon. But you've never had to live the way your father and I have. Life is not easy. The choices are not so simple.' She kissed me on the forehead. 'We do love you, son,' she said. 'But just because you know more than me and your father, and can read and write, it doesn't mean to say you know everything.'

35

Aunt Sarah had the Mahana haka team practising right up to the hour before the finals.

'Good,' she would say during rehearsals, 'but not good enough.'

Again and again she drove us through our new entrance and the new action song. She had fallen in love with the tune I'd composed for it, and she'd pulled out all the stops to create the appropriate words and actions.

'This is a gutsy composition,' she admonished. 'I want you all to put some guts into it. Come on, girls! Never mind about trying to look pretty. Get into it!'

I thought we had a smash hit on our hands. By the time we arrived at the Gisborne Opera House, we were ready to go for gold.

'We're on last,' Aunt Sarah announced. 'Ka pai! And guess what? Hukareka's on first!' She was triumphant. Now we'd be able to watch everyone else and tailor our performance accordingly. And the judges would have *forgotten* Hukareka by the time we'd finished. She bustled us backstage so that we could change into our costumes and queue up for Uncle Matiu to paint moko on us. Aunt Sarah hid the cloaks so that none of our competitors would see them until we emerged, resplendent. Then we went up into the balcony to join the other performers.

The view of the stage from the balcony was gorgeous. Flowers decorated the apron and sides. The Apirana Ngata Shield and Heni Materoa Cup dazzled in silver glory. The audience was dressed up to the nines. The men were wearing suits or sports jackets; the women were elegant in black, and some were wearing fake fur. The kuia were stunning with their greenstone earrings and pendants. The older ones had chiselled moko.

The lights dimmed. The compere came out. He was dressed in a tuxedo, and the audience whistled. He went offstage and came on again for another whistle. How we all laughed! Then he whistled at *us*.

'Ladies and gentlemen,' he said, 'from here you all look fabulous.

Not a black singlet or pair of gumboots in sight. Sorry, Auntie Mary, I didn't see you out there! Seriously folks, you look proud, beautiful and dignified. Yes, even you Auntie Mary. You all lend lustre to this occasion. For tonight we are going to witness the very best of our performing arts.'

We all started to preen.

In the distance I saw Poppy sitting with the Hukareka girls. She was vivacious in her black and white costume, her long hair curling on her shoulders. Her lips had been darkened and a moko applied to her chin. She looked like the daughter of a Renaissance prince. My heart gave a lurch –

NIGHT. A FULL MOON SHINES ON A BALCONY IN AN OLD ITALIAN CITADEL. A YOUNG GIRL COMES OUT, LOOKING AROUND AS IF SEARCHING FOR SOMEBODY.

GIRL Taku tane, taku tane, kei hea koe taku tane?
(Subtitles: Romeo, Romeo, wherefore art thou Romeo?)

A YOUNG BOY FROM WAITUHI, TRANSFORMED SO THAT HIS NOSE ISN'T AS BIG AND HE IS TALLER, DETACHES HIMSELF FROM THE SHADOWS.

BOY Ko ahau, kei raro nei!
(Subtitles: Down here, beloved, down here.)

Did Poppy see my adoring eyes? No, for the Hukareka group was hastening down to the stage.

'Good luck,' I said to her as she passed my seat.

She started to smile. Then she saw I was a Mahana and her eyes widened with surprise. With a flick of her piupius she was gone.

'But you don't want to hear *me* all night,' the compere said. 'So let's begin our competition with Hukareka first, followed by L.D.S. Mahia, Hauiti and Whangara. We'll have a break for a smoke –' The compere saw Grandfather sitting in the front row downstairs. 'Oops, sorry, Bulibasha.'

Grandfather waved the joke aside. Beside him, Grandmother Ramona was beautiful in that serene way of hers. She wore her long dress of white Spanish lace. She was like a dove among eagles.

'Then after the break Mangatu, Waihirere, Manutuke and Mahana. Break a leg, folks! And first on – *Hukareka*!'

The opera house erupted into cheers. We kept our hands under our bums. Clap for Hukareka? No fear.

The curtains opened. The stage was empty. On came Hukareka, proud and vigorous, executing that amazing scissors pattern. 'Karangatia ra, karangatia ra –' They moved in double time, hands outstretched and quivering, claiming the stage with assurance and authority.

'They *are* good,' Aunt Sarah nodded. 'They're going to be hard to beat.'

As the competition continued, Aunt Sarah revised her opinion. *Everybody* was going to be hard to beat.

'Ko Ruaumoko e ngunguru nei –' The L.D.S. Mahia men chanted. They were on one knee, gesticulating and slapping their chests red from every slap.

'Au, au, aue ha, *hiii*.'

The crowd was going wild. Old men were leaping into the aisle to face the men on the stage, confronting them and encouraging them to greater heights of vigour.

After Manutuke and L.D.S. Mahia came Hauiti and Whangara, and Aunt Sarah had been right; spurred on by the excellence of Hukareka, all the finalists had targeted *them* and were really pulling out the stops. Not only that, but every time the curtains parted the stage was empty. Everyone was copying Hukareka.

'Not fair, judge!' Agnes Poata called. 'They're all pinching our act.'

Hauiti had even gone one better, incorporating the entire marae ceremonial of welcome into their entrance – a karanga by the women, followed by a haka pulling everyone on to the marae, then the action song itself.

'E te hokowhitu atu kia kaha ra –'

The judges sat up in delight.

'Hauiti is *really* good,' said Nani Mini Tupara, who was sitting with us. She saw that Hauiti had changed their poi as well – a poi describing the coming of the canoes to Aotearoa. She burst into long applause.

'E ki! E ki!'

This was a moment that the Maori heart lived for – when music, words and action blended in perfection and brought the past surging like a sea into the present. My heart caught in my throat in recognition and thankfulness that I owed my life to those intrepid vikings of the South Pacific. The women in Hauiti's front row sat, using their short poi to mimic the motion of a canoe's prow plunging through the water. In the second row the women also sat and used the medium-long poi to depict the spray from the prow. Behind the women, the men were standing with peruperu sticks making paddling motions through stormy waves.

'Ka pai tena!' everyone yelled.

Whangara had their work cut out to claim the stage for themselves –

'Uia mai koia whakahuatia ake, ko wai te whare nei e? Ko Te Kani!'

By the time interval came, Aunt Sarah was looking sick. The foyer was buzzing. By common consent tonight was better than last year.

'We can only do our best,' Aunt Sarah said bravely as she exchanged mournful glances with the two tutors for Mangatu and Waihirere, who were also looking green at the gills.

Then the bells rang for the second half.

'Ah well, ka ka kakakaka –' Suddenly Aunt Sarah clutched her throat in horror. Halfway through saying goodbye to her friends, she had lost her voice.

Panic struck. The haka team relied on Aunt Sarah to set the note and volume for our items.

'Karangatia ra, powhiritia ra,' Mangatu sang –

Upstairs, Aunt Sarah was doing a dumb show. 'Where's a doctor?' she mouthed. 'Somebody get a doctor.'

'Pa mai to reo aroha,' Waihirere sang –

And there was Aunt Sarah, eyes bulging. 'Take me to hospital. Maybe they can operate in half an hour, stitch me up and bring me back in time for our performance.'

'Kapanapana,' Manutuke sang –

'I'm dying,' Aunt Sarah whispered.

Then it was time for us to go downstairs. Aunt Sarah heaved herself from one row to the next, as if on her way to bear testimony. It was clear to the entire audience that something was wrong in the state of Mahana. With heavy hearts the haka team went backstage. Aunt Ruth distributed the capes. We tied them on. Aunt Ruth sighed and turned to Haromi. Was that a wink?

'You better do the karanga for your mother,' Aunt Ruth said.

Did I forget to tell you that, as far as Aunt Sarah was concerned, there was only *one* star – herself?

'Oh no she won't!' she said, finding her voice. Have somebody else shine? Her own daughter? Get off the grass. She was her bossy self again.

'Okay everybody, *on stage.*'

But what about our new entrance song! The one we had been practising so hard?

'Everybody before us has done their entrance that way. Let's be different.'

So it was that when the curtains swished regally aside, there we were, in our long cloaks, in a V position. I couldn't see beyond the footlights, but the roar of approval was deafening.

Good old Mahana. Let the others be flashy. You could always count on Mahana to be solid!

We began our traditional chant. Not a muscle moved. Let other groups move if they wanted to – we were Mahana! Again there was a roar.

Then Aunt Sarah moved to the centre of the stage and let it rip. Everybody held on to their hats. The voice that could cut a ton of butter was made for the karanga. When revved up and covering all the notes from A to G, that same voice could circle the world.

Aunt Sarah was standing in the middle of the stage. To both sides of her, the wings of the V formation moved backward and forward, simulating the flying motion of a giant bird. Our long cloaks had been cleverly designed to look like black and white feathers. The women began to stamp their feet. No sound at all except for Aunt Sarah's voice, climbing to the stars. The men began to slap their chests. Aunt Ruth joined Aunt Sarah, her voice trying to catch up to Aunt Sarah's and finally intertwining with it to go higher into the heavens. Both men and women began to swing at the hips, our piupiu crackling like static electricity.

Haromi's sweet soprano came out of nowhere, speeding like a sparrowhawk after Aunt Sarah and Aunt Ruth, carolling up and beyond the universe. The three voices took the lid off the Opera House.

We began to sing: 'E Ngata e, titiro koe ki a matou –'

We lifted our arms heavenward, following after the three voices as they soared through the night sky. We searched for our ancestor among the stars and moons and, when we found him, we reached for him – Look at us, Apirana, your great work lives on.

This was our trump card. Our action song – a tribute to Ngata himself.

For a moment there was stunned silence. Then whistles of approval and foot tapping was heard throughout the hall.

The women sang – 'Titiro atu koe e Ngata!' The men sang – 'E Ngata e!'

The women sang – 'Titiro ki nga mahi ora!'

The men sang – 'E Ngata e!'

We brought the house down.

It would be nice to report that we won. We didn't. Neither did Hukareka. Hauiti got the palm.

However, both we and Hukareka were commended, and the Mahana action song was singled out for special praise. The judges said, 'Mahana's waiata a ringa showed both traditional and contemporary elements. Of particular note was the song's tune which indicated that Mahana was not afraid to embrace the music of today's young generation.'

For many years after, Aunt Sarah swore black and blue that even when we were practising the song she hadn't known the tune was 'See You Later Alligator'.

36

That winter, the competition between Mahana and Hukareka escalated. Apart from the haka competitions and women's hockey games there were great battles on the rugby field. When Mahana men's rugby team were drawn to meet Hukareka senior men at Rugby Park, excitement was feverish.

Grandfather's approach to training was merciless. Two weeks before the game against Hukareka he had the team running every night from Waituhi to Patutahi and back – in hobnail boots.

On the first night of the marathon runs the rest of the family watched and tried to keep the mood light as the men assembled on the road outside the homestead. They were nervous – with good reason. Those from whom the scrum would be chosen were in the front row of runners. They included Uncles Matiu, Maaka, Ruka,

Aperahama, Ihaka and Albie, and the sons of Ihaka Mahana. Behind them were the potential backs: Dad, Pani and Mohi – a new inductee – and a good number of the Whatu clan. Grandfather Tamihana sat in the De Soto with Aunt Ruth in the driver's seat.

'Keep the speed at five miles an hour,' Grandfather instructed her.

She started the car. 'Move out!' she called.

The men began to run in front of the car. The first half hour was easy as everybody chugged along at a steady mile every twelve minutes. After that, some of the men began to feel the strain. The horn of the De Soto blared. They had to regain their wind pretty fast. The option was to be run over by the De Soto.

Grandfather's rationale was that if the team could run at normal speed with heavy footwear, they would run twice as fast when they had their lighter rugby boots on. He did not doubt the strength in the men's upper bodies. Shearing, farming and fencing kept shoulders, chest and upper arms at optimum strength. Put a Mahana scrum down on a field and nothing could move it – the Mahana scrum could push the opposing scrum from one goal post to the other if it had to. The clan's weakness, however, had always been in motive power. Sure, the Mahana backs were speedy, but they couldn't keep the speed up. Thus the rugby team learned to apply the same tactics as the women's hockey team – get out there, *hit* the other side with all you had in the first half and get all the tries you could while you still had the legs to do it. The infusion of men from the Whatu family, who had more leg power and stronger running skills, was another of Grandfather's tactics. A third was to hope that some star centre or winger would turn up to work in the Mahana shearing gangs – Tobio had been one and Pani was the latest in line – or graduate like Mohi from junior football. The last hope was to pray to his American angel. Meantime, training was relentless. *Sting* was needed in the backline.

The night before the game against Hukareka, the family met with the team in the drawing room of the homestead. The atmosphere was strained. Mum was holding Dad's hand. Pani was standing beside Miriam until Grandfather sent a message via Mohi from the throne that he should take a few steps back. Pani crimsoned.

Grandfather knelt to pray. 'Oh God our eternal father,' he began. 'Tomorrow our rugby team has its big game. Succour our team and, if it be Thy will, bring victory to us, Amen.'

With a sigh, Grandfather stood up again. 'Okay, boys, get a good night's rest.' He gave a slight smile. 'Early to bed, no drink, no smoke and no sex.'

Later, while everybody was inside having a drink of cocoa, I went outside for air. I had found Grandfather's prayer and the constant drawing of battle lines to include Heaven somewhat claustrophobic. Did everything have to include God?

I was watching the moon when Grandfather came across to me from the verandah. A mood of arrogance possessed me.

'Why didn't you pray for a saviour?'

'Ae, we need a Jesse Owens,' he laughed. His voice was good-humoured and relaxed.

I looked at him, incredulous. 'Jesse Owens is black.' In our church, black men could not hold the priesthood.

'So?' Grandfather asked, puzzled.

'He bears the mark of the children of Ham. You wouldn't want a man like that in your godly team, would you?'

Take *that*, you bastard.

'E hara, grandson,' Grandfather sighed. 'Do you want a fight? You know I'm stronger.'

'You might be stronger,' I answered, 'but that doesn't make you always right.'

'Right? What do you know about right and wrong? You live a little longer, and maybe you'll get to be wiser.'

I wasn't going to take *that* one lying down. 'Why is it that older people always think that just because we're younger we don't know something? Your way of being right is to always say *we* are wrong, to keep us from knowing anything about the world outside Waituhi or to try to deny the world is changing. You can burn all the books you want, Grandfather, but that won't stop us. Nor will we believe anything you say, for instance, about the mark of Ham, just because you say so. You don't hold the power of life and death over us.'

Grandfather stared at me. 'We are a family of God,' he said, 'and I am the leader. Whether you like it or not, Himiona, I lead according to my beliefs and my faith in God that we will prosper *if* we obey His commandments. There's always got to be somebody who leads and others who follow. I'm the one who decides.'

'And if I don't like your decisions?'

A star fell from the sky.

'Then one of us,' Grandfather said, jabbing at me with a closed fist, 'is going to lose.'

The next day Grandfather hired two buses so that everybody from Waituhi, including Maggie and old Uncle Pera, could come to the game. This was how he distributed his largesse. When the buses arrived at the field, Grandfather was there to greet everyone as they alighted. He was like an Italian godfather, his wife by his side, waiting while everyone kissed his hand or embraced him. I marvelled anew at his charisma.

'They don't play rugby like they did in our day,' the old-timers said to Bulibasha as they stepped off the bus.

Grandfather was magnanimous. 'Let's see how the youngsters shape up anyway.'

Grandfather was so clever to have the old ones there. Whatever happened out on the field, nothing could damage Grandfather's mana. If the team lost, the old ones would say, 'There, didn't we tell you? These young ones are not as good as Bulibasha was.' If the team won, the old ones would say, 'Aha! You see? It's Bulibasha's training that has won the game.' He was the reference point by which all history was judged.

Just as the Waituhi crowd was seating themselves, the Hukareka supporters arrived. Rupeni Poata had travelled on the bus with his people and, as he stepped down, he offered his hand to Poppy. Laughing, she accepted his assistance and bowed prettily to him. At that instant I looked at Grandfather and Grandmother – and I saw Grandmother sway, as if she were a reed in the wind. A slight swaying motion, and that was all.

The Waituhi oldies pretended not to see the Hukareka oldies as they ascended the stand.

Uncle Pera started sniffing. 'Can you smell anything?' he asked Maggie.

'Yes,' she said. 'It's coming from *that* side of the stand.'

The Hukareka oldies weren't going to take that. 'Oh is that so!' one of them replied. 'How strange that the wind is blowing from *your* direction to ours. Somebody forgot to wipe their bum before they got here.'

Women could get away with saying such things in a way that men couldn't, but Maggie's feathers were ruffled. She scowled and was just about to reply when Zebediah Whatu said, 'Don't waste your time, Maggie. They're not worth it.'

The grandstand soon divided into *us* and *them*, a definite space ran right between the two factions. I felt surrounded by refugees from an old people's rest home.

'Let's get outta here,' I muttered to Andrew.

He nodded and we raced down the steps as more Hukareka people came up. Immediately I barrelled into Tight Arse Junior and Saul, and we began to trade blows. Saul got a lucky punch in and I reeled away, but somebody caught my arm in a vice to stop me from falling. He was short, squat and ugly.

Shit, Rupeni Poata.

'Hey, watch it, boy!' he laughed.

I coloured and pushed away from him. My heart was thudding in my chest like a cannon. Before Rupeni Poata could say anything more, I was off and away.

Later I remembered that his face had a scar running diagonally across the left cheek. Yet, in the story that Aunt Ruth had told me, when Grandfather Tamihana stole Grandmother Ramona away it was Grandfather who was slashed across the face. I raised the question with Andrew.

He shrugged. 'Maybe Grandfather's scar has faded,' he said.

The battle began in the dressing room under the stand. Nobody knows who started it, but somebody on one side said, 'Hey, I didn't know their cocks were so small.' His friend only made it worse by saying, 'Yeah, but their arseholes are huge, man.'

The inference to homosexuality was anathema to Maori men: the first punch-up of the day erupted. The fisticuffs were short, sharp and vicious, and Mohi ended up minus a tooth.

'Oh shit shit *shit*,' he cursed, spitting blood. He had a date that night and would have to keep his mouth closed whenever he smiled.

That was not the end of it. Everything quietened down for a second, then someone on the other side said, 'I went out with one of their women once.'

'Oh yeah?' his mate said.

'What a dog she was, man, even with a pillow over her head.'

This time, when the fists flew, it was a Hukareka man who was downed by rabbit punches to his kidneys.

'Cut it out,' the ref yelled, 'or the game is off before we even start.'

The ruckus was heard in the stand above the dressing rooms. Grandfather and Rupeni Poata looked at each other, and came down to see what the problem was.

'Tell your boys to back off each other,' the ref said.

Rupeni Poata bowed in assent. 'A truce for the day?' he asked Grandfather.

'Yes,' Grandfather answered.

'I want a clean game out there,' Rupeni Poata told his team.

Clean game, ha. He was such a double-faced bastard – just like Scarpia in *Tosca*, who tells his lieutenant to use blanks rather than real bullets in the mock execution of the hero Cavaradossi. When the squad fires, Cavaradossi falls down dead.

When the teams came out of the dressing room, World War Three was only narrowly averted.

'Come on the maroon!' the Mahana oldies yelled.

'Come on the black!' the Hukareka oldies responded.

'Maroon!'

'Black!'

'*Maroon*!'

'*Black*!'

The ref threw a coin in the air.

'Heads,' Caesar Poata called. Heads it was.

The Hukareka team took the advantage by electing to play with their backs to the sun.

'You'll need more than the sun to help you,' Uncle Pera yelled. He was a cocky little terrier lifting his hind leg against a fence post.

The strong, fierce Hukareka forwards were like racehorses champing at the bit. They grouped around Augie, Tight Arse Senior and Alexander Poata. Caesar Poata took the kick-off. The Hukareka supporters roared their approval.

The game began.

From the very beginning there was no doubt that Mahana was the heavier side. When the ball was kicked off, a solid wall of Mahana men was waiting underneath. The Hukareka forwards, expecting to dent that wall, bounced off like rubber balls.

'E koe! *E koe*!' the Mahana supporters yelled. They loved nothing better than a show of strength.

The ref ordered a scrum-down. Mahana to put in the ball. Mohi, at halfback, zapped the ball in quickly. The Mahana forwards gouged the ground like bulls, goring the ball back through the scrum to where Mohi was waiting. He was downed by his opposite half.

'Offside, ref!' the Mahana supporters screamed.

The ref agreed. Mahana got to kick the ball. My father Joshua took the kick. He found touch deep in the heart of Hukareka territory.

Good old Josh, the oldtimers nodded – almost as good as his father at kicking the ball.

Now a lineout. The throw-in was crooked. Another lineout was ordered. The whistle. Another scrum. The suspense was killing as each side tested the other, trying to probe for weaknesses.

Rupeni Poata went down to the sideline. Seeing this, Grandfather followed him down.

'Wait for the break, boys,' Rupeni said.

'Settle down, boys,' Grandfather said. 'Settle down. There's plenty of time. Plenty of time.'

And wasn't that just the best advice, the Waituhi oldtimers agreed. Bulibasha was the King of Rugby all right.

Out of nowhere Hukareka made the break. A lucky possession at the lineout. Quick spinning of the ball along from first five-eighth to second five-eighth –

Look! Titus Poata at halfback had slashed around as an extra man in the backline, drawing the Mahana opposite number to him before passing the ball out to Alexander Poata at centre –

Alexander kicked ahead and over the Mahana backs and was chasing after the ball. Whu, he was fast.

But there was good old Josh streaking over to get the ball on the bounce and –

Good boy, Josh! Takes after his father all right. Kicking for touch again, way down the side and back into Hukareka territory.

Great rugby, man. Not as good as the old days, but good to see the ball moving around. Somebody better keep an eye on Alexander Poata, though. Man, he was dangerous.

The whistle blew for halftime. The score was nil-all. The frustration on the field and off was reaching fever pitch. The atmosphere was heavy, like a front before the weather changes. Grandfather kept an unperturbed exterior, but I knew he was worried. He had expected Mahana to be up by at least ten points.

'You're doing good,' Grandfather said during his pep talk, 'but not good enough. I want to see more possession. I want to see more penetration by the forwards and better handling among the backs. Watch those Hukareka backs. They're opportunistic. They will take advantage of any breaks they can get. Ka tika?'

'Ka tika,' the Mahana men nodded.

Two minutes into the second half, the Hukareka backs made

another break and executed a scissors movement similar to their entrance on haka night. Titus Poata made a dummy pass and suddenly changed the direction of play by running *into* the gap between his position and second five-eighths. He cut through the lumbering Mahana defence players as if they were a piece of cloth. Before Mahana knew it, Alexander Poata had the ball and the Hukareka players were through and streaking for a try.

'Anei! Anei!' the Hukareka supporters yelled. Some of the women began a hula of delight, their ample bums wobbling like jelly. The stand started to sway with them. There were a lot of heavyweights among Hukareka women.

Caesar Poata took the kick at goal. Hukareka was ahead by 5 to nil.

Clouds began to gather above the space where Grandfather Tamihana was standing. I thought of the scene in *The Ten Commandments* where Charlton Heston looks up into the sky and calls, 'My God, my God, why hast Thou forsaken me?' God must have been listening, because four minutes later the Mahana forwards, led by Uncle Matiu, charged down the field with the ball. They pushed through the Hukareka men, knocking them aside like skittles. The try wasn't the most elegant in the history of rugby, but when Uncle Ruka put his hand over the Hukareka line and touched the pigskin down, bedlam erupted in the grandstand. There were *our* women doing the hula.

Dad converted the try. Five-all.

That was when the game took off.

Grandfather Tamihana gave a sudden cry. His bad leg buckled under him and he collapsed. The ref blew his whistle for the St John's men to assist. Rupeni Poata too went to Grandfather's aid. The whole of the Waituhi part of the grandstand were on their feet in alarm. Bulibasha was more important than the game.

Grandfather waved the helpers away and bravely he stood up. He indicated that he should like to be assisted up into the grandstand. A wave of applause greeted him. Tears sprang to Uncle Matiu's eyes.

'Our father's knee,' he gulped.

It was like the Mahana version of the rallying cry at the Alamo. As soon as the scrum went down it was obvious to the Hukareka players that Mahana had gone into top gear.

'Neke neke!' the scrum roared. 'Neke neke!'

My God they were thrilling – like an ancient warrior war party.

They pushed the Hukareka players before them, dribbling the ball as they went.

'Neke neke! Neke neke!'

Hukareka players came charging from all sides. No way could they get into that solid force and extricate the ball. On and on they went, until –

'Anei!' old Pera cried.

The scrum had pushed over Hukareka's goal line. Another try.

With a cry, Uncle Matiu held the football aloft – 'This one's for you, Bulibasha!' And slammed it into touch.

When Dad kicked that ball at the goal to convert the try there was no way he would miss. In one minute flat, Mahana had gone ahead 10 to 5.

At that point the focus on the part of Mahana for vengeance and attempts at resistance by Hukareka unleashed the old blood lust. When play resumed and the scrum went down, the curses and accusations from both sides about women, sisters and mothers could be heard in the grandstand. When the ball came flying out and the backs had already taken play halfway down the field –

Huh? Fists were flying back at the scrum.

'Break it up!' the ref yelled. 'Break it up!'

Tempers flared all over the field. Uncle Ruka and Titus Poata had their own private battle going – they butted and punched each other at every opportunity as if, by some process of attrition, one would knock the stuffing out of the other. Caesar Poata tackled Uncle Matiu. While Uncle was still on the ground, Caesar grabbed his balls and gave a strong *twist*. A few minutes later Caesar happened to be lying on the ground and Uncle Matiu happened to be trotting back onside. Oh dear, Uncle couldn't have seen Caesar because he ran over his thighs, stomach and chest in his sprigged boots –

'Oops, sorry chief, I didn't see you down there.'

Players were eyeing their assailants and taking every opportunity to pay back. They gave the bugger a shove as they went past. They brought their elbow up into his face. They chopped accidentally on purpose at his windpipe when the ref wasn't looking. Then my father Joshua scored a brilliant try. He ran from way back, joined the back line as extra man as it surged forward and dived over for our third try of the game. When he converted it, Mahana was 15–5 in the lead.

Then Mahana suffered its first casualty. At the next scrum, when the play moved on, Uncle Ruka remained on the ground, clutching his stomach in agony. The Mahana men went after Titus Poata, the bastard who had done it, and next minute three players had fists up and were brawling. Another two men hit the dust.

'That's enough!' the ref yelled, blowing his whistle. 'Quit it or I'm stopping the game.' Didn't anybody tell him that blowing his whistle wasn't going to stop a *massacre*? By the end of that little sortie, four players were being carted off the field and two reserves from each side were being called on.

Only one reserve trotted on for Waituhi. Where was Charlie Whatu? The ref wasn't waiting around. He blew the whistle to resume play. We were one man down. Hukareka scored and converted. Now Hukareka were only five points behind.

Uncle Matiu roared at me, 'Tell that *fucking* Charlie Whatu to get his arse *out* here!'

Andrew and I ran into the dressing room. St John's Ambulance men were treating the wounded. We found Charlie Whatu vomiting his guts out in the toilets.

'I've eaten some bad fish, boys. *Real* bad.'

Just then we heard a volley of booing from the Waituhi side of the stand. There was a drumming of outraged feet, and dust started to fall through the ceiling.

'What the hell's happening!' an ambulance man asked. 'Is that an earthquake?'

The door opened and Uncle Maaka appeared, swearing and cursing. He had been ordered off for a flying tackle. Our team was down to thirteen men. Oh shit.

Glory would have said, Do something.

Outside, I heard the Hukareka supporters screaming again as Alexander Poata, taking advantage of our misfortune, went over. 15-all.

I looked at Andrew. 'Be my guest,' he said.

I nodded. 'Take off your jersey,' I told Charlie.

Adults sometimes make the mistake of thinking that a fifteen-year-old boy is just a kid. If you're the fifteen-year-old in question, you know that you are a man – and most often you *look* like a man.

The ref saw me coming out of the dressing room wearing the Mahana jersey. He nodded, waited for play to go into touch and then waved me on.

'Are you crazy?' Mohi said. 'You'll get trounced out here.'

My father Joshua came up and said, 'Get off the field, son.' Blood was pouring from a cut on his forehead.

'I'm not your son,' I told him. 'I'm Charlie Whatu.'

Uncle Matiu understood. 'Ka tika, Simeon,' he said. 'Well, even Goliath was felled by David, ne? You don't happen to have a slingshot do you?' He laughed. 'You play at left wing. Any time you get the ball, *kick*. Or pass it to somebody else. Never mind about being a hero.'

I wasn't planning to be a hero. But in my own way I thought that my being on the field and making our side up to fourteen might make a difference. Even so I prayed to God, Please Lord keep the play on the *other* side of the field.

Boy, did He lay His bundle on *me*.

All the scrums seemed to be on my side of the field. Poor Mohi didn't know what to do. Whenever our scrum won the ball, he would pass it straight to the second five-eighths rather than me. Then, accidentally, he forgot I was there and shot the ball my way.

'Oh no,' he groaned, hiding his eyes.

He knew I was the worst kicker in the entire western world. What he had forgotten was that I was jack rabbit scared. No w*a*y was I going to be smashed to smithereens by those Hukareka men.

I saw a gap.

I went through with my eyes closed.

I took Hukareka by surprise and found myself in the clear.

Oh shit, what now?

Mohi was there. 'Pass it out!' he yelled. 'Pass it out!'

Believe me, I would gladly have done that, except Alexander Poata was marking him.

'Pass it out, you stupid fucker!' Mohi yelled again.

'Don't call me stupid, arsehole!'

I waited. Oh no. Now another two Hukareka players were zeroing in on me.

Come on, Alexander, come to me too. Now I knew what kamikaze fighter pilots felt like. But I'd done it. Alexander Poata joined the other two Hukareka players in chasing after me. Just before they slammed into me I let the ball go –

'All yours, Mo-'

It was no compensation to hear the roar as Mohi took the ball under his arm and, ten yards later, went over.

When the final whistle blew, Mahana had beaten Hukareka by 18 to 15. Grandfather came down to the dressing room to offer his

173

congratulations personally. He was pretty sprightly for a man who had collapsed at the sideline. He patted Mohi's back for his try.

Then, just as Grandfather was turning to leave, Pani called out, 'And what do you think of our little champ here?'

Grandfather paused. He looked at me as if he was seeing me for the first time. 'That was a stupid thing to do, boy. We could have been disqualified for the rest of the season.'

You're damned if you do and damned if you don't.

'Go easy on Simeon,' my father Joshua ventured.

'No, it's okay,' I jibed. 'I only went out there for the family. Not for anybody else. The family always comes first.'

The dressing room went quiet. I had gone too far again.

Just then, old Pera came hopping into the dressing room.

'Kei te pai, boys,' he wheezed. 'Good on you! Those Hukareka people are all having a good cry out there.' Then he saw me. 'E Himiona! That was a nice little run you had.'

He turned to Grandfather. 'Reminds me of the time when you were his age, eh? When you jumped in to help out a senior team. Just like him, eh –'

Wheeze, cough, splutter.

'Just like *him*.'

Afterwards, I said to my father Joshua, 'Dad, I'm sorry. I don't want to come between you and Grandfather Tamihana.'

He put a reassuring arm around me. His voice was thoughtful. 'You're not, son,' he said. '*He's* coming between me and my son.'

My father was growing up too. We turned to leave the dressing room, and there, suddenly, was Rupeni Poata. He looked amused.

'Well done, Charlie Whatu,' he said.

37

Shortly after the rugby game against Hukareka the weather cracked down with a vengeance. Gone were the colours of autumn; clouds brooded greyly over our landscape. Torrential rain came across the hills behind Waituhi, wave after wave of unforgiving assault. The rain funnelled down from the backcountry, following the contours of the land towards the Waituhi Valley. There, with a whoosh of landslips and erosion, the water poured into the Waipaoa.

'Wail-e-ree, I can hear the river call –'

My sister Glory and I would stand on the river bank, our faces whipped by the stinging rain. We had taken to singing the song from a western movie called *River of No Return* about a surly hero, a good-time girl and a young boy, and their adventures on a broad rolling river that roared across the screen from left to right. We felt the story had been about *our* river.

'If you listen you can hear it call, sometimes it's peaceful and sometimes wild and free –'

Mud so thick that you could walk across it surged and roared past us. Within its depths were logs as big as steamships. Trees as tall as two-storeyed houses cracked and yawed past in the yellow avalanche. Sometimes a dead sheep or horse, swollen like an obscene balloon, dipped and rolled within the water as if being basted in mud. The very ground we stood on thrummed with the turbulence of the Waipaoa. We knew that the river could be unforgiving. People trying to cross on horseback had drowned in the Waipaoa. A car had missed a bend, careered over and into its depths. Neither the car nor its driver was ever seen again. A rahui, a temporary prohibition, was placed on the river.

'I've lost my love on the river, gone, gone forever down the river of no return –'

We were a young boy and his younger sister standing on the river bank, in love with the river.

One morning, Red was missing from our herd of milking cows. When Glory found her, she was down the river bank. The front part of her body was out of the water, but the back half was stuck in the mud. The river raged around her, trying to suck her in.

'You've done this on purpose!' I yelled at Red. 'Just to make my day.'

Leaving Glory on guard, I ran back to the quarters, hitched up our stallion Pancho Villa and brought him to the river bank. I took a rope down to Red and tied it around her midriff.

'You stupid bitch!' I screamed at her.

'Mooo,' she answered unconcernedly.

To get the rope around, I had to get into the water itself. Suddenly a log or something hit me from behind. Glory screamed. Then Mum was there. She had seen me and Glory from the window of the quarters. She scrambled down the bank and joined me in the river.

'Here,' she cried. She had brought the whip with her.

'Glory,' I yelled, 'kick Pancho Villa to pull us out now.'

Glory jumped on to Pancho Villa's slippery back. 'Hup!' she screamed. 'Hup!'

Pancho Villa whinnied and strained and pulled too quickly. The rope *thwanged* and Pancho Villa reared in fright.

'Hold on, Glory!' I thought my sister would fly off and be gone, gone to the river. But Glory caught at Pancho Villa's mane and tried again.

'Hup! Hup!' My mother and I pushed Red from behind. Pancho Villa began to slip. I had to use the whip.

Dear God, direct the lash.

I laid the whip out and suddenly made it curl toward Pancho Villa's flank. The sting was enough to make him *jerk*. The mud gave a slow, slurping motion as Red's hind legs came free. She started to use her front legs to help herself out and up the bank, dragging Mum and me with her.

In all that time, not once did my mother say to let the cow go. Red was an important part of our lives. We depended on her for her good rich milk. Nor, when my mother and I emerged caked with silt and mud, was there any sentimental embrace. We had simply done our job.

My mother went back to the quarters and Glory and I carried on with the milking. Half way through, I found Glory shaking like a leaf.

176

'You won't ever leave me, will you, Simeon?'

'No.'

I thought of her, so small, kicking Pancho Villa and no doubt saving our lives.

'Ever ever ever?'

I held her in my arms. 'I promise,' I said.

Did Red thank us? Are you kidding? As I was milking her she arched her back and did a huge cowpat.

'Next time, you drown,' I said.

Later I went down to the river and gave a prayer of thanks to it for not taking us. Glory joined me.

'Wail-e-ree –'

As Dad predicted, our savings dwindled fast. With Grandfather's permission Dad left all the work at the homestead to me and went looking for work around the district.

My father was one of many men looking for itinerant work and he found knocking on doors a dispiriting business. Sometimes in the past he had been able to count on doing some fencing or horse breaking or mustering – always the worst stretch of fencing or the most vicious horses to break or the most difficult slopes to muster on – and he hoped that the quality of his work would be remembered. One night he came back with the news that he had managed to secure a one-man contract to cut scrub up the back of beyond.

The work was a six-week contract, and Dad decided to camp up there in a lean-to tent. Mum didn't like the idea, but there was no option. Dad saddled Pancho Villa and, pulling a packhorse with all his equipment and provisions, set off into the back country. During the first two weekends Mum and I joined him in the scrubcutting, taking up with us the provisions that would continue to support him.

The third weekend Mum and I arrived in the middle of torrential rain to find the lean-to vacant and the packhorse standing by with Dad's slasher and other equipment still tied to the saddle. My mother knew immediately that something was wrong. We rode down the track to the river.

'Joshua? Joshu-aaa!'

My mother gave a cry. She pointed through the rain. I couldn't make out what I was meant to be looking at. Then I saw that the track on the other side of the river had fallen away. I followed the slip and, there, at the bottom, was a small figure trapped beneath a fallen horse.

The swingbridge was down but that was no deterrent to my mother. She spurred her horse forward and into the torrent. 'Joshua! Kei te haere atu ahau ki a koe!' Of course I had to follow the crazy woman.

'Hang on, Huria!' my father cried. 'Let the horse bring you across.'

By that time I was busy trying to keep *my* head above water too. I saw a bend coming up and yelled at Mum, pointing it out to her. She nodded and started to urge her horse towards a place where the water was not running so strong. We both touched ground.

'You could have been killed,' Dad said.

'Well I wasn't,' she answered.

Two days before, Dad had been riding up to the scrub on Pancho Villa, pulling the packhorse after him. The rain was so heavy he didn't notice the unstable track, and the ground crumbled from under him. With a whinny of fear Pancho Villa tumbled down with the landslide. Dad tried to pull the horse's head around so that it pointed down. He thought he might be able to ride the stallion all the way to the bottom. But a sharp tree stump pierced Pancho Villa's stomach, ripping his guts out. Bawling, Pancho Villa spun and fell, pinioning Dad beneath its weight.

Pancho Villa was still alive. Huge blowflies were buzzing and maggots were already hatching in the dark stomach wound.

'I think my right leg is broken,' Dad said.

We set his leg with two branches and bound it tightly. Even so, he screamed and lost consciousness when we levered him out from under Pancho Villa.

'We only have two horses,' I said to Mum. 'We'll strap Dad onto my horse. You take him back to Waituhi. It's too dangerous for the three of us to cross the river together.'

She nodded. 'I'll come back for you tomorrow,' she said.

Just as they were leaving, my father's eyes flickered. His lips were quivering.

'I couldn't reach the –' He motioned to the rifle, still in its pouch, strapped to Pancho Villa's flank. 'Thank you, son,' he said.

He had loved Pancho Villa.

I watched until Mum had forded the river safely, pulling Dad's horse after her. On the other side my father motioned Mum to stop, as if he was waiting for something.

I went down to Pancho Villa, put the rifle to his head and pulled the trigger. The sound echoed around the hills.

My father's leg was fractured in three places. The doctor put a plaster cast on it to help the bone to knit, but Dad was worried about finishing the scrubcutting. We needed the money.

'I'll have to hand the job over to Pani,' he said. 'We'll share the contract money with him.' He and Mum were whispering in the bedroom.

'How many more weeks before the job's finished?' Mum asked.

Faith and Hope, followed by Glory, came to join me and listened through the wall.

'Three weeks, might be four.'

'Then I'll do it,' Mum said. 'I'm as good as you at scrubcutting. Four weeks is not long.'

'Kaore,' Dad answered. They began to argue.

Glory looked at me: Do something. I knew what she had in mind.

I took my sisters by the hand and we knocked on Mum and Dad's bedroom door.

'You should all be in bed,' Mum growled.

'Dad,' I said, 'there's no need for you to get Pani to do the work or for Mum to go out there for four weeks by herself –'

'Were you kids listening?' Mum asked, irritated.

'Do you think you can handle the milking?' I asked Dad.

'Ae,' he nodded.

'Then Mum and I will finish the scrubcutting together. Faith and Hope will take on her chores in the homestead. Together Mum and I should get the job done in half the time.'

'What about your schooling?' Dad asked.

'I'll only miss two weeks –' Glory jabbed me. 'Oh yes, and so will Glory. She wants to come with us.'

'Why?'

Glory was offended. What a silly question. 'I can cut scrub too,' she said.

The next morning Mum, Glory and I saddled up and headed into the back country. Dad said a prayer for us before we left. He was finding it difficult to let us go. All his life he had been the one to go out to work and now he was watching us take his place.

'The only reason why Glory wants to go,' Faith said, 'is to get a rest from the cows!'

Glory poked her tongue out.

'Look after your mother and your sister, son,' Dad said.

'We'll send Glory back in the weekend for stores.'

We left, moving quickly through the morning glow, over the hills, past the lake, climbing higher and higher. Just before we turned the bend which would obscure the homestead, Glory turned and called –

'Bye –'

Her voice echoed around the hills. It was just like the closing scene in *Shane*.

I wish I could say that the weather improved, but it worsened. Every morning we woke at six to face another day of rain. Cutting scrub was hard enough at the best of times, but working in the rain was many times worse. Mum was disheartened, but –

'Time to start, son,' she said.

We left Glory to make breakfast while we started on the scrub. Glory was always good at making a fire with only one match. We worked till eight, my mother always a little ahead of me. She *was* good at cutting scrub, and I remember how Dad often complained about her speed. He sometimes accidentally on purpose forgot to sharpen her slasher, just to slow her down. Glory brought us our breakfast – a billy of cocoa, fried bread and porridge – riding across the river with the food packed safely in the saddlebags. She stayed to help us until midday – and she was good too! But I can remember how Mum's lips trembled when, one day, she saw that Glory's hands were blistered and raw. At midday, Glory returned to the lean-to to make our lunch – usually mashed potatoes, pumpkin and sausages. Then back she would come, joining us until we stopped at four. By that time, sweat and rain had made us sodden.

My mother never liked riding back in the dark. She never liked camping out overnight either – a canvas tent was no protection from kehuas, not to mention Dracula. At nights, after dinner and sharpening our slashers for the next day's work, Mum was always in a hurry to put out the kerosene lamp so Dracula would have a hard time finding us.

Even though we were separated from our father and sister, Glory still kept up her usual custom of calling out –

''Night Dad, 'night Mum, 'night Faith, 'night Hope, 'night Simeon.'

'Goodnight Glory,' I answered.

The first weekend, just as Glory was saddling up to go back to Waituhi, we heard a voice shouting. 'Huria! Himiona!'

Coming up the hill to us was Grandmother Ramona. She had brought our stores, her sleeping gear and another slasher.

'More hands will do the job quicker,' she said. 'My bees are all nice and warm inside their hives and don't need me, and your grandfather is driving me around the bend with his being at home all the time.'

Grandmother Ramona brought kinder weather – a break in the rain. During that respite the earth warmed, the scrub dried out and became easier to cut. Although the work was hard, we established a rhythm which somehow heightened my senses to all that was happening: moments of beauty and humour as we worked together, epiphanies of illumination –

Glory, learning how to cut scrub left-handed because her right hand was swollen. Grandmother losing her footing, and laughing as she slipped and slid on her bum all the way to the bottom of the hill. My mother working ahead of us, never stopping to rest. Most of all, I remember three generations of women bending and chopping through the scrub, the steam curling off their workclothes as they ascended the hills. They wore wide-brimmed hats to stop either sun or rain from getting into their eyes, and layers of clothes to keep in their body warmth. On their legs, knee-high gumboots.

'We're your three women,' Grandmother said to me one day at smoko. 'Eh girls? We're all Simeon's women.'

I have never felt so proud.

Eight days after we had left Waituhi, we were finished. I put a match to the cut scrub. *Whoomph* and it burst into flame, bonfires of celebration. Then –

'Me haere tatou ki te wa kainga,' I said.

Time to go home.

38

Mum, Glory, Grandmother and I were glad to come down from the back country and see the smoke from the chimneys of Waituhi. Grandmother, despite her earlier reassurances, was worrying about her bees and decided to detour to her land. Mum, Glory and I continued along the gully which would take us to the homestead.

'Simeon,' Mum said, 'let Dad know we're on our way home.'

I lifted the rifle to the sky and let out two shots. The sharp reports surprised the air. When we reached the bend, pulling the packhorse after us, there was the Waipaoa River in the distance – and Dad and our sisters were racing across the paddocks to meet us. Our father was waving and yelling like a madman.

'Huria! Huria!'

We watched, laughing, as he came run-hopping on his crutches through the mud. My mother was still laughing when he pulled her from her horse. He kissed her with so much passion that she blushed –

'*Joshua*. The kids –'

After dinner that night, Aunt Miriam told me that Grandfather had been very scornful of Dad whilst we were away, saying things like, 'So your wife has to go out and work for you, eh Joshua?' or 'I suppose Huria wears the pants in the family now?'

The jibes had gone deeper than Grandfather could possibly have anticipated. In his own way, Dad started to rebel. One night he even took my side in one of my verbal skirmishes with Grandfather. This time I was having him on about the vexed question: when does life begin?

'Life begins when a baby takes its first breath,' he said.

'So abortion is all right then?' I answered.

'No, all life is sacred.'

'But you've just said that –'

'I *know* what I said,' Grandfather stormed.

Out of nowhere, Dad said, 'You don't have to shout, Father. My son was only asking a question.'

Grandfather stared at Dad open-mouthed. So did we.

When Glory and I returned to school, Mr Johnston was gentle in his reprimand.

'Just don't make this a habit,' he said.

Then Miss Dalrymple announced that she planned to take the senior school into Gisborne for a day's visit to some of the important industries and city departments.

'Some of you will be leaving school next year,' she said. She looked at Mita Wharepapa and I, both fifteen. 'You should know what possibilities await you in the big wide world.'

Ha! What possibilities could await any young Maori departing school at fifteen and without qualifications other than shearing or working on a farm?

The trip was an annual fixture, and the word was that the best tour to go on was to D.J. Barry's, the local manufacturer of aerated drinks – you got to taste some free samples. If you couldn't get on that tour, the one to Watties Canneries was second best. Try to avoid the visits to the abattoirs – stink, man – the Gisborne Harbour Authority or Gisborne City Council – bor-*ing*. At all costs, avoid the visit to the courthouse.

Guess who got picked for that?

'Simeon,' Miss Dalrymple said, 'would you give the speech of thanks, on our behalf, when we leave the courthouse?'

It wasn't a question either.

The only person who was pleased about the prospect was my mother Huria. When I told her about the speech she got it into her head that I had been singled out by sheer brilliance, and she gave the occasion more importance than it warranted.

'Simeon needs a pair of long trousers and a blazer,' she told Dad firmly. 'He's not a boy any more.'

It's true my school pants had seen better days, and I *was* growing. Dad agreed, but the money for the scrubcutting was slow in coming. There was no way there'd be money for clothes unless Grandfather was approached for an advance.

'We'll pay you back soon, Father.'

'It's a waste of money,' Grandfather answered. He was smarting over all the arguments we were having and all the corners I was pushing him into. I had developed the art of asking questions that had no answers or had not one but a number of answers. 'The boy is

183

getting too whakahihi. All this education is turning his head. You should take him out of school. Put him out to work like Mohi.'

'Is that your last word, Father?' Dad asked.

'Don't *you* start,' Grandfather warned.

So it was that my mother made her first visit that winter to Miss Zelda. She put on her hat and gloves and stood breathing deeply before entering the store.

'Why, hello Mrs Mahana,' Miss Zelda greeted her. 'Scott? Daisy? Mrs Mahana is here!'

Miss Daisy came scurrying from the back room. 'We haven't seen you for ages,' she said. 'We heard about your husband's accident. Is he recovering well?'

Mum was swaying back and forth. Sweat beaded her forehead. Her eyes glazed over.

'How can we help you, Mrs Mahana?'

'I – I – I –'

She had a piece of paper in her hands with my shoulder, waist and leg measurements written on it. Scott, noticing the paper, took it from my mother's hands and asked, 'Is this what you want, Mrs Mahana?' His voice was gentle and reassuring. He was a mild man who hid his gentleness behind glasses and a bluff exterior.

'I – I – ' Her eyes blinked. 'Yes. Thank – you –'

Pakeha customers came into the shop and, birdlike, Miss Zelda and Miss Daisy swooped on them.

'You take care of Mrs Mahana,' Miss Zelda told Scott.

'It's my department, anyway,' Scott said to Mum, escorting her along to menswear. Together they chose a suitable dark jacket and long trousers.

'Oh my,' Miss Zelda said when Mum returned to the front counter. 'You have such wonderful taste. Will you be paying by cash?'

'I – I –'

'Mrs Mahana would like to charge her account,' Scott said.

Miss Zelda's manner changed. 'Daisy?' she called. 'Is Mahana, Joshua, in the red?'

The Pakeha customers stopped to listen in. My mother looked down to the floor. Miss Daisy investigated.

'No, sister.'

'That will be all right then,' Miss Zelda smiled. 'It's only when our customers are in the red, Mrs Mahana, that we cannot advance credit. You understand.'

She was firm and businesslike. She took the ledger book and

entered, 'One blazer, £21; one trousers, £6, comes to £27 exactly –'
She wet the end of a pencil and began to inscribe the amounts.

Scott coughed. 'No, sister,' he said, 'the blazer is £15.'

Miss Zelda glared at him. 'It says *clearly* in the stock book
that –'

'It's my department, sister,' Scott reminded her. 'We have
overcharged Mrs Mahana by £6.'

Miss Zelda rubbed out her pencilled amounts and changed them.

'I wish you would run your department more efficiently, Scott.
What will our customers think, eh, Mrs Mahana?'

39

From the moment I boarded the school bus at Patutahi for our day
out in Gisborne, Haromi and Andrew kidded me mercilessly about
my new mocker – not that they had any reason to worry about my
eclipsing their style. They had scored the visit to D.J. Barry's.

'Why tempt Fate?' Andrew was intent on rubbing salt into the
wound as I fumed about having to go to the courthouse.

'And I'm the only Maori with the group going there,' I groaned.
Andrew shrugged his shoulders. 'Shit happens,' he said.

Miss Dalrymple was a stickler for being on time. We dropped
the other classes off on the way to the courthouse – the bus was
getting whiter and whiter – and at five to ten we were pulling up
outside.

'Should you be addressed by the judge, you must refer to him
as "Your Honour",' Miss Dalrymple said. 'This is the title by which
he is known. Everyone else may be addressed as either "Sir" or
"Madam". Our guide while we are at the courthouse is Clerk
Simpson and he may be addressed as "Sir".' On she went – blah blah
blah yackety yack. Slowly I was aware that she was looking directly
at me –

'*No Maori is to be spoken.*'

Jeez, can't a guy even breathe?

'I am very pleased to welcome you,' Clerk Simpson said as we
assembled outside the bus. 'Court is in session right now, but there
is so much else to see. I think we shall start in the chambers, shall
we?'

We followed him dutifully around the side of the building. Just then two policemen came out with a young man handcuffed between them. He was about nineteen, and Maori. Our eyes connected. I knew him immediately. He'd been Haromi's date on Christmas Eve.

'Oh dear,' Clerk Simpson said. 'I'm sorry about that, girls and boys.'

We watched as he was pushed across the front lawn. I heard Miss Dalrymple clucking away when Clerk Simpson told her, 'The boy has just been sentenced to jail for assault. He swore at his employer.' As the police van sped away, the young man's mother came running from the courthouse screaming his name.

'Mihaere! Mihaere!'

The chambers were cool and comfortable, gentlemanly and tastefully decorated. Photographs, diplomas and plaques adorned the walls, reminding me of the drawing room at the homestead. The judge came away from the courtroom to greet us.

'Judge Forbes,' Miss Dalrymple explained to us, 'has a short break before the court reconvenes. We are very lucky to have him say hello to us. Please thank him for taking the time.'

Thank you Judge Forbes Judge Forbes Forbes orbes orbes es.

His eyes twinkled.

'Well, ladies and gentlemen,' he said, 'thank you for coming to see me on the *right* side of the bench.'

Ho ho ho, what a funny fellow.

Judge Forbes proceeded to tell us how important he was, why justice was important and why the judicial system in New Zealand was the best in the world.

'Does anybody know why?' he asked.

'Because it is based on the Westminster system,' said Bobbie Brown, who had been primed to respond.

'And the Westminster system,' Angela Simpson continued, 'is practised throughout the British Commonwealth.'

'Very good,' Judge Forbes answered. He beamed at Miss Dalrymple. 'We may have the makings of two fine lawyers here, what?'

Haw haw haw, jolly boating weather and all that.

Just to show how *busy* and *important* he was, Judge Forbes asked Clerk Simpson to show us the schedule of cases he had dealt with during the month.

'Well,' he ended, 'I must read up on the next case. I understand you will be sitting in on my court?'

'Yes, Your Honour,' Miss Dalrymple answered. 'But we will be quiet, won't we, boys and girls?'

Yes Miss Dalrymple Dalrymple rymple pimple imple.

The judge swept out of the lobby, Miss Dalrymple bobbing as he went past. Clerk Simpson guided us to Judge Forbes' schedule. One by one we filed past and oohed and aahed at the number of cases on his plate.

JUDGE FORBES
Presiding Judge

9 am
White v. *Hakopa*
10.30 am
Crown v. *Wharepapa*
1 pm
Crown v. *Karaitiana*
2 pm
Williamson v. *Heke*

On and on and on. Page after page after page of cases involving being drunk and disorderly, murder, intent to obstruct justice, manslaughter, casting offensive matter in public, grievous assault, car stealing, domestic dispute, indecent behaviour, theft, petty larceny, land dispute, attempt to defraud, and so on.

'Simeon?' Miss Dalrymple interrupted. 'Don't take up all the time. Let someone else look.'

I stepped to one side. The rest of the class had their turn. When we had become suitably impressed Clerk Simpson said, 'Well then, let's go into the public gallery, shall we?'

We filed into Courtroom No. 1.

This was the place of judgment. Here in this large quiet room panelled with polished wood and hushed with the weight of legal process, people were put on display, like deers' antlers, their futures determined with a stroke of the gavel. Over there, higher than anybody else, was where the judge sat. In front of him sat the recording clerk. To the right and left were the prosecuting lawyer and the lawyer for the defence. At right a small corridor led to the room where the defendant waited to be called for trial. In front were the seats for the public.

'Not a word,' Miss Dalrymple hissed.

The public gallery was packed. I knew just about all the people

187

there. All of them stared straight ahead, down a narrow funnel of vision, as if afraid to see who was sitting left and right. That suited me fine. I hunched down, hoping I wouldn't be seen either. I felt as if I was on the wrong side.

The session that morning seemed to be one where the defendants had already pleaded guilty and were being processed for sentencing.

'How do you plead?'

'The defendant pleads guilty, Your Honour.'

'Fined £100.'

The judge lifted his gavel, and *bang*. A pair of antlers on the wall.

'How do you plead?'

'The defendant pleads guilty, Your Honour.'

'Term of imprisonment, one year.'

Bang, the gavel again. Another pair of antlers.

'How do you plead?'

'The defendant pleads guilty, Your Honour.'

This time the judge paused and looked gravely down at the defendant. 'Your crime is a particularly heinous one in our society, young man. Assault on another person with intention to commit grievous harm must carry with it the maximum penalty available to the law. Five years imprisonment.'

Bang. More antlers for the wall.

At each sentencing the defendant bowed his head and nodded as if all this was to be expected. His family group did the same. They were passive in their acceptance of the law and of te rori Pakeha. The Pakeha's place was to be the punisher and the Maori's place to be punished. There was a sense of implacability about the process, as if *they* were always right and *we* were always wrong.

Why didn't we fight back? We didn't know how.

Bang Bang BangBangbang ang ang

By the end of the court session my whole world had been shattered. When Miss Dalrymple asked me to give my speech of thanks to Judge Forbes I shook my head –

'No.'

'Just do it,' Miss Dalrymple commanded. The judge was still in his chair, waiting.

Do it do it it ititit it.

The courtroom was not quite cleared. A family group was sitting waiting for their son to come out from the holding room. He had been found guilty of indecent exposure. I knew the family and was embarrassed to have witnessed their shame. For most of the proceedings I had kept my eyes on the floor, flexing and unflexing my fists.

'Simeon!' Miss Dalrymple hissed again.

I wasn't angry, really. Just lost and bewildered. I looked at the judge in his ridiculous wig and –

'Sir, I am fifteen years old. I mean no disrespect. All my life people have been saying to me, "Do this, do that," and I have for the most part appreciated their advice. But there must come a time when you have to do something not because other people tell you to but because *you* want to do it yourself. I have come to that time in my life.'

I tried to swallow. There was a huge stone in my throat.

'Your Honour, I want to make choices for myself. To say "No" if I do not believe what is happening is right, even if other people are telling me to do it and that it *is* right. To say "Yes", if I believe it is right, even if other people are telling me don't do it. I have to start listening to *me*. I thank you for enabling our class to visit. But I cannot thank you for what we have seen today.'

By this time Miss Dalrymple was trying to get me to shut up.

'There is something wrong, Your Honour, with a place like this, if the majority of the cases which come before you are Maori and are placed by Pakeha against Maori. I cannot thank you for being part of a court which enables this to happen. I cannot.'

Someone in the family group began to sob.

'How can I thank you for all the Maori people you have jailed or sentenced for one crime or another? All those names in your book, do you know that I am related to all of them? Or that I know them? Sir, what is more, I know them as good people, not as names that you bang your hammer at or put in prison or make pay huge fines. That boy we met when we were just coming in, he was my cousin's boyfriend, Your Honour. And what was his crime? That he swore at his employer! You call that assault? Are you telling me he should be sent to jail for that? If I thank you, what am I saying to my relations? My aunts, uncles and cousins who have appeared before you this month? That they deserved it? They didn't –' It was a cry from the depths of my heart. '*They didn't.*'

I was almost done.

'Therefore, Your Honour, I will *not* thank you.'

189

Miss Dalrymple was grim-faced as she apologised to Judge Forbes. He was thoughtful and answered –

'No, the boy is entitled to his opinion. I commend him for that.'

I was told to go out to the bus *at once* and wait there.

The family group of the boy found guilty of indecent exposure was waiting beside the kerb, hoping to see him before he was taken away. The boy's mother nodded at me, and as I passed she laid a hand to stop me. She kissed me and I felt her tears against my cheek.

Then somebody else was there. I knew who it was.

'Ka pai tena korero,' he said. 'Ka pai. Kia kaha e tama. You spoke very well, young one. Very well. Your grandmother would have been pleased. Continue to be strong.' He shook my hand and motioned that we should hongi. Then Saul Poata came out, and his mother, Agnes Poata, began to call to him.

I touched my nose and forehead in hongi with Saul's grandfather – Rupeni Poata.

40

It was my misfortune that somebody from Waituhi saw Rupeni Poata shaking my hand outside the courthouse. When I tried to explain to Grandfather, he wouldn't listen. He raged and vented his anger on Mum and Dad for allowing me to go to Gisborne that day. His reaction, however, only added to my father's rebellion against him. Grandfather insisted that Dad give me a beating, but Dad refused, saying I was too old to be thrashed.

Then, one night, I heard Mum and Dad whispering together. When Glory joined me to listen – I put a glass against the wall to hear the conversation more clearly – we realised that something was going *on*.

'We can't keep on like this,' Mum said.

'We must bide our time,' Dad answered.

'For how long?'

'When the right moment comes, we'll take it.'

At the family gathering that month, the moment came. Our father, haltingly, took it and changed our lives for ever.

Dad made his move just as the meeting was ending. The korero had, as usual, mainly been between Grandfather and Uncles Matiu, Maaka, Ruka and Hone. The rest of us – the younger aunts and uncles, spouses and children, grandchildren and friends – were the respectful audience, bound together by a common fear that Grandfather would turn his attention to us – and by relief that we had escaped some censure or other. Grandfather had asked my uncles to give an accounting of the contracts for the next season – how many contracts we had received, how many still had to be negotiated, whether there were any problems now that the agreement with the Poatas had broken down, and so on. The meeting had subsided into small-talk and my aunts were getting up to go into the kitchen to prepare the family kai.

Then I noticed Miriam, who was sitting scared-eyed and staring across the room at Pani. Grandfather was laughing with Mohi, remembering the brilliant sidestep the boastful bastard had made in the rugby game against Hukareka. Sitting next to Grandfather, Grandmother Ramona was serene and as silent as always – Grandfather and his Queen. From the corner of my eye I caught again that scared-eyed look of Aunt Miriam's, this time directed at my mother. Aunt Miriam was in on something.

'Kaati ra,' Grandfather Tamihana said. 'Kua mutu?' I saw the light dying in Aunt Miriam's eyes. 'Are we finished then? Good. Let's have the karakia and grace. This champion of ours –' he slapped Mohi proudly on the back, 'he's getting hungry, ne?'

Grandfather went to kneel in karakia. We were following him down on our knees. Somebody coughed. Everybody looked up. Grandfather, surprised, wobbled and then stood. So did the rest of us. Aunt Miriam's eyes widened with terror as if to say, No let's forget the whole thing.

Somebody coughed again. Grandfather's eyes swept the room. He saw my father Joshua next to my mother. Both of them were still kneeling, their eyes on the floor.

'Is that you, Joshua?' Grandfather asked. He seemed surprised. His voice was dark. 'He aha te mate?'

My father and mother inched on their knees toward Grandfather. I saw my mother breathing deeply, her eyes firmly closed. When our father began to speak she exhaled a soft sigh.

'I would like a piece of land, Bulibasha,' Dad said.

I should remind you that my father was already thirty-three and my mother thirty-one. Dad was the ninth-born of Bulibasha and Grandmother Ramona. As far as male succession was concerned, he was the seventh son. His eldest brother Matiu was ten years older than he was. His eldest sister Ruth was six years older. In the way of all things he could be easily overlooked –

'Oh, what's your name again? Joshua?'

When the eldest children grow up, they are the ones who inherit the mana, the prestige, the land, the succession. When that is gone, what is left for the younger ones? The ones like my father, Joshua, or my spinster aunts Sephora, Miriam and Esther? Born to elderly parents, their role is to stay at home when the others have left. To look after the parents and, in the case of my aunts, to remain unmarried.

But let me ask you, can you realise what it must be like to be the seventh and last son. To be on your knees in front of your elder brothers and sisters? In front of your parents?

Yet there he was, Joshua who never said anything or asked for anything. Thirty-three years of age. Ninth child. Seventh son.

Joshua.

Grandfather returned to his seat next to Grandmother Ramona. He waited.

'Korero mai, Joshua,' he teased. 'Korero mai.'

My father began. 'All my life, Father, I have lived in this house and I am grateful for you and mother Ramona for the roof you have put over our heads and the food you have put in our bellies. The time has come when, like my brothers and sisters before me, I should leave your kindness and make my own home.'

His words were stilted. Careful. Respectful. I wished he would look up at me so that I could flash him a sign, Yes Dad, you can do it.

'What,' Grandfather asked, amused, 'have you done that I should even consider your request?'

'I have done nothing –' my father answered.

'Good,' Grandfather interrupted. 'I'm glad you are aware of it.'

My father's elder brothers smiled.

'Except,' my father continued, 'to obey your every wish.' His voice was like a guitar string struck right at its centre where the note would vibrate loudest. 'Like my brothers before me I have obeyed you in every respect. Like my sisters before me I have acknowledged and loved your authority. I have stayed under your roof and been your hewer of wood and tiller of soil and have done all of this because of my love for you and my mother. But the time has come when Huria and I –'

'Did she put you up to this, Joshua?' Grandfather asked. 'Is she the one who has turned your face against me?'

My mother shook her head. 'No, Bulibasha,' she said. 'We do not turn our faces away from you. We have four children now and the quarters we live in are too small for a growing family.'

'I will build another room on to the quarters.'

'We wish to be on our own,' our father said.

Grandfather sighed. He was dismissive. 'Enough of this nonsense,' he said. 'I need you here, Joshua. I need you to cut the wood, to plough the soil, to bring in the meat, to look after me, your mother and your three younger sisters. If you go, who will do the man's work?'

The question hung on the air. I thought my father Joshua's cause was lost.

'I will do it,' a voice said.

Grandfather's head swivelled toward the voice. He gave a quick laugh of astonishment as Pani stepped forward.

'I will do it,' Pani repeated. He took his cap off his head, came forward and knelt beside Mum and Dad. 'It would be a great honour to serve your family, Bulibasha.'

Pani was handsome, shy and, at that moment, aglow with strength.

'But why would you do this?' Grandfather asked.

Pani turned crimson. 'Bulibasha, I wish to marry your daughter Miriam.'

'Miriam?' Grandfather laughed out loud. 'Surely, boy, you know she must be ten years older than you.' He turned to Miriam. 'How old are you, daughter? Thirty? Is your womb still ripe or has it already dried up?'

At that moment I hated Bulibasha more than I had ever hated him in my life.

'Why don't you ask for Esther?' Grandfather asked Pani. 'She's more your age.'

Pani lifted his eyes to Miriam. 'Although I have respect for Esther, as indeed I do for Sephora, my feelings for them are as I have for sisters. The one I love is Miriam.'

Made radiant by Pani's love, Miriam came and knelt beside him. Grandfather became very angry. He stared at my father and pointed a finger at him.

'You put your sister up to this,' he said. 'Well, it won't work. Even if I was able to let you go, where would you go? There is no land left. I have nothing to give you. Nothing. It has all gone to your older brothers and sisters. Yes, once there was land, a little piece of the broken biscuit that the Pakeha left us. But the major portion of that land has gone to Matiu, for he is the eldest and the one who will carry on after I am gone. And what was left has already been divided up. You were born too late, Joshua. There is nothing left.'

All I could feel were tears of frustration and my sister Glory jabbing me with her elbow: Do something.

What could I do? Nothing, except take Glory's hand and together with Faith and Hope go to kneel beside our father and mother, Miriam and Pani.

'We too ask this of you, Grandfather,' I said. 'If you won't take Pani, take me. I will remain behind if you let my parents and my sisters go.' Glory pulled at my arm. 'And Glory will stay too.'

Grandfather roared with laughter.

I began to rage inside at our helplessness – my mother and father, kneeling here with Aunt Miriam and Pani, they would never be able to get away. Never escape. Never.

Then Grandmother Ramona stood up.

'Enough, Tamihana,' she said. 'Stop playing with them like a dog does a cat.'

She began to walk across the room to where my mother and father were kneeling. She paused a moment beside them. The hem of her long skirt brushed beside my mother.

'You might not have any land left,' Grandmother Ramona said to Bulibasha, 'but I do.'

My mother gave a moan and began to shake her head. But Grandmother was firm. Her voice softened and she patted my father on the shoulder. My mother caught at the hem of her skirt.

'You can have *my* land, son.'

At the words, Grandmother swayed as if the giving of the land were a giving of some part of herself. My mother began to cry because she knew how Grandmother loved that land and its fruit trees and hives: it was Grandmother's heart and sanctuary.

Then Grandmother recovered. Resolute, she swept the room with her gaze. Her voice was authoritative.

'All of you are witness,' she said. 'The land down by the river I give to Joshua, Huria and their children.'

She was gone out of the room before Bulibasha could speak up against her.

41

At the end of that winter, my father Joshua and mother Huria moved Faith, Hope, Glory and me from the homestead to the land down by the river.

Grandfather was angry at letting us go, constantly arguing with Grandmother and trying to force her to change her mind. He gave my father Joshua more and more to do, saying it all had to be done before we left. Dad was stoic and patient, despite the fact that Grandfather always found a reason to delay our departure. Finally, exasperated by our wilful and stony silence, Grandfather said to Dad –

'Go then, go to your mother's land.'

Mum suspected, though would never say it, that Grandfather wanted us to suffer through next winter. There was little time to prepare the land for crops that would take bud and be ready for the next harvest.

Grandfather was compensated when Pani moved in to take my father's place. Poor Pani, he agreed to Grandfather's terms – after one year, Grandfather would offer him 'my daughter's hand in marriage' – without really knowing the extent of his impending servitude. Every morning he was up at six. He was always at Grandfather's beck and call. He did chauffeuring duties when required. If he was lucky he managed to get into bed by nine. One stipulation, however, Pani fought. This was that he was never to be alone in Miriam's company. Pani obtained half an hour after dinner to sit with Miriam on the verandah.

Love kept Pani at Grandfather's stern wheel for the agreed year. At the end of the year Grandfather did indeed offer his daughter's hand – but Sephora's hand and not Miriam's. Was not Sephora the eldest and therefore the one to be wed before her sister? There was something biblical about Grandfather's gesture, a rightness that was nevertheless vindictive to the course of true love. Yet Pani persevered and agreed to work another year for Miriam.

On the day we moved to Grandmother's land, my mother found it difficult to leave the quarters. She was a sentimental person and, as the afternoon wore on, became more tearful. No matter what it looked like or how small it was, the quarters had been the place to which she was brought as a young bride. Here she and my father Joshua had shared their passionate life and, from it, become the parents of four children. They had nursed, raised and loved us when we suffered through whooping cough, flu, an ailment which the Maori called puku and other sicknesses. On one occasion Mum had called in an old kuia with healing powers to succour the rasping breathing I developed – Grandfather would have had kittens if he'd found out. The kuia hooked a small finger deep into my throat and pulled out string after string of dry yellow phlegm.

A house, no matter how small or old, is filled with memories.

My spinster aunts were also unhappy about Mum and Dad leaving. We were moving only three miles down the road, but the farewells between Mum and Sephora, Miriam and Esther were agonising. The women had grown to depend on each other. Aunt Sephora, for instance, had been midwife at my birth when I came prematurely into the world. She had always considered herself to be my other mother. As for Aunt Miriam's romance with Pani, that would never have happened had it not been for Mum telling Miriam to take the chance and forget about the difference in age, that here was a young man who saw beyond physical years to the person beneath.

Our spinster aunts were afraid too. They didn't want to be left alone with Grandfather Tamihana, whose rages and periods of irrationality could never be anticipated. But Pani would be there, living in the quarters, and he would keep Grandmother and my aunts safe at the homestead.

Dad filled the car with all our possessions, a pitiful assortment of bedding, pots and pans, clothes and a few ornaments and trinkets, and drove on ahead while the rest of us walked along the road, herding Red in front of us. Glory rode Dad's palomino and pulled the packhorse behind her. Our dog, Stupid, kept barking excitedly.

Grandmother Ramona accompanied us. When we arrived at the land she asked if she might be given a moment to say goodbye to her bees. Of course we agreed, expecting that even though we lived there she would continue to come down to the meadow to keep her hives.

'No,' she said. 'When I gave you the land I relinquished all claim to it.' When she said it like that, my mother started to cry again, the tears streaming like a river down her face.

The sun was hot that day and the meadow was brilliant with spring daisies and other wild flowers. A slight breeze rippled the long stems, making waves of yellow and green. Grandmother Ramona was not wearing her beekeeping clothes. She walked into the middle of the field and stopped for a moment, breathing in the fragrance. Then she began to karanga to the bees, to call them hither –

'Haramai, haramai, e nga pi aroha haramai –'

At first there was silence. Then, from the four corners of the meadow rose a humming sound as wave after wave of bees came shimmering and swarming like golden clouds towards her. Grandmother lifted her arms, her lips and her face to the honey bees. They came to rest in her open palms, to kiss her lips and taste her tears.

Afterward, she said that she had only two requests. The first was that we would never cut the meadow. The second was that we would love the bees as she had loved them. They, in their turn, would give us the sweetest honey in the world.

Then Grandmother turned her back and started to walk away. I swear to you that the honey bees made such a sound, such a loud buzzing, that you would think they would *die* of love.

Since then, whenever I have had to let go of anything or anybody in my life, I have always tried to remember Grandmother Ramona on that day.

She never returned.

That night we had the earth for our floor, the stars for our ceiling and the Waipaoa rustling at our doorway. Strangely enough, my mother was not as perturbed about sleeping in the open as I thought she would be.

'No vampire in his right mind is going to turn up when we have all of Grandmother's bees to protect us,' she said.

There was a derelict house on a small western rise which Dad planned to restore for us to live in. It had three bedrooms, a verandah which had been partially closed in as a fourth bedroom, sitting room, dining room and kitchen. One wall was completely exposed and would have to be rebuilt, and the roof over the back part of the house was missing. Elsewhere there were areas which would have to be patched. There was no bathroom or toilet, and washing would have to be done in the river. Nor was the old outside windmill operable; we would have to repair the vanes and pump to enable water to be drawn up from the river along the rise to the house.

The next morning, when the sun came up, we were ready to begin. The house had been used for storing hay and old clapped-out equipment – heavy pieces of iron, car and tractor parts, all the junk associated with farming. Sheep, birds and dogs had left copious droppings. Huge spiders' webs were strung in all the rooms. The first task was to clean the whole place out –

'Let's get to it,' Dad said.

I had been given another job – the digging of a drophole for the outhouse toilet.

Just then we heard the sound of cars driving up the track. Our gang, Mahana Four, had come to help us – Uncle Hone and Aunt Kate, Aunt Ruth and Uncle Albie, Pani and Miriam, Sephora and Esther, Sam Whatu and his sons Willie, David and Benjamin, Auntie Molly, Haromi, Peewee and Mackie.

'Don't tell Father,' Uncle Hone said.

'My name is Charlie Whatu,' Aunt Ruth winked.

'Just keep Mother Ramona's damn bees away from us!' Aunt Kate added.

By nightfall, the place had been swept and scrubbed, and repairs made to broken window sashes and doors. David and Benjamin had helped me with the drophole and Uncle Sam had rigged up a small private enclosure as a bathroom. An inventory had also been made of what had to be done to the house – new roofing, replacement of rotten wallboards and floorboards, glass for broken windows, new doors and so on. We also needed some fences; Mum wanted to keep some fowls. The list seemed endless.

'There's a lot of work to do, Josh,' Uncle Hone said. 'I'm glad you've got plenty of money.'

My mother and father tried to keep up a brave front, but the *real* situation was that we were hardpressed for cash, what with the repairs on the car and the extra tithe we were paying.

Then David said, 'Hey, I think Dad's got an old window frame you could have.'

And Benjamin said, 'What about that old roofing iron stacked behind old Pera's place? He doesn't want it any more. That'll do for now for the holes in the roof.'

Auntie Molly said, 'I've got an old wood oven you could use,

Huria. Oh yes, and a bath that is too small now – and don't *anybody* make a crack about that, thank you.'

Even Haromi came up with something. 'I'm going into town next Friday,' she said. 'I could steal some curtains from Melbourne Cash!'

One by one the inventory of what needed to be paid for began to reduce. By the end of the first week we had a real roof, doors that opened and closed, windows which had sugarbags over them and – a home.

Visitors began turning up with furniture they thought might come in handy. Maggie brought a coal iron. Uncle Pera brought a kerosene lamp and one day he asked me to go around to his place for a wardrobe with a *full length* mirror!

'What do I need one of these for now?' he wheezed. 'I only gets a fright when I go past it and see that old man in it.'

The visitors would come to visit, pretend to be looking at nothing, but think, 'Hmmmn, Huria and Joshua need a rooster for their hens –' When they came back they would just happen to have whatever it was they thought we needed.

My mother was embarrassed about such magnanimity. 'I've got nothing to give in return,' she said.

'Nothing?' the visitors would say. 'You don't think we want anything in return, do you?' But some of them would pause. 'Well, actually, if you happen to have any of Mother Ramona's honey to spare –'

Grandmother Ramona had gifted us not only land but also honey to barter with.

There were some items, however, that nobody could give us – fence posts, glass for the window panes and a new pump for the windmill. These things had to be purchased. I can remember clearly how proud we were, after many hours of frustration, when the windmill vanes began to revolve. We had been just about ready to give up and reconcile ourselves to carting water up from the river by drum when there was an imperceptible change in the wind's direction. The machinery gave a *jerk*, loosening all the joints, and there was a wheezing like Uncle Pera. The sound of water came slowly gurgling through old systems and flushing up into the house.

Despite the fact that we began to go into debt with the wood mill and hardware store in Gisborne – and we plunged quickly into the red with Miss Zelda, Miss Daisy and Scott – such moments were magical. The final touch was Glory's.

'I want you to put this up,' she said. She had a hammer and the sign she had given Mum and Dad at Christmas.

'Whereabouts?' I asked.

'Over the front door, silly.'

42

Spring came again, and with it the shearing. Once more the family gathered at the homestead with the families of Ihaka Mahana and Zebediah Whatu for the September thanksgiving meeting. The telling of the Mahana shearing history retained all its power and mana. At church, Grandfather gave his usual reading –

> The Lord is my shepherd I shall not want,
> He leadeth me beside the still waters,
> He restoreth my soul –

Shortly afterward Haromi left school, tossing aside her school uniform with one hand and turning into an instant nymphet.

'Watch out, world,' she squealed, 'here I come.'

Haromi tried to get a job in Gisborne, without success. She started to hang out with the bodgies at the Starlight Café. Two weeks later Aunt Sarah caught her sneaking in through the window after being out all night.

'That's it,' Aunt Sarah said. 'You're coming out shearing. I'm not having you turn into the real Salome and shedding your veils for boys.'

Haromi and Aunt Sarah ended up fighting each other. Haromi moved to Mahana Four.

Dad resumed shearing and I was again the sheriff looking after the one-horse all-women ghost town of Waituhi. Grandfather didn't let up on me either. One year in a boy's lifetime, however, can make a big difference in the boy. I was sixteen now, and the ease and assurance with which I tackled the chores sometimes took my *own* breath away. Without realising it, I had filled out. I had also become taller and muscular and, ironically, seemed to be physically taking after Bulibasha himself. I loved it when old Pera told him this one day.

200

'That boy's the spitting image,' Pera chortled.

Grandfather hated that. He hated the whole idea that I, the least malleable of his mokopuna, should become the one who resembled him most. I'm sure this is why he really *rode* me while the others were away.

'You finished chopping the wood, Himiona? Good. We need three more beasts killed for the gangs. Then after that I want you to shift the cattle to the hill yard. And after that we need a long drop for the new lav –'

He tried in so many ways to run me into the ground. But something else had happened to me. As well as growing stronger and taller I had become resistant to his control and his mind games. Moving away from the homestead to our land had given my family freedom from Grandfather's constant tyranny. In the wide gap that was developing between him and me, I was able to build a sense of independence, a sense of my own self. It was not just a matter of distrusting his decisions. It was a matter of trusting my own. That, though, did not stop him from hassling me, particularly on the question of my still being at school.

'You're useless, Himiona,' he said. 'Your father and mother are out there working their guts out. You're old enough to leave school. What do you want brains for? You've got strong hands. Why don't you help your parents?'

He almost won. One night when Dad came home from the Wi Pere station and our family were eating dinner I tried to give destiny a push.

'We've got big bills,' I began.

'The shearing will put us right,' Dad answered.

'But we have no savings, and we still have to plant our crops for next year.'

'I'll do that,' said Mum.

'No,' I answered. 'It's time for me to go out and work.'

'Where?' Mum asked.

I shrugged my shoulders.

'In the shed with your father?'

Perhaps the way to win them over was to parrot Grandfather back at them. 'Look at Bulibasha,' I said. 'He's managed all right. If God had wanted me to have more brains, He would have given them to me at the start.'

'No,' Mum said.

'But –'

'Kaore. I don't want you ending up in the shed, son. You deserve better. You and all of my children.' Mum was trembling. She looked at my sisters. 'All of you deserve better. Your dad and I want you to stay at school and get qualified. We want you, Simeon, to try for your School Certificate. Then maybe we'll talk about your leaving school.'

'But why?' I asked.

'Why?' Mum echoed. 'You want to know why?'

She pushed her chair, stood up, and got a piece of paper and a pencil. Then she sat down and slashed an 'X' with the pencil.

'That's why,' she said.

Apart from not being able to read, my mother was unable to write even her own name. My father couldn't either.

The next time I saw Grandfather I wanted him to know he had lost. I grabbed him with my parents' obstinacies and wrestled him to a standstill.

'I'm staying at school,' I said. 'Don't try to make me feel guilty, because it won't work. Mum and Dad want to support me.'

'What a waste of money.'

'It's their money and their decision.'

'And when you all starve over winter, boy? Words come easy when your belly is full, ne?'

I couldn't help it. I laughed. 'Why are you so frightened, Grandfather? Do you think I might be better than you?'

Grandfather was enraged at the suggestion. 'You'll never be better than me, boy. Whakahihi, that's your trouble. Whakahihi.' He raised his fists. I was no longer afraid. Sure he could still beat the *outside* me, but the *me* I was inside? He'd have a hard time there.

Our antagonism increased. Grandfather was always in my way, casting his shadow. He was like a giant wall of Jericho. I wanted to take up a trumpet and make that wall tumble down so I could get on with the business of growing up and becoming myself.

At the end of 1958, two events took place which brought competition between Hukareka and Waituhi to a climax and put thoughts of Bulibasha temporarily on hold. One was the seven-a-side Maori hockey tournament. The other was announced in the *Gisborne Herald* just before Mum, my sisters and I joined Mahana Four for the season:

NEW GOLDEN FLEECE AWARD

The New Zealand Wool Board today announced the holding of a national competition to select the best shearing gang in the

Dominion. A substantial cash prize of £5000 and the Golden Fleece Shield will be awarded the winning gang. A gold statuette, christened 'Jason', will be given to the best shearer of the year, not necessarily from the winning gang.

The new competition has been inaugurated to focus attention on the wool industry and to encourage quality in shearing.

'As a country which relies on its wool production for its overseas receipts,' Mr Williams, Chairman of the Board said, 'it is only appropriate that we should recognise the contribution of the shearing gang to New Zealand's economy.'

Regional finals would be contested in all the provinces, Mr Williams said. Two finalists from each province will travel to Masterton for the semifinals and finals.

43

It was the visionary Apirana Ngata who in the 1940s encouraged the seven-a-side Maori hockey tournament. What a man! His fingerprints were to be found everywhere throughout Maoridom – in politics, business, religion, education, culture and sport. A true Renaissance man for the Maori.

'Tamihana,' Apirana Ngata had said when he went to see Grandfather. 'I have done you one favour and now I ask you a favour in return – a favour for a favour, ne?' Tamihana agreed. 'Our people need the spirit of competition to keep our pride and mana and to improve and develop our culture. This is the reason why the haka nights were started, and the hui topu for Maori Anglicans. I want the same thing started up in sport.' Apirana Ngata's eyes creased into amusement. 'I've already been to see Pera Smiler and his sister Mini Tupara here in Waituhi. They have suggested hockey as the sport for the tournament because it is a game that all can play, men, women and children. Kua pai?'

'Kua pai,' Tamihana said.

Apirana Ngata was clever all right. Sport was just the excuse to get Maori together. Once that happened, the protocols of ceremonial gatherings took place and, before you knew it, a hui was happening.

Ngata well knew that Maori people loved to meet each other and loved to talk. In the formality of meeting, genealogies were exchanged so that one person could find the blood connection between himself or herself and another. Once that was achieved entire histories were exchanged. The tournament was therefore the place where the older people could reaffirm their personal and political relationships. Some hadn't seen each other for years, so it was important to redraw the map of the present by finding out what had happened, who had died and who had been born. Over five days people discussed the past and the present – land problems, cultural issues, old grievances – all in the language of the iwi. At breakfast, lunch and dinner the old people talked and talked and talked. They would say, 'Now that we have had kai for our bodies, let us now have the food of chiefs.' They would lie in the meeting house way after everyone else was asleep, discussing and debating matters affecting the history of the Maori.

Meanwhile the younger men and women were playing sport and, coincidentally, falling in love or having sex. The old people were quick to see who was falling for whom. If they were caught sleeping together, there was nothing for it except to get married. The old people were stern that way. They loved nothing better than to sit around a young couple who had overslept in the morning. When that couple woke up: marriage bells.

In some cases the old ones went further. Sometimes a girl was introduced to a boy she had never seen in her life and told she had been taumau'd to him – promised to him as his bride. This was the way political alliances were maintained.

Apirana Ngata was one of the most successful marriage brokers of all Maoridom.

'Come on, Mum!' Faith and Hope yelled. Although I had grown taller, my two sisters hadn't grown any prettier. They lived in hope and wanted to get to the tournament before all the boys were taken.

This year the seven-a-side tournament was held in Nuhaka. Grandfather and Grandmother – everybody in Waituhi – had left already, taking with them the shields and trophies that were stored in either Mini Tupara's or Pera Smiler's house. As usual, we were the last ones left to turn out the lights. Why did we still have to go over to the homestead, lock up and check that the stock were well fed? Would Mum and Dad ever finish?

'Wait your hurry!' Mum laughed. Her complexion was rosy and she was giddy with delight.

'All set?' Dad asked.

'We've been ready for ages,' Hope moaned.

'Let's put our foot down then, shall we?' Mum said. With a zoom and a bit of a skid we were off.

By the time we arrived in Nuhaka the main meeting house was packed to capacity. Other marae were taking people in, and it was a matter of going from marae to marae to find our own iwi.

'Where's Waituhi sleeping?' Dad asked.

'Down the road at Hemi's pa,' we were told.

Before we even got there, Mum's sister, our Aunt Jackie, saw us and screamed a welcome to Mum. 'I've saved a place for you with us!'

As soon as Mum saw Aunt Jackie they burst into tears. They hadn't seen each other for years. It was so embarrassing to see adults acting like children. Oh, the *shame*.

'Didn't Bruce come with you?' Mum asked. Bruce was Aunt Jackie's fourth husband.

'Him! I think I might trade him in. There must be another man here for me. The local people are expecting to feed a thousand.'

'Where have they all come from?' Dad asked.

'Palmerston North, Whakatane, you name it and they're bound to be here. I saw Ruatoki and Murupara arriving earlier this afternoon and –'

'Excuse me,' someone said. A red-headed young man blushed as he walked past.

'He's come with the team from Auckland,' Aunt Jackie said. 'If there's any red-headed kids born next year we'll know where the shotgun wedding will be held.'

We unpacked, made our beds on the straw mattresses and hung our clothes on the line which ran down the middle of the meeting house. People always brought three or four outfits – hockey clothes, formal wear for the dance, and informal wear for lounging around in. The women took the socialising very seriously, making beautiful dresses of tulle or organza and painting their shoes with glitter. The men wore sports jackets to the dance – literally a white sportscoat and a pink carnation.

Glory started to sneeze – oh no, hay fever.

'Kia ora!' people called. 'Kei te pehea koe?'

Within the melee I saw more dazed blond Pakeha wandering around the meeting house wondering what had struck them. They had been brought to the tournament by whanaunga who were now

205

living in the cities of gold – Auckland, Wellington and Christchurch. They were just ripe to be caught by some young Maori girl or boy. My cousin Moana met David, her naval officer husband, when her brother brought a team from the naval base at Devonport.

'He just fell into my arms,' Moana laughed, 'like an apple from a tree.'

'Actually,' David whispered, 'she had to give the tree a good shake first.'

The dinner gong sounded. Over we went to the wharekai to join the throng and marvel at the meat, pork, fish, crays, watercress, kumara, potatoes, pumpkin which graced the long trestle tables.

'Haramai konei!'

The local people urged us into their dining hall. Wasn't the smell of hangi food, fresh from the earth oven, delicious? Look at all that other food! Titiro! Mmmm, Maori bread, fried bread, paraoa rewana, kina, oysters, pupus! And over there, pavlovas, steam puddings, trifles, jellies and soft drinks. Truly, the horn of plenty. How would we be able to lift our hockey sticks in the morning!

I saw more relatives – my cousins Donna, Cindy and Chantelle who used to be Don, Sam and Charlie Jones from Te Puia.

'Hello, Auntie Huria,' Chantelle said, and kissed Mum on both cheeks. She left more lipstick on Mum than Mum did on her.

'What are you doing home?' Mum asked.

'We couldn't miss the hockey tournament,' Donna said. 'Anyway business is slow –' Chantelle hit Donna with her handbag. 'Oops,' Donna said. 'Uh, we decided to come home to see how the folks were.'

My cousins worked days at Carmen's Coffee Bar and nights up around the strip joints in Vivian Street.

Meantime, Cindy was eyeing me up and down. 'This isn't little Simeon?' she breathed.

'Yes,' I squeaked.

'Oo la la, enchant-é, formi-dable, mon enfant,' Cindy answered.

'Take no notice of that one,' Chantelle whispered in my ear. 'She went out with a French sailor last week and hasn't been the same since.'

I saw Saul Poata ogling my cousins in a derisory fashion. Poppy was next to him and she jabbed him in the side: good on her. Most people were used to Donna, Cindy and Chantelle. Although they were loud and bright, like brazen and brilliantly coloured birds of paradise, they were still hometown boys. I was just about to go over and take a poke at Saul when Aunt Sarah's voice cut through my anger.

'We're all wanted back at the marae,' she told Dad. 'Come quick. Now.'

In the meeting house the entire Mahana clan was clustered around Grandfather Tamihana, who was lying on his mattress. His eyes were wide and staring. Aunt Sarah was beside him, caressing his hands. We thought he had been taken ill.

'What's the problem?' Dad asked Aunt Ruth.

'Father has just found out that Rupeni Poata has been made chairman of the Takitimu Maori Council.'

The Maori council framework had also been a creation of Apirana Ngata. The Takitimu Maori Council represented the Gisborne tribes and was the forum through which Maori views could be channelled to government.

'Why didn't the other chiefs ask me?' Grandfather said. 'Why didn't they consult me? Why didn't I know that this was happening? Why have they done this to me?'

I had never seen Grandfather like this before. This was worse than mere physical illness. Somebody had made a voodoo image of Grandfather and was sticking pins in the doll. Here a pin at his right kneecap. Here another pin at his left leg. Now more pins thrusting through from front to back, viciously impaling eyes, mouth, ears, throat, loins – heart, head and soul. The doll was bristling with pins like a human hedgehog. Grandfather was in a state of psychic collapse.

By all rights, Grandfather should have been chairman and not Rupeni Poata. Somehow, Rupeni had persuaded the other elders to choose him. Was it because Grandfather was Mormon?

Grandfather raised his throat and howled. 'My sons, my daughters, I feel so betrayed.'

In one fell swoop, Rupeni Poata had entered Maori public life and become top man in Gisborne. In doing so he had stolen Grandfather's mana from him.

'We must restore our father's mana,' Uncle Matiu said. 'We must retaliate. We must shame all those who were involved in making this decision. We must also stand up for our religion. This year we must win the tournament.'

'Hukareka must be beaten.'

44

Mahana was putting two women's and three men's teams into the tournament. Neither Andrew nor I was picked for any of them, although we were school representatives. Grandfather didn't think we were good enough.

Grandfather was still preoccupied by the news about Rupeni Poata. His eyes followed Rupeni wherever he went; he stiffened whenever his rival was congratulated for his new appointment. The thought came to me that Rupeni Poata *defined* Grandfather's life. He had never dreamed that Rupeni would sidestep him by going into Maori politics – *his* exclusive arena – and that the other elders of Gisborne would agree to it.

'You can do what you like,' Grandfather said when I tackled him about Andrew's and my omission and suggested we make up a fourth men's team.

I saw Nani Mini Tupara from the non-Mormon part of the Waituhi Valley. She had entered two teams in the tournament.

'Will you support me if I register a team?' I asked.

'Rebelling again?' She laughed. 'Sure I will. But if your team wins, I don't want the trophy in a Mormon house. It comes to *my* house. Deal?'

'Put it there, Auntie.'

When the tournament began next day with a parade on the main field, bystanders were left in no doubt as to Mahana's intensity of purpose. There was something awesome about our march past the grandstand. Aunt Sarah had bullied us into wearing maroon sashes over our good clothes. She had inspected the Mahana teams and arranged them in height and order. Now, right out front, Aunt Sarah was bearing the flag which she had spent all night making – a huge golden angel glittered in the centre of a maroon satin banner. The angel was blowing a trumpet and, as the wind caught the flag, the angel appeared to be flying.

'Whu –' the crowd murmured.

Mahana won the march-past.

But who was making the presentation? When Grandfather went up to get the cup, Rupeni Poata shook his hand and then turned it into an Indian wrestling match. How the onlookers laughed! As for us, we should have felt triumphant that we had won the parade. Something in the mere fact that Rupeni had made the presentation made our triumph hollow.

It was all very well for Andrew and me to decide to field a team. The problem was, where would we find players at this late hour? Out of sympathy Dad and Pani said they would join us, but everyone else except Granduncle Pera, Mackie and Peewee had been taken. I was running out of time and out on the fields the games were beginning seriously.

Did I say seriously?

Two of the fields were paddocks from which you had to shoo the cows, sheep or hens before you could play. Sometimes the ball landed in the middle of a huge cowpat or down a rabbit hole. Some teams didn't have enough hockey sticks, so either borrowed them from other teams who weren't on their particular draw or played with battens or anything they could hold.

'This is *hockey*?' the red-headed Pakeha from Auckland asked, stunned. He was playing against the oldest hockey players in the world and, because they couldn't run, three of them were standing in the goal. At least they were better than the players who hopped on, never having played at all. They were *dangerous*, slashing at the ball as if they were playing golf.

The majority of teams had uniforms, but some didn't. Pity the poor referee: when two teams without uniforms played each other, he never knew who was on which side. They got confused too.

'Which is our goal?' they asked. 'Are you on our side?'

People expected the preliminary rounds to be a hard case. People cheerfully lost by 50 to nil to the better professional teams. I was losing my battle, too, to find three players.

Then Chantelle came up.

'Uncle Pera says you're looking for players,' she said. 'The women don't want us in any of their teams.'

'Well –' I hesitated, dumbfounded.

'Honey,' Donna said kindly, 'we may shave our legs but we're your last resort. Take us or leave us.'

'We can run faster than Uncle Pera too,' Cindy said. 'All that practice running away from the police, eh girls!'

'And most of the time in high heels,' Chantelle added. 'Well?'

'I'd love to have you,' I said.

The Waituhi Rebels were born.

As expected the professional teams started to come through the ranks, and by Saturday afternoon bystanders were barracking for their favourites. In the women's division it was clear from the beginning that the major battle would be between Mahana and Hukareka. Every time one of the Mahana women's teams met a Hukareka team everybody in Nuhaka could hear it. At first people laughed off the intensity of the Mahana teams as excess energy. Then Aunt Miriam hit a raised ball at the goal and caught Agnes Poata in the stomach.

'Hey! Mahana! Go easy there!' bystanders called. People at the tournaments were quick to be put off by bad manners or lack of fair play.

However, when Aunt Sarah fell on the ball and was attacked by Poppaea, The Brute, while she was on the ground, sympathies swung our way again.

'Hoi! Play the ball! Leave the old bag alone!'

Then Aunt Sarah made us all laugh. She jumped up from the ground and came running over to the sideline. 'Who said that! Who called me an old bag!' She didn't mind being called a bag, but she hated being called old.

Mahana won the women's division.

So far so good. But the men weren't faring as well. All the Mahana teams got through the first round, but in the second round Mahana Three and Mahana Four were knocked out by Hauiti and Hukareka. In the third round, Mahana Two succumbed to Te Aowera. In the second round that afternoon, the frontrunners were Hukareka, with two teams still in the championship, Te Aowera and Mahana One. A ding-dong battle was fought between Mahana One and Hukareka and, to great scenes of storm and agony, Mahana lost. The finalists were Hukareka One and Two, Te Aowera and –

Did I forget to tell you that the Waituhi Rebels surprised everybody?

There were two playoffs. One between Hukareka One and Te Aowera and the other between Hukareka Two and the Waituhi Rebels. The winners from each playoff would compete against each other for the top trophy.

That's when Grandfather Tamihana and I had a showdown.

Five minutes before Waituhi Rebels were due for the first playoff, he started to heavy the team.

'Joshua,' he said, 'I want you to change the name of your team to Mahana and to sack some of your players.'

What? My father wasn't captain of the team!

'You haven't a hope of winning against Hukareka. Not with those three takatapui among you.'

His voice was loud and carried to where Donna, Cindy and Chantelle were standing. Maori homophobia had always been the worst part of their lives. When they heard Grandfather's words they changed and seemed to diminish.

'I want them replaced,' Grandfather said. 'Ruka, Aperahama and Mohi will play for them.'

'But –' Dad began.

'No buts,' Grandfather continued.

My father stood his ground. 'I'm just the halfback,' he said. 'My son's captain.'

'Then you tell him,' Grandfather answered.

'No.'

'Joshua, I'm ordering you –'

'You tell him yourself,' Dad said.

Furious, Grandfather turned to me. 'Did you hear me, Himiona? You change the name of your team and get rid of those three.'

A crowd had begun to collect around us and Grandfather, aware of the attention, wanted to get the matter over quickly.

Chantelle trotted over and whispered in my ear. 'We don't mind, honey,' she said.

The trouble was, I did. 'No change,' I told Grandfather. My heart was thudding in my ears. My mouth was dry.

'What did you *say*?'

'There will be no change in either the name or the team.'

'You will make a laughing stock of me,' Grandfather said. 'I am ordering you to –'

'Have you ever taken the time to watch us, Grandfather? No, you've been too busy watching Mahana.'

'This is your last chance, Himiona.'

Just then, Nani Mini Tupara, alerted to what was happening, came running over. The light of battle was in her eyes and her temper was up.

'Are you trying to muscle in on my team?' she asked. 'They're registered under me, Tamihana, not you.' I could see Nani Mini was enjoying having Grandfather on. She loved to get her own back on him for splitting the valley with that Mormon angel of his. 'Anyway, cuz, it's all the same, isn't it? We're all Waituhi, aren't we?'

Meantime, the ref had heard what the ruckus was about and hurried over to assert some authority.

'Sorry, Bulibasha,' he said. 'Mini's right. This is her team, not yours.'

Grandfather knew he had lost.

'Himiona,' he whispered. 'Why did you register under your Nani Mini? Why not under me?' His voice sounded so adrift, like an anchor that has failed to take on the sea bed. I felt ashamed. 'One day,' Grandfather said, 'you and I –'

He walked away.

Ask anybody who has played seven-a-side hockey and they will tell you that it is a difficult and punishing game. With only seven players each, teams have to be fast and fit to last the distance – fifteen minutes first half and fifteen minutes second half and not just for one game, either. In a tournament you played eight games or more a day. No good pulling all the stops out at the beginning and running out of steam as the day progressed. The main secret to success was having and keeping possession of the ball. As long as you had possession, you could control the speed and the destiny of the game.

Over the preliminaries I had developed an enormous respect for Donna, Cindy and Chantelle's abilities to keep possession. Although they were transvestites there was nothing feminine about the way they slammed that ball. They were massive – and they could run.

Could they what!

I had every reason to expect that Waituhi Rebels would give Hukareka Two a good run for their money. What I hadn't anticipated, however, was that Donna, Cindy and Chantelle would be so devastated by Grandfather's dismissal of them that they would give up. From the moment they walked on to the field they didn't even try. They thought everybody was laughing at them.

The Hukareka Two team, led by Alexander Poata, swiftly took possession. Despite attempts by me, Andrew, Dad and Pani to stop the fast Hukareka Two men – Alexander, Tight Arse Senior, Tight Arse Junior, Bill, John and two others I didn't know – Hukareka

Two scored one runaway goal after another. By halftime Hukareka Two were ahead by 15 to nil – a goal a minute.

'Chantelle,' I pleaded. 'We've got to turn this game around. Please –'

By now people *were* laughing at Donna, Cindy and Chantelle. All along the sidelines, men were beginning to heckle us. Some were making effeminate gestures and mincing along like women. Grandfather, having washed his hands of us, was standing like a monument to morality and righteousness.

Nani Mini came over. 'Huh? What's wrong with your players?' she asked. 'They better pull their stockings up.'

Then I saw Mohi blowing kisses at us and I saw red. I walked up to him and socked him in the mouth. 'You leave them alone, Mohi.'

'Whu –' the crowd rumbled.

Before Mohi could hit me back, the ref had blown his whistle to start the second half. Dad, Pani and Andrew were silent as I trotted back. I started to rearrange the team.

'Why don't we just throw in the towel?' Pani asked.

'No,' I answered. 'If we keep possession of the ball we can keep the score down. I'll play centre forward; Dad, you play left inner; Andrew, you play right inner, and Pani, you play at centre half.'

'What about –' Andrew jerked his head at Donna, Cindy and Chantelle.

I shrugged my shoulders.

'Play ball!' the ref cried.

Tears of rage were stinging my eyes. I barged back and pushed Chantelle away from the centre forward position.

'You bitches,' I yelled at my cousins. 'If you don't want to fight for yourselves, get off the field. Go crawl back into your holes and die.'

I settled down to bully against Alexander Poata. All I could think of was winning the bully, shooting the ball out to Andrew, streaking into Hukareka territory and –

I felt a hand on my shoulder.

'You better step aside, honey.' Chantelle's voice was kind, but there was steel in it. 'You're standing in my position and *I don't like it.*'

I looked at Chantelle, uncomprehending.

'Off you go now, there's a good boy. Me and my girls are going to work.'

I moved back to centre.

'Are we ready, girls?' Chantelle asked.

'Any time, any place, any *way* you want it,' Donna and Cindy responded.

'So why are we waiting?' Chantelle said. 'Let's kick *ass*.'

The game took off. Chantelle bullied so fast that Alexander Poata was left literally standing in the middle of the field wondering what had happened. He looked like one of those cartoon characters who lose their pants and cross their legs: Eek. She pushed the ball past Tight Arse Senior and yelled to Cindy, 'Go, girl!'

The ball cracked from Chantelle down the middle of the field. Cindy took off after it, picked the ball up and swerved and dipped past the remaining Hukareka Two players. Like an avenging angel she sprinted down the field and *slam* –

Hukareka 15, Waituhi Rebels 1.

'One down,' Chantelle yawned, tossing her hair, 'fourteen to go. Ready, girls?'

The onlookers were stunned into silence. Then they let out a surprised roar. Nani Mini was laughing so loud she almost lost her teeth.

Hockey one, hockey two, hockey three and –

Again the ball cracked from Chantelle, but this time to Donna who hit it into the far corner and sped after it. Did I tell you that Donna had been a champion sprinter? None of those Hukareka players had a chance. Donna was there to pick up the ball and leisurely dribble it into the Hukareka goal.

'What took you guys so long?' Donna said as the panting Hukareka players caught up.

Alexander Poata was so pissed off about being beaten by a takatapui that he took a swing at Donna who ducked, kneed him in the balls and asked the other men, 'Next?' It was the kind of strength that people on the sidelines understood – even Grandfather Tamihana. They cheered and stamped their approval. Donna went to take a bow.

'Never mind about that,' Chantelle yelled. 'We've only got another twelve minutes.'

Hukareka 15, Waituhi Rebels 2. We would never make it.

The game got harder, but we had the crowd with us all the way. People like to see born losers clawing back. Against all odds we managed to draw 15–15 in the last second.

214

'Extra time!' the ref allowed. Now the game would continue until the first goal was scored.

Nani Mini was beside herself. She upbraided Chantelle. 'Why didn't you fellas play like this in the first half?'

Chantelle looked at me with tenderness. 'We can fight our own battles, Auntie,' she said. 'But sometimes it takes us a while to remember what they are.'

Today people still remember that semifinal game and the one that followed. They remember it not with laughter but with admiration for the team that came from the back and ended in the front. Mind you, people thought Waituhi Rebels had decided on our tactics from the very start.

'That was clever,' Granduncle Pera said, 'to get Hukareka Two all tuckered out first!'

For two minutes the fight of the champions see-sawed from one end of the field to the other. There always seemed to be somebody from either side able to stop the ball from going into the goal. Then the ref blew his whistle and announced that the first team to hit the ball from the circle anywhere over their opponent's back line would be the winner.

Hockey one, hockey two, hockey three.

I was so exhausted I could hardly stand.

Alexander Poata won the ball. Hukareka were on the attack. Then from out of nowhere Pani stopped the ball. He saw Donna waving from afar and hit it to her. But Donna was tired and the Hukareka players were catching up –

Suddenly Chantelle yelled, 'Cops, Donna! Cops!'

You should have seen Donna take *off* – like a rocket. Over the circle and *slam*.

Oh yes, we won the finals too.

45

In the early evening both Nani Mini Tupara and Grandfather, on behalf of Waituhi Rebels, went up to receive the coveted silver-studded shield at the prizegiving ceremony. I had mentioned to Nani Mini earlier why it was imperative that Grandfather join her.

'All right,' she agreed. 'But your grandfather can fight his own battles, you know. Just remember our bargain – I get to take the shield to my place. That'll fix the old paka.'

So Grandfather *did* win against Rupeni Poata, sort of, in the end. Not that Rupeni Poata seemed to care. When the official photograph was taken and everybody applauded he caught my eye and raised his arms to indicate his personal applause.

Dad was standing beside me. I turned to him and –

'Thanks, Dad,' I said.

'You were the captain,' he answered. 'Not me. Father was wrong in thinking he could change the name of the team and the players. Sometimes there *is* no choice.'

'There's always a choice, Dad.'

'Not when there's only one right answer. You were right, son, and Father was –'

Dad still could not make the admission.

The community hall was packed that night for the celebration concert and dance. We young ones were looking forward to letting off steam – the Black Shadows were playing, which meant we'd be able to rock and roll.

Andrew and I had a long shower and doused ourselves with two bottles of cologne; Andrew also drank some. He hoped he would get lucky in Nuhaka. My thoughts, as usual, were on Poppy. I was combing my hair into a duck tail – in those days I had enough hair – when the toilet flushed and Chantelle came out hitching up her skirt. We looked at each other in the mirror. Nothing needed to be said. Chantelle winked and was gone.

I had brought my new pair of grey pointed shoes – they were so long in the toes the only way I could walk was with my feet splayed out at right angles. Andrew lent me his bright red shirt and lime green pants. When I walked into the hall I looked like traffic lights trying to make up their mind whether to show Stop or Go.

By eleven the dance was in full swing – and no sign of the Hukareka crowd. Then Poppy walked in on the arm of Rupeni Poata, and they started to waltz. Everybody went, 'Aah.'

All of a sudden Rupeni stopped just in front of where Grandmother Ramona and Grandfather Tamihana were sitting. He bowed to Grandmother and, turning to Grandfather, congratulated him on the Waituhi Rebels' win. I think it was only then that Grandfather considered his mana had been restored.

Just as he was leaving, Rupeni almost fell. As he passed by I saw that he was trembling.

The dance turned *hot*. Waituhi's sense of competition against Hukareka was still running high, and the dance hall split down the middle. Waituhi lined up facing our partners – girls in one line and boys in the other. Hukareka did the same. We began to show off our dancing skills, trying to outdo the other side.

'You think you guys are so great? Take *this*.'

The music got hotter and hotter. The steps grew more and more complicated. People started to leave the floor to the gun partners, and soon boys were throwing their partners in the air, leaping and falling into the splits and gyrating like tops. The Puerto Rican dancers on the rooftops in *West Side Story* had *nothing* on us. The hall was awash with verve and excitement. Haromi took my hand and pulled me into the middle. The band erupted into 'Rock, rock, rock.'

'Oh no,' I said.

'Oh yes, cuz,' she answered. 'All you have to do is stand still. I'll do the work.'

Haromi was wearing a red dress that flared whenever she spun. She had learnt how to do French rock and roll and nobody could dance like she could. The floor cleared for us as Haromi dipped and circled and jumped into and out of my arms.

'Go, girl, *go!*' everybody chanted.

For one shining, elated moment both Waituhi and Hukareka forgot our differences. When Haromi span like a top – shedding her veils, as Aunt Sarah would have said – we were simply young men and women who felt so lucky to have been born in these modern times. We were kids from many villages, roaring our heads off.

Afterward, Poppy came up to Haromi and said to her, 'Next year I get to wear the red dress.' She turned to me. 'You were pretty good too.'

The dance ended at one o'clock in the morning. Both Andrew and I had struck out in the girls department. I had met a few whom I liked but shyness always had a way of tying my tongue into knots. So my cousin Andrew and I wandered off down the road towards the meeting house. Half way along we heard rustling in a paddock and the sound of a loud *slap*. A red dress came through the furrows towards us.

'*Men*,' Haromi said. 'Always after one thing. Look at my dress. Gotta smoke?'

We went to sit on a bank, watching the crowd as they drifted to the complex of marquees around the meeting house. The mood between the three of us sweetened and I felt absurdly happy.

'Hey guys,' Andrew said, 'did you know –'

This was the way he always began whenever he had found something out.

'Know what!'

'You won't believe this –'

'Believe what!'

The moon came out and flooded the nightscape.

'Grandfather and Grandmother aren't married,' he said.

'Bulldust,' I answered.

'They had all those kids,' Haromi added.

'It's *true*,' Andrew said.

I scoffed at the notion. 'Grandfather is too religious to live in sin.'

'I heard Aunt Ruth telling Aunt Sarah,' Andrew insisted.

'So are you saying,' I began, 'that after Grandfather stole Grandmother away from the church they *didn't* get married?'

'Yes.'

'But why not!'

'Search me.'

Haromi, Andrew and I stared at each other, unable to comprehend. Haromi began to laugh and laugh with absolute and unyielding delight.

'Oh *fu-uck*!' she yelled. As if she'd heard the most marvellous news of her life.

46

Everybody in Poverty Bay was talking about the Golden Fleece competition – everybody, that is, except Grandfather Tamihana. When Uncle Matiu raised the matter at our family meeting and asked Bulibasha if Mahana was entering, Grandfather laughed and said, 'Why should we go into a Golden Fleece competition? We're already the best! Waste of time even having a competition. They should give us the prize and save money.'

'Father,' Uncle Hone answered, 'we have to be in to win.' All the families in Waituhi were feeling the pinch and had pinned their hopes on this shearing competition.

'In?'

'In the competition. If we don't register we can't compete.'

Grandfather stood up. 'This is nonsense,' he said. 'I will hear no more of this. If the Wool Board want the Mahana family to compete, they can come to ask me.'

In the end his hand was forced. Rupeni Poata, who never stood on his dignity, made it clear that Hukareka would enter the competition.

On Friday night, the closing day for entries, the Mahana clan gathered at Waituhi and drove together to Gisborne to register for the Gisborne-East Coast provincial finals. The venue for registration was the city council chambers, and the mayor had decided to make an occasion of the event. He'd even organised a local orchestra to play oldtime songs just outside the signing area.

Outside the chambers, Grandfather took Grandmother Ramona's hand, and arm in arm they walked up the entrance to where the mayor was waiting. Grandmother was wearing a hat with a veil covering her face.

'How do you do, Tamihana,' the mayor greeted him.

'All this trouble just for me?' Grandfather responded curtly. 'Why didn't you just nominate one of my gangs to represent the province?'

'Are all of them entering?' the mayor asked.

'Yes.'

The forms were duly signed. The mayor kept talking to Grandfather until –

'Ah, here he is,' the mayor said.

Pulling up outside were Rupeni Poata and *his* family. It was clear that the mayor had arranged a publicity stunt. Rupeni, resplendent in pinstripe suit and with a white carnation in his hand, got out of his Buick with a radiant and proud Poppy.

'I see,' Rupeni Poata said when he reached the signing area, 'that my old friend Bulibasha will be endeavouring to claim the prize.' His tone was light, but Grandfather took it as a challenge. He stiffened and made ready to escort Grandmother out. At that moment a photographer from the *Gisborne Herald* called out –

'Gentlemen, can we have a photograph?'

'I wish you the best, Tamihana,' Rupeni Poata said. He extended his hand in friendship. Grandfather had no option but to shake it. The flashbulb *flashed*.

'Let us go,' Grandfather said. He took Grandmother's arm again.

Just as we were leaving, the wind lifted Grandmother's veil so that we could see her pallid, grief-stricken features. The orchestra struck up another song. Until that moment Rupeni Poata had maintained his diplomacy and manners. The melody came soaring out of the violins.

– Ramona, I hear the mission bells above –

Oh no.

When I looked back, Rupeni Poata had regained his composure. Poppy by his side, he watched as we stepped into our cars and sped away into the night.

The next day's edition of the *Gisborne Herald* carried the photograph of Grandfather shaking hands with Rupeni Poata on the front page. The accompanying report was headlined:

FRIENDS WISH EACH OTHER WELL IN GOLDEN FLEECE COMPETITION

Pictured above are two of the best known Maori citizens in the district, Mr Rupeni Poata and Mr Tamihana Mahana. As a young man Mr Poata was a well-known sportsman and he and Mr Mahana were often pitted against each other. Their friendly rivalry will again take place when their shearing gangs compete for the Gisborne and East Coast Golden Fleece provincial finals . . .

The photograph showed a handsome Rupeni Poata and a scowling Bulibasha. You can just see my face peering between the two of them. Grandfather was annoyed that he was mentioned after Rupeni Poata and that it was Rupeni whose sporting exploits were mentioned.

No useful purpose will be served by describing the Gisborne and East Coast regional competitions in full, except to say that thirty gangs entered, including four from Mahana and three from Hukareka. The mayor was disappointed that not more teams had put themselves forward. His publicity stunt backfired. He had hoped that the photograph of the Mahanas and Poatas registering would encourage others. Instead, when other gangs saw we had both entered, they decided not to bother.

The shear-offs were held at the Gisborne Show Grounds. Grandfather's entire energies went into supporting Mahana One. He had never seen Poata One shearing and, when he did so, he was alarmed at their speed. He began to crack his whip over the heads of Mahana One to encourage them to increase their speed too. Again, Grandfather was applying the age-old Mahana tactics – get out in front while you can, and stay out in front.

Public interest in the regional finals was so high that each shear-off was fully packed. Every Saturday for a month, cars and trucks turned in at the main entrance. Ticket sales increased as the regional semifinals approached. The competition appealed to the pride of the Gisborne and the East Coast citizenry – of course a Poverty Bay or East Coast team would win the coveted Golden Fleece award! After all, Gisborne was the home of the best shearers, wasn't it?

Local bookmakers had a field day accepting bets on this shearing gang or that. The punters were favouring Poata One, Mahana One and the Lawson Syndicate, a Pakeha gang which had been specifically brought together for the competition. Suffice to say that in the finals the Lawson syndicate lost out to a Mahana and a Poata shearing gang.

Poata One, of course, led the field. Much to everyone's surprise, however, it wasn't Mahana One that won through but – wait for it – Mahana Four.

With the Gisborne and East Coast provincial finals behind us, the family gathered to celebrate at the homestead. The meeting was one of the largest ever. As always, the other patriarchs, Zebediah Whatu and Ihaka Mahana, were in attendance with their families. Then Grandfather Tamihana entered with Grandmother Ramona and the mood was shattered. Grandfather called Uncles Matiu, Maaka and Ruka forward into the middle of the floor.

'I am very disappointed in my sons,' he said. Disappointed? Grandfather was appalled that the gang to which he himself was attached had missed out. It was incomprehensible that the premier Mahana shearing gang should have lost.

Bulibasha stood up and looked down at his kneeling sons. None of them dared to look up at him. 'What happened to you three? What happened to your shearing gangs, eh?' His questions lashed out. Uncle Matiu flinched. 'What happened to Mahana One! Mahana One is supposed to be the top gang. *You* should have been in the finals. Not Mahana Four.'

'Ma te wa,' Zebediah Whatu intervened. 'It wasn't entirely their fault. Who was to know that Mahana One and Mahana Two would draw to shear against each other in the first round? One knocked the other out. Then Mahana One had to face Mahana Three in the second heat. Same thing. The luck of the draw, Bulibasha.'

'I don't like luck,' Grandfather thundered. 'Luck isn't going to help Mahana Four. What hope have they got against the top Poata team? Poata One is the best I've seen.'

The entire sitting room was startled at this admission.

'All in the past, Bulibasha,' Ihaka Mahana said. 'At least we have a team in the finals.'

Grandfather Tamihana would not be pacified. He raised his left hand in a chopping motion.

'I'm *very* disappointed. You've let me down. One of you should have got through. We should have two Mahana teams in the finals. All our best shearers are in your teams – our best wool classers, sheepos, the works. Instead Mahana Four must battle with Poata One. My constant foe is the front runner. There's only one thing to do.'

Grandfather sat down on his throne and looked at each one of us in turn, staring us down, trying to impose his will. I would not turn away from his glance.

Grandfather laid it on us. 'I want you, Matiu, to take over from Hone as leader of Mahana Four. Matiu, Maaka and Sarah, you three are to replace some of the members of Mahana Four.'

Thus saith the Lord. No ifs, no buts, no maybes. Trying exactly the same tactics as with the seven-a-side hockey tournament. There was absolute silence.

Grandfather looked to Zebediah Whatu and Ihaka Mahana. 'Do you agree? You know, don't you, that ever since I started the Mahana shearing gangs, we have always been first in the district? If Poata One wins, I will never be able to hold my head up in this province. I am not going to trust to chance. The Poata team is fast and good. They are much faster than Mahana Four. The reputation of the Mahana shearing gang rests entirely on our ability to take the crown – the Golden Fleece.'

The family, abashed, nodded in assent.

Yes Bulibasha Bulibasha basha basha asha.

'Then it is done,' Grandfather said.

I was sitting at the end of the room, way down by the kitchen.

'No it isn't,' I said. I stood up, my head higher than the Lord of Heaven's.

'Let it be, Himiona,' my father Joshua hissed.

'Listen to your father,' Uncle Hone added. 'It doesn't matter who leads the team as long as it is a Mahana team.'

I was not going to let Grandfather get away with it. 'Mahana Four has deserved its place in the finals. It was judged to deserve that place and was given that recognition.'

'Mahana Four got lucky,' Grandfather said. 'Luck will not win this competition.'

'It was not luck,' I answered, standing my ground. 'Mahana Four trained hard for the provincial finals, as hard as anybody else in this room. I have to stand up for that and for the members of Mahana Four.'

'There will be *no* discussion,' Grandfather said.

'Yes there *will.*'

'*Himiona,*' Dad called.

I had taken a step past my kneeling uncles. I took another step to where Zebediah Whatu and Ihaka Mahana were watching. No more would I approach Bulibasha on my knees. No more would I be subservient.

'Why are you doing this, Grandfather? Why must you always make the world go your way? Why don't you admit that you can be wrong? All these dictatorial commandments –'

'Whakahihi, Simeon,' he shouted. 'Whakahihi.'

'And that word,' I continued, 'why do you always beat me over the head with it? What's wrong with being whakahihi? Your world is changing, Bulibasha. I'm one of the ones who is changing it.'

I paused. I took a breath. I had gone this far; I may as well go the whole hog.

'Legally, Mahana is bound to send the same team to Masterton that won. That team is Mahana Four. The rules do not allow substitutions.'

'Rules are made to be broken. I *am* the law.'

'No you're not. Even if you were, you are not above it. If you persist, Grandfather, the authorities will disqualify us.'

'What they don't know won't hurt them.'

'But they will find out.'

My mouth was dry. I was about to commit the ultimate heresy.

'Tell me how?' Grandfather asked. He was dangerous. His eyes glittered.

'I will tell them.'

'The family always comes first, Himiona.'

'Yes, Grandfather, it does.' I answered. 'But not even the family is above the law.'

I knew that I had gone too far – over the lip of the known world and into insanity. Behind and around me was a forbidding hush. I realised I was alone on this issue. When Grandfather Tamihana came for me, hip-hopping across the room, I knew that this was just between me and him – nobody would come to my defence.

Grandfather lifted me up by the scruff of the neck. He pulled me out of the drawing room, past Mum and Dad and into the kitchen. He threw me out into the back yard. When Grandmother tried to stop him, he roared, 'Stay out of this.'

He turned to me.

'Ever since you were born –'

Jabbing me like a boxer.

'You have been like a viper at my bosom –'

Hitting my stomach, my chest.

'Every time I want something –'

Feinting at my face.

'You are always there to confound me –'

The first hit to my temple. Blood pouring from the cut.

'Not any more.'

Slowly and methodically Grandfather began to take me apart. Oh, I could have fought back, but what was the use? Grandfather would have beaten me to pulp in time. Better to let him get it over with. It was faster this way. I tasted blood on my lips. I saw everything in a haze. The family had come out to watch, standing there on the verandah.

Yes, I suppose I had this coming. After all, the family did come first and I had challenged that commandment. Yes, I suppose I did deserve it, but *oh shit* standing up for your principles *hurt* –

Then I heard somebody screaming and yelling. Someone small was running across the back yard.

Glory.

'You leave my brother alone!'

She jumped onto Grandfather Tamihana's back. She put her legs around his waist and began to claw at his eyes.

'Run, Simeon,' Glory cried. '*Run*!'

She was a raging cyclone of fists and fury, spitting like a kitten. I tried to warn her that she was in danger, but my mouth was filled with blood.

No, no, Glory. Play dead, darling. Play dead.

The bastard was hitting *her* too. He reached behind, tore Glory from his back and threw her against the pump. She squealed with shock.

'Glory, no –'

I ran to my sister. Grandfather was after us.

'That's enough, Father.'

A strong arm came behind Grandfather to restrain him.

'These are my children, Father. So help me God, I will kill you if you raise another hand against either of them.'

My father, Joshua, was standing between us. His voice was all choked up. He was trembling with sorrow.

'Get out of the way, Joshua,' Grandfather threatened. 'That boy needs to be taught a lesson.'

'Please don't make me do this,' Dad said. 'Please –'

Grandfather tried to push past him. My father's fist came up. He cracked Grandfather on the jaw. Grandfather fell. He was like a huge tree, crashing in slow motion to the ground. The silence surrounding his fall was thunderous.

Dad started to sob. 'Oh God forgive me –'

Slowly, the family emerged from the verandah. My mother and Grandmother Ramona came to me, Glory and my father Joshua. Zebediah Whatu, Ihaka Mahana and aunts and uncles gathered around Grandfather to help him up and into the house. Uncle Hone put an arm around me.

225

'It will be all right,' he said.

A spell was broken that night – a spell that had been cast for a long time. The spell had to be broken so that we could all grow. But as with all momentous changes, the breaking of the spell came with great sadness. The children of Ranginui, when they separated their father sky from their mother earth so that they could walk upright, must have felt exactly as we did on that night.

47

Three weeks later a huge crowd from Gisborne and the East Coast came to farewell the special steam express which was travelling from Gisborne to Masterton via Napier, Hastings, Waipukurau and Dannevirke carrying the two teams from Gisborne who were representing the province in the Golden Fleece competition. The whole town was caught up in the excitement, no doubt assisted by the local newspaper editor who likened our journey to that taken by the Greek hero Jason and his valiant argonauts, who sought and finally won the golden fleece. Even the mayor could not resist the opportunity for some classical allusion of his own.

'The hopes of the district go with you,' he said. 'On your return, we will look for a white sail of victory rather than the black sail of disappointment.'

The brass band played. Red and blue bunting fluttered in the breeze. The train conductor called, 'All aboard!', and the express began to chug out of the station. The people on the platform were like tiny flags. We burst out of the suburbs into the green country. The steam from the engine was a white pennant curling in the sky.

All of Waituhi was on that train. Carriages five and six were taken by the Hukareka people, including Rupeni Poata. Behind them were supporters from all over the province. We took up carriages three and four, both the Mormon and non-Mormon sides of the valley. Among us was Nani Mini Tupara. Stay at home while everybody was at Masterton? Get off the grass. Religious differences aside, we were *all* family, deriving common ancestry from Mahaki, the leader of our iwi.

Grandfather Tamihana and Grandmother Ramona, being VIPs,

were up in the first carriage with other provincial officials. Aunt Ruth was with them. She had the pip with me and was still siding with her father.

I think all of us were glad that Grandfather was not sitting with us. After the family meeting Ihaka Mahana and Zebediah Whatu had tried to reconcile him with the legal situation about Mahana Four: no substitutions would be allowed. He remained adamant. In the end I suggested a show of hands be taken and, for the first time, Grandfather Tamihana realised he had lost against his own family. Is this how democracy begins?

'Mahana Four will never win,' he said when the results of the vote were read to him. 'However, if that is what all of you want – to support a losing team – then so be it.'

When I think back on it, I know that Grandfather Tamihana was right to be anxious about the composition of Mahana Four. We had gone into the provincial competition with our usual crew – Uncle Hone, Dad, Pani, Uncle Albie and Sam Whatu as our shearers; Haromi and Frances as sweepers; Aunt Sephora as our wool classer aided by Mum, Miriam – Aunt Ruth had gone back to Mahana Two – and Esther, and David and Benjamin on the press. I was still the sheepo with my two mates Peewee and Mackie and, even though she hated the attention, Glory was a grim presence concentrating on her dags. By contrast, both Poata One and the Lawson syndicate were made up entirely of adults. The Brute was doing the *dags*, for goodness sake.

Being in the national finals was different. No *way* could we hope to compete and expect to win – not with Haromi still throwing the occasional fleece upside down or Uncle Albie's slow pace. But there was no turning back. It must have been luck, after all.

At the last moment, Hukareka asked the judges if *they* could make two substitutions. The judges agreed on condition that Waituhi also have that option available to them. Thus Uncle Albie stepped down in favour of Uncle Matiu and Aunt Ruth replaced Frances. Grandfather at least got part of his way. Wily as he was, he also tried to have Mohi take over either David or Benjamin's position on the press. Their father Sam would not have it.

Even at the railway station Grandfather was still scheming, trying to convince Uncle Hone to relinquish his rights as leader to his eldest brother Matiu. From somewhere in the stratosphere Uncle Hone found the strength to say, 'No, Father Mahana. You gave me Mahana Four. You said it was mine. You cannot tell me to step down from being the head of Mahana Four. It is *my* family.'

I had indeed brought down Olympus.

Publicity about the special train to Masterton had spread over all the island. Whenever the train stopped along the way people were there to wish us luck and congratulations. Some were relatives from Waituhi who were pining just for a short glimpse of a mum, dad, aunt or uncle. In the end – what the heck – some jumped on and came down with us.

At Waipukurau there was a surprise visitor – Lloyd, in a wheelchair, trying to make sounds with his mouth. Mahana Two were overjoyed to see their old friend. The women shed a tear or two. The men yarned to him as if he was the same old Lloyd. When he saw Grandfather Tamihana and Grandmother Ramona he tried to take Grandfather's hand to kiss it.

'Th-*an*-k y-*ou*,' he enunciated. He was still on the payroll.

The carriage was quiet after Waipukurau. Lloyd had reminded us of our mortality. He had also made me remember the deep love and respect that people had for Grandfather. When had my relationship with Bulibasha started to go wrong? Or did the 'when' really matter? The relationship was broken – that was the reality. And it was not entirely my fault. Grandfather just did not want the world to change. I was a new generation. Somewhere between both lay the reason.

'Masterton next stop,' the conductor called.

'Here we go,' Uncle Hone gulped.

We started to clean up our carriages and change for the reception we knew was awaiting us. When the train steamed to a halt it seemed that all of Masterton was there – including, to Haromi's delight, an international film crew who asked her to pose for them on a bale of wool. In a trice her cleavage deepened and her skirt developed a split up the side.

'I'm the mother! I'm the mother!' Aunt Sarah cried. She tried to join her daughter in the photograph. Like a true professional Haromi just happened to cross her legs – and kick Aunt Sarah off the bale. There were no flies on Haromi.

The mayor of Masterton said a few words of welcome and offered us all the hospitality of the town.

'I hope you will not mind,' he said, 'but we have a ticker tape parade arranged for all the teams and supporters tonight.'

Did we *mind*? Not a bit.

People were lined on either side of the road, cheering like mad as we joined the other finalists in a cavalcade of floats down the main street. For this inaugural contest the floats comprised a historical pageant, showing the coming of the first sheep to New Zealand and the development of the wool industry. Some of the floats had models parading woollen garments. Others had bands playing songs like 'Click Go the Shears Boys, Click Click Click'. There were marching girls, high-stepping along with us, and highland bands playing Scottish songs. Way up front were the Kahungunu Maori Culture Club, singing their hearts out.

The buses were going so slow that Andrew and I pleaded to be let off to march along with the parade – our legs needed the exercise. At that suggestion everybody wanted to pile out too, even old Uncle Pera. Somewhere along the way Haromi got lost, and when we next saw her she was being filmed blowing kisses at us from a long white limousine. How did she manage to get there?

Somebody bumped into me from the back. Poppy. She was laughing and so excited that we did a little dance together in the middle of the street. Full of bravery I pulled her to me and kissed her. She struggled but I held on. I was enjoying it. I had heard that you were supposed to put your tongue down the girl's throat, but Poppy's teeth were clamped tight. Aha, but on the side *there* was a gap and – ouch! Poppy was furious.

'Oh, you –'

She pushed me away and slapped me hard. Then she ran off.

At last the parade reached the showgrounds where the competition would take place. Streamers were flying, banners were waving and at the entrance was hung a huge golden cloud, glowing with fluorescent lights. The Golden Fleece. Just at that moment three jet planes from Ohakea airbase *whooshed* across the grounds and vertically into the sky. The planes took my heart up with them.

Later that night, following the official reception, fireworks lit the showground.

'Are we really here?' Glory asked.

'Yes,' I answered.

She saw that I was lost to the stars. 'Don't forget your promise,' she said.

'What promise!'

'You said you would never leave me, Simeon.'

I took Glory's hand.

We had arrived.

48

Imagine this if you can. A bright Wairarapa morning. The sky has just been washed, rinsed and hung out to dry. A traffic officer, all spit and polish in white uniform, directs the line of cars which, today, are all heading to one place – a stadium with a sparkling golden cloud hovering over the entrance.

'There it is!'

The traffic is directed to park in fields next to the stadium. Family groups are walking swiftly to the entrance, queuing for tickets, bustling through the turnstiles to get a good seat.

'Let's find a good seat, Dad. Over there! See?'

The women wear floral dresses and hats. The men wear long trousers and sports coats. The teenagers and children assume an insouciant air, dressed in fashions straight out of the *New Zealand Woman's Weekly*. Families have brought hats against the sun, and picnic baskets.

'Would you like a programme, madam?' The programme sellers are pretty teenage girls from the local schools. They wear Golden Fleece sashes across their shoulders.

'Thank you, dear!'

The children want ice creams and pink candyfloss. They settle down for the curtain raiser about to begin.

'What's first on the programme, Dad?'

A marching team is performing intricate manoeuvres on the green, right in front of the main seating area. The girls look smart and pretty with braided military jackets, white skirts and white boots. Their leader twirls her baton and blows short sharp whistle commands. The team's choreography dissolves from military two-step into a ferris wheel pattern, a high-stepping box pattern and back into a perfect single line slow-marching towards the stadium.

'Oh well done, girls!'

While the girls are marching, local carpenters are still hammering away and adding the final touches to the three stages which have been erected in the middle of the arena.

'Goodness, will they be finished on time, Dad?'

The stages, marked Stage 1, Stage 2 and Stage 3, are arranged facing each other in a horseshoe shape. This way the shearing gangs can keep an eye on one another as they compete in the heats. The arrangement also means that no matter where you are sitting in the audience, you will have a good view of all the stages.

At the front of each stage is the shearer's board, with five positions for the shearers in each gang. The board is just wide enough for the sweepers, wool handlers and person on the dags to do their work.

'They'll have to be careful, love, otherwise they'll fall off!'

To one side of the board is the fleecos' table, where the fleece will be thrown and the sacks for the skirting pieces. Close to the table is the wool press. Behind the board are the shearer's holding pens and behind them are the bigger pens where the sheep are already waiting to be shorn. That's where the sheepos will work. When the sheep have been shorn, down they'll slide to the front of the horseshoe, where the judges will look at them and judge the quality of the shearers' work.

Shearers shear twenty-five sheep each. The best overall shearer in the competition will get the Jason statuette.

'Goodness me, how will the judges be able to choose!'

'It's going to be ber-loody close, love.'

Let's have a look at the programme.

Twenty-seven shearing gangs have made it to the finals of the first Golden Fleece championships.

'Doesn't that just make you feel so proud to be from Masterton?'

The shearing gangs have come from way up north of Whangarei to way down south of Invercargill. There's even a gang of Aussie shearers come all the way from Darwin. Doesn't that just take the cake?

Today are the preliminary heats – nine heats, with three gangs competing in each. At the end of the day there will be nine winners. Tomorrow, the nine winners will face each other in the three semifinal heats. Three days after that, the three winners of those will face each other in the finals.

'Which shearing gangs are in the first heat, love?'

The spectators begin to place their bets. Let's see -- Morrison (Wanganui), Karaka (Christchurch) and Simpson (Bay of Plenty).

Let's put five quid on Morrison! Oh, and our own Wairarapa gang, the Gregsons, are in the second heat, we must bet on them. Who are they up against? Oh dear, that shearing gang from Otago is supposed to be very good ... Ah well, that's the luck of the draw.

Now, when are the Maoris on? You know, the family whose photo was in the newspaper? Ah, there, heat 6 this afternoon. Wilson (Hawke's Bay), Jelley (Southland) – and Mahana Four (Gisborne).

Ah yes, the photo in the newspaper. If you ask people today what they remember about that first Golden Fleece championship in 1958, it's not the name of the shearing gang which won but 'Oh yes. The family of God.'

The photograph was a lucky snap taken by a photographer from the New Zealand Press Association and wired to all the newspapers in the country as well as to Australia and England. The London *Times* picked the photograph up and put it on the front page under the headline: THE FAMILY THAT PRAYS TOGETHER SHEARS TOGETHER.

The photograph shows Mahana Four at prayer the night before the heats. Uncle Hone, Uncle Matiu, Dad, Sam Whatu and Pani are standing at the back. Aunt Sephora, Aunt Ruth, Aunt Miriam, Aunt Kate, Mum and Haromi stand within their protective arc. David, Benjamin, Peewee and Mackie are on the left. Glory and I are on the right. In the foreground, Grandfather Tamihana has his hand upraised. Behind us flutters Aunt Sarah's flag, the maroon one with the golden angel at its centre. None of us even knew the photograph was being taken. We had our eyes shut.

The photograph caught the public imagination.

In the photograph Mahana Four looks the very picture of serenity and calm. The reality was – hardly. No sooner had we arrived at the stadium than Aunt Sarah, who had been watching the heats all day, came running into the dressing rooms like a chicken with her head cut off.

'Oh my goodness, oh heck, oh –' She acted as if it was the end of the world.

'Now what's this all about, sis?' Uncle Hone asked.

'I knew I should have brought the cloaks,' Aunt Sarah gasped. 'Or at least the sashes.'

'What for?'

'Have you seen what the other gangs are wearing? They've made new outfits! Bright red singlets. Or yellow shirts with their own insignias. Even Hukareka had the presence of mind to bring their hockey shirts. And what is Mahana Four wearing?'

We looked at Aunt Sarah blankly. Didn't she know? Our usual rough woollen pants held up with string, of course! Our black singlets and sack moccasins, naturally! And Mum and the fleecos were wearing what they always wore – their dresses with coveralls and bedroom slippers.

'This is how we always look when we're at the shed,' Aunt Ruth shrugged.

'You will look like hobos!'

'Well,' Haromi yawned, 'I wouldn't say everybody.' She had teased her hair up and planned to wear high heels.

Uncle Hone tried to calm Aunt Sarah down. 'This is a shearing competition, sis, not a beauty contest.' He looked at Haromi. 'No high heels. You throw the fleeces crooked enough already.'

To top is off, Uncle Matiu started to panic too.

'Look, bro,' he said, 'we're the only gang with kids in it.'

'What's the fuss?' Uncle Hone asked. 'This is the way Mahana Four has always been. We're a family shearing gang.'

'Don't you understand?' Uncle Matiu said. 'Of the twenty-seven gangs here, all except us are composed entirely of adults. Even Rupeni Poata's gang. What hope have Simeon, Peewee and Mackie against adult sheepos? Those other sheepos are fast. They're not worried about beating each other. All they're worried about is beating the clock. Father wants Mohi to come in as sheepo –'

Uncle Hone sighed.

'Then,' Uncle Matiu persisted, 'having Glory on the dags will make a laughing stock of us, and –'

Uncle Hone had had enough. 'No,' he said. 'The trouble, Matiu, is that you and father have never actually seen Mahana Four in action. You've both been too busy burying your heads in the sand to even *see* how good we are. Mahana Four is a good team, Matiu. We're all used to each other's ways. We know each other's strengths and weaknesses. You're just a ring-in for Mahana Four. I will not have you and Father upsetting my family like this. Things stay as they are. That is final.'

Way to go, Uncle Hone!

'Well,' Uncle Matiu shrugged. 'Okay, bro, you're the boss.'

He smiled sickly at us. 'But I think we better all stay clear of Bulibasha for a while and let him think he's had his way!'

He looked across at Grandfather and waved cheerily. How Grandfather wanted to interpret *that* was his business.

Even so, by the time our heat began we had seen enough of the other teams to know we didn't look like being in the running at all. We also heard that Poata One had won their heat by a mile, outgunning the competition like Machine Gun Kelly's gang. Although the news was expected it didn't make us feel any happier. Nor, on a personal level, was I feeling happy either. Since that first kiss Poppy seemed to be avoiding me. Every time I looked at her she looked away. Then, just before we were ready to go on, she came up to me.

'You're a Mahana,' she said. 'I'm a Poata. We're on opposite sides.'

The loudspeaker blared. 'Heat Number Six –'

Six six ix ix nix ix.

'On Stage 1 the Wilson gang from Hawke's Bay; Stage 2 the Jelley gang from Southland, and Stage 3 the Mahana gang from Waituhi, Gisborne –'

Gisborne scorn forlorn orn orn or.

I gulped and clutched Glory's hand. She looked up at me, puzzled. What was all the fuss?

The two other gangs came running out in their bright scarlet and blue mocker. They looked like silver people, smiling and bowing to the audience. We were still cowering in the wings. Aunt Sarah was right. We did look like hobos, even worse than Fred Astaire and Judy Garland singing 'We're Just a Couple of Swells' from *Easter Parade*. The Vanderbilts would never have asked *us* out to tea.

'Ah well,' Uncle Hone said, 'let's say a prayer to make us feel better.'

And there we were, praying again, our heads bowed to the Lord. We didn't realise that everyone in the stadium could see us. Had we known, do you think we would have done it?

Oh look. So it *is* true. They *do* pray.

'Okay,' Uncle Hone said, 'let's get it over with.'

When we shambled out, me holding Glory's hand, we were unprepared for the warmth of our reception. We climbed on to the stage and did what we always do. Uncle gave his string belt a tug – and the stadium hummed with amusement.

'Well I don't want you people to get a good surprise,' he said.

Then Aunt Ruth started putting her hair up into a scarf and Aunt Kate shuffled into her old slippers and said, 'E hika, my toes are poking out.'

Again, laughter rolled around the audience.

Finally, Mum kissed Glory, who ran across the stage between everybody's legs and sat on her box waiting for the dags to come her way. When people laughed, her face grew grim. She scowled and then poked out her tongue.

Peewee, Mackie and I went to the big pen ready for the race to get the obligatory twenty-five sheep into the shearers' holding pens.

'Are you guys ready?' I asked. Peewee was taking huge gulps of air. 'I'm counting on you both.'

They grinned.

The starter had his pistol pointed to the air. His voice reverberated across the stadium.

'Are you ready?'

Ready ready eady eady dy dy.

'Steady?'

Steady steady eady dy dy.

The pistol crack echoed in the air.

'*Go*!'

49

Well blow me down and tie me to a lamp post. Mahana Four actually won our heat.

Grandfather was sitting with Grandmother Ramona, Zebediah Whatu and Ihaka Mahana when the winners were announced, and he just about fell out of his seat. Nani Mini Tupara, sitting behind the men, laughed and laughed.

'Ana! Take that!'

The victory was trumpeted in the newspapers. The publicists for the championships knew a good angle when they saw one. On the morning of the second day there was the mayor of Masterton patting a scowling Glory on the head:

FAMILY OF GOD MAKES SEMIFINALS.

On that second day, however, the news was not so good. The

semifinalists were *fast*, and we were up against the Robinson gang from Northland, Horopura gang from Nelson and Christie gang from Auckland. To bolster our confidence Aunt Sarah presented us with our maroon sashes – she had rung home for them and had them sent down. We were appreciative, but –

'No, Sarah,' Uncle Hone said. 'We still look like hobos. The only difference is that we now look like hobos with sashes on.'

Walking out on Stage 2 was a different experience from the day before. Amidst the applause individual voices were calling out –

'Come on, Hone!'

'Show them how to throw a fleece, Auntie Miriam!'

'Attagirl, Glory!'

As if people knew us personally.

When we lost our semifinals heat to the Robinsons, who finished way ahead, the audience was disappointed. Grandfather was shaking his head. Our luck had run out.

But what do you know? Our marks for quality work took us to the front. Another photograph – Aunt Sarah managed to insinuate herself into this one of Mahana Four sitting on a wool bale – flashed across the Press Association wires:

HALLELUIAH, THEY'RE IN!

Golden Fleece fever hit Masterton. All the shearing gangs were feted, invited to functions and treated like royalty. We were always surprised to be stopped and congratulated. Glory was very popular and hated it. People thought she was just adorable and asked for her autograph. Aunt Molly didn't escape the limelight either. Although she said she was 'Just the cook' she attracted the attention of a food journalist who asked her what she fed Mahana Four.

'Oh, dumplings, watercress, boiled spuds, kamokamo –'

The article on Auntie Molly came out the next day and said that 'Auntie Molly's pièce de résistance is a bouillabaise of a Hungaro-Romanian flavour in which carefully moulded boules of flour enriched with natural spices are marinated with cress au naturel, potatoes à la Provence and a piquant tuber found only in exotic surroundings –'

'I'm keeping my mouth shut from now on,' Auntie Molly said.

Grandfather was in his element, his pride puffing up his chest like a pouter pigeon's. Wherever he and Grandmother Ramona went they commanded a respectful audience. Grandfather had not lost his misgivings, but he had been surprised at the efficiency and precision of Mahana Four. As far as the finals was concerned, though, he didn't think we had a hope in Hades. Mahana Four was competing against the Gregson gang, the home team from Wairarapa – and, of course, Poata One, who were widely expected to win. Caesar Poata was the fastest shearer at the championship.

Grandfather's obsession with the Poata shearing gang had increased during the few days we had been in Masterton. In some respects he seemed more intent on their losing than our winning. I was watching him when he attended the semifinal shear-off involving the Poata gang. I swear that Grandfather never moved a muscle, and yet he seemed to be sending down thunderbolts of psychic energy designed to cripple their shearers or set fire to their wool. The effort was burning him out, turning him into an empty husk. As the finals approached, Grandfather became more jittery. Zebediah Whatu and Ihaka Mahana tried to keep him calm, but the publicity was having an adverse effect on him. The more Mahana Four got the spotlight, the more he worried about the reaction when we lost.

'The Poatas have the better team. I know they have, because I've timed them. They are five minutes faster than the Gregson gang and six minutes faster than us. They will leave us in the dust.'

'Ma te wa,' Ihaka intoned. 'What the Lord wills will be.'

Aunt Ruth tried to jolly him. 'Father, you never know. One of their women just might eat something the night before and get as sick as a dog –'

'Or one of their shearers might have a little accident –' Uncle Hone winked.

'Just remember the angel,' Aunt Sarah said. 'Didn't the angel promise that the family would prosper?'

'Ae,' Grandfather agreed. 'But it didn't say we would win the Golden Fleece championship! Anyway, we need more than an angel to win.'

'You should have more faith,' I said.

'Don't preach to me, Himiona.'

'We will try our best for you, Grandfather, but that's all we can do.'

'You *must* win.' Grandfather would not let go.

'Whether we win or lose,' I said, 'is out of your hands anyway.'

'Oh is it now?'

Grandfather was still trying to manipulate destiny. Not content to allow history to take its course, he was trying to write it according

237

to his dictates. He had decided to take up the pen, forcibly cross out the intended outcome of our lives and alter our destiny to suit his own expectations. The arrogance of that assumption was breathtaking. Driven by the history of the Mahana shearing gangs, and his active role in it, Grandfather could not contemplate anything other than a triumphant ending.

Then the roof fell in.

For some reason, perhaps to do with excitement, it never occurred to us to look at the date on which the finals would be held. Sunday night: the night the family went to church. None of the Mahana shearing gangs ever sheared on a Sunday.

Grandfather called an urgent family meeting, and in a flash resumed control. Once again his decision would determine our course. I hated relinquishing our freedom.

'Are you sure the final is on Sunday?' Grandfather Tamihana asked. He could barely conceal his glee. This was a wonderful excuse, the perfect opportunity, for him to withdraw the team. There was even dignity in such a proposal, and it would prevent all the embarrassment of a loss. I knew he would take it.

'There's only one thing to do,' Grandfather Tamihana said. 'Mahana Four will have to pull out of the championship.'

The newspapers had a field day:

THEY WON'T SHEAR ON SUNDAYS.

Across the nation editorials applauded Grandfather's stand. From the pulpit churchmen preached the rightness of the decision to their flocks. Even the Anglican Archbishop sent Grandfather his congratulations. Hasty and urgent meetings were held between the Golden Fleece officials. Delegations of one kind or another trod their way to Grandfather's door.

'We can understand your Christian principles, Mr Mahana,' they began, 'but is there not a way around all this?' In other words, Can you change your mind?

Part way through all the furore I happened to have a second with Grandfather.

'Congratulations,' I said.

'What for?' he asked, surprised.

'Well of course Poata One will win now,' I said. Take *that*, you sanctimonious bastard.

Soon after that, Grandfather became very silent. When delegations came to him he was not available. Finally he said:

'Nobody can change my mind – except God Himself.'

He locked himself in his room.

'What's he doing?' the reporters asked.

Aunt Sarah dipped into the room to find out. When she came out she looked as if she'd died and gone to Heaven. A thousand-piece Hollywood orchestra and chorus blasted us with holy music.

'My father –' she looked holier than usual, her hands clasped in prayer and eyes seeking a vision, 'is asking God what to do.'

The headlines were predictable:

TAMIHANA SEEKS GOD'S ADVICE.

Grandfather stayed holed up in his room for two days. The press contingent at the Golden Fleece increased daily. The whole of Masterton, New Zealand, Australia and Great Britain held its breath. Sometimes during his period of contemplation and prayer Grandfather came out of his room and went for a walk.

'Any news for the public, Mr Mahana?'

'Nothing.'

'Will your shearing gang be in the finals?'

'I don't know.'

Aha. A 'Don't know' wasn't a 'yes' but it wasn't a 'no' either.

Then one night as he was walking, Grandfather happened across Rupeni Poata. They talked and separated. The next morning, Grandfather went for another walk. He met Rupeni Poata again. Rupeni shook Grandfather's hand, as if congratulating him for his firm moral stand. I didn't place any importance on the meetings until much later. As for me, my thoughts were as heretical as ever.

A TELEPHONE BOOTH. GRANDFATHER TAMIHANA APPROACHES, ENTERS, PUTS COINS IN THE PAYPHONE AND DIALS A NUMBER.

HEAVENLY VOICE Ko wai koe e karanga nei?
(Subtitles: Who is calling please?)
TAMIHANA Ko ahau a Tamihana he pononga o te Atua.
(Subtitles: A servant of the Lord.)
HEAVENLY VOICE Ah, kei te pirangi ahau ki te korero ki a Pa?
(Subtitles: Ah, do you want to speak to Dad?)
TAMIHANA Ae.
(Subtitles: Yes.)

THERE IS A CLICK, A PAUSE, AND JESUS IS TRYING TO TELL HIS FATHER TO GET OUT OF THE SHOWER TO ANSWER THE PHONE. THEN A VOICE COMES BOOMING DOWN THE TELEPHONE LINE.

TE ATUA He aha to hiahia!
(Subtitles: So what do you want now!)

Finally, the night before the finals, when suspense was at fever pitch and the officials had pulled out all their hair, Grandfather came out of the hotel room. The reporters crowded around. I looked across at him.

Okay, Grandfather, break our hearts. Be holier than thou. Save your face and hide behind the church –

Whaddyaknow, he surprised me.

'Mahana Four will shear in the finals,' he said.

The headlines announced:

GOD SAYS YES!

50

How we kept our heads in all that circus I'll never know. Although it was fun at first, the movie-star treatment began to drive us up the wall. Glory summed it up. 'Are we going home straight after this?' she asked.

'Yes,' Mum answered.

'Good,' Glory said. 'I miss our river.'

Only Haromi and Aunt Sarah, who was dying to get into Mahana Four, seemed to enjoy the stardom. She also pleaded with us to get some new maroon singlets or at least belts to replace the string on our trousers.

'We are who we are,' Uncle Hone said.

Why bother? We knew we wouldn't win.

The night of the finals the traffic outside the stadium was bedlam and people were being turned away from the gates. The Golden Fleece officials were ecstatic. We weren't. A full house meant more people to look at us and we were tired of being seen as freaks. Then Aunt Sarah burst out that three crews had arrived to film the finals. Oh great. Now our string belts, baggy pants and holey singlets would be seen in America, Europe, Asia and Outer Mongolia.

'Ah well,' Uncle Hone said. 'Last time up, folks. Then hoki mai tatou ki te wa kainga.' He was terrific. In one phrase he'd lifted our spirits.

Grandfather and Grandmother Ramona came down from the grandstand to say prayers with us. Grandmother looked so beautiful she made my heart ache. She was wearing her dress of Spanish lace. Her necklace glowed like moonstones.

'I know you will do your best,' Grandfather Tamihana said. Nothing more, nothing less. Then, escorted by Grandmother Ramona and Aunt Sarah, he returned to his seat.

The loudspeaker blared. 'Ladies and gentlemen, welcome to the finals of the Golden Fleece award –'

Award award oh lord lord ord.

The teams were introduced. Poata One was on Stage 1. The Gregson gang was on Stage 2. Mahana was on Stage 3. At each announcement the teams ran out into the middle of the arena and bowed. The Gregsons had all been to the hairdressers and the shearers had shiny new equipment. The Poatas were spruced up too and they had woollen jackets given by a local sponsor. Then it was our turn. Same old rough-as-guts us.

'E hika,' Aunt Ruth whispered.

Under the arc lights we felt like ants being looked at from a microscope. Towering on all sides were the stands of people, hushed, waiting, filled to the brim. Every now and then a battery of flash bulbs would go off. We felt completely forlorn. Mum, I could tell, was just about ready to take off and run away from it all.

Good old bossy Aunt Sarah saved us. Seeing us standing there, so far away, she was moved to tears of pride. She stood up in her seat and let rip with a powerful karanga that soared through the darkness. The karanga told us how proud our people were, to remember that we were from Waituhi and to come forward now. Nani Mini Tupara, then Grandmother Ramona, joined her. Before we knew it, Mahana Four had slipped into a haka, moving forward under the arc lights like a travelling ope. Fearless. Commanding. Unafraid.

'Ka mate ka mate ka ora ka ora
  Ka mate ka mate ka ora ka ora –'

I felt so proud. Aunt Ruth was doing the pukana for all she was worth. Aunt Sephora, Aunt Miriam, Aunt Kate and Haromi were quivering their hands and stamping their feet, and when they advanced you knew you'd better look out. Uncle Hone, Uncle Matiu,

Dad, Sam Whatu, David and Benjamin went out in an arrow formation to protect the women. They were gesticulating with what they were carrying – handpieces, broom handles, whatever. Peewee, Mackie and I brought up the rear. Oh yes, and Glory too, spitting and squealing her warning to all.

'Tenei te tangata puhuruhuru nana nei whakawhiti te ra
A haupane! Kaupane! Haupane kaupane whiti te ra!'

And all of a sudden there was a wave of applause and people were calling out –

'Come on the maroon!' 'Let it rip Auntie Ruth!' 'Rattle those dags, Glory!'

Before we knew it, the darkness was filled with people calling us by our names. People whom we wouldn't have known from Adam. People who had been following our progress and saw in us something of themselves. Something to do with people who could come out of nowhere and try to get somewhere. Something about reaching for the unreachable, touching the stars with your fingertips, searching after an impossible dream.

The starter came out with his starter gun. Big jolly Uncle Hone, a lump in his throat, pulled his pants up and turned to us.

'You know me,' he said. 'I leave the big speeches to Father or my older brothers.'

'Kia kaha,' we answered. At that moment we would have followed Uncle Hone to the end of the world.

'Work cleanly,' he said. 'Don't worry about speeding. Those other fellas have it over on us when it comes to that. Mahana Four has always had a reputation for good work. I don't care if we come last as long as we do a quality job. I have *never* been so proud of my family as at this moment.'

Uncle Hone did not know that microphones were picking up his speech and taking his words via radio to every listening household in the country. From somewhere far away the response came back. Wave after wave of acclamation.

The film crew was ready for action. All of a sudden lights blazed throughout the arena. Aunt Ruth did a double take and brought out dark glasses. Haromi primped her hair in readiness. Aunt Sephora smoothed her overalls. Dad, looking self-conscious, winked at Mum. I gave a special look to Glory, sitting on her stool waiting for the dags. The starter raised his pistol to the night sky.

'Oh my giddy aunt,' Aunt Ruth said, 'doesn't he know that God lives over there?'

She broke us up and made us laugh.
'Are you ready?' the starter asked.
Ready as we'll ever be –
'Are you steady!'
No, but that's not going to stop –
The pistol cracked.
'*Go*!'

Peewee, Mackie and I had been born for this moment.

'Hut!' Peewee was yelling. 'Hut!'

There were three judges, one at each of the stages. They sprang to action, watching the sheepos and taking notes on our sheep-handling skills. We pushed the one hundred and twenty-five sheep from the large back pen into the holding pens.

'Get in there!' Mackie was whistling.

The strategy was that I would fill Uncle Hone and Dad's pens; Mackie and Peewee together would fill Uncle Matiu's, Pani's and Sam Whatu's pens. Not until each pen had twenty-five sheep in it could the shearers begin. Our job was to try to give our shearers a head start, get them out front so that they could stay out front.

'Come on, Molly!' I was trying Uncle Hone's trick out on the sheep, pushing them gently into the pens. Peewee was casting a look at how the other sheepos for Gregsons and Poata One were getting on. 'Don't bother about them!' I called. But I couldn't help sneaking a look myself. The Gregson sheepos were manhandling their sheep over the fences rather than pushing them through the gates. The Poatas were using small sticks to get the sheep through.

Ah well, each to his own technique. I had my own worries to think about. Getting twenty-five sheep in each pen was difficult. The count could easily be wrong.

'Twenty-five in Pen 5!' Mackie called.

'Twenty-five in Pen 4!' Peewee called.

'Twenty-five in Pen 1!' I called.

Already the Gregson and Poata One gangs had finished their counts. No, hang on, the judge over at the Poatas was raising a red flag to indicate their count was wrong!

'Twenty-five in Pen 2!' I called.

Finally, 'Twenty-five in Pen 3!' Peewee called.

The crowd was roaring. The Gregson shearers had started on their first sheep; we were just behind them and now the Poata shearers had started. However, the job for Peewee, Mackie and me wasn't over yet. Not until one of the judges had checked our count could we let go our breath.

'Well done, lads,' he said.

Phew. But we still had to remain alert. Sometimes when the shearers came in for a sheep, another one would try to get out.

Oh look, that was happening over at the Gregsons! There was pandemonium on the Gregson board as the sheepos tried to catch the culprit and get it back into the shearer's pen. I gave a look at *our* sheep.

We love you, Auntie Molly, we really *do*.

Now it was up to the shearers. The Gregson shearers were positively *ripping* through their first sheep. Now they were on to their second, rushing with a slam into their pens. The sheep kicked and baa-ed with fear under the arc lights. The Poata gang had drawn level with us. They were fast all right! No, *wait*, one of the shearers hadn't quite clicked off his handpiece! It was buzzing like a wild thing out of control and clashing with the other handpieces.

As for us, Uncle Hone was shouting above the noise. 'Just take it easy, boys. No need to look up at how the Gregsons and the Poatas are doing. Feel the rhythm. Concentrate on your own sheep. We've got a long way to go yet.'

'We've got to increase the pace,' Uncle Matiu shouted back. 'Otherwise we'll get too far behind.' Uncle Hone simply smiled at him. 'Bro, you do as I say or else –'

Oh it was good to see our shearers moving their handpieces through the sheep's wool. Then one by one the sheep were going down the slide and our shearers were walking swiftly in to get their second.

Halfway through our second sheep the Gregsons were ahead and going for their third sheep. The Poatas too had pulled ahead of us. They caught up to the Gregsons, shearing neck and neck. The crowd was thrilled. But cries of 'Tar!' were going up on their stands.

'Easy does it,' Uncle Hone said. 'Don't get rattled, boys. We're here to do a quality job.'

The judge on our stage nodded and made a note.

An instruction came over the loudspeaker: '*Change judges.*'

The judge from Stage 1 went to Stage 2. The judge from Stage 2 went to Stage 3. The judge from Stage 3 went over to Stage 1. The audience loved the fairness which allowed the judges to get a good overview of the work of all the shearing gangs.

Aunt Ruth and Haromi had begun sweeping in and around each shearer's sheep.

'Dags away!' Aunt Ruth yelled. She pushed the dags over to Glory.

'Go for it, Glory!' one of her fans yelled.

Haromi was waiting for Uncle Matiu to finish his sheep. She flicked with her broom at the falling wool – face wool to one side, stomach and underside wool somewhere else. She put aside her broom and started to guide the fleece gently to one side, clearing it as Uncle Matiu shifted the sheep on to its back.

Along came the fleecos, Mum and Miriam, to take the fleeces to Aunt Sephora and Aunt Kate on the table. Oh no, now Haromi had decided to help them. Pulling the fleece clear. Bundling it up in her arms. Then a huge throw like a net and – perfect. The fleece glittered as it unfolded, seemed to pause on the air before falling squarely on the table. No wonder. Haromi had seen the cameras coming to film the action on our board.

'Talk about lucky!' Aunt Ruth laughed, hands on hips, forgetting where we were.

'If you've got it, flaunt it,' Haromi yawned.

They heard the laughter from the stadium and blanched.

'Oh shi-ucks,' Haromi said, making it worse. She did a little curtsy to the judge and the crowd.

The Poatas were neck and neck with the Gregsons on their fourth sheep. The crowd roared again as five Poata men on Stage 1 and five Gregson men on Stage 3 went into their pens together, dragging out their fifth sheep. 'Tar!' a Gregson shearer cried. *Our* shearers were just starting the fourth sheep. I took the chance to say to Peewee and Mackie, 'Thanks, guys. Next season you're both on the payroll.' They gasped and reddened. Being on the payroll was even better than coming down to the Golden Fleece. They gulped and shook each other by the hand.

There was a clatter of laughter from the crowd. One of the Gregson shearers, when turning his sheep, had knocked one of the fleecos off the stand! What a hardcase.

'Never mind about what's happening over there,' Uncle Hone said. 'Let's get on with our own job.'

'We've got to increase the pace!' Uncle Matiu said again.

'Don't panic,' Uncle Hone answered. 'Did I ever tell you about the tortoise and the hare?'

'*Change judges.*'

The shearers on Stage 1 and Stage 3 were settling into their sixth, seventh and eighth sheep, and into their rhythm. Caesar Poata was fluid as oil, shearing like a dream. Uh-oh, his brother Alexander was stopping and changing his blades – they were making too many cuts, the blood spurting from the whiteness of the shorn sheep.

'Tar!'

Our own Mahana shearers were steady and, in their steadiness, commanded respect. I felt so proud of my dad, holding the handpiece as if he had been born with it. Stroke after stroke, surely and calmly, the sheep's fleece peeled magically away. And here was Haromi again, pulling the fleece away from Dad's sheep. Gathering it in her arms. The suspense was awful.

'You must be in love,' Aunt Ruth said as yet another perfect fleece was cast.

'Well, someone is,' Aunt Kate interrupted. She nodded to where Miriam was waiting for Pani to finish shearing his ninth sheep. They had eyes only for each other and didn't give a tuppenny piece whether we won or lost. Meantime, peering at the dags and getting every piece of wool that she could from her collection was Glory. The camera team shone a bright light in her direction –

'Go away,' she said.

The cameraman poked his camera right into her face, so she got a dag and threw it at him. The stadium ricocheted with laughter.

'I'm doing my job,' Glory said, 'and it has to be the best job I've ever done.'

'You tell him, Glory!'

I realised that one of the reasons why the crowd always yelled out to us was because we talked all the time we were working. Not just about shearing either, but about love, life and the whole damn universe. The trouble was that we forgot the audience was there and let out the most awful secrets.

'*Change judges!*'

'Sheepo!' Aunt Sephora was calling. Like a hare, Peewee tore away. He jumped into the sacking to press down the neck pieces and side pieces. Mackie was helping David and Benjamin pack the fleeces into the press.

'Hang on a minute,' Aunt Sephora called. She went toward our pressmen. The judge followed her. 'This fleece is all right,' she said to Benjamin, 'but all right is still not good enough. Leave it aside for the second-class bales.'

'Good on you, Sephora!' someone called, approvingly.

The judge paused to take in Aunt's decision and scribbled something in his book.

'*Change judges!*'

The competition was coming to the home straight. Goodness, we'd only just started! The Gregsons were ahead with only two sheep to go, and the Poatas were in second place with three sheep to go. We were trailing with five sheep apiece.

'Steady does it,' Uncle Hone kept reminding us. 'The only competition that's worth anything is with ourselves. As long as we better ourselves, I'll be happy.'

Sweat was pouring down the shearers. The heat from the arc lights was stifling. Dark patches were appearing at Aunt Kate's armpits.

'Oh what the heck!' Aunt Kate said. She opened up her overalls and flapped air in. How everybody laughed at that!

The Gregson and Poata shearers were quickening their pace. They were looking across from their stages and going blow for blow down one side of the sheep and then down the other. They didn't bother to check us because we were so far behind. When shearers raced, something thrilling happened. The racing was like watching gunfighters – like Glenn Ford in *The Fastest Gun Alive* or Gary Cooper in *High Noon*. The race was a chance to say: 'Okay, folks, this is how the top guns do it. Watch how we *draw*.'

Now the audience was clapping as the last of the Gregson shearers finished his sheep. They clapped again as the Poatas finished. Our shearers droned on.

'Easy does it,' Uncle Hone said.

The Gregsons and the Poatas finished classing their wool. Their pressmen had a mighty race – clank, clank, clank went the presses – and were in the last stages of baling their wool when our shearers came to an end. Then the Gregson head shearer raised his hand to indicate that they were finished. Applause came down from the stadium. Caesar Poata soon followed. His pressmen finished sewing their last bale. Up came Caesar Poata's hand. More applause. Only a matter of minutes separated the Gregsons and the Poatas.

Uncle Matiu, meantime, was trembling in sheer frustration. He wanted Uncle Hone to cut corners. Uncle Hone always insisted that Mahana Four was never finished until we left the board the way we found it. So even though David and Benjamin had finished the baling, we still worked on, Aunt Sephora and the women cleaning up around them, and me and Peewee and Mackie unhooking the sacks and tidying up the work areas. We were four minutes behind the Gregsons and six minutes behind the Poatas. The stadium was absolutely silent. The moon was wan. We worked on.

Glory was the last to finish her job. Amused, Uncle Hone waited until she had nodded her head. Then he raised his hand too. In the gathering tumult, Glory did a little curtsy.

We didn't hear or care. We had eyes only for each other.

'We did our best,' Uncle Hone said to us.

'Did we what!' Aunt Ruth answered proudly. 'I'm changing gangs and coming over to Mahana Four. You fellas are the *best*.'

We were all sweating and crying like mad and couldn't tell what was sweat and what was tears. Then we just held each other so tightly so that no cold wind could come between us. Ever. It was over.

After all that, the judges' decision was a formality. The three teams were asked to wait on the stages. The stadium became hushed. The judges took *ages*. Then, just as the suspense threatened to kill all of us, the presiding judge took the microphone in front of the main stand. I cast a look at Grandfather Tamihana, sitting with Grandmother Ramona. Zebediah Whatu and Ihaka Mahana looked as if they accepted our fate; Grandfather looked as sick as a dog.

'Ladies and gentlemen,' the judge began, 'boys and girls, we have just witnessed a moment of history.' People began to clap. 'Ever since the beginning of our country, at least the beginning of Pakeha history, we have been a land which has been associated with agriculture. In particular, we are known as a country of two million people and six million sheep.' Laughter rippled the crowd. 'Thus it is fitting, ladies and gentlemen, that we should have a championship devoted to the art of shearing, for it is upon this art that we depend for our wealth, our overseas income and our economic wellbeing. On your behalf, I applaud all those in the shearing industry.'

The judge began to clap. He was joined by the thousands in the stadium.

51

'We've been away too long,' Aunt Ruth said as the train steamed through the mountains, and the plains of Gisborne spread out to claim us. Twelve days, but it had seemed like a lifetime.

Glory was sleeping in my lap. 'Wake up, Glory,' I said. 'We're almost there.' She yawned and stretched. The country unfolded before us. Far off – was that the red bridge? Was that the Waipaoa, glittering far away?

– Wail-e-ree, I can hear the river call –

Aroha, aroha –

Off in a corner Haromi was dreaming of the stardom that had almost been in her reach. Beside her, Mohi was strumming a guitar, plucking sweetness from the air.

We've lost our hearts to the river –

To the river Waipaoa –

Then the conductor was coming through the carriage. 'Five minutes to Gisborne, folks.'

Scattered farms came into view. Then suburban houses, and as we sped past people waved and tooted the horns of their cars. They captured the sun in their smiles. Then there was Gisborne station ahead, a *huge* banner: WELCOME HOME WINNERS OF THE GOLDEN FLEECE!

Did I forget to tell you?

This is what the presiding judge continued to say –

'The judges have found the judging throughout the championships a very difficult task indeed. In the process we have had to think clearly about our criteria. Speed, for instance, should not always be equated with being the best.' There was a murmur of agreement. 'To get there first,' the judge went on, 'many teams used unorthodox methods. I am not pointing a finger, but manhandling sheep over rails rather than pushing them through gates may get the job done faster but does not win points if we are thinking of sheep as an export product. Nor is shearing flat out but shearing badly conducive to the wellbeing of our industry. The object of the Golden Fleece competition was not to give the award to the fastest shearing gang but to the *best* shearing gang. Shearing just to get the wool off the back of the sheep was not what we wanted.'

The audience was beginning to prick up its ears.

'Perhaps the most critical area of all is the wool classing. If our wool classing is bad, how can we expect to maintain our good name as a wool country abroad? Our judges inspected all the bales and found great disparities in the quality of wool classing. Again, classing for speed does not necessarily pay good dividends.

'And finally, the pressmen. We have seen some wonderful displays of muscle tonight. But again, the emphasis has been on speed. It has been easy to tell a bale that has been packed down inadequately and sewn badly. Our bales of wool must survive journeys of long distance, during which wool is prone to expansion under tropical temperatures before it gets to our markets. Those bales must look good. The buyer must be able to be guaranteed a good quality product – not something which, like cheese, might have holes in the middle.' The audience laughed. The judge waited for them to stop. 'All this may be a long speech, ladies and gentlemen, but my fellow judges and I have felt it necessary to spell these things out clearly. May I reiterate that the New Zealand Wool Board was not looking for the fastest shearing gang. We were looking for the best.'

The judge coughed and cleared his throat. 'Ladies and gentle-men, the best quality work comes from those areas where tradition and a history of practice has meant that skills have been honed, refined and distilled over many years. It should therefore be no surprise that the Jason statuette for best shearer and the first Golden Fleece award, carrying a cash prize of £5,000, go to the Gisborne East Coast and Poverty Bay district.

'Could I ask Mr Caesar Poata to come forward to receive the Jason Award for best shearer for 1958.'

So Hukareka had won. I watched Grandfather Tamihana's crestfallen face and, at that moment, I loved him. He was human. Vulnerable after all.

Caesar called his father, Rupeni Poata, to share in the glory of the award. They looked so fine and handsome together, standing in the arc lights.

'Ah well,' Aunt Ruth said to Uncle Hone, 'better luck next year.'

That was when the judge went on.

'Now, ladies and gentlemen – the premier prize. It is not often that the gang that comes third is awarded first prize –'

What?

The stadium erupted. People were on their feet stamping and yelling with joy. The judge kept on talking above the uproar.

'The Mahana Four gang epitomises all the qualities of our shearing industry. They are of a Maori family with a tradition of shearing that goes back to the early part of this century. They are the only team to have entered as a family. Their work has been of the utmost quality. The judges could not fault their teamwork and their commitment to the job of good shearing. Their ages ranged from, forgive me Aunt Ruth, somewhere around fifty to seven years of age. I will remember young Glory's concentration on the task before her for quite some time. Ladies and gentlemen, *none* of Mahana's sheep was marked, cut or nicked in any way by their blades. The wool handling and sheep handling was of the highest standard. The wool classer, Miss Sephora Mahana, should be employed by the Wool Board immediately. Throughout the championship her work has been consistent with excellence. Special commendation should also be given to the pressmen, and, oh yes, the sheepos. Who needs sheepdogs when you can have such speed and finesse as was shown by Peewee Mahana and Mackie Whatu under the guidance of their team leader, Mr Simeon Mahana?

'May I please ask the Mahana Four shearing gang to come to the stage to receive their award.'

Uncle Hone was overcome. He couldn't speak. Then –

'Will someone go over and get Dad?' he asked.

I nodded and walked across the field. I bowed in front of Grandfather. 'Bulibasha,' I said. 'Your family awaits you.'

His lips were trembling. He stood and walked with me into the limelight. The stadium was on its feet in standing ovation. It was the greatest moment of his life – the culmination of all of his years as a shearer, and fitting tribute to his dream. And when, in the gathering roar, Rupeni Poata came over to congratulate him, Grandfather Tamihana attained apotheosis.

'You are indeed above us all,' Rupeni Poata said.

Grandfather could go no higher. Acknowledged by Rupeni Poata as his superior, and therefore above even Hukareka, he had assuredly become in prestige as well as in name Bulibasha, King of the Gypsies.

52

Although the joy and tumult was still ringing in our ears, my mother and father wanted to escape the civic reception in Gisborne and get back to our land down at the bend of the Waipaoa.

'Come on children,' Mum said. 'Let's get out of here.'

Just before leaving, however, I managed to have another few words with Poppy.

'I don't *care* if we're on opposite sides,' I said. I was remembering my friendship with Geordie and how that was supposed to be wrong too. I was angry at Grandfather for having constructed a world in which some matters had already been decided for me.

Poppy looked at me. Her eyes welled with tears. Then she gave me the most wonderful grin. 'There'll be other girls for you,' she said.

'Yes, I know,' I answered, 'but you'll always be the first.'

I hugged her, and didn't give a damn who saw. Then I ran out to where Mum and Dad were waiting. We had parked our old Pontiac by the station and cheered when Dad started the engine. Then we drove on home to sweet Beulah land. Oh it was good to see the meadow, the windmill turning, our house on the rise and our eternal Waipaoa.

That night, after dinner, our father Joshua looked across at Mum and coughed. My sisters and I were beside ourselves with excitement. Dad laid down his knife and fork and put his hands in his pockets. Mum wouldn't look at him. Dad made a great play of searching in one pocket and then another as if he couldn't find what he was looking for.

'E hara!' he said. 'I think I lost it. It must have fell out when I was –' Then his hand pressed against his heart and, 'Anei,' he whispered. He drew out a small packet and put it on the table. He pushed it toward our mother.

'Enei nga moni.'

It was £500, our share of the winnings.

My sisters and I whooped and yelled and screamed with delight. Mum breathed a deep sigh.

'I accept this token of aroha for me and our children,' she said, 'and return it to you as head of the household. I pray, however, that you allow me to take £200 for myself.'

Dad nodded in agreement.

The next day my mother, sisters and I drove into Patutahi. Mum wore her best dress and hat. She put on her white gloves and, at the last moment, applied lipstick. We stopped at the general store.

'Why look who's here!' Miss Zelda cried, putting her hand to her mouth. 'We listened to all the news on the radio! We just couldn't believe that our Maoris had won the Golden Fleece award! Congratulations!'

Miss Daisy and Scott came from the back to extend their congratulations. Other Pakeha customers in the store surrounded us to shake my mother's hand and pat Glory on the head.

'I – I – I –' My mother opened her purse.

'My mother wants to pay –' I began.

Mum put a gloved hand over mine. With a great effort she said, 'I – Yes – I – want to pay in – in – full.'

'Oh why not leave it for a while?' Miss Zelda smiled. 'There must be a million other things you want to do with the money. Go around the world perhaps!' She laughed out loud at the thought.

Mum was firm. 'No,' she said. 'Now.' Her tone communicated authority. The other customers looked somewhat put out.

'Well,' Miss Zelda said, 'if that's the way you want it.' She took out the ledger book and totalled the amount. 'Two hundred pounds,' she said.

Mum peeled the notes in front of Miss Zelda's astonished face.

'I think you'll find it all there.'

Miss Zelda nodded. Then, just as my mother was about to leave, Miss Zelda's voice came out of some dark place to *strike*.

'Oh dear, I forgot to add on £6 interest.'

It was such a small thing really. All we had to do was to say to Miss Zelda that we would come back. But my mother recognised it for what it was – a sneer at her back, a piece of spite, a play of power. My mother turned to Miss Zelda. She walked back through the other customers and looked Miss Zelda straight in the eye.

'You have made a mistake,' she said.

Pakehas *never* make mistakes.

'Yes,' Mum said, determined. 'You have made a mistake' – she pointed at a ledger entry – 'here.'

I thought, How can Mum know? She can't read, she can't do sums, she hasn't had any schooling. Miss Zelda would have her for mincemeat.

'Let me see that,' Miss Zelda said. She picked up the book and took it to the window. 'I can't see where –'

'There,' Mum said, 'where the ink is smudged. I remember clearly the day I came in. You charged me too much, got your rubber and rubbed it out, and put the right amount in. There. You overcharged me.'

'But I would never do such a thing,' Miss Zelda said.

'Well you did,' Mum said. She was trembling. 'You did that day.'

There was silence. Everyone was staring at my mother. I felt like I wanted the floor to open up so that I could disappear.

Then Scott came from the back. 'I remember,' he said, nodding at Mum, confirming what she had said. 'Mrs Mahana came in here and she looked at new clothes for her boy and we overcharged her by' – he paused – '£6.'

The exact amount owing on interest.

Zelda and Daisy looked at each other.

'Well, Scott, if you say so –'

With that, Miss Zelda wet her pencil with her lips and slashed a diagonal line across the tab.

'Paid in full and discharged,' she said slowly. She handed the tab to my mother. Her eyes were angry but her lips smiled. 'Thank you, Mrs Mahana. I must also apologise –'

My mother nodded her head. She turned and left the general store, walking as fast as she could towards the shade of the oak tree near the school.

When we caught up with her she was at the pump, pushing the handle frantically up and down and washing her face. We knew she had been crying and was trying not to let us see her tears. She turned to us.

'Isn't this a marvellous day?' she said. Her lips were still quivering. Then she gave a whoop and a holler. 'Kia tere! Let's get to town! We mightn't be able to buy anything, darlings, but nobody is going to charge us for looking.'

She was free. She was no longer a slave.

53

At the end of 1959 the faithful and stalwart Pani finally ended his two years' servitude to Grandfather Tamihana. He again sought Miriam's hand in marriage. Grandfather, still glowing in the success of the Golden Fleece, and Pani's part in it, agreed. He was proud to have Pani as his son-in-law. Miriam was thirty-four and her hair was beginning to grey. She and Pani were married at the registry office in Gisborne. They were overjoyed to be together. Nor was Miriam's womb barren. Within eleven months of their marriage, Miriam bore a lusty, squealing son.

Not long after Miriam's wedding, my cousin Mohi was drinking late at the Patutahi Hotel with his latest girlfriend Carol and four friends. He had put a down-payment on a red Ford Zephyr convertible with a white canvas hood and white painted tyres; it was the only one in Poverty Bay and looked like it had been driven straight out of *Rebel Without a Cause*. It was the appropriate car for the sex machine that was Mohi, and it was his pride and joy. That night Fraser Poata from Hukareka happened to be in Patutahi and challenged Mohi to a re-match race across the red suspension bridge. Perhaps Mohi was worried about scratches on his new car. He lost.

According to the coroner's report, 'No blame should be attached to the publican, Mr Walker, who refused to serve the young Mohi Mahana and his friends after 6 p.m. closing. It is a tragedy blah blah blah.'

The facts are that the said Mr Walker slipped a crate to Mohi, who was angry at having lost the race against Hukareka, on the understanding that the transaction would remain secret between them. Mr Walker was fortunate that the survivors of the accident kept to that understanding. Around five o'clock in the morning, after drinking steadily all night, Mohi failed to take the corner just past the bridge to Waituhi. My father Joshua and I, up early and on our way to a cattle sale in Matawhero, were the first to come across the car. The Zephyr was upside down in the huge drainage canal which ran parallel with the road. The bodywork had crumpled; the windscreen was starred with broken glass. Week-long rain had filled the canal, and floating upside down were the bodies of Mohi, Carol and a young man called Jake. The other three boys were sitting on the side of the canal, drinking and laughing as if the party was still happening, man, and yelling to Mohi, 'Hey you black bastard, wake up! Don't be a piker!' Brown beer bottles bobbed up and down unbroken in the water.

My grandfather Tamihana Mahana, Bulibasha, King of the Gypsies, took Mohi's death very badly. Mohi had been his favoured one; in him could no fault lie. His grief was only compounded by the way in which the newspapers made a big fuss of Mohi's promise as an athlete and of his relationship to Grandfather: this was 'the grandson of Tamihana Mahana, one of the best known Maori citizens of the district and patriarch of the family which last year won the Golden Fleece'. He was outraged that the local *Gisborne Herald* reporter should use the opportunity of Mohi's death to editorialise on the danger of alcohol abuse among young Maori. Grandfather was, after all, a respected elder of a church to which alcohol, tobacco and other abusive substances were anathema. A cynic like myself would have said that Grandfather was concerned only for his own reputation. But even if that was true, there was no denying the depth of his grief.

I mourned for my bastard of a cousin. After he died I could never look in the mirror in the bathroom without expecting him to come up behind me and shove me to one side –

'Get out of the way, Useless.'

I hadn't expected him to die, ever. Mohi had existed outside the rules because that was where Grandfather had placed him. He walked higher than the rest of us and was not subject to the same laws of gravity that made us walk the earth. There he floated in supreme confidence that, whatever happened, Grandfather would always support him. I think of him, drowning in the canal, his eyes wide with surprise, the air bubbling from his lips –

'But this cannot be. This *cannot* be. I am the grandson of Bulibasha –'

54

In 1959, still determined to prove Grandfather wrong about my abilities, I sat School Certificate for the second time. At seventeen I was two years older than most of the students sitting the examination, and Miss Dalrymple had hinted that perhaps I should give up any pretensions to te rori Pakeha.

The day the results came in the post, Andrew telephoned early to say that he had just received his and that he had failed. I thought, 'Boy, if he's failed I'm a goner too.' By the time Mum handed me my letter, I was convinced of it. I opened the envelope. I thought I saw a blur of Fs for Fail.

Since her brush with Miss Zelda at the general store Mum had started to learn the alphabet. She took the letter from me and, in her halting hesitant way, began to read out the results.

'P, Biology. Pass ne? Ka pai, kotahi P.'

She held both my fists up in the air and made me put one finger up from the right fist. She read the next line.

'P, English. Pass ne ra? Kapai, e rua P.'

Another finger up, right fist. Next line.

'F, Geography. Aue, he raruraru! E rua P, kotahi F.'

One finger up, but left fist. Next line.

'P, History. Kia ora. Pass ano! E toru P, kotahi F.'

Three fingers up, right fist; one finger up, left fist. Final line.

'P, Mathematics. E wha P, kotahi –'

Mum's face quivered as she realised I had passed. She held the results in front of her. 'I think I'll get a frame for this,' she said, 'just to prove I'm not so dumb a mother after all.'

Naturally Grandfather was told and, while I foolishly expected a compliment, a crumb from his table, I was not crushed when it didn't fall into my eager hands. Grandfather still mourned Mohi who, by virtue of dying young, had become a kind of saint – the person whom no other heirs could hope to emulate. More to the point, Grandfather had always valued things he could see – strength, a well-formed physique, fortitude. Grandfather could see those, could see sweat, or a hillside after all the gorse had been slashed, or a fence where there had not been one, or the shorn sheep after a contract had been completed. But School Certificate results? Marks on paper? Those remained unseen to Grandfather, like chicken scratchings in the dust, and therefore without worth.

Grandfather's failure to acknowledge my success at the next family meeting was, I assumed, simply a sign that our relationship was taking its normal course. Whatever my achievements, I was still third child of his seventh son. Little did I know that Grandfather was preoccupied with his health. At sixty-seven he was faced with intimations of his mortality.

Grandmother Ramona suspected something was wrong with Grandfather when she saw him cleaning the toilet bowl after having flushed it two times.

'I can do that,' Grandmother said.

'Hei aha,' Grandfather answered. He motioned her away but she stepped past him. It was strange to see him on his knees doing woman's work.

'Didn't you hear me, woman? *Hei aha.*'

Grandmother backed away. But she had seen the blood rushing down the bowl with the water.

A week later Grandfather started to have stomach cramps, and although he never complained Grandmother Ramona knew he was in pain. Then Grandfather began to do his own washing – woman's work again – washing and rinsing his long underwear. She caught him at it and saw there was blood in the front and in the seat of his longjohns.

'How long has this been going on?' Grandmother asked.

'I feel like a woman,' Grandfather growled. 'It is only women who pass blood.'

'Yes,' she answered, 'but that is natural for us and only happens every month. It is not natural for the man to pass blood and so often.'

'You look after your business,' Grandfather said, 'and I'll look after mine.' Then, 'I am passing blood from my bum also, kui.'

'Kaati,' she answered. 'It's time to see the doctor.'

Even in 1959, when they should have known better, Maori used to say, 'The only time you see the doctor is when you want to be born and when you are about to die.' Accidental injury was permissible as long as the damage was visible – a fractured limb, a gunshot or knife wound. But something internal – like what had happened to Lloyd or what was now happening to Grandfather – was unseemly and to be feared. The invisible malady was a punishment, retribution for some evil committed when you were younger. So if you were ill from an internal disorder you pretended it wasn't there and willed it to go away. If it persisted you hid the illness from your close family. If you felt faint you rushed to the bedroom and lay down so nobody would know. If you wanted to vomit you excused yourself and tried to get to the toilet before you spilled your guts. You bore your symptoms with strength and fortitude, in spite of the pain. Much later in life my father Joshua showed exactly the same stupidity when his waterworks stopped and he couldn't urinate. He remained stoic until finally pain drove him to the doctor. He was lucky to be fixed – unlike Uncle Ihaka who died at forty-nine when the swollen appendix he had been hiding burst and killed him.

My dear cousin Haromi – she was another one. The only recourse for breast cancer in those days was to have a radical mastectomy and even then, according to fatalistic folklore, you ended up dying. When I visited my wonderful cousin in her last week she said to me, 'At least I will die a complete woman.' The removal of any part of oneself was a heresy.

Is it any wonder that, in the event of autopsy, the return of a Maori body unblemished by the coroner's knife and with all body parts in their place, is of such concern to Maori? I can still remember the outrage and agony which attended the tangi of my nephew Aaron, Haromi's second son, who died of an unknown malady at the age of three. The release of his body was delayed by the coroner. When Aunt Sarah went to bathe her grandson and prepare him for burial she found two neat incisions – one at the base of his neck where his scalp had been lifted, and another across his chest where his heart had been examined.

The body is tapu.

This attitude was the rule with Maori people. Was there any reason to expect that Grandfather would be an exception? No matter Grandmother Ramona's stern admonitions, he refused to visit the doctor.

When Grandfather's body began to rot inside, he clamped back the pain. Eating became a nightmare and he turned to the pure Waipaoa water, to kanga pirau, fermented corn, and puha mashed with kumara. When he felt an attack coming on he hissed and clenched his lips. Eyes bulging, he punched out blindly as if trying to render visible the attacker within.

Nobody went to help Grandfather. Nobody offered sympathy, because to do so would mean that Grandfather would have to admit his illness. And that would have meant facing up to that dark deed of the past, for which payment was now being demanded. Instead, a proud complicity of silence surrounded Grandfather as he crashed around the homestead and Waituhi. His body heaved, shat dark red blood, careened, vomited bile, fizzed, pissed poison, staggered, farted rotten stench and bawled like some huge and enraged bull.

Grandmother, Sephora and Esther cleaned up the mess.

This, after all, was Bulibasha. This was the way that such a man, King of the Gypsies, should die.

Bulibasha finally turned to medical help in the second week of April, 1960. By that time, I had been at the Mormon college in Hamilton for two months. When I left, Glory had dismayed us all by screaming, 'You promised! You promised me, Simeon!' She ran after the bus until she could run no longer, calling me to come back.

'You're a stupid, obstinate, foolish man,' the doctor said when he was called to Grandfather's side. 'I can't understand how you've lasted so long without drugs. You are a miracle of modern science. You have been in terrible pain and I am in no mood to compliment you on your fortitude. Stubborness doesn't win any medals, Mr Mahana.'

The doctor said he would arrange a nurse to give daily medication and administer pain-killing drugs.

'My daughters will be my nurses,' Grandfather answered. 'I'm not going to have any Pakeha looking at my bum. Anyway, I'm not going to die. Didn't you say I was a miracle of modern science?'

At the doorway, before leaving, Uncle Matiu asked the doctor whether there was any chance.

'I shall give that question the contempt it deserves,' the doctor replied. 'The man is riddled with cancer. If we had had the chance to operate and remove the malignancies earlier, perhaps –' He added that Grandfather had a week, ten days at most.

Grandfather must have overheard.

Had I not known him better I would have suspected that Grandfather made another wager with God or that American angel of his. Throughout that time he would not allow people at church to pray for him, persisting in his belief that 'I'm not going to die'. This same stubbornness, mixed with church disapproval, prevented him from seeking the help of a tohunga. Instead Grandfather turned to the things he knew best. He increased his diet and exercise. Now that he had drugs, he would pump them faster through his body to repel the invader. His body had not let him down before – why should it do so now? After all, he was Bulibasha. *The* Bulibasha.

Grandfather's problem was that he didn't understand that to everyone comes this season of death. Despite his religious upbringing he forgot there was a time to live and a time to die – and his time to die had come. It was as simple as that. His cancer was not an indictment on his life or on him as a person. It was simply his body saying, I am finished now and you must shuck me off as a husk from corn and prepare for your next great adventure. Grandfather never accepted that. He could not leave off asking the question, Why me? As if the cancer had somehow sneaked past God without God's approval. Or, as if that American angel, so many years before, was welshing on his promise. The cancer was an affront to Grandfather's ego. It was something else to be battled and triumphed over. And, oh, every breath of air was so sweet.

I could have told him that there was another reason why his time to die had come. He had already achieved the triumphs of his life. There was nothing left for him to accomplish.

Grandfather lasted for another three weeks. Then I received a telephone call from Dad asking me to come home to Waituhi. Grandfather was in the last stages of death.

'Haere mai koe, Himiona,' my father Joshua said.

The plane from Hamilton touched down at Gisborne airport late on a Wednesday evening. Glory rushed into my arms, an unruly and impetuous eleven-year-old. I hugged Dad and we kissed. We drove back to Waituhi. God, it was so good to see the Waipaoa River, darkly swirling in the falling light.

Mum, Faith and Hope were waiting at the house on Grandmother's land. It was nine in the evening, the right time for a departing soul to make its way from Waituhi, across the bosom of the land to the northernmost tip of Aotearoa. The soul would not need to wait too long for the sunrise, the opening of the way to the next world. Together Mum, Dad, my sisters and I walked across the

261

paddocks and along the road to the homestead. The moon was a crescent. There was no sound. No dogs, no cats, no possums squealing in the night. The silence was an indrawn sigh.

Lights in the homestead were blazing. Mourners, dressed formally in suit and tie or in long gown with scarves, waited outside for their turn to go in.

'Haere mai koutou ma,' Zebediah Whatu said as we approached.

'Ae,' Aunt Molly added, 'haere mai koutou.'

I stepped into the light and the iwi saw who I was. There was a moan, like banshees on the wind, and old Maggie came to cup my chin lovingly in her hands.

'Go inside, our father is waiting.'

I had been in the presence of Death many times before, but I was unwilling to be witness to my grandfather's death. I could still be persuaded, even at that late stage, that Grandfather was invincible. Indestructible. The iconoclast in me wanted to believe he would rise up like Lazarus, or like Christ, and resume his place among us. I could just imagine him doing that, saying, 'E koe! I fooled you all!' Laughing in that huge lusty way of his.

Once inside, there was no such delusion. My uncles Matiu, Maaka, Ruka and Hone were standing like first lieutenants at the death of Mark Antony. Aperahama and Ihaka were talking in hushed tones to the priest. I couldn't see my aunts Ruth, Sarah, Sephora, Miriam and Esther and realised that they – all Grandfather's women – would be with Grandmother Ramona at the bedside. Bulibasha *was* dying.

Uncle Matiu saw us arriving and motioned Dad to him. His eyes were red but he was not weeping. He was the eldest son. On him, above all others, would fall Grandfather's mantle. Others could weep, wail, succumb to the passions of grief, but not him. Never him.

Uncle Maaka joined us. He punched me on the shoulder and commented on how grown up I looked. Then, 'You should all go into the old man,' he said. 'He hasn't got long now. We've all been in to receive our blessing. It is your turn.'

My father burst into tears and, for a moment, I was embarrassed. But at the sight of his tears the iwi inside the sitting room were swept up in his grief. They began to wail like lost souls. My uncles hastened to surround my father, arms around each other like a protective circle. I had forgotten that although my father was seventh son he was also the youngest son. Vulnerable. The baby. Then Dad sighed.

He blew on his nose. He motioned Mum, my sisters and I to accompany him.

'No,' Uncle Ruka said. 'Just you, Huria and your girls. Grandfather wants to see Himiona alone.'

I felt fear drain into me. Alone? What for? What enmity still remained unspoken between us? Was damnation to be my blessing?

Mum and Dad went through the door. Grandfather was propped up among the pillows. Grandmother Ramona and my aunts were sitting at the foot of the bed and made room for Mum and my sisters to join them. Dad went to the bedside and knelt. He took Grandfather's left hand and kissed it. Grandfather placed his right hand on his head and whispered a few words, then Mum and my sisters joined Dad. Grandfather made a sign with his right hand. When Grandfather had finished, Mum kissed his forehead and signed to my sisters to do the same.

Then it was my turn.

The room was brightly lit, as if Grandfather had decreed that all should see him as he was. There was to be no pretence of shadows and curtains to veil the reality of the cancer. A sweet smell perfumed the air. Incense was burning, presumably to mask the rotting of Grandfather's wasting body. Smoke curled from tapers placed at the four corners of his bed. I looked down upon my grandfather. He still retained his hair and his frame was not skeletal. God had been kind to him, permitting the cancer to eat away his insides but forbidding it to take away the props to face, chest, arms and legs. His body might be scraped hollow inside but outside it still maintained the illusion of substance.

Nevertheless, something intangible marked him as not quite the same. Something to do with aura. His life was draining away, the candle of his life diminishing. The lamp was low.

'Ko wai ia?' Grandfather asked. His eyes searched around and I realised that he was blind.

'Ko Himiona, e pa,' Aunt Ruth answered.

'Aaa –' Grandfather nodded. 'The viper –'

Grandfather made a sign with his head that the door should be closed. Then he added another sign: Grandmother and my aunts were to leave us alone. Aunt Sarah shook her head but Grandmother Ramona said, 'Kaati. Haere atu.'

'Don't stay for too long,' Aunt Sarah said. 'There's other people more important than you has to see him.'

There was a click of the door as they departed.

'Himiona –' Grandfather sighed.

He shook his head and his lips creased into a grin. He put his right hand down to me. I wasn't too sure whether he was going to take a swipe at me or not. I decided to trust him, and lowered my head to receive his blessing.

'Kaore –' he said.

Puzzled, I saw his eyes gesturing at my own right hand. I wasn't too sure what he wanted. Then I realised: Grandfather wanted to Indian wrestle. He had *never* wanted to Indian wrestle with me.

I grinned at him and spat on my hand. Grandfather indicated with his eyes that he wanted me to spit on his, too. He opened his palm and, when I went to take it, gripped me with an iron hand. I was startled. This was not a man in extremis. Our hands wavered in the air, and with disgust I noticed that Grandfather was managing to bend mine back to the bed. I knotted my muscles and started to push his hand back.

Even if you're on your death bed, you bastard –

He laughed. A small quiet laugh, but there was joy in it. Then he said –

'Drop your pants.'

Drop my pants?

'Ae,' he repeated. 'Down your trou.'

I shrugged. A man's last wish is a man's last wish. I took my belt off. My trousers slid to the floor.

Grandfather's right hand reached down beneath my shirt. I gasped as his hand reached through my pubic hair. I had a sudden thought that maybe he was going to take his revenge by twisting my balls off and turning me into a eunuch. Instead he cradled my balls and took the measure of my cock. He gave a small tug and I was embarrassed to feel myself thickening and lengthening. His eyes looked into mine.

'Ae,' he said. 'Ae.'

There was a look which conveyed all that an old man must feel about youth and the sexuality of one's grandson. Regret that he will not be able to feel the bucking of another person beneath him in orgasm. Nostalgia for all those times of heated encounters and lust. And pride that one's own offspring has achieved a rightful inheritance.

'You and I the same –' he said.

Was this Grandfather's blessing? This acceptance that I was one of his? Had I now obtained his acceptance?

'Ah, Himiona –' he sighed. There was such regret in his voice. 'You and I –'

I bent to kiss his eyelids. My lips tasted the salt of his life, my nose felt the warmth of his breath and my skin took the warmth of his cheek.

He took his hands from my thighs. I buttoned myself up.

'You make the decision,' he said.

Nothing more. I left the room.

At the end of his life, Grandfather Tamihana was moved from the bedroom into the sitting room. A space was made for him where his throne had been. There, swathed in blankets and propped up by pillows, we looked upon him for the last time. Mother Ramona was by his side. The Mahana clan gathered, kneeling in homage around him, waiting for his last breath. Every intake of breath was ours. Every exhalation was also ours. The windows and doors of the homestead were all open. Outside on the verandah were the Whatus, the Tuparas, the Peres, the Horsfalls, the Kerekeres and all the people of Waituhi.

Grandfather laboured, sighed, coughed, hissed, held his breath and laboured again late into the morning.

'Maybe,' Haromi whispered to me, 'he's waiting to hear that old Rupeni Poata has dropped dead.'

I grinned at her. It would make Grandfather's night to know that his arch enemy had gone before him.

Still Grandfather hung on. Even when, at three in the morning, Grandmother reached across to him, patted his shoulders and said, 'You should go now', he kept breathing.

'E hara!' Grandmother Ramona continued. 'Go now and let us get some sleep!'

Around four, Grandfather's breathing levelled out. All of a sudden he took a breath. His eyes flickered open. He looked up and saw something awesome approaching from far away, flying down from the clouds, through an open window and into the room. The curtains billowed with the wind.

He watched alert as something blond and glittering, with blue eyes and lazy smile, flew around the walls, trying to find a way through his defences.

'Kaya-oraa, Tamay-hana,' the angel laughed.

The angel feinted, swerved and tested Grandfather to ascertain how it could get through.

'The best of three falls?' the angel asked.

Imperceptibly, Grandfather nodded. His eyes darted this way and that in quick flickering movements, following the rippling wings of the angel, waiting for a break. But the angel always seemed to keep out of his reach.

Grandfather became impatient. He let out his breath in one explosive '*Haaaaa* –'. He could wait no longer.

The angel opened its wings as if to claim Grandfather. With a cry the mighty Bulibasha, King of the Gypsies, sprang through its defences and started to wrestle with it.

'This time I'll defeat you!' he cried.

The room opened and Grandfather and the angel fell into searing light.

'Kua mate o tatou papa,' Uncle Matiu said.

The dogs which until that time had been silent all started to howl.

55

Maori people say that when Death's angel visits he sometimes takes two people rather than one. I don't know why this should be so. Perhaps it's God's way of saving on travelling. Whatever, when the news spread that Grandfather had died, people associated his passing with the death of my cousin Mohi. They said that Mohi had gone ahead to make ready the way for Grandfather.

Grandfather's tangihanga was held at Waituhi, on Rongopai marae, and was one of the largest ever seen in the Poverty Bay and East Coast. This would have pleased Grandfather, who always placed great store on size and on ceremony, as if this was a measure of a person. Elders from all tribes travelled with large ope to mourn his passing. Indeed, he became a greater person in death then he had been in life.

During the three days of mourning references were made to Grandfather's many illegitimate children and to his having killed a man who had the audacity to walk over his legs, and his sporting prowess reached epic proportions. By the third day the family was almost convinced that Bulibasha had been a supernatural person. We kept on looking at him in his casket and thinking, He's going to get up and start haranguing us any minute for thinking he's dead.

By the last day over two thousand people had come to farewell Bulibasha. Over and over mourners praised his exploits as a Maori Samson and honoured our family. His links with Ngata were elaborated on. The establishment of the shearing gangs. The fairness, honesty and reputation of Mahana One, Mahana Two, Mahana Three and Mahana Four were all spoken of. References were made to the winning of the Golden Fleece. Finally, accolades were accorded Grandfather's status as the head of the family of God. He had, indeed, been a faithful servant of his God and, by his works, had been a living witness and testament that God lived.

During the final hours, Grandfather had a surprise visitation. From out of the sun, Rupeni Poata and the people of Hukareka arrived. Their ope numbered over a hundred and they came walking down the road calling and wailing to us. Poppy was on Rupeni's arm. She was proud, undaunted.

Aunt Ruth was outraged. 'How dare they come,' she hissed. 'Have they forgotten that they come to Waituhi only at their peril?'

'If they try anything,' Uncle Matiu said, 'they will surely pay. With their lives.'

We were all alert for any offence, any slight against our grandfather. We sent out our best women to karanga back to them. Then Uncle Matiu nodded to David and Benjamin to go out and challenge them. We offered up our most fierce haka to assure them that they were not dealing with mere mortals. We watched, our noses flaring and eyes bulging, as they walked onto our marae. The whole earth seemed to become charged with psychic energy. Hukareka, *watch out.*

Hukareka presented three speakers. All of them were intermediaries between the Mahana and the Poata clans and sought to reconcile us. We listened, our minds alert to their nuances. Was that a criticism? No? How about that one? Well, we'll let that one slide by –

Then Rupeni Poata himself stood up. He approached the porch where Grandfather was lying in state. He nodded in deference to Grandmother Ramona. Then –

'I'm glad you're dead, you bastard,' he shouted. 'You hear me? I'm glad you're lying there in your coffin. The sooner we get you buried the better.'

I couldn't believe my ears. My uncles and cousins wanted to run out and kill Rupeni right on the spot. We were held back by Zebediah Whatu.

'All of Hukareka rejoices that you're dead,' Rupeni continued. 'I rejoice. Now that you are gone there is space for us. You cast too big a shadow, Bulibasha. Take it with you and leave us the sun.'

Then Rupeni sat down. The sun polished his face with glowing bronze. He was like a proud statue.

'Don't you understand?' Zebediah asked. 'Of all the eulogies delivered, that one was the greatest. The greatest compliment, the greatest homage to Bulibasha.'

At the reading of Grandfather's will, all the land and shares were, as expected, left to my uncles Matiu, Maaka, Ruka and Hone, my aunts Ruth and Sarah and my uncles Aperahama and Ihaka. Grandmother was left the homestead and a large cash settlement for as long as she lived. At her death, the homestead and residue were to be shared equally by my aunts Sephora, Miriam and Esther.

My father Joshua was referred to as 'already having been provided for by his mother'.

56

A month went past. I came home from Hamilton for the holidays. I was falling in love so often at the college that my heart welcomed the rest of Waituhi, and the physical labour. Like all boys in their late teens I was tussling with who I was and what I wanted.

One day, after Dad and I had come in from fencing, my mother said, 'Something's happening up at the homestead. Mother Ramona is acting peculiar.'

'It's to be expected,' my father answered. 'After all, Father was Mother Ramona's entire life. They were married for a long time. She's bound to feel his loss.'

'This is different,' my mother said. 'You'd better find out what's troubling the old lady.'

I too had become aware of some change in Grandmother Ramona. Her daily visits to Grandfather's grave had been attended by some transcendence, some luminosity of appearance. I often saw her standing up there, a black silhouette against a blood-red sky, unmoving, eternal, appearing for all the world an icon of undying love.

There was a rightness about Grandmother's faithfulness to Grandfather. If the Mahanas had been Hindu, no one would have doubted that Grandmother Ramona would gladly have gone to the funeral pyre with him. Perhaps she was ready to die now.

But what was this?

'Mother's been talking to somebody on the telephone,' Mum said. 'Sephora has caught her at it a number of times now. Mother Ramona hangs up immediately. She has also started locking her door. One day Esther saw her through the doorway. Mother Ramona had taken that old wedding dress of hers out of her hope chest. She was ironing it.'

Later that month came the event we had all been dreading – the first gathering of the family since Grandfather's death. The full complement were present to confirm the ongoing nature of the Mahana clan. Zebediah Whatu and Ihaka Mahana had agreed out of respect to us that they would not attend.

'Where's Mother Ramona?' Uncle Matiu asked. Being the eldest, he was expected to take over the running of the family meetings.

'She's not ready yet,' Aunt Esther answered.

'Aue, poor Mum,' Aunt Sarah sniffed.

There was an uncomfortable silence while we waited.

'Are you going to take Father's seat?' Uncle Aperahama asked Uncle Matiu. He motioned to Grandfather's now vacant throne. Uncle Matiu gave a slight hop of alarm.

'No, that would be disrespectful. Next week I'll go into town and buy a new one.'

Then Grandmother Ramona arrived, regal in black gown and greenstone earrings. Aunt Sarah began to sob as if life had broken into tiny pieces. I watched Grandmother keenly as she made her way through the family to her accustomed chair. There *was* something different about her. Some resolve. Some sense of purpose. Her procession was marked by increasing sobs and wails from Aunt Sarah. Grandmother Ramona sat down and sighed – 'Oh shut up, Sarah,' she said. 'Carrying on all the time as if the world was going to end. No wonder your husband took to the bottle and your daughter has run away.'

Our mouths fell open.

Then Grandmother Ramona's eyes softened. Her demeanour became supplicatory.

'Your father is dead. You are his children. I am your mother. The dead to the dead. The living to the living. I have a request. I have done my duty by him, your father, and by you all. I want you to let me go now. Go back to him who I have loved all my life.' She paused. 'To Rupeni.'

To *Rupeni*?

There was a shocked silence, then Aunt Sarah stepped up to Grandmother Ramona and said, 'You're over sixty, you stupid old woman. What the hell are you playing at?'

Bedlam broke out.

It is very difficult to trust adults once you have found them out. All my life I was accustomed to the usual Mahana evasiveness whenever I had any questions. Answers like, 'Ask no questions and you get no lies.' Or, 'It's none of your business.' Or, 'When you're older we'll tell you.' These had always been the three main responses to any questions about the enmity between the Mahanas and the Poatas. So is my scepticism to be wondered at when a story turns out to be a complete lie from the start?

From the very beginning I had been brought up to fight the Poatas because *they* hated us. I had been told that this hatred stemmed from Rupeni Poata and his rivalry with Grandfather Tamihana on the sporting field and in haka. But God had always been on Grandfather's side and thus he was the one who always triumphed. Even where Rupeni Poata happened to excel, it was always because he was good at strategy or on game plan: Grandfather's physical strength allowed him to win in taiaha and mere, but Rupeni's intelligence enabled him to triumph in peruperu and haka.

Wrong. Rupeni was the better sportsman and Tamihana always had it in for him because, no matter how hard he tried, Rupeni was the one who consistently came first.

Again, I had always believed Grandfather and Rupeni Poata were natural competitors, never wishing to play on the same side and always playing against each other. The one arena where Grandfather was the clear winner was in the love stakes, where his outright handsomeness and sexuality sidelined Rupeni completely. In the shower room there was no doubt as to who was the more virile man.

Wrong again. Grandfather, despite his physical attributes, was not the clear winner in the love stakes either.

The keystone to the rivalry, so I had been led to believe, was that Rupeni hated Grandfather after he had taken Ramona, who loved Grandfather, from the doors of the church.

Wrong for the third count.

When the First World War came, it is true that Rupeni and some of his friends were advocates of Sir Apirana Ngata and heeded his call to enlist in the Pioneer Battalion. It is also true that Grandfather's mother refused to let him enlist. And it is true that just prior to leaving for France, Rupeni and Ramona were engaged to be married. But Ramona had never been in love with Grandfather at all. She had been faithfully Rupeni's for many years, and wanted nothing more than to marry him before he left to go overseas with the Pioneer Battalion.

The truth is: Tamihana had never even seen Ramona until the day before her wedding.

This is how it happened.

Waituhi was playing football in Ramona's village of Hauiti, and had won the game. On his way back to the pa, where the team was being billeted, Tamihana passed by a house near the church. He heard women inside giggling, and, attracted by the sound, crept up to the flax and peered through.

Tamihana saw a girl in white, her back to him, with her head completely covered by a veil. Her mothers and sisters were fussing over the hem of her wedding dress. The girl turned in profile and the sunlight lit through the veil. Tamihana could see that she was very young. Sixteen.

'E kare ma!' the girl trilled.

The girl laughed, her face to the sun, and the wind lifted her veil so that for a moment Tamihana could gaze on Ramona.

Tamihana was eighteen. He had had many women. But he took one look at Ramona and was pierced to the heart by the lightning rod of God. Other women in Tamihana's life became as nothing to Ramona's innocent beauty. In one look he devoured her lips, her body, her eyes, her breasts, her hair and her thighs. His physical desire was such that he felt his cock storming out of its phallic sheath like a sword. He knew without doubt that she was a virgin.

When Tamihana found out that Ramona was the ridiculous Rupeni Poata's bride, and that they were to be married the next day, he roared with laughter.

Came the wedding day and Tamihana, astride a white horse, watched from a hiding place near the church. He saw Rupeni arrive in his Model T Ford. He glanced down the road. Ramona was on her way to the church. The band was playing –

– Ramona I hear the mission bells above –

A woman among the wedding guests saw the party approaching. She began to karanga to Ramona, her mother and father and sisters, all coming along the road. Rupeni, aglow with love, stepped out to greet his bride. Tamihana spurred his white horse along the road. It was all so easy.

The wedding guests scattered as Tamihana galloped through them. He slashed Rupeni's cheek as Rupeni tried to catch the reins of the stallion. The blood flicked across Ramona's white dress like glowing rubies. Tamihana leaned down. He lifted Ramona up.

'Ko wai koe!' she cried. 'Who are you?'

Ramona fitted easily into his arms. Her perfume took his breath away and triggered his lust.

'Kaore,' she pleaded. 'Kaore.'

He placed her in front of him. His breath hissed. Even as Tamihana galloped away he had turned her to face him. He prised her legs apart. He heard her whimpering and saw her glance at Rupeni, so far away now.

He unbuttoned his trousers. Lifted her up and onto him.

'*Ruu-penne –*'

Screaming, Ramona's breath sucked the veil into her mouth.

Again Grandmother asked the family: 'I want you to let me go now, back to Rupeni Poata, the man whom I have loved all my life.'

The family argued all that night. They reached a decision.

'No.'

Grandmother stood up.

'I will abide by your decision,' she said.

57

A week after that fateful meeting I was digging in some fence posts at our farm. Glory was helping me.

'You have to do something,' she said during our smoko. 'Grandmother Ramona has decided to die.'

So it was true then.

'Why me?' I asked.

Glory shrugged. 'It's your job.'

'My job?'

She looked at me as if I was hopelessly dumb. 'Of course, silly.'

Since the family meeting, Grandmother Ramona had locked herself in her room and refused to eat. Every morning, noon and evening Aunt Sephora pounded on her door. No answer.

'She'll come around,' Aunt Sarah said. 'When she gets hungry she'll eat.'

Grandmother never did.

'This is emotional blackmail,' Aunt Sarah said angrily. 'If Mother Ramona wants to die, then so be it. I will not have our father's name and mana trampled on. If Mother goes to Rupeni it will be like shitting on all our father stood for. There has always been war between the Mahanas and Poatas.'

Glory's words were still ringing in my ears when I went around to the homestead. I tapped on the window. Grandmother came to it but wouldn't open it. Her face was ethereal.

'What's this all about, Grandmother?'

'You must help me,' she said.

I went back to work. My father Joshua had taken over digging in the fence posts.

'Dad,' I said, 'if you hadn't met Mum, would you have been able to fall in love with somebody else?'

He paused. He looked at me strangely. My father has always been a man of the soil. The earth is something he knows. Emotions? Those too he knows with his heart. He does not need to explain with words. There is a language of the heart which is more profound than words from the lips. He tried his best.

273

'There's never been anybody else for me but your mother,' he said.

That settled it.

'We have to have another family meeting.'

So it was that the entire family gathered again to discuss what to do about Grandmother Ramona. Grandmother had agreed to come out of her bedroom to listen, but she was so fatigued she had to be helped to her chair.

The discussion didn't get off to a good start. Straight away Grandmother's sons and daughters took over, as was their right, and nobody else could get a word in edgeways. The first hour was filled with argument and counter-argument between them.

Aunt Sarah got hot under the collar. 'Why should we be discussing this?' she asked. 'Mum has already said she will abide by our decision. We have made that decision. If she wants to starve to death, that's *her* decision. Let it be on her own head.'

'How dare you say that,' Aunt Sephora interjected. 'How dare you let our own mother die!'

'Don't be stupid!' Aunt Sarah scoffed. 'There's no way the old lady will kick the bucket. This is just a try-on –'

'Now wait a minute –' Uncle Jack, Aunt Sarah's husband, tried to intervene.

'Who pressed your button?' Aunt Sarah was withering. 'You're not part of the family. Speak when you're spoken to.'

Uncle Jack's nostrils flared. My mother looked down. In one fell swoop Aunt Sarah had re-established the pecking order, reducing all the spouses of Grandfather's sons and daughters to people whose opinions came second. This was the way it had always been.

'You've said enough,' Aunt Ruth said. 'I'm the eldest of the girls, Sarah. Get back into line.'

Then Grandmother Ramona made a slight movement of her head, as if the wind had lifted a veil from her face. It was significant enough to make everybody look at her.

'He took me against my will,' Grandmother Ramona said. Her voice knifed up from the past. 'You're all old enough to hear the truth. Your father stole me away from Rupeni and took me against my will.'

Esther started to sob. 'No, Mum, I don't want to hear –'

Aunt Ruth, sensing what was about to happen, waved her arms at us who were the grandchildren –

'All you kids clear out.'

It was too late.

'You,' Grandmother Ramona pointed at Uncle Matiu, 'are the first one born from his taking of me against my will. And you,' she pointed at Uncle Maaka, 'are the second.'

'Didn't you kids hear? Out of the room, all of you!' Aunt Sarah was beside herself. 'Everybody out. Everybody except the family.'

But Grandmother was merciless. 'Stop ordering everybody around, Sarah. This is not your house. Everybody *stay*. You should all hear this.' Her eyes glittered. Her voice, when it came again, was precise, matter-of-fact.

'He took me into the scrub and he kept me locked up in a shearing quarters. He had planned it all along. He took me. Six times the first day. Six times the second. It hurt. It always hurt with him. He was like a bull. So big. He gored me. Trampled on me every time. I pleaded with him to stop. I knew I was already pregnant. As soon as he did it to me that first time, I knew.'

Uncle Matiu's face was quivering.

'Shut your ears, all of you,' Aunt Sarah said. 'Mother doesn't know what she's saying.'

'Don't you tell me what I know and what I don't,' Grandmother Ramona answered. 'You know nothing, Sarah. Nothing. I tried to get away from him. I knew that Rupeni must have been looking for me. Once I heard somebody in the scrub and thought it must be him. On the third day I managed to get free, but' – her voice drifted – 'Rupeni was already on his way to France. I thought that Tamihana would let me go, after he'd had his way. But he wanted to keep me. What for? I don't know. Who knows how a man is or how he thinks? Anyway, it was too late. I was hapu. I couldn't go back to anybody – to Rupeni or my father and family. A week after I was stolen away, Tamihana brought me down from the bush. My father was waiting with a shotgun and wanted to kill him. I said, "No, e pa, for I am with this man's child. It is too late." He asked me, "How do you know?" A woman always knows. When the seed gets planted inside here' – Grandmother pointed to her thighs – 'a woman knows. She is supposed to feel joy. But for me there was no joy. There was only shame. You know, four years later when Rupeni came back – I had three babies by then – he asked me to be with him. Did you know that? He said he didn't care that I had been taken by Tamihana. But I knew if I went to him that he would always have pictures in his head of your father sleeping with me, and raping me, and they would always come between us. All my children would be reminders that Tamihana had taken me first.'

Grandmother looked across at Matiu. She raised an arm to him. 'It was not your fault, son, that you were born of rape. It was not mine either. When I was carrying you, I hated you. I wanted to take a stick and push it up inside me and kill you. When you were born I hated you because you looked so like him. Every time I looked at you I would think, "You should have been Rupeni's. You should have grown from Rupeni's seed." But my breasts were heavy with milk and, after a time, I grew to love you because you had nobody to defend you.'

Grandmother gestured to all her sons and daughters. 'I grew to love you all.' Yet she was firm. 'But all of you, even my grandchildren, all of you are the result of couplings in which Tamihana took me against my will. It is the truth. I swear it before God.'

Uncle Ruka snorted in contempt. 'I don't believe any of this. Dad wasn't like that.' He looked at Grandmother Ramona. 'You're telling us that he raped you every time?'

Grandmother Ramona lifted her head. 'It is always like the male to think that women enjoy being taken when they don't want to be taken, ne? You think we will get used to it, ne? It's one of your fantasies, ne? Hear the truth then. It was always rape. Yes, I got used to it. I got used to closing my eyes and wishing he would get it over with. And of course there were times when he was good for me. Your father could make me tremble with need. He could look at me and I would start to moisten and flower for him. I am an animal, yes. But those times, too, were rape. At those times I would shut him away out of my head. I never initiated my times with your father. And when I cried out, it was always Rupeni's name that was on my lips. Your father hated that. You want to know why he always beat me? Because whenever we made love and he was enjoying it I would spit out Rupeni's name. Right to the very end.'

'Did Father ever love you?' Aunt Miriam asked. 'Did you ever love him, Mother?' Miriam was a romantic. She needed something to cling on to in the maelstrom.

'Ah, love,' Grandmother mused. 'That is a different thing. Yes, your father loved me. He asked me to marry him, but I always refused. When he found religion it was a release for me too. I said "Yes" when he asked me to be baptised with him. But I always said "No" when he wanted us to marry. To marry him would have been to bless that act of abduction, and you know our teachings: I didn't want to be tied to your father for all eternity.' Grandmother paused, thoughtful. 'Love? I think your father loved me because he wanted to possess me and he never could. There have only been two people in this family he was never able to possess. Me and Himiona.'

Me? Did that mean Grandfather loved *me*?

'But there was something else,' Grandmother continued. 'In the beginning he wanted me because he didn't want *Rupeni* to have me. You understand? He would never have taken me if I hadn't been intended for Rupeni. His jealousy of Rupeni was beyond understanding.' Grandmother paused again. 'Did I love your father? I stayed with him for over sixty years.'

'But you had all of *us*,' Uncle Ihaka remonstrated.

'Yes,' Grandmother answered drily. 'I didn't have any choice.'

'But why did you stay with him?' asked Uncle Maaka.

Grandmother Ramona smiled. 'I was his property. His possession. I was a woman. I had nowhere else to go.'

'And in all that time you still loved Rupeni?' Aunt Ruth persisted. The eldest girl. Trying to restore control.

'Yes, always,' Grandmother answered. 'Even when Rupeni married. After all, he was a man just like any other, he had the needs of all men. His wife Maata was a proud woman and I liked her very much. I was jealous of her for a while, especially since he seemed to love her. Most of all I was pleased for him that he had found a woman able to give him fine children. When she died, I suppose I could have gone to him then. I don't know why I didn't. I think, by that time, I was so old I'd forgotten that everybody has a second chance. I want to take that chance now.'

'Did Rupeni ever try to come between you and Father?' Uncle Hone asked. We needed to know, now.

Grandmother Ramona shook her head. 'Never. Oh yes, we exchanged a few words every now and then. I thought he had lost his love for me. We were always so formal with each other. I have never touched him since that day your father stole me. But there were times when we would tremble when we were near. If we touched each other I would be afraid –' She swayed. Recovered. 'Deep down in our hearts Rupeni and I knew that we loved and wanted each other. But I would never have gone to him. I was Bulibasha's. I was a mother with twelve children. I had respect for Bulibasha. He was the father of my children.'

'So why go to Rupeni now, Mum?' Aunt Miriam asked.

'Because Bulibasha is *dead*,' Grandmother said, 'and I am alive and Rupeni is alive.' She straightened. 'I say again, I have done my duty to your father and to the Mahana family. Nobody can say that I have not been dutiful. But now I have another duty. To put right what your father put wrong forty-five years ago. To go to Rupeni as I would have done when I was sixteen.'

'Have you talked to Rupeni?' Uncle Matiu asked. 'Has he agreed to have you?'

'Yes. He wants me. I want him. It is as simple as that. But he too has said he will abide by your decision.'

'We'll be the laughing stock of Gisborne,' Aunt Ruth muttered.

'That's all you can think about, isn't it,' Grandmother Ramona said. 'The mana of the house of Mahana. You think Rupeni's family wants this to happen too? Not a chance.'

'You've never loved us, Mum,' Aperahama said.

'Oh my son, love for you is why I will not do this unless you agree to it. If you don't, then let me die. But I beg of you, let me go to Rupeni. Besides, there's one more thing that you should know –'

Grandmother reached into her dress pocket and took out a letter. 'He sold me,' she said. 'Your father sold me to Rupeni Poata.'

There was a shocked silence.

'This is the proof. It is my bill of sale. Here –' She gestured to Uncle Matiu.

'You see,' Grandmother said, 'your father wanted to win the Golden Fleece so badly that he went to Rupeni Poata and said that if Rupeni threw the playoff he would give me over to him. As it happened, Rupeni Poata didn't accept, though he let your father think he did. Mahana Four won because it was the best.'

'Of course it was,' Uncle Hone snorted.

'Rupeni gave this bill of sale back to your father after the competition. I found it in his drawer. I rang Rupeni to ask about it. Rupeni told me he said to your father, "You should have trusted that angel when it said it would look after you." Your father never told me about this.'

'But it doesn't count,' Aunt Sarah said.

'No. But your father's *intent* was very clear. He would have sold me if he had to. I am angry with him for even thinking of it. It was the last straw. I do not feel obliged to him any longer.'

'Well, that was *then*,' Uncle Maaka said. 'This is now. There's a big difference. I don't think any of us need to take into account your story.'

278

He turned to the others. 'Kua pai?' he asked.

'Kua pai,' they agreed.

Glory was kneeling next to me. She jabbed me in the side and nodded:

Do something.

I frowned back at her. What could I do?

Then I remembered Grandfather's words. 'You make the decision,' he had said. Nothing more.

I coughed and tried to speak. My father looked at me, curious. I coughed again.

'I think we should vote,' I squeaked.

All eyes in the room swivelled around to peer at me. 'Hei aha?'

'I said,' I repeated, 'that we should all take a vote.'

Aunt Sarah pursed her lips and looked at me askance. 'Why is it,' she said, 'that every time you mention a vote, Himiona, I always feel like I'm about to be had! No vote.'

'Don't you believe in democracy?' I asked.

'Yes, but –'

'The vote is the only democratic way.'

'Listen to the boy,' Aunt Ruth snorted. She rushed to take Aunt Sarah's side. 'This isn't an election, Himiona. And who's *we*? If anybody is having a say in this matter it's the adults. Not kids.'

'I still think,' I said, 'that there should be a vote. Perhaps only – our parents?'

Glory nodded vigorously.

'Who do you specifically mean?' Aunt Ruth asked, enunciating each word carefully. 'And where do you get all this nonsense? School is making you whakahihi.'

Then Uncle Hone spoke up. 'I think Simeon has a point. We don't seem to be getting anywhere. Why don't we try it? How about all Mother and Father's children and our partners?'

Mum's eyes widened. So did Uncle Jack's and Uncle Albie's. Let the in-laws in on a decision? Are we hearing right?

Astonishingly, 'Sounds worth a try,' Uncle Matiu said. 'Agreed? Kua pai?'

There was a mumble which appeared to indicate agreement. The in-laws shuffled nervously.

'I'll give you a few seconds to think about it,' Uncle Matiu said, 'then I shall ask for a show of hands. How many of us? Twenty?'

'This is ridiculous,' Aunt Sarah exploded. But before she could elaborate, Uncle Matiu had called for the vote.

'How many for Mother Ramona?'

Eleven hands.

'How many against?'

Nine hands.

'Mother wins.'

'I knew it wouldn't work,' Aunt Sarah said. She turned to Uncle Jack, 'Why did you vote against me?' She looked at Uncle Matiu. 'Jack's just changed his vote. A draw.'

'I'll vote the way I want to,' Uncle Jack said. 'The vote stays as is.'

'Well, I don't like the vote,' Aunt Ruth said and folded her arms. That's that.

'So we should lock Mother up for the rest of her life? Or let her die?' Esther asked. 'Is that your solution?'

Aunt Ruth turned on her. 'We'll force feed her if we have to.' She turned on everybody. 'How can you all take Mother's side? We're talking about the mana of the family here, and don't any of you forget it. Our father is lying up there in his grave. He fought all his life against Rupeni Poata. Look what Rupeni did to our father's leg. I loved my father. Did any of you? You are being persuaded by a silly old woman who is losing her marbles. I can't let you do this.'

I raised my hand again, hoping to stop Aunt Ruth from turning the tide.

'Perhaps there should be three votes,' I said. 'You know, have three shows of hands and the majority vote wins.'

Aunt Ruth looked like she could murder me.

'Ka tika,' Uncle Hone nodded. 'The boy has some brains, after all. Maybe we should all go for our School Certificate.'

Everybody laughed.

'Well,' Uncle Matiu asked Aunt Ruth, 'does that sound fair to you?'

Come on, Aunt Ruth, come to Simeon.

'Oh, all right.'

Gotcha.

'Round number two!' Uncle Matiu said.

My heart was pounding. Glory was humming beside me. She looked totally unconcerned. What was the fuss all about?

'How many for Mother this time?' Uncle Matiu asked.

This time nine. Uncle Jack was still hanging out against Aunt Sarah.

'How many against?'

This time eleven.

Grandmother Ramona looked across to me, her face wan. She knew Aunt Ruth's impassioned defence of the Mahana mana had appealed to the family's sense of honour. There was only one vote to go. What should I do? There had to be some way of giving Grandmother a fair chance. Surely there were some of the family who, under other less public circumstances, would vote for –

Then I knew. I put up my hand again.

'The third vote should be by secret ballot,' I announced. 'Then people can really vote the way they feel.'

Aunt Ruth stared at me. 'If I ever get into trouble with the law, remind me to engage you as my lawyer,' she said.

'So,' Uncle Matiu asked, 'we take Simeon's suggestion? Kua pai. Then hand out sheets of paper and everybody vote. Simeon, you can count them when we've finished.'

'Not on your life!' Aunt Sarah exploded. 'If anybody's going to count the votes it will be me and Ruth.' Then she began to whimper, then sob, then heave. Tears ran down her eyes. She looked as if she was going to have a heart attack.

'Our father was a good man,' she wailed. 'We love our mother too, but Mum, you have only selfish desires in your heart. Our father is up there, dead. *Dead*! Nobody can speak for him except us. Even though he is dead, he is still Bulibasha.'

I thought, Oh shit, shit, *shit*.

Uncle Matiu coughed. 'Let's vote now,' he said.

The room was filled with the sounds of scratching. Then quiet descended and gradually the papers started to come my way. I recognised my mother's wilful 'Ae,' in favour of Grandmother. My father had also voted 'Ae.' So had Miriam, Pani, Sephora and Esther, Jack and Albie. But with growing despair I knew that Aunt Sarah's last speech had brought the sword of Damocles to hang above Grandmother's head.

Nine for Grandmother, eleven against. We had almost done it, but almost was not good enough.

'Well, Simeon,' Aunt Sarah, said, 'bring the papers for me and Ruth to count. Don't take all night.'

My feet had turned to lead. I started to walk across the room. Glory stopped humming. She gave a sigh of exasperation and glared hard at me. Her eyebrows knitted together: Well? What next?

I nodded: Play dead, Glory.

She fainted.

My mother rushed up to her with a cry. Aunts and uncles crowded around. Just for a moment the vote was forgotten.

Out with my pencil. Add two slips of paper with 'Ae' on them; subtract two slips with 'Kaore' on them.

'I'm all right,' Glory said, reviving.

Her look told me, You owe me one, brother.

58

Sometimes when I think of Grandmother Ramona now I imagine a silent film with people walking in the fast jerking way we used to laugh at when we were children. Dressed entirely in white, she is la paloma, a beautiful white dove, in an overdressed Spanish court. Her lover is a young man who demonstrates his love with his hands across his heart.

He has nothing to give Ramona. Not riches, not lands, not even a proud castle in Spain. Nothing – except his love. A love which will endure for ever.

The night after the vote was one of unparalleled beauty. The sky was so clear that you could see to the end of the universe. My father Joshua and I were standing with the men of the family at the bottom of the steps to the homestead. Through the wide open windows, their curtains billowing in the evening breeze, we could see the women. Grandmother Ramona was sitting in front of her mirror, combing her hair. My sister Glory was threading yellow daisies through it. Aunt Ruth and Aunt Sarah were still haranguing their mother, their voices like cicadas.

Uncle Matiu came out the front door. 'Rupeni's on his way,' he announced.

I flushed and had to hide my face in the shadows. Yes, I was ashamed. My manipulation had changed the course of family history for ever. There was something arrogant in the notion, something God-like in the assumption.

'You make the decision.'

But underpinning it all was a new emotion, a reckless disregard for the rightness of things. I could play with people as if they were toys. There was not so much difference, after all, between me and my grandfather, the Bulibasha.

Of course Aunt Ruth and Aunt Sarah had just about died when they counted the votes. They looked at each other and blanched and counted again. Then Aunt Ruth pierced me with a glance. She suspected something. She and Aunt Sarah continued to protest, but in the end they had to agree that the result meant Grandmother could go to Rupeni Poata.

I don't know how long we waited that night. Members of the family came and went. Zebediah Whatu turned up, and strong words were sent to Grandmother. Ihaka also had a go at her. Even Granduncle Pera wanted a few words. Every now and then there'd be the sound of yet another screaming match in the house as the women, too, argued with each other. Maggie came for a moment; so did Auntie Molly. Everyone had their own opinion.

Another hour passed. Uncle Hone looked at his watch and said, 'Rupeni's sure taking his time.'

'Maybe he doesn't want her after all,' Uncle Aperahama suggested with a laugh.

'Well,' Uncle Matiu said, 'maybe we don't want her either.'

Then a sound began to pierce the darkness – the phut phut oogle oogle of a vintage car. Now we knew why it had taken Rupeni so long to get to Waituhi. Along the road came the headlights of a Model T Ford, the one which Rupeni had locked in his garage for forty-five years. The car turned into the driveway; its bonnet and cab were festooned with ribbons. Two tiny dolls dressed in wedding clothes were affixed to the radiator.

The Model T coughed to a stop in front of the homestead. Rupeni got out. I didn't know what to think at first, because he was wearing a morning suit that was much too small for him and his pants were tight across his bum. There was a ripping sound from his coat as he strained to push shut the rickety car door, and to add insult to injury his wing collar burst open and he had to clutch at his bowtie to stop it from falling off.

'Ko ahau,' he said. 'It is I.'

'You stay there, Rupeni Poata,' Uncle Matiu yelled out to him. 'Dad never let you come across the threshold when he was alive, so don't think you can cross the threshold now. Your woman will come to you.'

Rupeni nodded.

'What's he doing now?' Uncle Ihaka asked.

Rupeni had gone around to the back seat of the car. He reached in and began cranking furiously with his arm. Then –

– Ramona, I hear the mission bells above –

Good grief.

Grandmother appeared on the verandah with her daughters beside her like a chorus of unwilling bridesmaids. My sisters were there too, as flower girls. Glory caught my eye and pointed at her artwork in Grandmother Ramona's hair. I gave her the thumbs-up. Grandmother Ramona was wearing the old wedding gown, pinned and tucked with safety pins, a simple white dress like a nightgown falling to her ankles. Glory's flowers were lovely, but the rest of Grandmother Ramona looked wrong, her attempt at turning back the clock a foolish and pathetic charade. Yet there was a rightness too in the challenge, an integrity in a gesture made in the face of Time.

'E kui, ma te Atua koe e manaaki,' Mum said. Mother, go with God.

'I'll never forgive you, Mum,' Aunt Ruth said.

In desperation Aunt Sarah yelled out, 'Hone? Matiu? For goodness sake, stop her.'

My uncles reacted without thinking to the peremptory demand, but in a flash Dad was there, stopping them.

'Let her go,' he said. 'Let her go.' He looked up at Aunt Ruth. 'She's already been through enough, sis.'

My father, Joshua. Finding his voice, his authority. And knowing that he owed Grandmother Ramona much for the piece of land she had given us.

'Go to him, Mum,' he said.

Grandmother nodded. She kissed Dad's hand as if he alone had made it right for her to leave. As she passed by me, she bent her head in acknowledgement.

I will never forget the look of love on Rupeni's face. His eyes were filled with tears, spilling with glowing moonstones. Then I looked at Grandmother Ramona, and it seemed that the years were folding in on themselves with every step she took from the verandah. She was getting younger and younger as time turned back forty-five years.

There was magic in the air that evening. It had the power to set things right.

And Ramona was coming along the road, a sixteen-year-old

bride-to-be, and dogs were growling and snapping at the wedding party. But Ramona didn't care about the kuri nor about the cowpats and horse dung strewn along the way. In the distance she heard a woman in karanga.

'Haere mai koutou, haere mai, haere mai, haere mai –'

Ramona saw the old Model T Ford standing there beside the church. She searched among the crowd and there was Rupeni gazing at her from afar.

Ramona thought, He should be inside waiting for me. Doesn't he know that this is bad luck for him to be standing there? Then she was there, facing him.

'Rupeni –'

'Ramona –'

She giggled because the band was playing her song.

'Ko taku aroha ki a koe kaore e mate,' Rupeni said. 'My love for you will never die.'

'Nor mine for you,' she answered.

Suddenly Ramona heard the drumming of horses' hooves. Something screamed in her mind. Her own voice called out to the gods: *Kaa-ooo-rrr-eee* – She turned, frightened, expecting to see a white horse coming down the road and a fierce man whom she did not know stooping to snatch her away. But it was only the wind playing tricks with her imagination. Only a white horse ambling riderless along the road. Nothing more. There was only Rupeni taking her hand.

I saw Rupeni open his arms wide to Grandmother Ramona. Some trick of light turned them into youthful bride and groom. It was almost as if the years between had been a mere delay.

Grandmother Ramona lifted a hand to Rupeni. They touched for the first time since that aborted wedding day. The lightning rod of God *struck*.

So that is what it's like. The tingling sensation compounded of love, desire, lust, yearning and aching for completeness. With a moan, Grandmother Ramona collapsed into Rupeni's arms. And they were again a man and a woman, both in their sixties, weeping, tracing their faces with each other's hands, not quite believing, holding each other.

The recording had stuck in the groove of the record –

– bells a-bove a-bove a-bove –

Rupeni took the needle off the record. He escorted Grandmother and opened the passenger door for her. She hesitated a second.

I thought, No, don't look back at us, Grandmother. Don't. Although you know the strength of Rupeni's love you still might change your mind. This is your chance, Grandma. Take back your life. Go for it.

'Hey, old lady,' Uncle Hone called. 'Haven't you got a suitcase?'

Grandmother turned to us. 'I came to your father's house with what I am wearing. I leave his house the same way. He owns everything else.'

'You are a foolish old woman, Mum,' Aunt Ruth cried. 'You, Rupeni, you are a stupid old bugger.'

Aunt Sarah began to sob again. 'Mum? Please don't go. It's not too late to stay. Mum?'

Grandmother Ramona seemed to waver. Then she took a deep breath and stepped into the car. Rupeni closed the door behind her.

'I thank you all, sons and daughters of the King of the Gypsies,' he said. Then Rupeni made a sweeping sign for me alone. 'And I pay my respects to you –'

He bowed low. His eyes were twinkling, as if he knew I had dealt in chicanery, taken a card from the bottom of the pack and put it on top. Theatrically, he flung his arms in the air.

'True heir of the great Bulibasha.'

Rupeni started the car. He turned it out of the driveway and along the road. Aunt Ruth began to run after it. Aunt Sarah ran after her. Then all the other sisters were running, Sephora, Miriam and Esther, running, running, running –

'Mum? *Mummee*!'

It was too late. The road was a ribbon of moonlight.

Epilogue

My parents Joshua and Huria still live in Waituhi. Lately, though, my mother has been pestering my father to move into Gisborne so she can be nearer to her mokopuna – Faith and Hope's children. My father, being the youngest son, has had the unenviable task of mourning and burying his elder brothers Matiu, Maaka, Ruka and Aperahama, and his sisters Sarah and Sephora. My father has taken it all in his stride, as if this is one of the natural blessings to befall the youngest son. It is his job.

'Better me to bury my brothers and sister,' he says, 'than some stranger.'

His brothers and sisters lie beside their father Tamihana Mahana in the hillside graveyard.

The homestead, although ravaged by age, managed to survive the effects of Hurricane Bola and is still standing. Uncle Hone lived there for a time, but then he shifted to Wellington where his daughters had gone to find work. Aunt Ruth lives there now, alone since Uncle Albie died. But she has my dear cousin Haromi's children to look after. When Haromi died of breast cancer, the children went to Aunt Sarah, but when Aunt Sarah died, they then went to Aunt Ruth. The childless one has been gifted children in her late years.

Aunt Ruth and Dad are the only ones left in Waituhi. The rest, Ihaka and my aunts Miriam, Sephora and Esther, have moved to Gisborne.

As for the grandchildren, we became scattered to the four winds by the world of the Pakeha. Its insistent clamour enticed us all away from the simpler pleasures of our lives. My cousin Andrew Whatu and I were sent to boarding school together, and we both managed to survive terrible marks and make something of our lives.

Somewhere in the middle of all this I lost touch with my sister Glory. I went to Auckland to work and it was a surprise to realise she was a teenager. One night I received an urgent telephone call from Dad in Waituhi. Glory had run away to Wellington. I left work to go to find her, and when I did so she ran to me and started to hit me with savage blows.

'You promised,' she screamed. 'You promised you would never leave me and you did.'

We wept in each other's arms.

I felt like saying, No, Glory, I didn't leave you. We had to grow up, both of us. That's what happened, Glory, we simply grew up.

Contrary to their expectations, my sisters Faith and Hope never managed to improve on their looks. What they lack in beauty, however, they have made up in personality. And do they both have heaps of children! Hope's husband, Zac, has always bemoaned the fact that he should have listened to his mates when he took Hope into the bush. The fertility of the Mahana women remains unabated.

My sister Glory and I resumed what turned out to be a volatile brother and sister relationship. Glory ran away again and became a ship girl. I found her again, lost her again, found her again. For a while my cousin Chantelle was there to pick Glory up whenever she fell. Then Chantelle fell victim to HIV and was soon dead.

Glory got into a number of relationships with Maori men, all like me but nothing like me. I am too frightened to think about the implications, but I know that I love my sister Glory more than anyone else in the world. In her mature years she has settled down to a single life which, from time to time, admits a man. Ours will always remain one of those tumultuous sibling relationships, defined by the fact that we have always been too close to each other. We need times away from each other, but when we are together it is an emotional fusing of such fierceness that all the times apart are rendered meaningless.

Glory is forty-nine now and matronly. She has a parcel of kids from different fathers. Sometimes, just for fun, I'll say, 'Play dead, Glory.' Instantly she will keel over, faint and lie on the floor, pretending to be unconscious. What Glory's kids feel about these performances I shudder to think. Then she'll laugh out loud and we will hug each other. What happened that night when Grandmother left the homestead is a secret between Glory and myself alone.

I now live in Auckland. I met Erana when I first arrived there and we married soon after. We have a son, Mark. Erana was curious about Poppy, who was the first girl I ever kissed, and began writing to her. It is through this link that I keep in touch with the way Hukareka is feeling about Waituhi. Poppy has married and raised children – three sets of twins – and ostensibly taken over leadership of the Poata clan, having been accorded this role by Rupeni Poata himself.

For a time there was an expectation that I should return to Gisborne, as if Grandfather had marked me in some way to be his successor. As time has passed this expectation seems to have faded. Anyway, Uncle Hone is still alive and my father Joshua too. There is no need for me to engage the question yet. My Aunt Ruth acts as messenger between us.

The great Mahana family of God has enlargened and become a wonderful tribe of young men, women and their children. Some have married with the Whatu family and most of them still work for Mahana One, Mahana Two, Mahana Three or Mahana Four. There is now talk of a Mahana Five which can travel to Australia, America and Scotland for shearing. Uncle Hone's eldest son is expected to take over. Grandfather would have been proud of that.

Although shearing is now an all-round profession, there is always an October meeting at the homestead. There my father Joshua and dear Aunt Ruth preside over the history, the telling of the dream that Grandfather Tamihana had many years ago, and the great Golden Fleece win of 1958. Zebediah Whatu, Ihaka Mahana, Granduncle Pera, Maggie, Nani Mini Tupara and Auntie Molly have all gone now, but are remembered in the Mahana Shearing Hall of Fame. Lloyd is still living.

Since 1958 there have been triumphs aplenty for the Mahana clan, but those earlier times are remembered with reverence, thanks and joy. To Aunt Ruth has fallen the task of being the scolding termagent, the one who reminds us of the past and of our duty to the family. The family comes first and it comes last. The family is *for ever*.

And to my father Joshua has come his time. He is no longer ninth child and seventh son but respected head of the Mahana family in Waituhi. That is, unless Uncle Hone comes to visit.

I am still a member of the church which has been so central to this story. Despite my waverings, nothing has shaken my conviction of its truth and beauty. The church has suffered my waywardness with infuriating patience. The way to God is not always straight and narrow, and mine has been as crooked as a dog's hind leg.

The Waituhi Valley survived the split caused by Grandfather, and these days we are stronger than ever. Nani Mini Tupara would have loved to have seen that return to unity.

I believe my grandfather did, indeed, see an angel.

My Grandmother Ramona and Rupeni Poata married in a registry office and lived happily together for seven years. When Rupeni died at seventy-one, he was buried at Hukareka and it was our turn to go there and abuse him in the same way that he had abused our grandfather. We all thought that Grandmother Ramona would return to us but she said, No.

Grandmother Ramona died three years later. She had wisely stipulated that she should lie on her own family marae at Hauiti rather than at Waituhi or Hukareka. At her tangi the Mahana and the Poata families eyed each other angrily, one family on either side of her casket, while Grandmother's own Hauiti people tried to mediate between us. Some people say Grandmother's was the worst tangi they have ever been to; others say it was the best because of all the arguments and fighting. It seemed the only place we wanted to bury the hatchet was in each other.

The arguments took place over three nights and were always on the question of where Grandmother Ramona should be buried. Next to Tamihana, the man with whom she had lived most of her life but who was not her husband? Or next to Rupeni, the man she had always loved and who was her legal husband for only a short time? When I suggested, jokingly, that we should have a vote, Aunt Ruth looked fit to murder me.

A swarm of bees, coming across the hills like a golden cloud, only complicated matters. For a moment all was bedlam as they entered the tent where Grandmother was lying in state. There they kissed her arms, drank from her lips and, from their immense buzzing, sounded as if they could die for love of her.

'You and your bees, Mum,' Aunt Ruth cried.

For some reason, it was to *me* that everybody looked for a decision on that night before Grandmother was buried.

'You make the decision,' Grandfather had said. Nothing more.

When I saw the family waiting for me to say something, I looked for Glory, hoping she would faint for me. For the first time in our lives she didn't.

Sorry, bro, this time you're on your own.

I thought of Bulibasha, the King of the Gypsies, and realised that he had put my feet on a difficult path. There are people who lead because they have the courage to make decisions. The test for all leaders is whether they are able to accept responsibility for changing people's lives for ever.

I took that responsibility. For Grandmother's sake I had already, once before, let my heart rule my head. Was it not time for me, in all my arrogance, to now place my head above my heart? To acknowledge that Grandmother had had her time of truancy but that it was over? To remember that, dead or living, the family always came first?

Cinderella had danced at the ball not once but twice, for I had forced the hands of the clock back before midnight to allow her to dance with her prince again. Midnight was gone now. Was it not time for Cinderella to make utu, make payment? Or could I, being the romantic, continue to place her above the Bulibasha? Above even family?

– Ramona, I hear the mission bells above –

I can never hear that song without thinking of my Grandmother Ramona and her great love story. Nor can I ever dissociate it from those times in the 1950s when the Waipaoa River so ruled our lives. The sound of the river is like a cry in my soul – aroha, aroha – and I know that both Glory and I will love the river until we die. And my father is right. It *is* the sweetest-tasting water in the world.

Everybody accepted my decision about where Grandmother should be buried, though not all agreed with it. I suppose this must be Bulibasha's last laugh on me. I can just imagine him up there, chortling his head off and saying, 'So you're the leader now, Himiona? See if *you* can do better.'

And the decision? I'll let you work it out for yourself, though I'll give you a clue. It has become yet another reason why, today, the Mahana and Poata families are still fighting each other.

Author's note

This novel is dedicated to my father, Te Haa Ihimaera Smiler Jnr, my grandfather Pera Punahamoa Ihimaera Smiler and the great Smiler family of whom I am a member. It is also written in memory of my fabulous grandaunt, Mini Tupara, Uncle George Tupara and the Tupara family.

Bulibasha is a work of fiction. Although Waituhi is a real village, Hukareka is not. For geographical purposes Hukareka has been situated somewhere between Manutuke and Bartletts. The Golden Fleece championships is modelled on the Golden Shears competition.

The novel was written when I was the Katherine Mansfield Fellow, Menton, France. My thanks are due to the Katherine Mansfield Trust, the Electricity Corporation of New Zealand, Mrs Marguerite Lilley, and Professor Albert Wendt and the University of Auckland for leave from the English Department.

From the bottom of my heart I thank William Rubinstein, trustee for the Katherine Mansfield Fellowship in France and secretary of the New Zealand France Association, Nice, and his wife Nelly. Thanks also to the New Zealand France Association, Monsieur Frederic Billy and the Maire of Menton, my French teacher Monsieur Alain Roman, Jean and Olga Franc de Ferriere, Jacqueline Bardolph and Jean, William Waterfield and Angelique, Annabelle White, Gordon Stewart, Maarire, Terry, David and Guillaume for their support – and to Jane, and Jessica Kiri and Olivia Ata, the best daughters in the world.

There was no better place to write *Bulibasha* than in the south of France, close to Italy, where verismo – temperament, passion, pain and laughter – is so much akin to the Waituhi Valley's own passionate involvement in life, death and history. I pay tribute to the sun, mountains and peoples bordering the great Mediterranean Sea.